FEAR CALLER

BEVERLY HAMOWITZ

FEAR CALLER

Print ISBN: 978-1-09830-395-2
eBook ISBN: 978-1-09830-396-9

FEAR CALLER

FEAR CALLER

Colorado Territory 1866

"First, you must walk the rabbit out," Red Moon told sixteen-year-old Ned Harper when she agreed to teach him to hunt with bow and arrow. Her black eyes crinkled when she added, "And, in hunting, as in all things, you must learn the patience of a spider as she reweaves her broken web."

Ned nodded, but they both knew patience was not part of his make up.

Of course, he'd hunted rabbit and deer with a shotgun since he was old enough to lift one and aim it accurately, but after serving as a Union drummer boy, he'd developed an aversion to guns. Couldn't tolerate the feel of a rifle butt against his shoulder, or the crack and thunder when it fired, or the stinking haze of spent powder that hung in the air after. For a time, he couldn't even look at one.

Standing boot-deep in snow, the old Ute woman watched from a distance. Emerging from the trees a moving shadow in thin mid-winter dusk, Ned took ten noisy paces, then halted and drew back the black-fletched arrow in his short bow. Hands almost numb with cold, lean arms stretched taut, he waited in silence until a cottontail—frightened from the safety of its nest by the crunch of his steps—scurried for a few seconds, then stopped, its body still as a brown stone in a field of white. Ears perked, nose twitching, the rabbit's glistening dark eyes scanned the clearing. Before it could make a move to save itself, Ned's arrow pierced its neck, killing the animal instantly.

Closing his eyes, Ned exhaled, grateful for the quick death. Rabbits could make the most god-awful din when they were distressed. Another thing he couldn't abide since the war was the sound of any creature screaming. He lifted his hat to brush back the dark hair—sweat-damp despite the cold—that fell across his forehead. Trudging toward him, Red Moon gave a quick nod of approval and he flashed her the tight half-grin that had come to pass for his smile.

Kneeling beside the dead rabbit, he drew his knife and had begun to dress the carcass by the time the Indian reached his side. As Red Moon had taught him, he apologized to the animal for taking its life and thanked it for giving him warmth and food. He'd never understood why a rabbit would leave its hiding place when it sensed danger. He'd seen soldiers do the same on the battlefield—walk right into what they knew would be the hail of bullets or cannonballs that would kill them.

Red Moon hunkered beside him. "The People say Rabbit is the Fear Caller." She looked with pity on the dead animal, its once liquid eyes now dull. "Hawk's eyesight is keen, just like your aim is true. But Rabbit is so afraid of being caught his fear is very loud. It shouts to the things he's most afraid of: 'Here I am, Hawk! This is where I'm hiding, Mountain Lion! Come find me, Arrow!"

The onyx eyes in her weather-lined face shone bright as they met and held Ned's. "And so, his fears come to him."

Knife in one hand, fingers of the other stroking the cottontail's fur, Ned bowed his head. Not to hide tears, he had none, but to absorb the words he knew to be meant for him.

CHAPTER ONE

Spring 1875

Ned Harper grimaced as the proprietor of Cuthbert's Mercantile examined beaver pelts a trapper had piled on the counter. He watched the merchant test the weight of each and dig his fingers into the thick fur. After Horace Cuthbert nodded to the grizzled trapper, he raised his eyes above the man's broad shoulders and caught Ned's icy blue glare. Narrowing his own eyes, he muttered, "And don't you be giving me none of those foul looks of yours, Harper. Dead is dead."

Shaggy dark hair fell to Ned's shoulders and several week's growth of beard shadowed his even features. He'd come across too many half-dead animals mangled in the brutal traps to keep his disgust silent. "And torture is torture."

With a scowl at Ned and an apologetic shrug to the bristling fur trader, the proprietor hefted a snaggle-toothed bear trap and a ten-pound sack of Cuthbert's Flavor-Full Pemmican bars onto the counter in trade for the pelts. The heat and activity in the busy store had turned his jowled face florid and, Ned noted, his shortish temper shorter. In a corner, two men tested white ash baseball bats that had just arrived from Louisville. They swung the cudgels with such blind exuberance that other Saturday shoppers were obliged to cut them a wide swath or risk being struck.

"Take those infernal toys outside!" Cuthbert snapped, glowering at the barber and the banker. With a bat over one shoulder, a new horsehide-covered ball in hand, and a swagger in their steps, the men did as they were told. To the trapper and other patrons crowding the store, he grumbled, "Grown men carrying on like puddin'-headed boys."

As the fur trader shouldered past Ned, Cuthbert folded the mahogany pelts and slid them onto a shelf behind him. A hunter and trapper himself, Ned had come to town to trade two deer hides, a side of dressed venison, and the pemmican he'd made—the same Cuthbert labeled and sold as his own—for a month's worth of provisions: The best coffee the store carried—Arbuckle's Ariosa Blend, several bottles of Old Overholt's Rye Whiskey, canned goods, salt, sugar, lantern oil, and other sundries. He'd take the rest in cash.

The merchant rapped a thick knuckle on the list of supplies Ned set on the counter and made a show of opening his till. "That there trapper has as much right to make an honest living as you," he said, counting out Ned's payment and slapping it on the counter. "And so do I."

"That can be done," Ned replied, "without resorting to those cruel contraptions to do it." Horace's frown didn't stop him from adding, "Or by selling them."

From the time he was a youth, Ned had used humane cages to trap, hunted with a bow and arrow, and swore he'd never take a shot unless certain it would deliver a swift, merciful kill.

Hands pressed flat to the wooden counter, Cuthbert bowed his head, then looked up and folded heavy arms across his broad belly. "No matter how you feel about it, Harper, trappers are gonna keep using those traps and storekeepers are gonna keep selling 'em."

With a conciliatory grin, Ned pocketed the money and made peace with his friend over their long-standing disagreement. "And, no matter how you feel about it, Horace, I'm gonna keep hoping they won't."

Ned was relieved to find himself able to banter. Over the last year or so, the once ordinary act of coming to town had become difficult. Months had passed since his last visit, but dwindling supplies forced him to face the questioning glances or averted eyes of the town folk he'd been avoiding. He knew they meant well—for the most part—but their interest and overtures struck like unintentional blows to a still tender bruise. Cuthbert's gruffness and the store's familiar smells—sawdust, pickle brine, the musk of animal pelts, lye, coffee, and other odors harder to identify—brought a welcome reminder of what had once been normalcy.

Mrs. Charles Hanover stepped to Ned's side and laid a gloved hand on his buckskinned arm. "As you surely know, I often tell my children and my husband, that hope is one thing, but expectations are quite another." Her green velvet hat matched the silk of her bustled visiting dress. The plump matron was always attired in the latest fashion imported from Boston, her graying auburn hair always coiffed beneath a stylish fanchon. Delicate gloves, of no practical use in Solace Springs, graced her hands. In the crook of one arm, she clutched Dash, a squirming black and white King Charles spaniel, also imported from Boston. "You must take heed to manage yours, especially when they pertain to a merchant and his profits."

"Morning, Mrs. Hanover." Ned gave her the best smile he could manage and stroked the dog's silky head. Mother of his closest friend, Jane Hanover had known him since he and her son Will were youths. A critical woman by nature, she'd been kind to Ned when his behavior met her standards and not so when it didn't. "I'll bet Dash hopes you'll let him come out hunting with me and Cloud one day," he said. "Spaniels are bred to flush game."

Keeping his eyes on the dog, he avoided her probing look, but the muscles in Ned's shoulders bunched at her attention. For months he'd sought the shelter of shadows—the long, slanting silhouettes of tall trees that surrounded his cabin, a corner table jammed against a wall at the saloon, a lowered hat brim. Just to avoid looks like those.

"One must always strive to have hope, my dear." The matron lifted her gaze to Ned's, as did the struggling dog—whose luminous brown eyes seemed to beseech him to help it gain its freedom. "But, expectations, as Dash would tell you himself, are a sure path to disappointment."

Without the effort it took to keep his expression unchanged, Ned's own smile would have faded into the shadow it had become. He'd long since given up on both.

A few feet away, Alexandrina Victoria Hanover—Allie to everyone but her mother—fingered the silk ribbons she pretended to examine and waited to hear Ned's response. Moments before, he'd greeted her with a nod and a finger to the brim of his dark hat, had met her eyes briefly, then turned his attention elsewhere. No more and no less than he'd exchanged with the young men wielding the baseball bats who had once been his good friends. He's not himself, she thought, hasn't been for some time. A twinge of something she couldn't name caught her by surprise. What she felt, she assured herself, must be compassion.

Tall and slender, Allie wore her brown hair simply and—unlike her mother—her clothing plain. Despite her intentions, her eyes lingered on Ned. Maude Mary, her twelve year-old sister, who should have been absorbed in the pleasant task of deciding how to spend the penny their father had given her, jabbed an elbow into Allie's ribs with an infuriating smirk.

Before Allie could give her the withering look she deserved, a querulous voice drew all eyes to a young woman standing in the doorway. "It's Joseph, Pa." Sarah Findlay tilted her head back toward the street. "I couldn't stop him."

CHAPTER TWO

Without a word, Luke and Martha Findlay pushed through the crowd in the store and out the door. New to Solace Springs, the family had kept to themselves since taking over the Evans sheep ranch a few months ago. No one knew what to make of the girl's urgent statement, so after an exchange of curious glances, Allie and several other patrons followed them. Her mother and sister remained in the store rather than join the undignified rush.

Outside, a knot of town folk—mostly children—clustered at the side of a buckboard wagon across the dusty street. A young boy stood petting an enormous grey and white dog who sat on its haunches and clearly enjoyed the attention. Granted, it was Ned Harper's white wolf dog—long-legged, more than three feet tall at the shoulder, and weighing over a hundred pounds—but everyone knew Running Cloud to be one of the best-natured creatures around. Unless he sensed that his pack, which included Ned, Ned's friends, and a few canine companions of his own, was being threatened. The dog alone would not have drawn much interest.

Nearing the wagon, onlookers could see what had caused the fuss. The boy looked to be about eight years-old and small for his age. He held one thin arm pressed to his chest, the hand contracted into a claw. One leg, bent at the knee, twisted inward. His head bobbled and wagged and his thin mouth twisted into a grimace with a spot of drool glistening in one corner.

"What's wrong with him?" a youth asked, gaping at the child.

Another boy stepped back, waving an arm in warning. "Don't let him touch you—you'll catch it!"

Their companion gave a derisive snort. "Aw, come on, he's just feeble-minded. You can't catch that." With a snigger at his friend, he added, "Especially not you. You've already got it!"

The target of their comments seemed oblivious to the taunts. Raising a flailing arm and aiming it at the top of the dog's head, while struggling to maintain his balance, appeared to require the boy's full concentration. The contact was more swat than stroke, but Running Cloud accepted the blows as the gentle pats they were clearly intended to be. When the child dropped his arm, the dog nuzzled his elbow as if to encourage him to continue.

At the sight of his son and the wolf dog, Luke Findlay charged across the street. At the sight of the charging man, Running Cloud sprang in front of the boy, the newest member of his pack, in a fierce, protective stance. Ears back, fangs bared, a menacing growl rumbled deep in his chest. Drawing up short, Findlay stumbled backward and grabbed a rifle from his wagon.

Weapon cocked and aimed at the dog, his finger tightened on the trigger. His wife, Martha, halted close behind him, both hands pressed to her mouth. Sarah stood beside her mother with her head bowed and cheeks flaming.

Golden eyes feral and fixed on the man's throat, Running Cloud snarled and crouched, the thick fur at his shoulders bristling. In the next heartbeat, Ned faced Findlay and shoved the gun skyward as it fired. Crazed by the blast, the dog lurched back and forth, yowling and snapping.

Flattening his other hand in front of him, Ned signaled his dog. "Calm," he commanded, as every muscle in his own body tensed for action. Cloud froze, locked incredulous eyes on Ned's, then sank to his haunches. Still aiming the rifle upward, Ned slid murderous eyes toward Findlay. "You, too."

His own expression just as lethal, Findlay kept one hand clenched on the upraised barrel and a finger of the other hooked on the trigger. The wolf's gaze stayed riveted on his throat.

"Settle," Ned commanded. Cloud huffed, stifled a growl, and hunkered down to his belly. Turning to Findlay, Ned released his grip on the rifle. "Put that back in the wagon. Slowly." In control of the situation and his own emotions now, it still took everything he had to keep his voice steady. Tilting his head toward Running Cloud, he said, "He's tame, but guns try his patience. Mine, too."

Nothing moved. Then, yapping pandemonium erupted from the mercantile. Dash had gained his freedom. The loud and unaccustomed noise of a gunshot in town had caused a commotion in the store allowing the spaniel to free himself from his mistress's embrace and tear across the street. Yelping and leaping, he scampered in ecstatic circles around the larger dog. When Cloud did not join in the play, the panting pup settled on his own belly, paws forward, feathery tail swishing expectantly.

With several people peering over his shoulders, Horace Cuthbert watched from the doorway of his store. "It's all over." He assured his patrons no one had been hurt and that they could all safely return to their shopping. "Look out there," he told Mrs. Hanover, "that poor ragdoll of yours is finally getting to act like a dog."

Through sun-squinted eyes, Findlay scrutinized Ned—a rugged young man, dark-haired and lean. He appeared to take special interest in Ned's calf-high buckskin moccasins, the badger claw fixed to his hat band, and the leather medicine pouch on a thong around his neck. Apparently convinced the wolf dog was no longer a threat, he tossed the gun into his wagon and swung around to face Ned, glowering. Mrs. Findlay hurried to comfort Joseph, who cowered fear-frozen behind Cloud.

"Tame?" Findlay demanded in a derisive drawl. "You tellin' me that mangy wolf's tame?" Fair-haired and freckled, anger mottled his weathered features. A stocky man, his thick arms hung at his sides. He flexed his hands, as if undecided whether to ball them into fists or not.

Ned exhaled slowly. "Mostly." Despite the other man's obvious scorn, he extended his hand. The rifle blast had startled people to the doors and windows of all the stores along both sides of Commerce street. He felt too many eyes on him in the unrelenting morning light to let this get out of hand. "Ned Harper. Sorry for the fright. "

Findlay's eyes lingered on the badger claw. "Tamed by you, I suppose?"

Withdrawing his hand, Ned struggled for the patience that so often eluded him. His nerves had been raw at the prospect of coming to town, but he hadn't anticipated this kind of trouble. The sun was weight, not warmth, on his shoulders. "Yes."

Findlay's mouth twisted. "Well, isn't it a sore pity someone hasn't seen fit to tame *you*."

Blinking once, Ned absorbed the jab. He sized up his adversary. The man was about his own height, but broader through the shoulders and heavier. Older. Slower. Tensing to strike, Ned knew he could take him, knew he had the advantage of youth and speed and fury. The urge to attack without thought or restraint had always come too easily. The badger claw on his hat had been given to him as a reminder of just that.

Willing his pounding heart to quiet, Ned summoned a smile. When it came, it didn't reach his eyes. "Some have tried. I s'pose there's too much wolf in Cloud and me for it to have done either of us much good."

The onlookers quieted. Some stared at Ned and shifted nervously, others turned to walk away. Findlay broke the silence with a snort. "Just see you keep that yellow-eyed varmint away from my boy."

Aware of all the eyes on him, Ned rested a hand on the dog's head and met the man's stony glare. One of old Heck Abernathy's admonitions came to him: "Kickin' never gets you nowheres, son, lest yer a hard-goin' mule." The thought settled him. "No need to worry on that account," he said. Then, to the boy, "His name's Running Cloud and we both thank you for the kindness you showed him."

Jutting his chin toward his wife and son, Findlay signaled them to climb into the wagon. With an arm around Joseph's thin shoulders, Mrs. Findlay steadied him as he lurched and stumbled toward the cart. A slight, tired woman with buried eyes, she gave no sign she heard the words that came next.

Making a warding gesture with her fingers, a young matron pulled her daughter close. "It's demons, I tell you. Hide your eyes."

"Now you all stop your staring. It's just plain rude," chided old Mother Foster—who was having one of her clear-headed days. She gave the Findlay boy a pitying smile. "Poor thing's afflicted."

Allie's younger brother, who had been among the children staring at Joseph, stood close at her side. About the same age as the boy, Albert watched mesmerized. He was the tender-hearted member of the Hanover family and she knew it would trouble him to see any living creature suffer. When Joseph passed by, he took a step toward him. "I'm Albert. My father's the doctor here. Doc Hanover. He helps lots of 'fflicted people." In a softer voice he added, "Maybe he can help you."

"He can't," Findlay muttered down at Albert and swung Joseph up onto the buckboard's bench. Seventeen-year-old Sarah Findlay had managed to stay out of her father's line of sight until that moment. "Get in," her father told her sharply. "Now."

"Yes, Pa."

Once Sarah was seated beside her brother, with eyes straight ahead and hands folded in her lap, Pa helped Ma into the wagon and climbed in beside her. With his snap of the reins, the buckboard jerked forward. Over his shoulder, he snarled at Sarah, "You'll explain how all this happened when we get home."

"Yes, Pa." The hot-eyed glare she darted at Joseph steamed with resentment.

The explanation should be simple enough. The huge dog sleeping in the shade of the cart next to theirs had awakened, shaken the dust from its coat, and stretched. Joseph managed to clamber down from the wagon to pet it without her stopping him because a jaunty young man toting a bat over one shoulder had approached the wagon and distracted her from her duty.

"You must be that new girl everyone's talking about," the barber had said with a smitten grin. Turning to his companion, he added, "They're sure right, aren't they? Why, this young lady's pretty enough to make a blind man blush!"

Engaged in the flirtation that followed, Sarah hadn't seen any harm in what Joseph was up to until the crowd gathered. By then, it was too late and she'd run to summon her parents. As the wagon swayed down the rutted street, Joseph's longing gaze stayed on Running Cloud. Sarah no longer had any interest in the men who'd been the cause of what was likely to be a lengthy and boring scolding. Or worse. She had the whole ride home to think up a more acceptable explanation.

For now, her eyes lingered on the man in buckskin who had somehow gotten both the wolf dog and her father to obey his commands.

The wagon clattered just out of earshot when someone said, "I tell you, it's a judgment from the Lord. That child bears the mark of Satan!"

Outraged, Allie wheeled to face the people she'd known most of her life. "It is most certainly not a judgment. Or demons. He's an innocent child whose brain was injured at birth."

She often assisted her father, the town doctor, with his patients and—at his urging and against her mother's adamant opposition—planned to apply to a women's medical college in the East. During slow times at the clinic, she immersed herself in Dr. Hanover's journals and had a keen interest in women and children's health. An article about what she believed to be the boy's condition had recently come across Doc's desk.

Aware people had quieted to listen, including Ned, who stood just outside the small circle, Allie lifted her shoulders and calmed herself. Dispel ignorance at any opportunity, her father had taught her. A quick swallow eased the dryness in her throat. "It's called Little's Disease or 'birth palsy,' " she said. Some people walked away, a few stayed to listen. She lifted her voice to be heard by those who had turned their backs. "Dr. Little says in a difficult delivery, the baby may get stuck in the birth canal for too long. Even if he survives, not getting enough oxygen can damage the brain and cause the limbs to contract and spasm."

Certain her father would approve and, truth be told, hoping Ned would realize she was a grown woman, not just Will Hanover's younger sister, she continued, "What you saw in that child are just the scars from that. I've helped Doc stitch up enough of you to know you all have a few of your own. Do those scars mean *you've* been touched by the devil?"

A spattering of shrugs and grins answered her question.

Albert slipped his hand into hers and tugged, drawing her attention down to him. "But Father can help him, can't he?"

Knowing the truth would trouble the boy, Allie hesitated before repeating the Chinese proverb her father had told her when she'd been distraught at a patient's failure to recover. "Medicine can cure only curable diseases, Albert, and even those not always." She laid a hand on his shoulder. "I'm afraid this is one that can't be helped."

In part to avoid her brother's crestfallen expression, in part to seek Ned's reaction to her speech, she straightened and searched the few faces still there. Neither he nor Running Cloud were anywhere to be seen. A hollow opened just below her ribs with the realization it might have been her own thoughtless words that had driven him away.

Quelling her disappointment, she returned her attention to the dispersing onlookers. "Sometimes," Allie told them, "it's the ignorance of others that does the worst crippling."

Docile after his adventure, Dash did not resist when Allie scooped him up, carried him back into the mercantile, and deposited him in her mother's arms. Mrs. Hanover, who did not seem at all perturbed by her pet's mutiny, received him with a fond smile. "I must agree with dear Queen Victoria—'were it not for the honest faces of dogs, we should forget the very existence of sincerity.' "

Since her childhood in Boston, Mrs. Hanover had been obsessed with all things pertaining to the Queen of England. She'd described to Allie how, in 1861, she had mourned the death of the Prince Consort as if he were a family member. All her children carried the given names of royal offspring: Her eldest son—William Patrick Albert, her first daughter, Alexandrina Victoria—named for the monarch herself. Alice Maude Mary had been followed by Albert Edward. Dash, of course, was named after the Queen's own beloved spaniel.

Unlike the Queen, Allie would have to concede, her mother found her own children neither burdensome nor unattractive. For the most part. Mrs. Hanover cupped a hand under her youngest son's chin and tilted it to study his face. With a satisfied nod, she released Albert.

Turning her attention to Allie, who knew full well she was her mother's most vexing child, she held her gaze for a longer moment. "I see you and your brother are unharmed by the unpleasantness outside. Gunshots in the middle of town! What could those men have been thinking? And what could you have been thinking to run into the midst of it?"

Before Allie could respond, her mother held up a gloved hand and answered her own question, as she often did. "Neither they nor you *were* thinking and that's all that needs to be said about that. Uncivilized is, as uncivilized does." With an accusatory eyebrow arched at Allie, she added, "I must say I am somewhat surprised Ned Harper had a part in it. I thought he was done with that manner of foolishness."

Heat rose to Allie's cheeks. Her older brother, Will, often teased Ned about his unruly past, but it irked her that her mother alluded to it now. "That was a long time ago."

A young child back then, Allie had been sheltered from Will's tales of his friend's dubious exploits. Most of the time. But one night, from her listening perch on the third step from the top of the staircase, she'd heard how the sheriff and Heck Abernathy had locked Ned in the barn overnight because of some sort of trouble at a place called the Tanglefoot Saloon. She recalled feeling sad and confused when, after that night, Ned had no longer been welcome at her mother's table for Sunday suppers.

"Ned only got involved because the other man was about to shoot Cloud." Allie swallowed, surprised by the tightness in her throat. "You know he couldn't bear for anything to happen to his dog especially after . . . everything."

Studying Allie's heightened color, the corner of Mrs. Hanover's mouth twitched downward and matched the disapproval in her tone. "I see."

"I assure you, Mother, there is nothing for you to see."

"Tone, Alexandrina, tone. Need I remind you . . ."

Albert, who had been rocking on the balls of his feet, interrupted. "Mama, there's a new boy and he's all bent and wobbly and the other boys were bothering him when he was petting Cloud and his papa got scared and Ned pushed the rifle up and it shot into the air so he couldn't kill Cloud!"

Stopping for a much needed breath, he went on more slowly. "Someone said he's marked by the devil and Allie," he gave her a proud smile. "Allie told them all 'No he's not'! He's my age and his name's Joseph and he's 'fflicted . . . Allie says even Father can't make him well, but I can still be his friend, can't I, Mama?"

Mrs. Hanover's face softened. Lowering her gaze, she pushed the brown hair back from his forehead. "Of course, you can."

Raising her eyes, she gave Allie the disquieting look that usually accompanied a statement to the effect that if she hadn't given birth to her eldest daughter herself, she would have no doubt the girl must be a foundling. Instead, her face took on a more neutral expression.

"My word," she exclaimed, "those poor Findlays! They clearly need a proper welcome to this town. I believe my Benevolent Ladies must be summoned to action. But first things first. Albert, I don't see a sack of candy in your hand. Do you still have your penny? And, Alexandrina—ribbons!" Her frown returned, deeper than before. "You will at least do me the kindness of pinning a spot of color to that drab frock you insist on wearing, please and thank you."

It's at least as trying for me to be your daughter, Allie thought, as it is for you to be my mother. To avoid an unwinnable argument, she reached for a bright teal ribbon.

Turning to the store's proprietress, Leonora Cuthbert, who was weighing the candy, Mrs. Hanover placed a calligraphied invitation on the counter and pushed it toward her.

"Leonora, I do hope you'll join us for tea at South Slope this time," she said, stroking Dash's silky ears. Allie knew it vexed her mother that the shopkeeper's wife had never attended one of her events. "Hats and gloves, of course."

Ten years ago, Dr. Charles Hanover had informed Mrs. Hanover he could no longer breathe in Boston. He felt compelled to fulfill his life-long dream to venture out to The Frontier where one could find an abundance of air and sky and land. While Allie and Will had welcomed the call to adventure, their mother had been outraged. Born and bred a Boston Brahmin, as was the doctor, she had declared she had no desire to leave her beloved city, nor the privileged life it afforded her. Most certainly not for the unknown, uncivilized Colorado Territories.

In the busy mercantile, Allie, who had only vague recollections of their home in Boston, and Maude Mary, who had been a toddler when the family came West, exchanged long-suffering looks. To them 'South Slope' was their home, nothing more than one of the larger houses in town. In truth, it was the grandest residence in Solace Springs and most neighboring towns. The showy residence was their mother personified.

"Hats and gloves, my word," the proprietress scoffed, as she tallied the cost of Mrs. Hanover's purchases.

As a young child, Allie had often perched on a step at the top of another staircase—that one in their elegant home in Boston—to listen unobserved to other conversations she wasn't meant to hear. She remembered strained, muffled discussions followed by louder arguments and long periods—days—of uncomfortable silences. One night, as the tone and volume escalated, two-year-old Maude Mary had crept out of bed to huddle in her lap. When their mother found Allie comforting the sobbing toddler clinging to her on the stairs, she grudgingly agreed to make what she always referred to as "The Grand Sacrifice." With the stipulations she be allowed to bring as much of Boston with her as possible, that she return home as often as she pleased, and that her sons be educated in the East, Mrs. Hanover agreed to her husband's wishes.

Now, side by side in the mercantile, Allie and Maude Mary's reactions to the reminder of the Afternoon Teas their mother hosted were as opposite as Melpomene and Thalia—the comedy/ tragedy masks of theater that hung in their father's study.

Maude Mary's eyes gleamed above her smile. "Oh, Mrs. Cuthbert, of course you must come." Her girlish voice mimicked her mother's manner perfectly. "Mama does serve such exquisite Victorian Sandwich Cake and sticky black ginger bread and Oolong tea. And the ladies do try their best to be elegant. Mama will wear her lilac and I my pink satin." She looked around the store, then back at its proprietress. "I do have so many questions and am just perishing to learn how you and Mr. Cuthbert manage to know exactly what the people of this town will want to purchase. For instance, how do you know how many washboards will be needed at any given time?" At Leonora Cuthbert's blank expression, Maude Mary said, "When you come for tea, we can discuss such things."

Imagining her own expression must be pained, Allie did nothing to alter it. Her sister and mother were who they were. Maude Mary would ask her endless, and often inane, questions. Their mother would never understand that the ladies of Solace Springs could not be deemed an elegant lot, by any stretch. Most were the wives of ranchers and farmers and storekeepers who owned plain sunbonnets and sturdy work gloves. Allie herself took no satisfaction in the frothy affairs. On those occasions—to avoid the inevitable unpleasantness—she grudgingly traded her practical calicoes and linsey-woolsey's for the frivolous fashions her mother favored. Maude Mary had never needed coercing. At a young age, she'd realized if she wore the frills her mother so loved, she could get her own way about almost everything else.

With her mother's hard gaze upon her, Allie surrendered to what she knew to be required of her. "What Mother means, Mrs. Cuthbert, is that you work so hard you deserve a few hours away from the store to enjoy tea and cake on the veranda." Her smile warmed despite her awareness of the inanity of words and she added what she knew to be true. "I'm certain all the ladies would be glad of your company."

Frowning at the scalloped invitation pinched between the thumbs and forefingers of two work-roughened hands, Nora Cuthbert shook her head. Tall shelves overflowed with canned foods. Dry goods and all manner of sundries lined the wall behind her, beckoning to be replenished. In the front window, a row of glass globes filled with colored water prismed the late morning light that spilled into the bustling store and begged to be dusted.

With a nod in Allie's direction, Mrs. Cuthbert said, "Thank you for the kind words, dearie. I know you—and your mama—mean well, but anyone hankerin' for my company knows right where to find me." Over the rims of wire spectacles perched on her thin nose, she addressed Mrs. Hanover with less warmth. "As I've told you for years, Jane, I can't just up and leave the store to Horace in the middle of the day to go drink fancy tea and eat cake." Raising her eyebrows higher, she added, "Not on the veranda of that fancy house of yours or anywhere else."

Jubilant at his wife's agreement to the move, Dr. Hanover had agreed to everything she demanded. He traveled west months ahead of the family to set up his practice and see to the building of their new home on two acres atop a gentle hill overlooking a town so small that, at the time, it had been little more than a sparse main street—motley with ramshackle stores, lean-to's, and a few trading tents—surrounded by ranches. He'd spared no expense on the construction of Jane Hanover's lavish residence, nor on transporting most of her furnishings, clothing, and household help to Solace Springs.

Mrs. Hanover started to speak, but Nora held up a hand. "And, no, Jane, none of those 'exquisite' items you ordered from that Harrods Department Store in London, England have come in yet."

"But it's been months," the matron protested, resettling the restless dog in the crook of her arm. To her daughters, she added, "I had so hoped to have the Lapsang Souchong and Darjeeling for this month's Tea. And that posh silver biscuit box from the catalogue . . ."

"It's been weeks," Nora corrected her, as she did every Saturday. "It'll be months before your order even gets to London, never mind months more until your 'posh' items find their way across the whole Atlantic ocean—and the better part of this continent—to show up here at plain old Cuthbert's Mercantile."

Mrs. Hanover lowered her eyes for a moment. Raising them, she said, "I must reprove myself, mustn't I? I do confess to allowing hope to become an expectation. Nonetheless," she lifted her plump chin, "nonetheless, I must say . . . we are not amused."

CHAPTER THREE

The day's events had left Ned Harper rattled for reasons he couldn't have predicted. And, he thought, surprised at how much it added to his uneasiness, Zeke's gone and brought baseball to town.

At the steepest incline on the switch back road to his cabin, he swung out of the wagon to spare Trickster, his black Morgan stallion, the extra weight. Running Cloud loped alongside, then darted in and out of thickets and up and down the hillside. Welcoming the solitude, Ned tried to put the hubbub of town and the ugly encounter with Luke Findlay behind him. He'd managed to call up enough patience to stop himself from doing anything he'd regret and was glad of that, but the effort had left him drained.

On one side of the wagon path, trees and brush climbed the slope, providing dappled shade to the road below. On the other, Solace Lake sparkled deep blue in the distance and livestock grazed the green and gold grasses of the ranch lands below. A stiff afternoon breeze blended the sweet scents of the pastures with the spice of the pines and the earthy aroma of mud hardening in the sun. Ned took little notice of the surroundings that had once delighted him.

When they reached the homestead, Cloud scouted a puddle of shade beneath a tree and settled there for a nap that would likely last until hunger sent him into the woods to hunt for his supper. Ned had chosen this piece of land three years ago—part hillside, part flatland, with his lower acres adjoining Will Hanover's pasture land. They'd begun to breed the horses they planned to sell to the army and their stock had grown to include two stallions, several mares, and five yearlings. This spring should see the birth of three more foals.

According to the Homestead Act, this autumn they could buy their 'up proved' land outright for a dollar or so an acre. Will had built a pretty little house for his wife and young family on the flatlands. Ned had chosen the wooded hillside to build his own. His log cabin and outbuildings nestled against a forest of blue spruce and limber pine. To one side of the house, a stream tumbled down the hill. From the front porch, he could see open sky meet tree tops with the lake and mountains shimmering beyond. Two large windows faced southwest, giving the house the benefit of afternoon light and warmth for most of the year.

Balancing an armload of provisions, he climbed the rough wooden steps to the covered porch and found a hamper at the door. Will and Hannah. A week didn't go by without one of Hannah Hanover's homemade woven baskets appearing at his door. Ned didn't need to lift the cloth to know what it hid: a crock of rabbit stew made from one of the brace of rabbits he'd given them a few days ago, fresh oat bannocks, potato pudding, and the inevitable vinegar pie.

Hannah, Will's fiery Scottish wife, informed anyone who would listen that, "Tis my vinegar pie, ye ken, that's the only thing standing between Ned Harper and scurvy!"

His one-room cabin, larger by several feet than most of its kind, was clean and well-kept, but felt dark and cramped to him. In one corner, a colorful quilt decorated a bed with a wooden chest at its foot. A National Excelsior Stove and a pie safe took up most of another wall and a small trestle table with two chairs stood in the center of the room. On either side of the stove, shelves displayed tin ware, crockery, and a few pieces of delicate bone china. Iron pots and pans hung from hooks attached to the lowest ledge. A pair of upholstered chairs faced a deep fireplace with an elk hide covering the wood floor beneath them. The hearth was cold, the woodpile neatly stacked. Neither had been touched in many months.

Ned had squared and chinked every log himself, built almost every piece of furniture, hung every shelf. But the place and everything in it gave him no pleasure. He kept his eyes and mind on his tasks. After storing his supplies and carrying the cream and butter down to the springhouse, he trudged back to the cabin. He dished up a plate of cold stew and potato pudding, poured a tin cup of whiskey, and brought the food out to the porch. Standing there in the dusk, he couldn't shake the memory of the crippled boy. Appetite gone, he set the plate and cup down sharply.

"Cloud!" he called into the woods. "To me!"

The wolf dog bounded out from a nearby thicket. With Cloud trotting at his side, Ned tramped through a maze of trees, tangled underbrush, and up and down rock-strewn hills. A recent cloudburst had left the ground slippery in some places, boggy in others, and the night air pungent with the scent of mud and leaf mold. The forest usually settled Ned, but there'd been times it took every bit of resolve he could muster to fight the urge to keep walking until there was no way out.

Tonight his will failed him. Mindless, he plunged farther and farther into the dark woods, insensitive to what was underfoot or overhead. When he reached the bank of Crooked Canyon Creek, cold and fast with spring thaw, an owl's plaintive cry roused him from his stupor. Soaked with sweat and legs rubbery, he didn't know how long he'd stood on the edge of the rushing freshet. Didn't care.

Ice in his heart, he muttered, "Dammit," and shook his bowed head. "What am I doing? What the hell am I doing?"

He knew the answer. And the answer shamed him.

Hours later, he and Cloud plodded up the porch stairs of his cabin, both spent. The dog ate the untouched food on the tin plate Ned set on the floor and was soon asleep at his feet, dreaming and twitching. Ned sipped Old Overholt's until the burn of the whiskey eased the tightness in his chest. When he knew he could put it off no longer, he entered the dark house.

Eyes straight ahead and Cloud at his heels, he strode past the bed and through a door that opened to an unfinished space. He'd begun work on a second room a few years ago, but had yet to complete it. His arms felt too heavy to lift a hammer when he tried. Two walls joined the back wall of the cabin, but where the fourth should stand nothing divided the house from the woods. Where the roof should be, there was only the dome of night sky. All the logs he needed had been split and squared, all the roof shingles cut and shaped and stacked in the barn. His building tools—broad ax, draw knife, adz and maul, and a bed roll—lay beneath an oilskin tarp in a corner.

Retrieving another tarp and blankets from the stable, he spread them over the hard-packed dirt and stretched out on top, pulling a blanket over himself. If it rained again, he'd shelter in the stable. Arms crossed beneath his head, he watched the broken moon make its slow descent toward morning. Cloud squatted on his haunches—nose high, ears pricked—alert for any scent or sound warning of unwanted visitors. Crickets chirped nearby and the underbrush rustled with the scurry of nocturnal critters. An owl hooted overhead, a comforting presence.

When he finally closed his eyes, Ned hoped for sleep, but had little expectation it would come.

I know it's my fault for getting out of the wagon, Joseph thought, drowsy in the thin light of dawn. Now Pa's all bulled-up, Ma's skittish, and Sarah won't even look at me. But, I'm glad I did it.

The man said to Pa, "Ned Harper. Sorry for the fright." But Pa wouldn't shake his hand.

He said to me, "His name's Running Cloud. Thanks for the kindness you showed him."

Pa won't even let me play with our own sheep dogs. He says they're working dogs and they'd just knock me over anyhow.

Pa don't like Ned Harper or Running Cloud, but I do. That's probably why I dreamed about them. We were walking through the woods just past sundown. When the dog ran ahead, I ran right along beside him. A white owl—big as the moon—watched us and who-whooed from a branch high above.

The only thing I was scared of was Pa finding out I'd gone outside our gate by myself.

CHAPTER FOUR

Dr. Charles Hanover had a penchant for repeating the sayings of famous men. "I am often informed, amused, and, on occasion, comforted by the words of those far wiser than myself," he had explained to his children more than once.

"We know, Papa," Allie and her siblings would always humor him, singly or in unison.

Carrying a steaming mug of his morning coffee down the hall, Allie approached her father's study. Much to the chagrin of her mother, Doc Hanover couldn't abide tea. "Our esteemed Founding Father John Adams said, " 'Tea must be universally renounced. And the sooner the better!' "

As Allie neared the room, the sound of his laughter quickened her pace. A quick rap on the door got her a warm, "Enter, please."

When she crossed the threshold, he beamed up at her and set his book on the Chinese tea table beside his chair. Bluster, his aging border collie, dozed at his feet. "Thank you, my dear," Doc said. "You bring two of my favorite things to brighten a grey morning—a cup of my preferred libation and my extraordinary daughter."

Lifting the thick tome, he tapped the page he'd been reading. "In this, his magnificent work, *War and Peace,* the brilliant Russian author Lev Nikolayevich Tolstoy sums up the profession of medicine just so: 'Though the doctors treated him,' Doc recited, 'and let his blood, and gave him medications to drink, he . . . nevertheless . . . recovered.' " Closing the book, he chortled, "Nevertheless, in deed!"

Her father had returned home late the night before after visiting his patients. Keen to share the events of the previous day, Allie had risen early to catch him before he left again. His study was her favorite place in the house—a refuge of mahogany furniture and thick Turkish carpets, all suffused with the rich aroma of leather, old books, and wood smoke. Handing him his coffee, she kissed his cheek and settled into the Chesterfield chair facing him.

"My dearest child, Tolstoy's words remind me how easy it is for those who do our work to take ourselves too seriously." His lean, patrician features softened with affection. "I implore you to please remember this: In all your pursuits—medical or otherwise—take yourself seriously only when, and if, you absolutely must."

"Papa," she said, with a rueful twist of her mouth, "you must not ask that. You know better than anyone that not taking myself 'too seriously' doesn't, and will never, come easily to me." Tilting her head, she gave him a narrow look. "Nor do I agree it should."

"I do know that, my dear," he said. "And, truth be told, I wouldn't have it otherwise." Tasting the coffee, he gave her an appreciative smile. The beverage was just as he liked it—scalding hot and bitter black—'barefoot'—as Ned Harper had informed him cowboys drank the invigorating brew. "You are all the more a blessing to me because of the depth of your empathy and wisdom. You are and always will be my . . ."

"Most favorite child. I know, Papa." Leaning forward, she reached for his coffee, took a sip, grimaced, and handed it back. "As is Will, because of his independent nature and zeal for hard work. And dear Albert, for his sweet spirit and generous heart. And, oh yes, our Maude Mary, because . . . because the insufferable, prying little hen . . . is so observant and curious." At his abashed look, Allie patted his hand. "Don't pretend you don't know all your dearest 'blessings' talk to each other about you as much as you talk about us."

Sunlight penetrated the early morning drear and streamed through mullioned windows to cast a checkered pattern on the dark wood of the desk. "I suppose empathy and wisdom must cut both ways," her father sighed, inclining his head half an inch. "I will be sure to remember that in all my future dealings with my favorite *eldest* daughter." Setting the coffee out of her reach, he raised a brow. "Now, I'm eager to learn to what I owe the pleasure of this visit."

"Well," she began slowly, "I had an interesting time at Cuthbert's yesterday. First, you'll be delighted to learn Zeke Foster is importing baseball to our very own Solace Springs. His long-awaited bats have arrived from Louisville."

"Excellent!" Her father had been an avid baseball 'crank' in Boston and Allie knew he missed the pastime dearly. "I surmise," he said, "that means Solace Springs will soon have its own team."

Allie lifted a disinterested shoulder. "I surmise you surmise correctly." Then, with a mock dreamy grin, she added, "Second, Zeke is, alas, in love again."

"Ah, our poor Lothario." Her father's graying brow arched. "I thought he was besotted by the new schoolmarm."

Doc Hanover took as keen an interest in gossip as any of the town folk. Zeke's love life always provided ample fodder for talk and speculation, couched in mostly good-natured amusement.

"That was last month. Ned says, 'The only thing Zeke Foster has ever been any good at is making bad decisions about women.' " The dapper barber, always desperate to find lasting love, was often defeated by his own fickleness. "There's a new girl in town and he's already spoony over her. Her family, the Findlays, bought the Evans's sheep ranch a few months ago."

Wrapping his fingers around his mug, her father studied her. "Somehow, I doubt my unrepentantly serious daughter came down at cock's crow just to report on Zeke Foster's latest romance." With his patients, Allie had observed, the doctor inquired about the smallest details of their physical complaints, their histories, and their concerns. In conversation, he rarely asked questions. He made observations and waited for more to be revealed. If nothing was forthcoming, he seldom pressed. "There must—please—be a more promising third thing."

"Well . . . yes. The girl—Sarah Findlay—has a younger brother who, I believe, suffers from Little's Disease." After rereading Dr. Little's monograph the night before, she was confident in her assessment and hopeful her father would be impressed.

"Little's Disease," he echoed, gazing at her over the rim of his spectacles. "You've made a diagnosis based on your observations."

Allie felt a small pinch in her chest. "And your journals, of course." It hadn't occurred to her until just that moment that he might find it over-reaching for someone with so little experience and no formal training to presume to do such a thing. "Not exactly a diagnosis," she corrected, irritated by the warmth she felt suffusing her cheeks. "Just a theory. Of sorts. I guess."

"Theory may be all we physicians have to work with much of the time," he said. Since childhood, Allie had taken a keen interest in all aspects of her father's medical practice. Without a qualm, she'd observed him stitch wounds, set bones, and perform surgeries. Fascination with his books and medical journals—*Gray's Anatomy*, in particular—had fueled her curiosity and helped her develop an extensive, if somewhat startling, vocabulary at an early age. When Doc realized she had a true passion for medicine, he'd allowed her to assist with minor procedures at his clinic and accompany him on calls. "Go on, my dear. Elucidate, please."

"A young boy, maybe eight years-old, though I think he might be small for his age," she began, picturing the child with his hand on Cloud's head.

"With involuntary writhing movements, twisting of the torso, tremors, and grimacing. Able to walk, but with an unsteady gait." Her father's nod encouraged her to continue. "He didn't talk, so I couldn't assess speech or intelligence."

With a pang, she caught herself describing the boy as if he were a clinical study in one of her father's journals, rather than an afflicted child determined to pet a large, friendly dog. "His name is Joseph Findlay. He has big dark eyes and raggedy yellow hair and he climbed out of the family's wagon because he wanted to make friends with Running Cloud."

"From your description, I must say I'm in agreement with your diagnosis of mild to moderate athetoid palsy. I'm even more impressed with your understanding that young Joseph is a person, not a diagnosis. Well done."

His praise brought more color to Allie's cheeks. Still, she was troubled on the boy's behalf. The article she'd read had been disheartening. "But Papa, is there really nothing that can be done for him?"

Doc shook his head. "Sadly, there's neither cure not treatment for his condition. Most parents would have placed a child like him in an asylum at birth, so his family must be credited for caring for him themselves. We can help him best by encouraging them to continue to do so."

"I don't think they need much encouragement, they—especially his father—seem very protective of him." She recalled the scene at the wagon with a knot in her stomach. "Some children, even a few adults, said cruel, ignorant things about him."

"Our world can be a most inhospitable place for those who are different," Doc acknowledged, then brightened. "Still, that boy did manage to elude his parents' protection long enough to make the acquaintance of a rather intimidating wolf dog."

"He did."

"A sign of spirit, I must say." When Allie didn't elucidate, Doc continued, "I assume Ned accompanied said dog to town."

"He did." Allie considered how much to say in answer to her father's unspoken question. He would be interested in all of it—Ned's still-guarded demeanor, his tense encounter with Joseph's father, his quick exit after. All of it left her heavy-hearted. "He's still not himself."

"A less clinical assessment in this case, I see."

The warmth in his eyes assured Allie his words were not a reproach. Before she could assure him it was, in fact, a clinical assessment, at least, of sorts, he set down his mug and leaned toward her.

"There is something I've been wanting to discuss with you for some time and your astute description of the child tells me the time has come." Her father's tone alerted Allie that the 'something' was serious. Curious, but not alarmed, she waited for him to explain. "I believe you're ready to have a case of your own to follow," he said. "One that you can assess and treat, as you deem necessary."

When she could, she exhaled. "Ready? To follow patients of my own?"

"Under my supervision, of course."

"Of course." Then, with small-voiced uncertainty. "You're sure I'm ready?"

"I am."

"I'll have a case to write up and submit with my applications."

"You will." When Allie could manage nothing more, Doc said, "Good, then. I'll fill you in on the Winnicott family later. Their situation may seem simple on the surface, but as you'll find time and again with your patients, their problems are complex and the solutions elusive." Lifting his coffee cup, he took a sip, then studied her with more intensity. "I have no doubts regarding your readiness, my dear. I do, however have one small concern."

Allie felt the color leave her face.

"Small, I said." His smile dispelled some of her uneasiness. "As I've said since you were a very small child, you have a tendency . . ."

She met her father's gaze. "I know, Papa. I have a tendency to, as you have put it, 'host the burdens of others.' "

"Yes, my dear."

He'd taken care to explain it wasn't a flaw, simply the 'least of her virtues.' And Allie had to admit her father wasn't entirely wrong. She'd never been able to tolerate feeling helpless. When others suffered or faltered, she'd always been quick to step in and try to set things right. Sometimes too quick. "And," she said, "you fear this family—these Winnicotts—will allow me to take ownership of their burdens, if I let them."

"Allow you? Let them?" As much as he avoided direct questions, he was quite free with hypotheticals. "Perhaps," he chuckled. "More likely, they'll insist on it."

"Then I assure you, Dr. Hanover," Allie said with a wry grin, "I will summon all my resolve and use this case as an exercise in learning to restrain that regrettable habit of mine."

"Do not mistake me, my dear. Your capacity to care is not regrettable. Far from it. But when people are taught to manage their burdens, rather than relinquish them to others, they become stronger. The Winnicotts, as you will find, are much in need of strengthening, among other more mundane things. Now, I must be off. I'll give you a little background this evening, then await your assessment based on what you find when you've met them." He rose, signaling their talk was over. "I'll tell them to expect your visit soon. They, and I, will look forward to it."

Pride and gratitude brought her to her feet and she threw her arms around her father. "No more than I, Papa." Resting her cheek on his chest, she breathed in his familiar scent—wool, wood smoke, always something medicinal, and a hint of her mother's attar of roses. His confidence in Allie thickened her throat. "Thank you so very much."

Releasing him, she pulled back and gave him the cocked-head, raised-brow look she had inherited from him. "But who, might I ask, is going to tell Mother?"

Mrs. Hanover lifted her chin and narrowed her eyes at her husband and daughter. "I forbid it."

She was as opposed to her daughter's aspiration to become a physician as her husband was for it. Like Queen Victoria, she believed marriage gave one one's position in the world like nothing else could and that the training of a young lady should be toward that one goal. The notion of a woman working outside the home was scandalous. "A travesty of all that is natural!"

She maintained that everything any daughter of hers would ever need to know could be found in *Godey's Ladies' Book* and that Allie had already had all the education a young lady needed to take her place where she belonged—in the home she would one day make for her own family. Most certainly not in a basement dissecting room in the company of male physicians and cadavers.

But the idea of a wife opposing her husband was equally unthinkable to Jane Hanover. She had voiced her opinion—she felt a slight palpitation when she realized she'd uttered the word 'forbid' to her husband—and would henceforth silently submit to his will.

That, of course, did not mean she would refrain from expressing her dissatisfaction to her daughter in subtle—and not so subtle—attempts to dissuade her from her foolishness.

CHAPTER FIVE

Solace Springs, Doc Hanover noted, had been infected with a virulent strain of baseball fever.

The younger men succumbed first, led by the barber, Zeke Foster. They were quickly followed by those of all ages and stages of fitness. With the arrival of the Louisville bats, potential players engaged in tryouts to ascertain who among them could throw, hit, or catch the ball. Some had one or another of the skills; few had all.

In the face of these obstacles, Zeke remained undaunted. "All we need is practice, boys," he assured them, tapping the ground with the bat he always carried. "And, a damned place to play. And, a damned name."

After a barrage of conflicting opinions, the team settled on an empty field a quarter of a mile from town on which to create a diamond. They took two days to agree upon the distances between the four bases and between the hurler and home plate. After even more heated discussions, they named the lot Elysian Fields—an homage to the site in Hoboken, New Jersey where the New York Knickerbockers had played the first recorded baseball game on October 6, 1845. With only one or two dissenting votes, they designated themselves the Solace Springs Sluggers and commenced their practices.

That, Doc had observed, was when the trouble began.

During early workouts, frustrations almost ended the Sluggers' hopes of being ready for a match against the Fountain City Nine by late September.

Strong farmers and able ranchers, the players were accustomed to long days of hard labor, but most were not athletes. Hitting a small brown leather ball with a stick did not come naturally. Whether thrown or batted, catching it was equally challenging. Sprinting around bases called upon rarely used muscles.

The team's hurlers were erratic. Some could throw hard, some straight. None did both with any consistency. They flung the ball over the strikers' heads or dangerously close to their bodies. Swinging desperately, batters tried to make contact with the invisible ball. Success was sporadic, at best. Will Hanover, who'd proven himself a decent hitter and an adequate first baseman, lamented to his father, Doc Hanover, "I'd say the odds of getting hit by a ball are about as good as hitting it."

If and when a pitch was solidly hit, the fielders were as apt to drop easy pop flies as to be struck by them. They tended to lose grounders between their legs, or worse. High fly balls to the outfield often caused collisions between two or more over-zealous players. When a ball had been caught, chances were the throw to a baseman would go awry. As one such afternoon wore on, the players became so irascible that old Reverend Carstairs, who was umpiring, was obliged to impose a six cent fine—payable on the spot—for swearing.

The formation of the baseball team caused an unexpected boon to Dr. Hanover's medical practice. After the games, he and Allie treated a line-up of players for sprains, strains, bruises, black eyes, and assorted jammed fingers—wounds caused by the combined efforts of grown men determined to take possession of one small ball. For day-after aches and pains, Zeke did a brisk business selling McLean's Volcanic Oil Liniment—"good for man and beast."

"It's fortunate," Doc had opined, as he splinted a finger, "that no one can hit the ball hard enough to do much real damage, else the name Elysian Fields might take on its more ecclesiastical meaning."

Nonetheless, he maintained his long-standing passion for the game. He and his youngest son, Albert, came to watch Will and the others whenever they could. Sporting matching news-boy style baseball caps, they stood on the sidelines, dodging foul balls and wild pitches. On this sunny Sunday afternoon, Doc was relieved to see that weeks of practice had improved the team's performance. He gave Albert and himself some credit for the progress. During one of the Sluggers' more disastrous early practices—one player had almost been concussed by a high fly ball that had landed on his head, rather than in his outstretched hands—Albert had turned to Doc with a troubled expression. "Are they afflicted, Papa?"

Shaking his head, Doc had chuckled. "No, son. That's just what Mark Twain would call, 'grievous awkwardness.' " But, after some thought and more observation, he added, "I do believe you have correctly diagnosed at least part of the problem. Other factors notwithstanding, it's clear these poor fellows *are* afflicted with sun-blindness."

Taking it upon himself to cure the problem, he ordered baseball caps with visors from the Peck and Snyder catalogue and he and Albert presented them to the team. Doc also insisted they keep a barrel of water available to help prevent dehydration and heat stroke.

Even if Will hadn't joined the Sluggers, Doc would have been an avid supporter. "I've been a baseball crank since I was a boy," he'd told him and Albert over one Sunday supper. "I attended as many Boston Tri-Mountain home games as I could. When Will was old enough, I took him along."

Will's eyes shone with the boyhood recollection. "I was what—seven—when we saw Boston play Portland on the Common? Their captain, what was his name? Crowell? He hit the only home run of the game. Then," a slow smile spread across his face, "the poor guy fainted dead away. You ran right out onto the field and took care of him."

"That I did." Doc stopped for a moment to savor the memory. He'd assured the worried team their man suffered only from sun stroke and would make a full recovery. "I also managed to wrangle myself an invitation to join those boys in their jollifications around the bar at the Cummings House that evening."

Now that the Sluggers were no longer afflicted by sun-blindness, and had gained more confidence in their skills, they encountered a new problem. Arguments about the rules often disrupted their much needed work-outs. The current practice game halted when Sam Hollister tried to get a runner out by throwing the ball at him.

"You can't do that!" Zeke railed.

"Can and will!"

"Doc," Zeke shouted, chest to chest with Hollister. "Come out here and settle this!"

When the men learned Doc had attended professional baseball games, they credited him as an authority and often called upon him to resolve their disputes. Will and the other players clustered around to hear his opinion of this current row.

With Albert at his side, Doc approached. "Difference of opinion?" he asked mildly.

"It's not a damned opinion," Zeke snarled. He had emptied his pockets and given all his money to Reverend Carstairs before the game. "It's a fact."

Sam balled his fists at his sides. "It's just not a *true* fact."

"Well," Doc said, "you're both right, to a certain extent. If you're playing rounders, throwing the ball at someone is called 'soaking' and it's a legitimate way to get a runner out. If you're playing baseball, it's not. You just have to agree on what game you're playing." He frowned at the red-faced men. "Whichever it is, remember it's just a game. It's supposed to be fun."

Both men looked askance at Doc. Almost in unison, they protested, "We are having fun."

Zeke turned glum. "Now that we've got the damned rules straight, all we need is a hurler who can throw the damned ball straight."

"And hard," Sam commiserated.

"And consistently," Will added, with a sigh.

"With a good eye and a strong arm."

"Steady, at least most of the time," Sam added.

Eyes alive with calculation, Zeke gave Will a meaningful look. "I don't know why we didn't think of this before."

At first, Will didn't seem to catch his meaning. When he did, he took a step back, shaking his head. "He'll never do it."

The other men stared him down. When Will looked to him for support, Doc's hopeful gaze matched the players'.

"All right, all right," Will snapped, "I'll ask him." After years of hunting with bow and arrow, Ned Harper had developed the arm strength, aim, and keen eyesight of a natural hurler. Doc was certain his son's next words were aimed at him. "Just don't blame me when he says no."

CHAPTER SIX

"I know you're not here 'cause you're 'concerned' about me," Ned chided Will, who had caught him off guard by showing up at his cabin on a weekday morning. He slanted cold eyes up at his friend. "Because you know better than that."

Head down, Ned focused on his task. It might have been a few days, a week or so maybe—he couldn't say for sure—since he'd last ridden down to the H&H to work the horses. But that wasn't unusual of late. "And I'm damn sure you didn't come up here to see if I finished the cabin yet," he added, still testy, "because that's none of your business."

His words matched the even cadence of the back and forth motions of scraping hair, fat, and flesh from a deer hide using the animal's sharpened thigh bone. Ned knew Will would never complain he wasn't pulling his weight at their ranch, though he had to admit there'd be truth in it if he did. The thought made him more irritable. Sweat stung his eyes and his back and arms ached in protest at the hours of toil he'd put in. He'd been preparing the skin for tanning for days—cutting the hide from the carcass, dressing the meat, then washing the hide, rinsing it in the stream, wringing it out, drying it on the rack.

Will had found him in the cleared space behind his cabin surrounded by the paraphernalia for tanning—a sapling frame to twist and warp the hide, a drying rack, a bucket of warm water and minced deer brains, and a couple of big-bristled brushes. Blue spruce and limber pine surrounded the small clearing, but the bright sun and cloudless sky allowed no slanting shade to give respite from the summer heat. No breeze dispersed the fetid odor that spoiled what should have been the fresh air of Ned's mountain retreat.

"What I do know is winter's only months away," Will countered. Looking past Ned into the roofless, three-walled enclosure attached to the cabin, his gaze lingered on the bedroll in the middle of the dirt floor. He frowned. "Now look here," he said slowly. "I don't mean to cross a line." He said it in the careful tone of a man who is about to do just that. "But snow and ice and wind are coming with it. If you're gonna be sleeping there," he tilted his head toward the bedroll, "you need a roof and four walls."

Ned knew what people thought, what they said amongst themselves, never to him: "He's taking it hard, of course," had changed to, "He's taking it too hard, for too long."

For a moment, the only sound was the rasp of bone against deer hide.

"Dammit Ned, it's time to finish that room." The words hung between them—the line had been crossed. Will sighed and crossed another. "There are plenty of folk who'd be glad to come up and help. We'd get it done in a day."

The scraping done, Ned stood and stretched the kinks from his back. Lifting his hat, he pushed back damp hair and wiped the sweat from his face with his forearm. Will's offer weighed like a four-by-four beam on his shoulders. Resettling his hat, he gave him a flat stare, then looked away. "I don't need any help."

Something akin to shame kept Ned from meeting his friend's eyes. It wasn't that he didn't want to finish the room—he missed the comfort of a warm, dry bed and a good fire in the hearth on a cold day. And he wasn't one to leave a task undone. Still, the cabin—finished room and unfinished—had come to feel like a cage. He couldn't bring himself to lay another log and close it up even more. "The barn's done me just fine whenever I've needed shelter," he said. "It'll do 'til I get to the cabin."

He'd wintered in the stable while building the homestead and again after Becky and the baby died. The small barn's walls were solid enough and hay stuffed into the cracks stopped most drafts. Heat from a three-footed stove and Cloud and Trickster's bodies had taken the edge off the deep chill of winter nights and their company eased his loneliness. The animals sensed his grief, he was sure, but had done him the kindness of not trying to comfort him.

Will lifted a shoulder in surrender. "That's pretty much what I told Hannah you'd say." Furrowing his brow, he sniffed the air. His eyes watered and he grimaced. "What the devil is that god-awful stink?"

Grateful for the change of subject, Ned favored him with a grin. The hide was ready for the next and most important step in the process. "Deer brains," he replied, eyeing the reeking bucket. "They're startin' to rot from the heat, but that won't hurt the tanning." Stretching the hide over the rack, he added, "If you really want to help, roll up your sleeves and slap some of that soup onto the hide. All we have to do is work it in with our hands and we'll have the softest buckskin you've ever seen."

"But why . . ." Breathing through his mouth, Will stifled a gag "Why brains?"

Cupping his hands, Ned scooped up the noxious mixture and slathered it on the deerskin. "I'd always favored neats foot oil 'til Red Moon taught me brain tanning. Brains don't darken the hide or let it get brittle like the oil does. She says every animal has just enough brains to tan its own hide—except the buffalo. With a buffalo, you might need to add a few egg yolks to have enough."

When he was a youth, the old Indian woman had shown him how to make and fletch his own arrows and shared her tribe's beliefs about hunting. She'd warned him never to take the first animal he saw. "Let it go. Chances are you'll see more. If you don't find another all day, your decision to let the first go was a wise one. When the number of animals in an area is down, killing the first may make it the last you'll see there for many years." Even more solemn, she'd added, "Greed and wisdom can't sit at the same campfire."

Ned carefully massaged the brain solution into the hide with Will attempting to follow his lead. "Slow down," he told him. "Best way to get a job like this done quick is to do it slow."

As always, Ned had honored the deer as Red Moon had instructed. After the kill he'd knelt beside it and given thanks to the animal spirits and the Creator. He'd apologized to the buck for taking its life. Where it had fallen, he left a gift for its cousins—a small salt lick.

When their work was done, he and Will stretched the hide on the roof to await another coat of brains, safe from critters. Lye soap and stream water did little to wash away the stench that clung to their hands and arms. "Don't you go telling Hannah it's my fault you've come home stinkin' like a buzzard's breath," Ned warned Will.

They escaped to the fresher air of the front porch to sip Old Overholt's and talk—or not—until the sun hung low on the horizon.

"Baseball team's comin' together," Will said. He refilled his cup and took a deep swallow. "More or less."

Ned slid him a sideways glance and shook his head. "Like Cuthbert says, 'grown men acting like puddin' headed boys.' "

"I suppose." Will sat a few minutes more, then rose to leave. He resettled his hat, jammed his hands in his pockets, and started to speak, then stopped.

With a mix of amusement and uneasiness, Ned sensed his usually forthcoming friend had something more on his mind. "What's makin' you so fidgety? More complaints?"

"No," Will said too quickly, drawing a sharp look from Ned. "No, it's just . . ."

"Just?"

"Well, I was wondering . . ." He rubbed the back of his neck. "I was wondering if you might be . . ."

It did entertain Ned to see Will tongue-tied, but not enough to press. "I sure wish you'd find something better to do than wonder about me." He cut off what he believed was likely to be more 'concerns' regarding how he was living his life. "Maybe you could try wondering about something more interesting—like what Hannah's fixin' you for supper tonight."

"Can't." Will's shrug told Ned he'd won. "I already know the answer to that." He pointed to the basket he'd set by the door. "Same as she sent you—cock-a-leekie soup and bannocks."

"Good," Ned said, feeling more affable. Whatever had been on Will's mind, it appeared he'd decided to let it go. Leaning back in the wicker chair, he put his feet up on the porch railing. "Get on home and enjoy it. Thank Hannah for me."

After climbing in the saddle, Will looked back at Ned, started to speak, then headed down the mountain. Ned poured himself another drink. With Cloud settled at his feet, he watched the sun sink out of sight. In the numbness of whiskey, he could bear to think of Becky and their baby, Benjamin Thomas. The life they might have had, should have had, together. The life he didn't want without them. He could feel Becky's head on his shoulder, her hand on his chest. He'd held her like that while life ebbed from her body.

The midwife had wrapped Benjamin in a blanket Becky had knit and laid him in Ned's arms. His son had never even drawn a breath. He'd held him until Doc laid a hand on his shoulder and the midwife eased the infant away from him. Losing that precious weight had left Ned's arms empty and aching and cold.

Reverend Carstairs, accompanied by a chorus of other well-meaning folk, had assured him he'd see Becky and his son again in the hereafter. Had he been churched as a boy, he might have had an easier time believing it.

But the Harper brothers had lived on their own far from town and to them Sundays were no different from any other day. Despite Ned's doubts, the Reverend's promise did give him some comfort. He found himself pondering the possibility more and more, as his days became increasingly burdensome. If it's true, he'd begun to think, why wait to join them? If it's not, it wouldn't matter—he imagined death to be a dark and empty place no different from the one he occupied now.

Topping his tin cup off with more whiskey, he downed near half and hoped the gut-searing heat would reach his arms.

CHAPTER SEVEN

"Well," Allie's mother huffed. She set the latest copy of *Godey's* beside her on the rose chintz sofa with enough of a slap to make her point, but not enough to be unladylike. "As you know, I strongly disapprove."

Standing in the doorway of the morning room, Allie was anxious to be on her way to make her first visit to the Winnicotts. Though she'd prepared herself for her mother's displeasure, it still rankled.

"Of course, I know," she retorted, hands clenched behind her back. It irked her that her mother's disapproval still stung. "How could I not? You've made it *ever* so clear. I was hoping just this once you might try not to." Her mother's tight frown reminded her that conflict would only prolong the unpleasant conversation. Taking a breath, she tried for conciliation. "I'm only doing what you've taught me by your example. Charitable works—bringing food and clothing and firewood to a needy family. And, as Papa explained, I may do a bit of doctoring—if and when it's called for." She lowered her eyes to say the next. "I hoped you'd be pleased."

Her mother's morning room was, as always, lovely. Sunlight gleamed on the silver tea set and lit the facets of a crystal vase of lilacs on the inlaid table. A spring breeze stirred through open French doors mingling the sweet fragrances of the garden with the sharp spice of brewing tea. In a room without shadows, a shadow darkened Allie's thoughts. She guessed the home she'd be calling on later this morning would hold nothing to please the eye or nose or spirit.

"Don't mistake me," her mother said more kindly. "I do credit your intentions, serving the worthy poor and all that. What does not please me at this particular moment is the thought of you visiting a hovel in the sorriest part of town all alone."

"I won't be alone." Allie relaxed, able to give her mother at least one less thing to object to. "Papa asked Norberto to drive me." The family's handyman would see to her safety and assist as needed. Though she knew it unwise, she couldn't resist a mild tease. "Of course, you're welcome to come along if you like."

"If I like?" Her mother's mouth tightened again. "Well, I am sure and certain that I don't like." With a beleaguered sigh, she leaned back against the cushions of the sofa. "My stars, Alexandrina Victoria." Mrs. Hanover gazed upward, as if petitioning the errant deity who had sent her such a difficult daughter to explain itself. Allie wasn't certain if her mother's next words were meant for her or the gods. "Why is it you must take such pleasure in trying my very soul?"

Doc Hanover, who had come up silently, stood behind Allie in the doorway. "Why, my darling," he said cheerfully to his wife, "it is the duty of our children to try our souls. Else, how will we earn our places in Heaven?"

Eyes alight, Maude Mary, who had taken in the scene from behind her father, skipped past him into the morning room. To Allie, she said, "A hovel? A real hovel? I've never seen such a thing and I am just perishing to visit one!" She looked to her mother. "Oh, Mama, please, please—I just must be permitted to go with Allie!" Swinging around, she beseeched her father, "Please, Papa? You always say we must take education where we find it."

A chorus of "No's!" answered her in swift unison.

The overnight squall had muddied the rutted main street of Solace Springs, slowing the cart's progress. As Norberto urged the horses to slog through the muck toward the Winnicotts' home, Allie realized she had some trepidations of her own about her visit to her first patients. What would they need beyond the food and clothing donated by the Benevolent Ladies? Would she be able to provide it?

Passing the respectable establishments that lined Commerce Street, she watched people hurry about their week-day errands at the tack and feed, land office, livery, and tailor. The bank, post office, and mercantile were the busiest, the Tongue Oil Saloon still shuttered. Behind the line of buildings, tree-studded knolls sloped and dipped up to the edge of the woods.

Horace Cuthbert waved to her as he set a cask of brine and pickles by the door of his store. In front of Zeke's Barber Shop, two elderly cowboys hunched on up-ended barrels, gossiping while they chewed and spat tobacco. Leaving the familiar behind, Allie noted the street grew more deserted, the scattered buildings more rundown, and the road itself more potholed.

Her uneasiness wasn't about visiting the 'sorriest' side of town, it was the nagging fear she might fail to help the Winnicotts, or disappoint her father, or, most galling of all, prove her mother correct about the limitations of women. Since learning of Allie's plans, Mrs. Hanover hadn't missed a chance to remind her of Queen Victoria's pronouncement that in this disappointing modern world their "poor, feeble sex was bent on forgetting every sense of womanly feeling and propriety." She had deemed Allie's intention of attending medical college and entering a profession a loathsome example of what the monarch cautioned against.

To remind herself to hold fast to her own beliefs, Allie's fingers went to the letter folded in her skirt pocket. Her father had arranged for her to correspond with the daughter of one of his former colleagues in Boston. A few years older than Allie, Miss Lydia Brennan was pursuing her education at Dr. Elizabeth Blackwell's New York Medical College for Women. Dr.

Blackwell, the first woman to graduate from an American medical school, had started a women's college with a small hospital attached. From Lydia, Allie got the encouragement she could not expect—nor hope for—from either the Queen of England or her own mother. As the cart jolted past the funeral parlor, she pulled the letter from her pocket and smoothed it on her lap to reread.

My dearest Allie,

As our esteemed Dr. Elizabeth Blackwell tells us, "If society will not admit of woman's free development, then society itself must be remodeled." Her words are my anchor whenever the prejudices of that society threaten to drown me in the tide of injustices women face in our pursuit of medical education. I came upon yet another troubling item in a popular periodical. I share it with you—not to discourage you, but to prepare you for what may lay ahead. It said: "The proposition that women, as a sex, are not fit to practice medicine—that their weak physical organization renders them unfit for such duties and exposures, and that their physiological condition during a portion of each month disqualifies them from such grave responsibilities—is too nearly self-evident to require argument."

Not fit! Because of the monthlies of our child-bearing years? My heart sank, but was buoyed when I found this response to such unfathomable ignorance: "When women students finally have access to the same education and the same facilities men have—then, and only then, can a truly sound conclusion on the fitness of women to medical practice be reached."

You see, my friend? There are those who oppose the 'arrogant arguments' against us and know we will prove ourselves when given the chance. Still, the few of us who do gain admission to a reputable medical school often find ourselves blocked from preceptorships under a licensed physician. If we are fortunate enough to attain one, we may still be refused admission to a medical society—which is the only means to become licensed as physicians.

But, as Dr. Blackwell reminds us: "It is not easy to be a pioneer, but oh, it is fascinating! I would not trade one moment, not even the worst moment, for all the riches in the world." Nor would I, dear Allie. Like your brave family and all the others who travel West, into the unknown, we too must endure hardship and, at times, hostility to establish a new world beyond the limits of the old!

Please write soon. Your lively descriptions of how medicine is practiced in your rustic village are so similar and yet so different from mine here in New York City!

You and I are truly Aesop's Country Mouse and Town Mouse, are we not?

Your sister in Pioneering,
Lydia Brennan

Folding the letter, Allie returned it to the safety of her pocket. After her visit with the Winnicotts, she would finally have work of her own to share with Lydia. And, she would ask her opinion about the child with Little's Disease. There might be treatments in New York they wouldn't learn of for years in the Territories. Since seeing the Findlay boy in town, he'd occupied her thoughts almost as much as the Winnicotts.

When the road wound past the crockery mill, the buildings became even shoddier. The wood-planked sidewalk ended—no one walked Commerce Street or its side lanes here. In a few hundred yards, Norberto turned the corner at a dilapidated cluster of shacks that housed Solace Springs' lowest saloons—the Sullen Bride, the Best Chance, and Miss Birdie's notorious Tanglefoot—where a painted likeness of a Bengal tiger glowered from a front window. All were tawdry sporting houses with a few back rooms for gambling and an upstairs where the 'calico queens and painted cats' plied their trade. Though the ramshackle buildings showed no signs of life so early in the day, Allie and Norberto both averted their eyes as they passed.

The Winnicott's slip-shod dwelling squatted a quarter-mile up the rise. A zigzag, rock strewn path—muddy or dusty, depending on the weather—had been worn to and from the saloons. The cart carved its own way with the horse's hooves sucking at the mud with each step. At what she guessed to be the Winnicott place, Allie saw three scrawny children squirm bare toes into the mud and—like the man and woman at their sides—stare at the approaching wagon. In front of one of the seedy huts dotting the hillside above them, an old woman stopped her work on a hardscrabble patch of soil to lean on her hoe and gawk.

When the wagon pulled up in front of the house, Allie had to admit she was taken aback by Ephraim Winnicott. Doc had described him as a feckless young man, a derelict who drank and gambled away the meager money he won at the faro tables or earned at occasional odd jobs—jobs that had become more sporadic as the ranchers who hired him found him to be lazy and inept at almost everything. What Allie saw was an affable, big-boned farm boy with his four-year-old son perched on his shoulders, the child's fingers twisted in his father's longish blond hair. He didn't look like a man who would choose his vices over his family's needs, but their circumstances argued otherwise.

"Why, Miss Allie Hanover," Ephraim said, approaching the wagon with a grin and an extended hand. "Ephraim Winnicott. This here's my wife Clarie and our little'uns Etta, Junior, Caleb, and Baby Grace. Pleased to make your acquaintance."

Taking his hand, Allie stepped down from the wagon and returned his smile. "I'm so glad to be meeting all of you."

After swinging the boy to the ground, Ephraim stepped back to scrutinize Allie from head to foot. Leaning close, he lowered his voice. "In case you don't know it, your daddy's 'bout as proud of you as a hen that's got itself a duck for a chick! Said he'd send his very own daughter to help us out—and here you are. Course, I never doubted him. I took my measure of the man when he come all the way up here to see to our sick baby." His face clouded. "We'd of lost Gracie last winter, but for him."

The unsmiling children were mottled brown from the sun and a coat of dirt that Allie guessed masked the pallor of malnutrition. Their arms and legs were sticks, their hair matted, and their cheeks hollow where they should have been round. "Dr. Hanover asked me to look in to see what we can do to keep you all stronger for next winter," she said, with a smile that took them all in. "I've brought some things I hope will help."

Clare Winnicott—not much older than Allie—was as tall, slender, and dark as Ephraim was fair. Standing silent at his side, her smile was bright, her eyes bleak. She balanced a toddler on her hip, with a begrimed three-year old boy huddled behind her tattered skirt and a solemn six-year-old girl planted protectively in front her, all skinny as sparrows.

"Oh . . ." Allie said to the children, with mock alarm. "I almost forgot . . ." Patting a pocket, she frowned. "Now, where . . ." She patted another. "Where . . . did I put those? Oh, here they are." The children stared saucer-eyed when she withdrew a handful of cherry drops (her brother's offering) and a piece of Zwieback for the baby. Like hungry nestlings, they tilted their faces up to their mother for permission to accept the rare treats. Not meeting Allie's eyes, Clare nodded.

"The Ladies' Benevolent Society has sent food, clothing, and a few sundries," Allie told her, gesturing toward the bags piled in the back of the wagon. Norberto jumped down from the cart to carry the goods inside, but Ephraim waved him away. At Allie's nod, the handyman stepped back and stood with his arms folded across his chest. Throwing the sacks over one broad shoulder, Ephraim tucked a load of fire wood under his other arm and strode toward the shack.

"Etta," he told the six year-old girl, "you stay out here and mind the babies don't fall in the crick." To Allie, he added over his shoulder, "The fewer folk inside, the better. It's about as close in there as dammit is to swearing."

Pushing aside the patchy hide that covered the door opening, he held it back for Allie and his wife, while kicking a few empty cans and some candle stubs into a drift of litter in one corner. In the dimly lit room—a light a grey haze filtered through a piece of ancient, oiled lambskin that served as the room's one small window—Allie was struck by the odors of wood rot and garbage. Muddy where the roof had leaked, the dirt floor reeked of urine. The stench of the neglected privy, too close to both the cabin and the stream that flowed nearby, found its way inside and stung the back of her throat. What Lydia would call a 'disease-harboring miasma,' Allie thought, fighting a grimace.

When her eyes adjusted to the near-darkness, she saw thin pallets on the ground strewn with clothing she assumed was used for bedding, a small, rusted monkey stove—without a stick of wood in sight, a rickety table, and three splintered chairs. Grease had congealed in a fry pan on the stove. Allie's skin crawled with the sensation of the fleas and lice she imagined must already be feasting on her.

Emptying the homespun sacks, Ephraim named each item he placed on the table. "Bacon and flour. Sugar, corn meal, beans, coffee, and cheese. Pie. Squash. Jam. A loaf . . . three loaves. of bread." He set a crock of milk and a basket of eggs nested in wood chips in front of his wife. "Look here, Clarie—eggs and milk just like you was hopin' for."

Clare finally met Allie's eyes. Her voice was whispery, even when she spoke up. "Thank you, Miss."

"Yes, Miss. We do thank you with full and grateful hearts for what you done. But," Ephraim ignored a sharp look from Clare, "I can't help but wonder why there's no meat here 'cept bacon. Children need meat for strength."

When Allie handed him one of several small dough pockets she'd brought, he eyed it with suspicion. "Meat pasty," she told him, thinking he appeared quite capable of putting meat in front of his children himself. "From my sister-in-law. She sent the vinegar pie, too. She swears it can prevent scurvy."

Clare lowered her eyes as a flush of what Allie took to be embarrassment colored her pale cheeks. After surveying all the foodstuffs, tossing the donated clothing on the floor, and piling the wood by the stove, Ephraim nodded his approval. "Like I said, Miss, we're much obliged for all you've brung." He lowered his eyes. The smile he gave her when he raised them was designed, she understood immediately, to charm. "I just can't help but wonderin'—and I sure do hope you don't take offense—if you and those Benevolent Ladies might find it in your big, generous hearts to spare us a few layin' hens? And a cow, maybe? It'd do these little ones good to have milk and eggs regular like. As you can surely see," he lifted his big hand and made a gesture that encompassed the filthy room, "we got more problems here than we can say grace over."

Determined not to host the burdens of this able-bodied man who chose not to provide milk or a laying hen for his family, Allie picked up the clean clothing he'd tossed on the floor, put it back in the flour sack, and set it on a chair. Eyes hard on his, she said, "Hector Abernathy—who has a heart for taking on men who want work whether he needs them or not—might be hiring out at the Golden Eagle Ranch."

"Golden Eagle?" Ephraim scoffed. "I'm not working for no man keeps a squaw in his bed." Puffed up with pride, he nattered on, " 'Sides, wrangling horses ain't for me. Faro's my fortune. When I truly twist that tiger's tail—and I surely will any day now—why, my winnings'll set me up in my very own establishment."

Flinching inwardly, Allie remembered her father's words. In large part, it was Ephraim's affinity for gambling that caused and continued his family's desperate circumstances. "Faro," Doc had said, " 'Twisting the Tail of the Tiger' is a dangerous and dishonest game of chance. It destroys families and reduces gullible men like Ephraim Winnicott to poverty. Because of their own weakness, to be sure, but also because of the rigging of the dealing boxes.

"I've heard that crooked faro equipment is so rampant many an unscrupulous sporting house—our own tawdry Tanglefoot included—uses 'gaffed' dealing boxes specially designed so the bankers can cheat the players. It's said—and I have no reason to think otherwise—there's not a single honest faro bank to be found in all of the entire United States. 'Twisting the tiger's tail' is a fiction, my dear, a damned—excuse the expletive—dangerous fantasy. The insatiable 'tiger' devours most of the poor souls who enter its benighted lair."

In the harsh reality of the hovel, Ephraim lifted his eyes and stared into the distance, as if watching his dream come true. "Plan to call my place, 'Clarie's Tiger Cage Casino and Tavern.' Not here, course, not in this no-account horse trough of a town. I've got my aspirations fixed on Blackhawk, or maybe Central City." Wrapping an arm around his wife's thin shoulders, his voice softened. "I'll see my Clarie has all the fancies she deserves one day, including a big ole feathered hat finer than the one Miss Birdie sports over at the Tanglefoot." He smiled down at his Clarie, squeezing her tighter. "You can mark me on that."

After promising to muck out the privy "whenever he got the chance," Ephraim absented himself, leaving Allie and Clare alone. Overwhelmed by the needs she saw, Allie set about to do what she could. First things, small things, first, she told herself. She took Clare and the children on a hunt to find fallen tree branches to use for brooms, then set them to sweeping debris from the shack. She convinced Clare to bathe the children once a week—in the cold stream for now, with the lye soap and chamomile shampoo she'd brought, with hot water in the wash tub she'd bring on her next visit.

Breathing in the scent of the shampoo, Clare murmured, "Reminds me of my Mama's house." Head bowed, she whispered, "She would be mortified to see how we live out here."

Allie took her hand. "There's nothing here that can't be made better. If you'll let me, I'd like to help with that."

Eyes averted, Clare nodded and squeezed her hand.

In the filth and cold, winter would be treacherous to the unwashed and malnourished little Winnicotts. Even in summer, they were red-eyed and sniffling. What should have been minor cuts and scrapes festered with green and yellow pus. Allie was sorry to have to introduce them to iodine on her first visit, but it had to be done. Hugs, smiles, and one more cherry drop each helped them forget the sting and, she hoped, forgive her.

She left the bottle of iodine with Clare and promised to return with a few more things they might need on her next visit. Might need? she thought, disheartened. What did the Winnicotts *not* need? The list burgeoned in her mind: a sturdy broom, wood and rope to build a bed frame, mattress ticking and clean straw to fill it. Tin cups so the family wouldn't all share the only one they had. A Dutch oven. Soap and candles. Flannel to make diapers for the baby—babies. A tub for washing. A shovel to muck out the over-flowing privy. And more food. And more soap, lots of soap. And, she resolved, she would bring two of South Slope's laying hens. They wouldn't be missed and Clare and the children shouldn't suffer for Ephraim's failings.

After promising to return as soon as she could, Allie and Norberto rode through a dove grey mist away from the 'sorry' side of town, back toward the part, she thought with new cynicism, that apparently didn't need to apologize for its existence.

When she arrived at South Slope, her father commended her efforts and encouraged her to assist when and how she could. As satisfying as the visit had been in some ways, it had disappointed Allie in others. Aside from the application of iodine to minor wounds, she'd found no opportunity to hone her medical skills in either diagnosis or treatment.

"Papa, all they seem to need is food, supplies, and some education about hygiene. I don't want to be a 'friendly visitor.' Mother's Benevolent Ladies could have done what I did today."

"Ah, my dear, don't worry about that. For now, you're laying the ground work of trust. I assure you your medical skills will be called upon in ways we cannot predict. Those poor children—as William Shakespeare has said—'are subject to every ailment flesh is heir to.' " He shook his head sadly. "And cruel winter hasn't even had its say yet."

CHAPTER EIGHT

In the great room of his rambling ranch house, Hector Abernathy leaned back in his chair, folded his hands over his ample belly, and released an appreciative belch. He'd finished off two large elk and cornmeal patties, two and a half bowls of Three Sisters Stew—beans, corn, and squash—and more slices of fry bread than he could count.

Red Moon, his Ute wife of forty-plus years, laughed her easy laugh. "You're welcome, Eats Like Two Bears."

Grinning at each other, the five Golden Eagle ranch hands seated at the long trestle table took that as their sign the meal was over. Scraping their chairs back, they thanked the old Indian woman for dinner and returned to their work. Snatches of their amiable banter trailed behind them as they ambled out of the house.

Heck's faded blue eyes followed Red Moon's trim form as she moved around the table to clear the plates. As soon as the men left, her cheerful demeanor had changed. His wife was a spirited woman with a fondness for fun, so her somber expression and the droop of her shoulders warned him something was amiss.

When she reached for his bowl, Heck's large hand caught hers and held it to his chest, his gaze warm with affection. "Darlin,' " he said softly, smiling up at her, "you are just as beautiful as the day I first laid these lovesick eyes of mine on those shining black braids and sparkling eyes of yours."

He pulled her into his lap and squeezed her bottom, hoping to lighten her mood. "And I still can't get my fill of this round, sweet . . ."

"Stop it, old man!" Giggling like a girl, she pushed on his chest and pretended to try to squirm away.

Great Basin Utes didn't even approve of intermarriage between separate tribes, so when strong-willed young Red Moon had wed the white rancher it caused quite a stir. The couple had been shunned by her tribe and treated with animosity by the town folk of Solace Springs. It had taken more than twenty years for both tribe and town to get used to the couple, but Heck's generosity and good humor and Red Moon's quiet wisdom had won most of them over.

"We have five grown daughters and seventeen grandchildren," she chided him, "and these braids are striped with white like a skunk and these eyes are not so keen as they once were."

Tightening his arms around his wife, Heck sighed and nuzzled her neck. "Just as well, Star That Fell From the Sky, I'm not much to look at these days anyway."

Turning in his lap, she studied him. Smoothing his long, white hair behind his ears, she cupped his weathered face with her two brown hands and kissed him on the mouth. When she pulled back again, he saw that the lines that curved down from her eyes and around her mouth had deepened. Searching her face for some clue as to what troubled her, he mirrored her frown. "I'm guessin' it's not the loss of my good looks that's got you so glum, is it, darlin'?"

Red Moon shook her head, stood, and smoothed the skirt of her long buckskin dress. Her hand toyed with the beadwork at her throat. Heck recognized the gesture that always meant she was about to speak of something difficult. Cautioned, he drew a long breath. His wife was a wise and practical woman and not easily distressed.

"Our son's heart is heavy with the water of sorrow," she said, head bowed. She and Heck exhaled as one, this was not a new worry. "Hannah Hanover came today to show me the baskets she wove. She learns quickly." For a moment, the humor returned to her eyes. "She's figured out how to weave in a ribbon with the plaid design of her Scotch clan."

They both chuckled at that, then Red Moon sighed and moisture brightened her eyes. "She told me Ned is no better. He comes down from his cabin to work the horses most days, but sometimes she and Will won't see him for a week. When he's there, he speaks little and keeps to himself. Will told her he still sleeps outside." She pressed her hand to her chest, as if the pain she felt was physical. "In the stable, when it rains."

Ned Harper wasn't their son. Ten years ago, at the end of the Civil War, the taciturn sixteen year-old with a bad case of 'soldier's heart' had shown up at the Golden Eagle Ranch looking for work. Heck had hired him as a ranch hand and Red Moon had taken him in like a mother wolf takes an orphaned pup into her own litter. In the time he'd spent with them, she'd nurtured, nourished, and scolded him, while Heck worked him to the bone. Together they'd helped him heal—with a few hitches along the way, some entailing a night or two in jail or locked in the barn—and watched him grow into manhood sure and strong. Or so they had thought.

"The souls of the dead cling to Ned because he won't let them go," she told Heck in a hushed voice. "Too much time has passed and he still mourns. When someone cares more for the dead than the living, the whole tribe suffers. That kind of selfishness angers the Spirits." Her eyes were as opaque as polished river stones. Red Moon lived in the white world, but held fast to the beliefs of her own Tewa people. She'd been given her name because she was born during an eclipse when the full moon had turned scarlet, but Snowy Owl was her spirit animal. Heck boasted that if she'd stayed with her tribe instead of marrying him, she would have become a powerful medicine woman.

"If Ned keeps on as he is, Spirit might call the Warrior in White Robes to come with his giant bow and arrows to hunt him and take him to the afterlife before his time."

"He's lost right now," Heck said, shrugging his broad shoulders to shake off the weight of helplessness. "But darlin', Ned's got to find his own way. There's nothing we or anyone else can do for him."

"There is something you can do, Two Bears." Red Moon placed both hands firmly on his shoulders and looked deep into his eyes. "You must take him up to the plateaus to chase wild horses. The mustangs will lead him back."

CHAPTER NINE

Driving the dainty green and gold surrey—built in Denver as a gift from her father to her mother—Allie had to admit she had doubts about her mother's plan to welcome the Findlays to Solace Springs. Mrs. Hanover had enlisted a contingent of her Ladies' Benevolent Society to pay a visit to the sheep ranch. The Ladies had been generous to the Winnicotts, as well, but Allie knew there would never be a caravan of Welcome Wagons converging on the shanties in the 'sorry side' of town.

With her mother beside her, bedecked in her canary-yellow silk visiting dress, and her younger siblings squabbling on the bench behind them, Allie hoped the Findlays wouldn't see the surprise visit as an intrusion. At least, a few Welcome Wagons would be less daunting than Afternoon Tea at South Slope. Mrs. Findlay and her daughter, Sarah, did not strike her as the hats, gloves, and "Isn't the oolong lovely" sort.

Aware of the range wars that had troubled other places, the previous owners of the sheep ranch had made certain to keep their flock confined to their own property. Miles of sturdy fences enclosed the outer perimeters of the modest ranch. Each paddock had its own well-constructed barriers to contain a handful of the two hundred or so Horned Dorset ewes and lambs grazing the land. A few fenced lots each held a lone ram. Where the road curved alongside the paddocks, the strident brays of a donkey and the panicked bleating of sheep bombarded the visitors. The horses shied at the cacophony, forcing Allie to rein them to a stop until they collected themselves.

When the spooked horses regained their composure, Allie urged them forward. Hannah, her brother's wife, settled her own palomino mare and resumed an easy trot alongside the surrey. Over one arm, she carried a basket containing a vinegar pie and a bouquet of flowers from her garden.

"Guard donkey!" Hannah called out with a big grin and a nod toward the paddock. Her wild red hair defied the bun that never tamed it for long. In her mild Scottish burr, she added, "Better protection than dogs, ye ken." Allie's skeptical look drew further explanation. "Aye, donkeys are verra protective of their wee darlin's. Why, they'll charge and chase any critter that threatens their sheep. When they're not riled, donkeys have as sweet a temperament as ye could hope for. And they dunna bark, nor do they dig, nor roam like dogs. Better behaved than some husbands, if ye ask me." With a sidelong glance at her unamused mother-in-law, she quickly added, "Except, of course, for my own bonny Will Hanover!"

Once, when Allie had expressed skepticism about one of Hannah's pronouncements, Ned, who'd known her since Will first began to court her, told Allie, "If Hannah Hanover says a rooster dips snuff, you can be sure if you look under its wing you're gonna find the can."

"Speaking of wee darlin's," Allie called to her, "Papa says there are big doin's at the ranch today."

Just six years older than Allie, Hannah had been born in the Free Territories of Colorado and raised in a home where her Grand-da Fergus spoke Gaelic, her da and brothers played the bagpipes and bodhrans, and her mam served oat bannocks with every meal. Trying to tuck strands of copper-gold hair back under her bonnet with one hand and manage the reins and basket with the other, Hannah said, "While I'm out here enjoying the pleasant company of the Benevolent Ladies, yon bairns will be in the able care of their da, their grand-da, and braw Ned Harper—who will be teaching Ian to ride."

"Ian? Ride a horse?" Mrs. Hanover gasped. "He's just a baby!" Leaning forward, she leveled a withering glare at her son's wife. "My dear girl, are you truly allowing such a thing?"

"Dinna fash, Goodmother," Hannah soothed. Dwarfed on the back of the mare, she rode as fearlessly as she did most things and handled her mother-in-law's many criticisms with equal confidence. "Will's set to look after the boys, Ned'll look after Ian and the horse, and Grand-da Hanover will look after Will and Ned. Of course," she added with a wink, "he'll see to the stitching up or bone-setting, if any's called for."

Allie's mother sat back, lips pursed, hands clasped in her lap. "I do suppose you and my son must raise my grandsons as you see fit." Staring straight ahead she then addressed no one in particular. "What I would like to know is just who will be looking after Dr. Hanover? He left South Slope this morning wearing cowboy boots!"

Before riding out to his son's horse ranch, Doc Hanover stopped at his surgery to trade a tailored topcoat and three-button vest for a long-sleeved cotton shirt, loose-legged, wool cowboy pants, and a Stetson hat. A tall lean man, the casual clothing suited him. To spare his wife undue distress, he stored certain items of contraband haberdashery in an office closet. She did not share his fondness for the trappings of country life. Once comfortably attired to enjoy a day outdoors, he tacked a note on the door of his clinic:

In case of EMERGENCY ONLY find Doc at Will's place. Minor bumps, bruises, scrapes, and bellyaches will be treated with a large and bitter dose of disdain.

Doc would have left Allie in charge of the clinic, but she was joining her mother in the welcoming of the Findlays. He and his daughter had discussed the young boy with Little's Disease and what Allie should look for to assess his condition further, if she had the opportunity. Much to his surprise, Albert, who would never pass up a chance to spend a day at the ranch with his older brother, nephews, and Ned, had been adamant he must go with the women. He was, he explained, set on befriending Joseph Findlay.

With his medical satchel secured to the saddle, the doctor rode out of town a happy man. Almost everyone he passed returned his smiles and nods. Solace Springs was small enough that every face was familiar. Still, the town was large enough to provide everything a man and his family could need: A well-stocked mercantile, a cobbler and tailor, a school, a decent hotel with a more-or-less decent restaurant, a garrulous barber who could assist with bone-setting, and a reliable bank. The jail was sturdy; the sheriff sober. And, the elderly undertaker had been calling the town's square dances—Frolics—for as long as most residents could remember. A steepled church graced one end of the dusty main street and too many derelict saloons and brothels—for Doc's taste—clustered at the other. Most important, he reminded himself often, Solace Springs was not Boston.

Holding his roan mare, Hippocrates, to a leisurely pace, the doctor reveled in the fields, forests, and meadows he passed. The morning air was clean and crisp, scented with ripening grasses. Although he knew it to be a scientific impossibility, he swore the sky rose higher and spread wider in Colorado than it could ever aspire to be back East.

Rounding the bend, he passed through the wooden gate with "H & H" scorched into its arched crown. The Harper and Hanover Ranch, Will and Hannah's home. His heart swelled with satisfaction at what they—and Ned—had achieved in just a few years. Two dozen mares with their colts and fillies grazed in a patchwork of pastures. Alone in his paddock, a chestnut stallion arched his powerful neck to survey his domain.

A white-washed house—small, but with plenty of room to grow—nestled in the shade of a trio of tall, blue spruces. What Hannah called her "wild-flower swither" framed the porch steps with a tumble of blue iris, violet mountain lupine, magenta aster, and lemon-yellow daisies. Raised with the help of friends and neighbors, the barn and stable stood behind and to one side of the house.

And, most of all, there were his three grandsons. None, to his wife's dismay, named for British royalty. When she had accepted his proposal of marriage, Charles Hanover had made Jane promise her affection for him had nothing to do with his surname. "You must understand, my dearest," he'd warned her, "by no stretch of your fertile genealogical imagination will any offspring of ours ever have the slightest claim to the throne of England."

"Of course, I understand," she'd assured him with the captivating smile that had won him. Still, there had been something in her bold brown eyes that kept him guessing to this day.

Tying Hippocrates to the rail of the training corral, Doc saw that the riding lesson had already commenced. Five year-old Ian, uncharacteristically solemn, concentrated atop Mollie, the gentlest mare in the stable. The boy had shared a saddle with Will since he was an infant, but this was the first time he'd hold the reins on his own. Ned stood in the center of the corral grasping one end of a lunge line that stretched to a halter over the horse's bridle. Turning slowly, he guided the boy and beast in a circle around the soft earth of the inner perimeter.

A week before, Doc had leaned against a wall in the stable to watch Ian and Ned—who he hadn't seen in months—curry the patient mare, dig debris out of her hooves, and saddle and unsaddle her. While they worked, Ned had told the boy, "No one deserves to sit a horse unless he knows how to tend it. Are you listenin' Ian? No one's ready to *ride* a horse until he knows how to fall off." Although the boy had proved himself adept at using the mounting block to get up into the saddle, Ned had insisted he dismount by swinging a leg over the horse's back and sliding off several times. "Best you get a feel for just how far it is to the ground and just how hard it is when you hit it," Ned had warned him, with a wry glance toward Doc, "so you're not too surprised when you fall off. And," he'd added, with no hint of humor, "you will fall off."

"Close your eyes, Ian," Ned now called from the center of the ring. The morning had warmed and a line of sweat darkened the back of his blue shirt. "Don't think about anything but getting the feel of the horse."

The boy did as he was told, swaying with Mollie's plodding rhythm. Over last Sunday's supper at South Slope, Will had confided to Doc that he knew he could teach his son to ride himself, but preferred Ian learn from his friend. "Ned taught me everything I know about horses, but I'll never *know* horses the way he does." Just a year older than Will, Ned had befriended him when the Hanovers first arrived from Boston and Ned had been working for Heck Abernathy. "I believe Ian's got that same kind of knowing in him. If it's there, Ned'll bring it out."

Long and lanky like his father, Will leaned against the corral fence with one arm wrapped around two year-old Angus, who perched on the rail with his chubby legs dangling over the edge. His other hand rested on the curly red head of four year-old Colum, who stood at his knee to peer through the middle slats.

Engrossed in the lesson, Will didn't acknowledge his father's presence until he was standing at his side. "Hey, Doc," he said with a startled grin, handing him the toddler.

Angus squirmed readily into Doc's embrace, threw his pudgy arms around his grandfather's neck, and pointed. Not at his brother on the horse, but at Ned. Even in the presence of his brothers, father, and grandfather, Ned always took precedence as the child's favorite. "Ed! Ed!" the toddler crowed. "Ed!"

At the age of fourteen, Will had informed his parents he would no longer call his father 'Papa' and would henceforth refer to him as Doc, as did all the other residents of Solace Springs. Although Doc had to admit he was pleased, his wife had not been. A few years later, when Will announced he would not be attending university in the East, but would stay in Solace Springs to homestead a horse ranch with Ned and marry Hannah McGregor, his mother had not spoken to Will or Ned—whom she declared clearly deserved a good share of the blame—for three days.

Doc had been relieved when she came to a grudging acceptance of the life Will and his high-spirited bride had chosen. After the birth of their first grandson, she'd even forgiven Will for marrying a Scot. In fact, she embraced this connection to Scotland as something she shared with the Queen, often referring to the H & H Ranch as 'Balmoral West.'

"You picked a good day to visit," Will told Doc, pulling his attention away from the center of the corral. "There's all kinds of excitement going on here. We've got Ian learning to ride. And," he reached down and ruffled his four-year-old's hair, "Colum will tell you what else is about to happen."

The boy tipped his head back to give his grandfather an upside-down grin, then pointed to a mare pacing at the far end of the next paddock, away from the other horses. "Ned says Josie's gonna *drop* her foal today, but Da says don't worry 'cause him and Ned'll be right there to catch it. "

"Then all will be well," Doc assured him. To Will, he added, "That'll make three born this season."

His son's gaze followed the pregnant mare pacing back and forth along the tree-shaded fence, twitching her tail. Her hide glistened with sweat and her udder hung distended with milk.

"If all does go well, that is." Will hesitated, frowning. "Ned's worried about this one. Josie's eighteen years-old, our oldest broodmare. He says we may have a long night ahead of us." An anxious grin lifted one corner of his mouth. "He's been edgy as that mare all day."

"I'll let your sister know it's time."

Will's frown deepened at the reminder. He'd told Doc that when Allie heard of the coming birth, she'd asked—begged—to be allowed to observe. She'd attended and assisted many human deliveries with Doc, but had never seen a foal drop.

"I agree it would be a beneficial chapter in your medical education," Doc had told her. "The animal kingdom can certainly teach us a many things about birth and death. As far as we know, they don't fear either, so manage both with much more equanimity than people."

It was no surprise to Doc to hear that when Will broached the subject of Allie watching the birth, Ned had given him a hard look. "Too many people in the stable. It'll spook the mare."

"We're talking about Allie, not Maude Mary," Will had pressed. "She won't spook either of you and you know it."

Jaw tight, Ned had drawn a breath and released it. "You and Doc have already made up your minds." Shaking his head, he narrowed his eyes at Will. "You've got me caught like a moth in a mitten, seems I've got no choice."

Will had shrugged and nodded. "Seems so."

"Then you make sure she knows to stay quiet and keep out of the way."

When Doc passed along the instructions, Allie had consented to all Ned's conditions. No surprise there, either.

Watching Ned, Doc noted that although he divided his attention between Ian and the agitated mare in the paddock, he showed no outward sign of undue concern for either. For the last year and a half, his closed expression had made it near impossible to guess his feelings. The thought reminded Doc of the task the baseball players had set Will to do. Doc cared first for his family, second for his medical practice, and a very close third for the Solace Springs team. "You haven't mentioned whether you've talked to Ned about hurling for the Sluggers."

"Tried."

Ned and Will worked the ranch together almost every day and Doc knew his son was not one to be easily daunted. With a sympathetic chuckle, he said, "That hard, I guess."

Will's short laugh matched his. "Harder."

"Open your eyes, Ian." Ned's voice drew their attention back to the corral. He'd acknowledged Doc's arrival with a finger to the brim of his hat, then returned his concentration to the boy. "Wrap those reins around the pommel and ride with your hands on your hips." When he mimed his instructions, Ian gaped at him for a moment, then did as he was instructed. "Good!" The horse and boy slowly circled the paddock. "Find your balance and keep it."

In his element in the training corral, Ned's straight back and agility gave no indication of the state of his spirit. Doc raised a questioning brow at Will. His son's wife had been Becky's dearest friend and had a close bond with Ned. "Hannah must have some thoughts on how he's doing."

"She says, 'poor lad's still blacker than the Lord of Hell's waistcoat.' "

If only a day in the sun could heal a blackened spirit, Doc thought. "Hannah does have a way of summing things up. I just wish she'd do us the kindness to be wrong every so often."

"I said that to her once and she told me she had," Will said. "Thought it might've been in the summer of '70."

When the young rider circled the corral and again rode past them beaming, Ned called to him, "Stretch your arms straight out at your sides." He demonstrated and this time the boy assumed the position without hesitation. "Use your knees now. Ask Mollie for a fast walk." The boy kicked the horse in the ribs. "Knees, Ian, not heels!"

When he sat the horse comfortably at the faster pace, Ned told him, "Point one arm at me and raise the other straight up over your head." Demonstrating again, he formed an 'L' with his own arms. "Keep your finger and your eyes aimed at me. Go around again."

Not taking his own eyes off his son, Will said, "Ian's catching on even quicker than I thought he would."

"Faster now," Ned ordered. Urging the horse to a trot with his knees, Ian earned a nod of approval. "Now, stop thinkin' about riding that horse and just ride her!"

Doc couldn't help but wonder what it must cost Ned to be teaching Will's boy what he'd hoped to teach his own son.

CHAPTER TEN

Allie's apprehension burgeoned as she led the small caravan of welcome wagons through the gate and into the porch yard of the Findlay home. Luke Findlay waited on the top step of the veranda with his arms folded across his chest and his expression grim. Mrs. Findlay and Sarah stood to either side and behind him. There was no sign of Joseph.

Broad-shouldered and thickly-built, his ruddy skin blotched from decades in the sun, Mr. Findlay met the ladies' friendly greetings with a scowl. "What's this all about?"

Shading her eyes with one gloved hand, Allie's mother stepped forward, her smile bright as her gown. "I'm Mrs. Charles Hanover, Mr. Findlay. We're here on behalf of my Ladies' Benevolent Society and all the citizens of Solace Springs to welcome you and your family to town."

The women carried pies, casseroles, and other small gifts. Folded in her own arms, she held one of the colorful quilts the Ladies stitched for all the town's brides and newcomers. Allie and Maude Mary had brought their precious copy of *Little Women* for Sarah, and Albert clutched a paper sack in which he'd saved most of his cherry drops to present to Joseph. In the long moment that Mr. Findlay remained silent, Allie half-expected to see him reach for his rifle.

When he spoke, his tone was as truculent as she remembered it. "You can see," he said, mimicking Mrs. Hanover's sweeping gesture to encompass his own simple, but obviously thriving, sheep ranch, "we don't need your charity. So I'd be obliged if you'd turn your benevolent selves around and head back to where you came from."

His wife stepped in front of him. Plainly moved, she spoke with what seemed to Allie forced boldness. "Now Luke," she said, eyes and timid smile directed away from him and toward the visitors, "this here is not charity. This here is our new neighbors come to call."

Linking her arm through Sarah's, she smiled at the ladies. "Me and my daughter are grateful for the kindness."

Ignoring her husband's dumbfounded glare, she motioned the women inside.

Leaning against the door jamb, Sarah watched with a bemused expression on what Allie realized was an extraordinarily pretty face. Like her mother, Sarah wore a shapeless Mother Hubbard dress, tied at the waist, with long leg-o-mutton sleeves. Her flaxen hair was fixed in a simple bun. If Allie hadn't been certain paint would be forbidden in this family, she would have sworn the girl—who was close to her own age of seventeen—had rouged her lips and cheeks and darkened the lashes that framed her green eyes. The drab calico print did nothing to diminish her beauty.

Joseph had edged out of the house and peeked out from behind his sister's back, eyes riveted on Albert. Still glowering, Mr. Findlay hesitated before moving aside to allow the ladies to pass. As the ladies of the entourage introduced themselves, he managed almost civil grunts in response, but didn't meet anyone's eyes.

Last in line, Albert offered his hand. "I'm Albert Hanover, Mr. Findlay. Pleased to meet you, sir."

Allie, who had been about to follow Sarah and Maude Mary into the house, stopped in the doorway and turned to watch. Everything she'd seen of him so far cautioned her to be wary of Joseph's father. Any rudeness toward her younger brother would not go unanswered. She prepared to speak up, if need be.

Shaking the boy's hand, Mr. Findlay's demeanor softened. "Now tell me something, Albert Hanover, what is it makes a sturdy fellow like you decide to spend his Saturday morning making social calls with the Ladies of the Busy-body Society?" He studied Albert, then recognition hardened his features. "You're one of those boys from town who tormented Joseph."

"No, sir!" Clutching the bag of candy, Albert said, "I was there, but I wasn't one of them." He held the man in his earnest gaze. "I want to be his friend. That's why I'm here, sir. I came to play with him."

Joseph hung back in the shadow of the house, eyes still fixed on Albert.

Mr. Findlay stiffened, a kaleidoscope of emotion playing across his features. "Well, I'm sorry to disappoint you." Looking into the distance over Albert's head, he swallowed hard. His shoulders slumped. "You've seen for yourself, Joseph can't play. It only shames him to be reminded he can't do like other boys." With a tight smile, he said, "I believe you mean well, but it's those that mean well do the most harm. Joseph just wants other children to let him be."

Albert raised crestfallen eyes to Allie. Before she could think what to say, Joseph's thick, halting voice stammered from the doorway. "I . . . want to play . . . with him . . . Pa."

Mr. Findlay swung around. "Go back inside, son."

The boy's mouth opened, then closed. His head drooped in resignation and a ragged thatch of wheat-colored hair fell across his eyes. Before he could obey, Sarah appeared in the doorway with Maude Mary in tow. Draping an arm over her brother's shoulder, she pulled him close and widened innocent eyes at her father. "Pa, the house is so hot with all those ben-ev-o-lent ladies crowded in there . . . May I please show our new friends the lambs and kittens?"

Maude Mary gave a start, as if she'd been pinched. Her blink and quick side glance at Sarah confirmed it. "Mr. Findlay," she said, "I do so adore kittens! They are just about my most favorite things in the entire world. How old are they? How many do you have? Do they get along with the lambs? Why, I am desperate to see . . ."

"We don't want to disappoint Albert, Pa," Sarah cut in. "Joseph can come along. He hasn't been out at all today." Her brother's head lolled from side to side, then twisted to look up at her with what Allie perceived to be disbelief. Sarah added sweetly, "It'll do him good to come outside."

Eager for an opportunity to observe the boy, Allie added her voice to the conspiracy. "On the way over, my sister and I were telling each other how much we hoped we'd get to see your lambs."

"And, Pa," Sarah's face remained turned toward her father, her gaze locked on his, "you know how much Joseph likes to visit the kittens."

With considerable effort, Joseph brought his waving hands together in front of his chest, a caricature of prayer. Allie noted this as evidence of intelligence and a sense of humor, both indicators of a healthy mind.

The boy's head drooped to one side and he lifted imploring eyes to his father. Struggling to form a word, he shaped the pout for a 'p,' but his lips collapsed to a frown. When he tried again, he managed: "Puh . . . puh . . . please."

"Please, sir!" Albert chorused, crossing his fingers behind his back.

With the discomfited expression of a man who realizes he's been bested by those he judged to be lesser adversaries, her father gave Sarah a stern frown before surrendering. "You look after your brother, hear?"

"Of course, Pa." Her lips tightened. "I always do."

Findlay gave neither his children nor the interlopers another glance. Stalking to his horse, he mounted and spurred it in the direction of the outer paddocks. Chickens squawked and scattered to get out of his way, while nearby sheep swung their heads as one to watch him go.

With a clearly besotted Maude Mary gazing up at her and clinging to one hand, Sarah looped her other arm through Allie's and pulled her toward the barn. "Kittens first. If you think they're cute," she said, her mood apparently restored by her triumph, "just wait 'til you cuddle a lambkin."

Glancing back over her shoulder, Allie saw Joseph stumble along behind them, struggling to keep up with Albert, who maintained a slow pace at his side. The aimless, amiable chatter of young boys passed between them—one speaking too many words too fast, the other too few, too slow. As far as Allie could tell, neither seemed to mind the difference.

When Allie, Sarah, and the children left the barn and headed back toward the house, it was almost noon. Albert tugged a bleating lamb by a rope around its neck and Maude Mary cradled a pair of squirming kittens against the beaded bodice of her blue dress. Unlike her brother's breeches and jacket, she and her outfit had remained remarkably free of hay and dirt. Joseph lurched at his new friend's side. Both younger Hanovers wore the slightly crazed expressions of soldiers about to do battle.

Their mother's smile froze at their approach. Raising a warning finger, she said, "No."

Maude Mary hurried to her. "Mama, you've been saying for months those cats of ours are old and lazy and good for nothing. They don't even *try* to catch mice anymore." The Hanover children had been taught that a convincing argument might get them what whining and wheedling certainly would not. In a voice loud enough to be heard by all the ladies, she added, "I do believe I saw a rat go under our back porch just yesterday."

Before Mrs. Hanover could protest, she held one of the balls of fur in her own hands. Allie knew the hard look directed at her meant her mother felt she had not done her duty to prevent this situation. "If I say yes to *this*, Alexandrina," she stroked the purring grey kitten, then raised an eyebrow toward Albert and his much more problematic prize, "what do you propose I do about *that*?"

Allie shrugged and both children beamed in triumph.

With a diffident smile, Mrs. Findlay said, "I know it was you arranged all this, Mrs. Hanover." She motioned toward the ladies waiting to make their farewells, then bit her lip and stared at the ground. Raising care-worn eyes, she added, "No one's ever done anything so kind for us before. Luke won't . . . well, he just can't . . . show it." A smile crinkled the corners of her eyes. "That being said, I've got some good news and bad news for you. Good news first." She stroked the tiny cat nestled in the crook of her guest's arm. "We're always glad to find homes for the kittens."

Dislodging the cat-to-be's needle-sharp claws from her canary silk, she handed it back to Maude Mary. "The bad news?"

"Sheep can pasture with horses and cows and they'll eat most anything grows in the ground. But," she said, "sheep are our livelihood. We sell weanling lambs for a dollar a pair."

As if to demonstrate its lack of pickiness, the lamb nibbled the weeds at Albert's feet. "Mama," he said, "I have fifty pennies saved. I can buy it myself."

"The bad news is," Mrs. Findlay said, "sheep just hate to be alone. They're likely to dwindle without each other's company. We never sell just one lamb."

Jamming his hands into his pockets, Albert tucked his chin in his collar.

"Well," his mother said, with a resigned sigh. "I suppose that means we must have the two. Dr. Hanover will be pleased, I'm sure. He already believes our three horses, milk cow, and flock of chickens make him a gentleman farmer. With a pair of sheep grazing in the garden, I'm sure he'll fancy himself a cattle baron."

The deal done and a promise extracted that Mrs. Findlay and Sarah attend the next Afternoon Tea, and bring Joseph along to play with Albert, the Hanovers and their acquired pets and livestock piled into the carriage. On the rear bench, one of the lambs squeezed between Maude Mary and Albert with its head on the boy's thigh. The other squatted on Allie's lap up front. The animal, it's fleece soft as silk, seemed to weigh as much as her youngest nephew.

Resigned to their fates, the sheep eventually stopped bleating and gazed up at their new owners with the trusting eyes and endearing half-smiles that were their permanent expressions. The kittens slept in Maude Mary's lap. Mrs. Hanover had taken the reins, in lieu of wrangling a lamb, and they proceeded home at a leisurely pace.

Free to review the events of the day, Allie's thoughts returned to the barn. Before the visit, her father had asked her several questions she couldn't answer about the boy with Little's Disease. "I give the Findlays much credit," he'd said, his face grim. "Most children born with that condition are so feeble of mind and body they're given up to institutions at birth. They live out their brief and miserable lives in circumstances that sicken my soul."

At the time, his words had chilled Allie, but watching Joseph with Albert heartened her. Her brother—quick, sturdy, and surefooted, and Joseph—slow, wobbly, and concentrating on every movement, had played happily together. In the barn, they'd enticed the kittens to chase lengths of straw. Outside, each in his own way, had gamboled with the lambs, creating what Allie thought a perfect choreography. She would tell her father that although the child's speech was impaired and his limbs contracted involuntarily, his intellect and emotions seemed undamaged. Engrossed in observing Joseph, Allie hadn't realized she was only half listening to his older sister. With a conspiratorial grin, she'd pulled Allie aside to sit on a bale of hay and grasped both her hands.

"Now tell me everything," Sarah had said, "I mean *everything,* about the men in this town."

Allie had blinked. "Men?"

"Yes, men!" Sarah's laugh was as pretty as her smile. "You know, males? Fellows? Grown-up boys with whiskers? This town is full of them."

Allie had wondered what she and Sarah Findlay might find to talk about, but hadn't imagined their conversation would take this turn. Minding her manners, she did her best to respond to what she could only think of as silliness. "You're right about that," she'd agreed. "Droves of them come through on their way to somewhere else more exciting. A few stay."

"A few? There's a good sight more men here than women, by anybody's reckoning." Sarah's expression went coy. Releasing Allie's hands, she dropped her eyes, then looked up from beneath thick lashes. "A fine young lady like yourself must have her pick. I expect you're already spoken for."

"Me? No," Allie had said, her eyes returning to the boys. It struck her that Joseph's awkwardness seemed to ease when he was active. She forced herself to turn back to Sarah and think of something to contribute to their chat. Without realizing she was doing so, she confided what had been most on her mind of late. "I hope to be leaving to study medicine in the East."

Since her visit to the Winnicotts, her father had been even more eager for her to apply to a women's medical college. At the same time, like Lydia, he seemed compelled to remind her of the prejudices she would face. Just a day ago, he'd shown her an article written by Professor Edward Clarke of Harvard in which the so-called learned man railed against advanced education for girls: "If young women study too much," the academic had written, "they will divert blood away from the uterus and toward the brain, thus rendering themselves irritable and infertile."

"That's absurd!" Allie had laughed. But the professor's opinion was too similar to her mother's ideas for comfort. She'd raised questioning eyes to her father. "Isn't it?

"Of course, it is." Wrapping an arm around her shoulders, he'd assured her, "In any case, I prefer my daughters to be irritable, rather than ignorant."

To counter his wife's ongoing protests, Doc had shown her and Allie an encouraging article he'd found in the pages of Mrs. Hanover's very own *Godey's Lady's Book*. It said, in part, "Talk about medicine being the appropriate sphere of men alone? With tenfold plausibility and reason, we might say it is the appropriate sphere of women alone!"

Without comment, her mother had pursed her lips and slapped shut the cover of the traitorous magazine she insisted was the authority on everything.

In the barn, Sarah folded her hands in her lap at Allie's revelation and prissied her mouth.

"School in the East? Well, isn't that la-di-dah." With a dismissive wave of one hand, she'd proclaimed, "I was done with school two years ago and there isn't a single thing would make me sit on a hard bench in a cold classroom for one single minute to listen to a frumpy Miss Stop-Fidgeting-And-Do-Your-Sums. I wonder what a person expects to find in the la-di-dah East that's any better than here." Lifting her chin, she thinned her eyes at Allie. "Unless, of course, she fancies herself just too la-di-dah for a place like this and the folk who live here."

Too much her mother's daughter to actually let her mouth drop open, Allie sat in stunned silence at the childish outburst.

"Oh dear," Sarah said quickly, widening remorseful eyes at Allie. "That sounded rude, didn't it? Ma says sometimes I'm rude as a bear, but I don't mean to. Especially not to you." She directed what appeared to be a sincere gaze at Allie. "I don't usually take to girls. They can be . . . well, you know. But, you're different. I just know we're going to be great friends." With a conspiratorial smile, she added, "I suppose we'll have to be. There aren't many women our age in this town, are there? Seems most are all dried up or still just children."

Allie could muster no response. Her eyes went back to the boys. Albert, tall for his age and tawny, long-legged and coltish. Strength and grace would come with time. Joseph, twisted, stunted and pale, his gait would remain awkward, his body contorted for the rest of his life. She was pleased to see her brother mold himself to the other boy's limitations. Moving only as fast as his new friend, falling to the ground when Joseph stumbled and fell, both hooting with laughter as if it were just part of their game, making it part of the game.

Forcing her attention back to Sarah, Allie did her best to listen, nod, and smile. But it was Maude Mary, who seemed most interested in the silly prattle. Enticing a striped kitten to follow a string, she had edged closer to the bale of hay. With a pang, Allie guessed the slump in her sister's shoulders indicated she'd overheard herself dismissed as a child.

"Before you go anywhere, Miss La-di-dah, may I ask you a favor?" At Sarah's words, Maude Mary stood still while the kitten batted at the string that had stopped moving. "I'm not really interested in *all* the men in town," she went on. "Mostly just one. And you must tell me everything you know about him. Everything." Lowering her eyes, she took a moment to smooth her skirt before looking up. Anticipating being asked about Zeke Foster, Allie mentally edited what she would reply. "Please," Sarah said coyly, "tell me about the man with the wolf dog."

An unaccountable dryness in her throat had silenced Allie for several heartbeats.

The mid-day heat, the excitement of the morning, and the gentle rocking of the carriage lulled all the Hanovers into silence on the ride home from the sheep ranch. As the wagon swayed and bumped along, Allie pondered Sarah's question and her own response to it. She'd remained quiet for so long that Sarah had prompted her, "You do know the one I mean, don't you? The man who told his dog—and my pa—to heel."

"To calm. He told them to calm." Allie couldn't begin to think why Sarah's question had unsettled her. Must be because Ned is such a private man, she told herself. Of course, that's it. Although she'd known him more than half her life, she didn't feel she knew him well. Even if she had, she would have little to say about him to this girl. "His name's Ned Harper."

"I know his name," Sarah had snapped, impatience stealing some of the prettiness from her mouth. "I was there when my pa wouldn't shake his hand."

Evasion was something Allie abhorred in others, so it surprised her how easily she employed it. Ned's story was his own to tell. "He's my brother's friend." When Sarah frowned, she'd added, "They raise horses together."

"A rancher. That's real good. It just might help bring my pa around some. He formed a poor opinion of him that day in town. "

"Around?"

"Why, when Mr. Harper comes to call on me, of course."

Beneath Sarah's beauty, Allie sensed something disingenuous. Bright as a false penny, her father would call it.

"That is," Sarah went on, "after you make the proper introductions." Her emerald gaze was as hard and bright as the gemstone. "You won't go and disappoint me, will you?"

Aware she was being manipulated, Allie could think of no gracious way to slip out of the net her new "friend" was casting. And, few things would give her less pleasure than presenting this irritating young woman to Ned.

Maude Mary's voice rose above the rhythmic clip-clop of the horses and interrupted Allie's uneasy reverie. "Mama, I'm going to name my kittens Milord and Milady, because that's what I want them to be when they grow up. Isn't that clever of me?"

Knowing her sister all too well, Allie didn't miss the edge in her tone. With minimal argument, Maude Mary had convinced their mother to allow her to keep both kittens, a grey and a tabby. The victory had satisfied her until Albert was granted permission to keep *both* lambs—a far greater coup. One, their mother had implied, that would please Papa more than the acquisition of a few barn cats. And Sarah Findlay had slighted her. Allie braced herself. When unhappy, the girl's cleverness often came with a honed blade directed at a random target.

"Very clever, indeed, dear," their mother affirmed absently. Allie recognized the echoed words that indicated her thoughts were elsewhere, as they often were in the presence of her squabbling children. Allie's were not. She waited with a mix of curiosity and dread to see where her sister's temper would strike.

"Albert," Maude Mary said, "what will you name your lambs?"

He studied the weanling's sweet faces for a moment, then shook his head. "I don't know yet."

"Oh, because I was just thinking," Maude Mary stroked the glossy fleece of the lamb wedged between them, "you should call them Leg-o-Lamb and Mutton Stew." Before he could voice his puzzlement, she added, "Because that's what they'll be when *they* grow up."

Pinned down by the ever-heavier lamb on her lap, Allie swiveled her head to glare at her sister. "That is a wicked thing to say, Alice Maude Mary." To her brother, who had gone wide-eyed, she added, "And it's not true. These are wool sheep, not meat sheep." Facing forward for a moment to allow her temper to cool, she turned back. The lamb in her lap stood and swung its head in the same direction, bleating in protest. "Besides, if names meant anything," she told her sister, "you would be called Smug or Smarmy. Or worse."

Maude Mary drew an affronted breath, then shot back, "And you'd be Miss La-di-dah-di-dah, wouldn't you?"

The rest of the ride home, Maude Mary sat with her chin propped on her fist gazing at the countryside. Sometime after they arrived at South Slope, and she and Albert had settled the new animals in the barn, she came to find Allie reading in their father's book-lined study. Late afternoon sunlight filtered through tall, mullioned windows and into the polished wood and leather-scented room. Standing motionless in the doorway, she was silent until Allie looked up.

"Sorry," Maude Mary mumbled in the forlorn, grudging way she always did when she made amends. With one finger, she twisted a lock of hair to painful tightness. "You were right to scold me."

Allie rose and smiled at her. "Well, someone has to."

The girl grimaced, then edged into the room and Allie's open arms. Resting her head on her sister's shoulder, she sniffed back tears. "I said sorry to Albert."

"I knew you would." Allie held the girl close. Remorse, as strong and swift as her anger, always followed her sister's outbursts.

Her head still on Allie's shoulder, she asked, "So which is it?"

"Which is what?"

A small smile played at the corner of Maude Mary's mouth. "Should I have been named "Smug" or "Smarmy" ?"

After kissing the top of her auburn head, Allie held her sister at arm's length and gave her an appraising look. "Hmm. Smug or Smarmy . . . I think it's the third one."

"'Third?"

Allie's own smile was affectionate, but grim. "Did you forget the 'Or worse'?"

Maude Mary left the study with her step lightened by Allie's absolution. As she always did. But it wasn't thoughts of her sister's erratic emotions that impaired Allie's ability to concentrate on Jean Charcot's article: "Lessons on Maladies of the Nervous System." Her own nerves felt singed, her chest tight, and her stomach invaded by writhing snakes. Sweet, sly, acquisitive Sarah Findlay had set her sights on Ned. Allie tried to convince herself it was none of her concern. That it didn't matter. But, with a pang she couldn't define, she had to admit that as much as it shouldn't, it somehow—absurdly—did.

Leaning back against the leather of her father's chair, she watched motes of dust float in the shafts of sunlight streaming onto the mahogany desk. She always came to this room in search of the comfort of logic and reason. Her father had taught her that every problem has a solution—often more than one—and that all that was needed was to define the problem and apply one's intellect to find an answer.

After several moments, it struck her that logic didn't apply to her current predicament. Reason failed her, as well. In all her father's books and journals and monographs, she realized with dismal certainty, she would find not one bit of information that could help her understand why talking about Ned with Sarah Findlay had left her so disconcerted.

At that moment, her father appeared in the doorway. "Josie's foal should come tonight."

My very first friend is named Albert Hanover, Joseph thought after the visitors left. He's my age, but bigger than me. He goes to school and he rides horses. I don't. Pa won't let me. But Albert likes me anyhow, I can tell. He listens when I talk and he talks when I listen. And we both laugh at the same time.

His sisters ignore him just like Sarah ignores me.

Pa don't know this—Ma says it's best not to give him too much time to think about some things or he'll get all bulled up and try to put the kibosh on them—but I'm going to Albert's house in a few weeks, to play with him. *To play.*

Pa says I can't do things like other boys and maybe he's right. But maybe he isn't.

I'm scared Albert won't still like me if I can't play.

But, maybe he already knows and doesn't care.

CHAPTER ELEVEN

The chestnut mare had been in the first stage of labor too long for Ned's liking.

For ten hours, Josie had paced the dimly-lit confines of the foaling stall looking at her sides and kicking at her belly. Slick with sweat, she'd lain down on the fresh straw, trying to position the foal, then struggled to her feet to resume her restless to and fro. She stood and lay down, stood and lay down. Again and again. The foal's head and one foreleg—in 'diving' position—should have appeared by now.

Ned and Will stationed themselves at the back of a nearby stall with Allie between them. Her presence irritated Ned, though he did his best to hide it. The three sat in silence in the hay to allow Josie her privacy—out of sight, but near enough to help if needed. The first time Ned had invited Will to attend a foaling, he'd cautioned him to be quiet and invisible. "Horses don't like company while they're in labor. Some'll hold off birthing for days just waiting to be alone. Mostly, they drop their foals in the night."

That first birth had been normal. Easy. Quick. As had all the others on the ranch over the last three years. Josie's was proving to be different. Fighting his own apprehension, Ned sensed the horse felt something was wrong, as well. When they checked on her, the whites showed around her large amber eyes and her sides rose and fell like a bellows. Pacing erratically, she seemed to be seeking a means of escape from the pain and confinement. Oiling his arms to be ready if he needed to intervene in the birth, he noted that Allie's alert eyes took in every detail. Good as her word, she remained silent.

They left the horse to her labor and again retreated out of her sight. Unable to sit still himself, Ned paced, leaned against the stable wall with arms locked across his chest, paced again. Time became a physical sensation to him. The space between every heartbeat lingered like a held breath. When he heard a hard thud from across the stable, he grabbed the lantern and hurried to the birthing stall with Will and Allie close behind. The sound had been ominous—not the careful easing of a heavy body to the ground, but the abrupt collapse of body and will. With that, Ned felt a rush of relief. There was finally something to do.

Hovering behind him, Will whispered, "What's happening?"

Ned silenced him with a sharp gesture, as Allie remained silent. Shining the light on the mare, he saw Josie motionless on her side in the hay. Her legs stuck straight out from her distended body and a moist red sack protruded from the fleshy folds between her hind legs. Ned's shoulders slumped at the sight. Handing Will the lantern, he pulled off his shirt and approached the mare, knife in hand.

The placenta's come first, he realized. If he didn't get the foal out immediately, it could suffocate. Kneeling at the exhausted mare's hindquarters, he positioned himself over her and to one side, carefully working his oiled arm up into the horse. The mare shuddered as he felt for the fetus. Sick with fear, he raised his head. Lantern light caught the anguish in his eyes and the tight line of his lips. "It's breech."

Slippery with sweat and blood, his arm almost numb from being pinched between the bones of mother and child, Ned strained to gain traction. When he thought he had a grip on the foal, its hind leg slipped out of his grasp.

Will watched grim-faced. Looking from the barely breathing mare to the widening circle of blood and tissue beneath her, his features went slack. "Josie's done, Ned," he said quietly.

Ned glimpsed Allie lay a warning hand on her brother's arm and give a small shake of her head. Will was silent for a time. Then, too soon, he said, "She's lost too much blood. Ned. She doesn't have the strength to push and you don't have the time to turn the foal and pull it out. It's over." His voice was flat with resignation. "It's over, Ned. Let them go."

Sights that freeze the heart harden the eyes, and Ned had seen too many. He raised clay-cold eyes to his friend and his breath came in short gasps. "Get . . . out."

Will drew back as if struck.

Head lowered, Ned pushed sweat-damp hair out of his eyes with his forearm and renewed his efforts. No lives will be lost this night, he thought. Anyone who believes otherwise doesn't belong in this stable. "Go back to the house," he told Will and turned-away, his face a careful blank. "I'll see to this." His eyes met Allie's and in that quick glance he knew she understood. As far as he was concerned, she could stay or go, as she pleased. Not looking up again, he told Will, "Go. Now."

Will swung around and left Ned to his bleak task with Allie to watch him at it.

The ranch house was dark, save for the light of one oil lamp in the kitchen. And silent. The boys had begged to stay up to greet the new foal, but after well-fought battles, each had surrendered to sleep and been carried to bed. Ian, the last. Hannah stood behind Will and rested a hand on his shoulder. Elbows on the table, he bent his head and rubbed his temples.

"Ye can't be surprised he's being stubborn, now can ye?" she said gently, pouring him a cup of coffee. "Not about this. After everything."

"If it was just about being stubborn, I wouldn't mind." Lacing his fingers around the cup, Will stared into the dark liquid. He'd known Ned for ten years. There was nothing either had experienced that hadn't been shared, darkest times included. Until the last year or so. "You didn't see his eyes."

Sitting down beside him, Hannah laid a hand his arm. "I have seen his eyes, *mo chridhe*. We both know what's there and why." Ned had always had a temper, but in the past it had shown itself in whiskey-fueled bar brawls, not harsh words directed at friends. "He must do this thing his own way and there's nothing to be done about that." Locking her fingers in Will's, she squeezed his hand. "Ye know it's not you he's angry at. Our Ned's never been one to say a thing can't be done if he's of a mind to do it, now has he? Stubborn as a stuck door, ye told me so yerself. I ken he's letting yer sister stay because he knows she has that in her, too."

Brushing his finger along the curve of Hannah's face, Will pushed a lock of coppery hair behind her ear.

"Ye'll see," she told him. "The wee scunner'll be standing at the kitchen door in the morning complainin' no one brought him bannocks and coffee all night."

"He said not to." Will lifted a corner of his mouth in as much of a smile as he could manage. "He said the smell of food might bother the mare." They both sat silent, contemplating the contents of their coffee cups. After several moments, Will said, "I should go back down."

"No, you should not," Hannah said firmly. "He asked ye leave him be and ye must do as he wishes. What ever happens with the horses, Ned'll bear what must be borne."

Will shrugged, hoping his wife was, as always, right.

Just after sunrise Ned and Allie appeared at the kitchen door, bloody from head to foot and grey with fatigue. Hannah and Will, who had kept vigil at the table all night turned wary faces toward them.

It had been a grueling night. After exiling Will, Ned had used all the strength he could muster to repel the foal back into the uterus far enough to reverse it. That done, he'd tried again to grasp a leg without success. Panic and despair had taken hold in his chest, when Allie stepped out of the shadows and knelt at his side.

"Let me," she said softly. "My arm's smaller."

He shook his bowed head, too spent to speak.

"I've done the same thing before with women in labor." She rolled up her sleeves and slathered oil on her arms. "We're wasting time."

He moved aside. There was nothing else he could do and he knew it. Allie bent her head close to the horse and worked her slender arm into Josie. Finding one of the foal's hind legs, she pulled hard with each contraction, trying to draw it out of its weakening mother.

The girl's face was streaked with sweat and blood and she grunted with exertion. Ned watched, allowing her to do what she could, but made himself face the likelihood the foal was dead. In that gut-wrenching moment, Josie gave a great heave and the foal shot out with Allie's arm wrapped around its body, flattening them both to the ground. Lying on her back, stunned, she held the newborn. When he himself could breathe, Ned lifted the colt off Allie's chest and laid it on the hay, still unsure if it was alive or dead.

After a few moments, the mare garnered enough strength to struggle to her feet and stand protectively over her feeble baby. As she rose, the umbilical cord broke cleanly away. A good sign, Ned thought, with measured relief as he tied it off. He gave Allie, who had pushed herself up on her elbows, a nod of approval. At least, it seemed, the mare would live.

Its mother's nuzzling encouraged the foal to roll onto its chest and draw its first weak breath. Another good sign. But when it fell back on one side and lay motionless, Ned despaired for the young horse's survival. As he braced himself to accept the unacceptable, the colt jerked and shuddered, shook its head, and snorted out the fluid it had inhaled during the difficult

labor. Still breathing, it lay where it had fallen. Taking a few steps back, Ned sat down heavily in a corner of the stall and forced himself to hold onto the hope that the foal was just resting to gather the strength to suckle. Beyond the limits of exhaustion himself, he drew up his knees and bent his head on crossed arms. Allie came to sit at his side.

Unsure how much time had passed, Ned was startled by a rustling of the hay. The colt lurched to its feet on spindly legs, wobbled beneath its mother, and began to nurse with surprising vigor. When it lay down in the hay again, he saw it was sated. Josie's milk was good and the colt had the strength to suck. He knew then it would survive.

Once satisfied that the entire placenta had been delivered and was normal and that Josie was no longer bleeding, Ned bowed his head so Allie wouldn't see his tears. When he looked up, she was grinning at him, her face wet with her own.

Ned leaned against the kitchen door jamb, his body backlit by the morning sun. Allie stood at his side. Flinching, he flexed his right hand to work the numbness out of his arm. Will and Hannah waited in silence. Ned avoided their eyes until a soft, slow grin spread across his haggard features. "H & H Ranch has a fine new colt," he announced. "Mother and son are a little the worse for wear, but doin' well. Thanks to Boston." He saw Allie blush at his praise and at his use of the nickname he'd given her when she was a child. Her presence in the stable had been a comfort he hadn't expected. "Much as it pains me," he said, "I've gotta admit she was the one saved that colt's life. Maybe Josie's, too."

Beaming at them all, Allie lowered herself into a chair at the table and wrapped her hands around the mug of coffee Hannah set in front of her. After reluctantly accepting Will and Hannah's hugs and backslaps, Ned made a show of inhaling the aromas of coffee and oat cakes that filled the kitchen. In truth, the smells turned his stomach. He and Allie had done

their best to wash most of the blood from their hands and arms, but the sight of the dried gore that still coated their clothing unleashed a wave of emotion in him. Lowering his eyes, he gripped the back of a chair to steady himself, while trying to banish memories of the night Becky and Benjamin had died.

Forcing a grimace into a grin, he donned the mask he'd learned to wear. "I'm filthy and beat and just about hungry enough to eat the south end of a northbound mule," he said, intending to flee. "I'd best go wash up."

Hannah drew him into a chair. "Ye'll do no such thing. Yer both clean enough for now, we'll see to your clothes later." He caught the quick alarmed glance she exchanged with Allie and shame thickened his throat. They understood the cause of his distress. He felt Hannah's hands on his shoulders, as if she sensed his urge to escape. "You'll stay right where ye are, just as ye are. Food and coffee'll settle ye."

The steaming coffee and warm, yeasty aroma of the bannocks soon made his stomach grumble informing him, to his surprise, that he was, in fact, hungry. At the same moment, three sleep-tousled, but nonetheless exuberant, Hanover boys burst into the kitchen. "Is it born?" Ian asked, searching all their faces as he reached for a bannock.

Colum, the worrier in the family, chewed the corner of his lip and asked his father, "Did you and Ned catch it when Josie dropped it?"

Ignoring his parents, brothers, and aunt, Angus toddled toward Ned, arms lifted. "Ed!"

Taking the child onto his lap, the warmth and weight of the boy's body anchored Ned to this time and place.

"It's a fine colt," Will told his eager sons. "You'll all meet him after breakfast and chores. Then, we'll have to decide what to call him."

"Aye." Hannah stood behind Ned to refill his cup. "I've been pondering the subject of names, myself. " With a wink to Will and Allie, she said, "I ken we must call him Scunner."

"Scunner?" It was one of the few Gaelic words Ned knew. Turning to frown up at her, he cleared a crumb from his throat. "Nuisance? Why would you want to name the new colt 'Nuisance'?"

Hannah raised an auburn brow. "The colt? Now what is it, I wonder," she asked, cocking her head at him, "makes ye think it's the wee colt who's the nuisance around here?"

Grimacing at the reminder of his harsh behavior toward Will the night before, he gave him the repentant look and sheepish grin he knew was all it would take to earn his friend's forgiveness. He ate heartily, asked for more coffee, stood to toss Angus—squealing with delight—into the air, and caught him just in time.

With the baby's pudgy arms tight around his neck, he realized that even here—in the warmth and light of the best place that existed in his dark world—he could no longer bear the aching emptiness that had become his life.

CHAPTER TWELVE

On her second visit to the shanties, Allie found Clare outside on a rickety chair mending the torn lace of a faded blue camisole. A gaudy collection of corsets and too-sheer-to-be-decent shifts filled a basket at her feet. Up the hill, the children crouched in the dirt to help the old woman tend her garden.

"Baseball?" It wasn't just a stunned echo—Allie truly didn't believe she'd heard correctly when Clare explained that Ephraim was off playing baseball. Setting the heavy, galvanized tin wash tub she'd carried from the wagon onto the ground, she stood with hands on hips, stony-eyed. And angry. The stench of the still filthy privy was worse than it had been before. "He's playing baseball."

"Yes, Miss." Clare's hands had gone still, her eyes fixed on her sewing. "With the men in town. They say he's good at slugging the ball."

Norberto, shorter than Allie by half a head and built like a barrel, stood at her side with coils of rope looped over one shoulder and planks of wood balanced in his arms. His usually amiable face mirrored Allie's displeasure. He'd offered to help Ephraim build a rope bed frame for the straw-stuffed mattresses the Ladies' Benevolent Society had donated, so the family wouldn't have to sleep on the vermin-infested floor. Now it appeared he'd have to do it alone.

"Ephraim says workin' so hard at faro— bein' cooped up at the Tanglefoot and all—gives him a hankerin' to get outside and move around some." When Clare raised her eyes, Allie saw her misery. "To keep up his strength."

"I see." Allie flinched inwardly at how much her tone resembled her mother's. To give her temper time to cool, she watched the children help the old woman weed and hoe. But her attempt to reserve judgment failed. Anger buzzed through her veins. It didn't help that she saw Etta pull what might have been a rock or weed from the baby's mouth.

With a shrug, Norberto shifted the weight of the wood and headed toward the shack. "No problema, Senorita Allie," he said over his shoulder. "I make the bed myself. For la Senora and los ninos."

"Please wait, Norberto," Allie said quickly. She saw the Winnicotts had done nothing she'd asked them to do to prepare for her visit. "First, we have to sweep the place out." She'd brought a sturdy, Shaker broom—taken without asking from the barn at South Slope. She hoped her next words wouldn't offend Clare. "We must burn all the old bedclothes. I've brought fresh blankets and quilts." Old, but clean—taken without asking from the soon-to-be rags shelf of her mother's linen closet.

When the sweeping and burning were done, Norberto set about constructing the beds. Allie brought another wobbly chair outside, set it next to Clare's, and eyed the colorful garments in her basket. "Oh, these aren't mine, Miss," she explained with a soft giggle. "I do some mending for the girls at the Tanglefoot when I can get it."

Allie laughed with her, glad to see the reticent young woman let down her guard. Picking up a thread-bare shift, she studied the torn bodice. Ripped. With a start, Allie remembered how the 'girls' at the disreputable saloon made their living. "If you have another needle, I can help."

As they sewed, Allie drew Clare out by asking about each of the children and listening to her descriptions. The baby had always been sickly, the toddler sunny and serene—until he flew into one of his screaming fits. The older boy was either pensive or mischievous, depending on which way the wind was blowing. And Etta, she said with a proud smile, was a caution. "Bossy, just like my mama, but bright as a button."

Then, her shoulders slumped. Bowing her head, she dropped her mending in her lap and pressed her hands to her cheeks. Allie laid a hand on her shoulder. "As I told you last time, there's nothing here that we can't make better."

Lowering her hands, Clare shook her head. "I know you mean it, Miss. But I just don't believe that's so. It's not the dirt or the want, it's . . . I am twenty-three years old and I've birthed six children. Buried two." Tears welling, she dried them on the shift she'd been stitching. "I love my babies, I truly do. But . . . they just keep coming and I can't . . . I just can't keep having more. I don't know if Ephraim'll ever be able to feed the ones we've got."

Collecting herself, she managed a rueful laugh and resumed her sewing. "Mama did warn me not to marry him. 'Clare Louise,' she said, 'Ephraim Winnicott may look like a man, but he's stuck somewhere between grass and hay. If he's not fully growed by now, he never will be.' "

Tying a knot in her thread, Clare pulled a taffeta gray bodice that Allie guessed had once been violet from the basket and began reattaching a lace ruffle. "I thought she was just being bossy, as usual, but I s'pose she was right." With a sideways glance at Allie, she said, "My pa he was mean. Real mean. You understand? Poor Mama, bless her, she don't know what it's like to be in love like me and Ephraim. I know what my husband is and I know even better what he isn't and it makes no never-mind to me." Tilting her chin up, she held Allie's gaze. "That man'd give me and our babies the full moon and every single one of the brightest stars, if he could."

Clare's words were the opening Allie had been waiting for. An opportunity to provide health care, not just charity, had presented itself and she was determined to make the best of it. Anxiety and excitement ran in tandem through her veins. Broaching the delicate subject, she felt her face redden and summoned the confident spirit of Lydia Brennan to guide her. With halting sentences and awkward pauses, she suggested abstinence—the easiest and most effective method of avoiding pregnancy—what Lydia called "voluntary motherhood."

"Oh, Miss!" Clare laughed and rolled her eyes. "My Ephraim? Why he would not abide such a notion for one minute."

That came as no surprise to Allie. When she assured Clare there were other solutions, the young woman's face went somber. "Is such a thing really possible, Miss?" Allie understood the depth of her desperation when she added, "If it ain't truly so, please don't say it is."

"It is," Allie assured her. But other methods would be difficult to come by and none were guaranteed. The Comstock Law—"The Suppression of Trade In, and Circulation of, Obscene Literature and Articles of Immoral Use"—made it illegal for physicians to discuss ways of preventing conception. Lydia had informed Allie they'd solved that problem at her clinic by addressing issues of 'feminine hygiene' instead.

Allie kept her outrage that such a personal matter could be prohibited by law to herself. Doc had informed her that in recent years, Goodyear had developed a product for men that was so popular it was advertised in the penny press. He said they circumvented the Comstock Law by calling it 'Rubber Goods for Gents' and 'The Married Woman's Friend'—meant to be used to prevent venereal disease.

"The rubber condom," her father had informed her in the same clinical tone he used when he taught her how to cauterize a wound, "has proven more reliable in preventing conception than sheep intestines and other similar materials that have been used since antiquity. "

Allie swallowed the dryness in her throat and told Clare, "A rubber sheath is a new . . . um . . . device." Lowering her eyes, she tried to sound matter-of-fact. "It's very effective. A man puts it on his . . . on his . . ."

Clare held up a hand. "Miss Allie. This is Ephraim Winnicott we're talkin' about here."

Trying not to sound daunted, Allie said, "I understand." But she didn't. Not entirely. As an unmarried woman, all she knew of such things was what she'd read in books, mostly *Gray's Anatomy.* "Vaginal sponges are . . ."

Much of the optimism faded from Clare's face. "Soaked in vinegar. Or you can take half a lemon and stick it . . . up there. The girls at the Tanglefoot told me those might work, but that's how we got baby Grace."

"Douches afterward can . . ."

Clare shook her head. "Caleb." Her thin mask of hope began to disintegrate, revealing the despair beneath it. "Please, Miss Allie, you said it was possible. I just can't keep havin' all these babies." Her voice caught. "You said you know a way that'll work."

Praying that Clare had not been failed already by the last and only thing she had left to offer, Allie asked, "Have you ever tried a womb veil?"

"A womb veil?" With a furrowed brow, Clare contemplated the words. "Why no, I can't say as I have."

Hoping what she was about to say would prove true, she said it as if it were a certainty. "It's like the sponges, but much more effective. If you like, I'll bring one next time I visit."

"Yes, thank you, Miss." Clare's eyes shone with the brittle brightness Allie associated with fever. "And, please, please come back soon. Real soon."

Gratified to have won Clare's trust, and optimistic she'd found a way to make a medical intervention that might truly help her, Allie felt slightly giddy. "I will," she promised. She'd have Doc order the womb veil as soon as she got home. And she'd write to tell Lydia about her success that very night. "I'll have to send away for it, so it may take some time. But I'll bring it as soon as I can."

"Sooner, please," Clare begged.

As Norberto drove Allie back down the dusty hill toward Commerce Street, squeals of carefree laughter came to them from where Clare and the children splashed in the creek. Allie knew her father would share her triumph and would gladly order the illegal rubber device.

Also, she had to admit, it did please her far too much to muse on what her mother's reaction might be if she found out that her disappointingly un-Victorian daughter was about to break the law.

CHAPTER THIRTEEN

"Jackstraws?" Albert asked.

"No."

"Hopscotch?"

"No," Allie said again. Albert was trying hard, but his suggestions brought them no closer to solving their problem of what games he could play with Joseph.

From the shade of the deep, covered porch that faced the white barn, she and her brother swayed back and forth on a wooden swing. They watched Doc, Will, Ned, and Norberto construct the fence for a grassy enclosure for the lambs. A squall had brought drenching rain the night before, breaking a spell of heat and humidity, but had left the ground sodden and difficult to work. Every posthole the men dug quickly refilled with mud.

The addition of the sheep meant more mouths to feed at South Slope come winter. Cloud, Dash, and Bluster—Doc's old border collie—dozed beneath the wagonload of hay Will and Ned had brought from the H & H Ranch. With his mistress occupied, the spaniel had been free to spend an ecstatic morning frolicking with the bigger dogs. Now, filthy and bedraggled, Dash had been banished from the house until someone bathed him—which no one seemed inclined to do—had anyone been able to catch him.

Folding his arms across his chest, Albert faced forward, kicking his feet to propel the swing. He turned to Allie. "Marbles?"

She shook her head. It was the morning of the Afternoon Tea and she felt the need to prepare Albert for his visit with Joseph. In helping him think of games the boys could play together, she'd already vetoed hopscotch, dominoes, and jump rope as impossible for his new friend. She feared chasing lambs would not entertain them for very long.

"Cup and ball?" Albert ventured.

"He could only watch you play."

The men, working ankle-deep in mud, drew the boy's attention. Allie's eyes lingered on Ned's strong back and shoulders and his sweat-soaked shirt, as he lifted timbers for the split rail fence and nailed them to wobbly posts.

"He does draw the eye now, doesn't he?" Allie recalled the words she'd heard Hannah whisper to Becky years ago, when she'd caught her watching Ned at a barn dance, a blue bandana tied around his arm. Allie had giggled with them, though the comment had been somewhat lost on her. Then. Now she understood full-well what Hannah had meant.

With a sigh of defeat, Albert ejected himself from the moving swing. "Gotta go help Will and Papa." Hopping down the steps, he turned back to Allie. "Maybe Joseph'll have some ideas when he gets here."

"He just might."

While she was culling ideas from her own childhood pastimes, Allie was startled by a sudden, loud, string of irritable oaths that burst from Ned. Another timber had pulled free of its post and dropped into the muck. Glaring at it, he lifted his hat to smooth back the damp, dark hair stuck to his forehead and wiped his face on his sleeve. When he caught Allie staring at him, his exasperated frown gave way to an apologetic grin. Before she could think to return the greeting, he'd returned to his work.

The night she'd helped him deliver the colt had left her with a mix of feelings. Shared accomplishment at the end of a shared ordeal. Gratification at his approval. A poignant sense of his still raw grief. And something else.

Something she barely understood—and had been unable to dismiss—that brought pleasantly unpleasant warmth to her cheeks.

Chastising herself for embodying a cliché she'd always found silly, she hurried into the safety of the house where preparations for the Afternoon Tea were well underway. Dressed in lilac satin, her mother supervised Mrs. Olney, the now elderly cook who had accompanied them from Boston, and stony-faced Miranda, the kitchen maid. They prepared the delicacies that would be served on linen-covered tables set in the shade of the wide, semi-circular veranda outside the great room. Three large pitchers of lemonade perched on the sideboard.

Prim in her pink satin dress, a knee-length version of her mother's gown, Maude Mary hummed as she arranged sweet peas and white roses in porcelain pitchers, setting them in the center of each table. When that was done, she arranged name cards, china plates, and floral teacups at each of ten seats.

Allie arrived in the kitchen so flushed her mother's eyes widened. "Has the day turned so warm already?"

"Oh, no," Allie said, tucking an errant strand of hair behind her ear. "It's a fine day!"

"I'm glad to know it," her mother observed drily. "Then may I ask the cause of your high color, Alexandrina? It can't be that your corsets are too tight or your silks too steamy, as you're not wearing them."

Allie had been granted a reprieve from the required Afternoon Tea finery. She'd volunteered to watch the children—Albert, Joseph, and her three nephews—a task which necessitated practical clothing. Pressing her hands to her cheeks, she settled her nerves. "I suppose it's just I can't imagine what Albert will find to do with Joseph."

"Of course, that would be what has you blushing," her mother said, directing an arch look at Miranda, who was licking icing off two of her fingers. The maid returned her mistress's glare, wiped the offending fingers on her apron, and applied herself to frosting the sandwich cake with insolent strokes of the knife. Mrs. Hanover started to say something to her, but apparently thought better of it. Instead, she called out the door to Maude Mary. "Come along, my dear girl, I'm in need of your wise counsel regarding our surprise for Sarah Findlay."

"Surprise?" Allie shifted her gaze from her mother to her sister.

Maude Mary stopped in the door way. "I thought you knew."

"Knew what?"

"I suppose you must come along too, Alexandrina," her mother sighed. "This concerns you, as well. Hurry now, both of you."

The guests were due at three o'clock, except for Martha and Sarah Findlay who were to come at 2:30 to give Joseph time to get settled. Ignorant of anything that might be construed as a surprise, Allie followed her mother and sister into the morning room where a teal dress with pink rosebuds embroidered on the bodice was draped over the chintz sofa. Allie recognized it as one of her gowns from last season. Or the one before. She didn't remember which and wouldn't have cared if she had.

"Will it suit her complexion?" her mother asked.

"Mama," Maude Mary said, "Sarah's such a pretty girl, I can't think of a color that wouldn't suit her."

"Yes, that's what I thought, too." Lifting the dress, she held it up to Allie. "She will certainly do this lovely frock justice. Although it was quite becoming on you, Alexandrina. When you deigned to wear it, that is."

She will do it justice, Allie thought, surprised that she'd felt stung by her mother's thoughtless words. Allie had no illusions about her own appearance. She didn't think herself plain, nor did she think herself pretty. Tall and slender like her father and older brother, thick brown hair—not the lustrous auburn of Maude Mary's—high cheekbones, large hazel eyes, and, as her mother had once told her, a good mouth.

"We're born with our eyes, Alexandrina," she had said. "But we make our mouths." It had been one of the rare occasions on which Allie had received her approval. "Intelligence has shone from your eyes since the day you were born and, I daresay, your mouth is quite pleasant, if not somewhat stubborn."

Of course, Allie had had suitors, several. Sarah Findlay was correct—with five men to each woman, there were no spinsters in Solace Springs. But, none of the men had interested Allie. Which was just as well. None, she'd been told by her mother, would have been deemed suitable anyhow.

"Alexandrina!" her mother's irked voice cut through her thoughts. "I asked if you think the dress will fit her. She's not as tall as you are." Pursing her lips, she looked from the elegant frock to Allie and back. "Plumper, too."

"Well," Maude Mary said in a miffed tone, "if you were to ask me, which is what I thought you called me in here for, I would remind you that Sarah Sue Findlay is exquisite and will be a perfect vision in this, or any other frock."

Allie turned a critical eye on the dress. "The length's not a problem, you can baste it up for today. As for the rest," she was sure Sarah's curves would fill it out in a way she herself never could, "I'm sure it will be just as Maude Mary said."

When they returned to the large, sunny kitchen, Allie saw that most preparations for the Tea were complete. The cakes and sandwiches stayed cool in the large oak and glass ice box that was Mrs. Olney's pride and joy. The cook addressed herself to arranging platters of the tamales and beans Norberto's wife, Anjelita, had sent for "El Doctore and los trabajadors."

Doc Hanover had developed an appetite for the flavors of the southwest and Norberto and his wife took great pleasure in satisfying it. Another favorite of his, a pitcher of café de olla—coffee with sugar, cinnamon, orange peel, and milk—joined the pastries in the ice box. It would be heated and served in earthenware mugs when the day cooled. The doctor required his bitter 'barefoot' coffee in the morning, but café de olla was a pleasure he couldn't resist at the end of the day.

"Alexandrina," her mother said, surveying the kitchen, "run outside and tell the men dinner will be served at the trestle table as soon as they've washed. Please and thank you. Then come right back up to help Miranda bring out the food and plates. Those weary souls must be ravenous. Oh, and do be sure they have all the necessary cutlery. Miranda," she tilted her head toward the dour maid, who was close enough to hear every word, "tends to forget things just to be perverse when she's asked to work outside the house."

Carrying covered crockery and utensils out to the waiting men, Allie smiled at Miranda. "You know she thinks the world of you."

"I know she's my mistress and I know I'm lucky to have the place I have here, Miss." A closed-mouth smirk hid her bad teeth. "I also know the town folk call her 'Lady Jane' behind her back."

Allie, who'd heard the same whisperings, slid another quick smile at the maid. Her mother would not be displeased by the nickname.

The men, with Albert sitting tall among them, welcomed the hot, hearty food with enthusiasm. Working since just after sun-up, they were, as predicted, ravenous. Cake and bread-and-butter sandwiches, delicious as they might be to the ladies, would not have sufficed at this table. The pungent aroma of exotic spices and herbs filled the air when Allie uncovered the dishes Anjelita had prepared. Ladling beans onto their plates, she caught snatches of conversation as they unwrapped the corn husks from their pork tamales. The sheep pen was almost complete, they agreed, and they were relieved the work would be done before the worst of the afternoon heat and the storm that would follow were upon them.

"Done, at least for now," her father said. With a look of comic alarm, he cocked his head in the directions of the barn. "You can be assured Mrs.

Hanover will insist that fence be painted white as soon as she realizes it's not."

The small barn had been an item of contention when it was built. Mrs. Hanover abhorred the idea of having such a rustic structure on the property, but Doc insisted it was necessary to shelter the cow and horses and to store their feed. After much, often heated, debate, she had relented on the condition that it be built in the same Gothic Revival style as the house and painted to match.

When Allie returned with lemonade, she was pleased to hear Ned and Will bantering as they'd done since they were youths.

"Baseball? Again?" Ned groused. "Sure, you just run along and play with your friends. Seems whenever you're of a mind to shirk your responsibilities . . ." He held up a hand to silence Will's attempt to protest. "They fall square on my shoulders. But, someone has to unload all that hay and someone has to pitch it up into the loft and someone, you of course, has to sashay into town to whack at a little brown ball. It's a good thing you Hanovers keep me well fed, or I just might start to feel poorly used."

Though Will cringed dramatically at Ned's teasing, Allie knew he and her father were as gladdened as she to see a glimpse of Ned's old spirit. "The hay can wait," Will said with a cajoling smile. "Come with me."

At that, Ned's face closed.

"No," he snapped, abruptly getting to his feet. The sharpness of his reply startled Allie and hushed the other conversations at the table. After an awkward silence, Ned managed an awkward smile and softened his tone. "No thanks." Eyes on the lowering sky, he said, "Storm's coming. I don't want to lose a load of hay to the rain."

Allie's baffled expression matched her father's and brother's as they watched Ned's retreating back. Despite his inexplicable reaction to Will's invitation, she was pleased to know he'd be staying at South Slope for the afternoon. Making her way around the table to fill lemonade glasses, she was perturbed to find she had to concentrate to steady her hands.

In the shade of the wide veranda that wrapped around the exterior of South Slope, Allie and Maude Mary rocked in white wicker chairs to await the Findlays' arrival. Albert had been sent to clean himself up and change his muddy clothes before joining them. Their mother had instructed—please and thank you—that Maude Mary bring Sarah and Mrs. Findlay to the morning room for the 'surprise' and that Allie and Albert entertain Joseph outside.

Still at a loss for how to accomplish that, Allie only half-listened to her sister's grievances. For months Maude Mary had begged to be allowed to put up her hair and let down her skirts—like the proper young lady she believed herself to be. Apparently, hearing herself referred to as a child by Sarah Findlay had inflamed her impatience.

"I just don't understand why I must continue to suffer this humiliation!" She stood to shake a few tiny leaves from her immaculate, albeit calf-length, dress. "Mother keeps telling me, 'Alice Maude Mary, my dear, to everything there is a season.' I have no idea whatever that has to do with anything. What does she mean, Allie?"

At Maude Mary's age it hadn't mattered a whit to Allie whether her hair or hems were up or down. In this, as in all things, her sister would not rest until her questions were answered. With the enigmatic smile she knew maddened her, Allie said, "When the time is right you'll know."

"The time is right, right now!" Maude Mary huffed. After a moment, she faced Allie. "Everyone makes it sound like there's some mystery to it. Please, please, just tell me what it is. If I have to wait, I will. But I must know what I'm waiting for and why."

Allie hadn't had the benefit of counsel from either her mother or an older sister in this matter. Hannah had been the one to fill her in on the mysteries of womanhood. In a solemn whisper she now told Maude Mary, "You're waiting to flower from a girl to a woman."

"Flower?"

"To become a maiden. A young woman."

"A maiden?" Maude Mary pondered this. "How do you know whether you're a girl or a maiden?"

Her own face reddening, Allie regretted broaching the topic. Recalling her father's 'in for a dime, in for a dollar motto,' she resigned herself to the fact that Maude Mary would not stop asking questions until she got an answer. "You'll know you're a maiden when you get your courses." At her sister's baffled stare, she explained, "When you bleed."

Eyes wide, Maude Mary sat back in her chair and folded her hands in her lap. "Bleed?"

Allie and Maude Mary shared a bedroom, so Allie was certain the girl had some notion of what she meant by 'bleeding.' She guessed her sister hadn't realized it would happen to her someday, too. Or that it could have anything to do with being allowed to wear long skirts.

"So that's it? That's what Mother meant?" Her awed smile matched her eyes.

Allie had only half-noticed that a presentable Albert had slipped out of the house and plopped onto the top step. Watching the road, he picked honeysuckle blooms from the vine twining around a porch post, pinched them, and pulled the stamens to suck the nectar. "Who's bleeding?" he asked.

At that moment, the Findlays' buckboard pulled into the circular drive. With a whoop, Albert leapt down the steps and dashed across the sloping lawn to greet them. Maude Mary gave Allie a long hug, then—head high and every inch the demure young lady, short skirt notwithstanding—gracefully descended the steps with Allie following.

Each dressed in her best linen hoopskirt, blouse, and bodice, Martha and Sarah climbed from their wagon and adjusted their bonnets. Refusing their help, Joseph clambered down. Once he was steadied, all three faced the house and stared at the Gothic Revival structure that was South Slope. Imitating the architecture of the castles and cathedrals of Europe, the large, two-story home had a pitched roof, steep cross gables, and mullioned windows with pointed arches. Carved posts stood at intervals around the covered veranda encircling the house. Mrs. Hanover liked to say that her home—dove grey with white trim—"has more decorum" than the often garish 'painted ladies' built elsewhere.

As Allie and Maude Mary exchanged warm greetings with their guests, Albert turned to Joseph. "We don't have to go to the tea party, but we still get cake! My papa might even let us have some café de olla. We can play with the lambs or the kittens, if you like. We're building them their own pen. I helped! Do you want to see it?"

Joseph, timid, nodded.

"He's shy to be in such unfamiliar and such . . . such grand surroundings," Mrs. Findlay explained. She glanced at Sarah who had also gone silent. "I suppose we all are."

Allie laughed. "Don't worry, you'll get used to it. We did." Making their way up the grassy slope, she told them. "Papa built this house so Mother wouldn't miss Boston too much. Truth be told? The rest of us wish we could live on a beautiful wide-open ranch like yours."

Albert hung back to walk with Joseph as Allie led them down the main corridor, past the parlor, her father's study, and the dining room. At the end of the hall, they entered the great room with its tall, arched windows, marble hearth, and Kermanshah carpets. Enameled Chinese jars the size of toddlers squatted on inlaid tables in front of the windows and a spinet piano graced one corner. Comfortable seating—a jade green velvet settee, overstuffed chairs, and two plush ottomans—furnished the room and an ornately-carved walnut staircase led up to the second floor, where a wide corridor overlooked the space below.

Mrs. Hanover awaited them at the door to her morning room with Miranda at her side, balancing a tray of lemonades. Presenting them each with a tall glass, Allie's mother said, "So pleased you could join us."

"We're pleased . . . honored to be here." Mrs. Findlay intercepted the glass meant for her son and held it while he drank. "We've never been inside such a . . . such a splendid place before. It's like a dream."

"A dream come true," Sarah murmured. "And I never, ever want to wake up."

As the women spoke, Joseph edged closer to his mother and clenched a piece of her skirt in his hand. She wrapped an arm around his shoulders.

Mrs. Hanover beamed at Sarah. "How lovely of you, my dear girl. You do give truth to the saying 'beauty is as beauty does.' " Turning to Allie, she said, "Alexandrina, you and Albert have been plotting all day about the mischief these boys might be able to get into, if given half a chance. So, outside at once, please and thank you. I have my own mischief to make with Sarah and Mrs. Findlay and we don't have much time before the other guests appear. Ladies," she said with a mysterious smile and a broad gesture, "come into my parlor."

When his mother attempted to move away, Joseph's fingers tightened on her skirt. When Albert stepped up to comfort him, he twisted away. Mrs. Findlay looked to Sarah, who would not meet her eyes. Bending to whisper reassurances to her son, she tried again to detach his now two-handed grip, to no avail.

After a few moments of this, she shook her head. "I'm sorry. It's just . . . he's not used to bein' away from home. Strange places frighten him. Not that this place is strange. I don't mean that, of course. It's just so big. And different." She lowered her eyes. "Luke was right—this is a mistake. I'm sorry. We best . . . I think we best just go home."

"Oh, no!" Maude Mary exclaimed. "Please don't go. Mother will be so disappointed."

Sarah lowered her own eyes. "Ma, please," she whispered. "Mrs. Hanover asked us here early because she has a surprise for *me*. Just once can't something be about *me*?"

"Alexandrina."

Her mother clearly expected Allie to forestall the disasters looming on all fronts. Bending her head so it was near Joseph's ear, she said, "Albert and I were hoping you could tell us if we're caring for the lambs properly. We've never had sheep before, so we've got so many questions." Speaking softly, she untangled Joseph's fingers from his mother's skirt and transferred them to her own hand. "Those little lambs are so dear, aren't they? We wouldn't want to be feeding them wrong or not doing all we should to make them happy. Will you come outside and give us your opinion on the new pen?"

With a firm grip on his hand, Allie straightened and waited for Joseph's answer. She guessed he wasn't often given choices. His head drooped and lolled from side to side, but he managed to lift it to give his mother and sister a questioning look. When they both nodded encouragement, he waggled his head toward Albert, who nodded back.

Eyes still on Albert, he said, "Oh . . . kay."

Following Maude Mary into the sitting room, Sarah looked back over her shoulder. "Thank you," she mouthed to Allie.

CHAPTER FOURTEEN

When Allie and the boys completed their journey to the back yard—made arduous by Joseph's halting gait—they found the pen complete and Doc and Norberto surveying their handiwork.

"Papa," Albert said, "this is my new friend Joseph."

Doc grasped the boy's hand. "Call me Doc. I'm pleased to meet you. I must thank you for your part in our acquisition of the first two sheep in Albert's flock."

Although he gave no outward sign, Allie knew her father was assessing every aspect of the boy's condition. With renewed diffidence, Joseph stared at the ground, until Ned came trudging out from the barn with thirty pounds of bleating lamb struggling beneath each arm and Cloud at his side. The wolf dog had sniffed and licked Allie and Albert earlier in the day, so Joseph's less familiar scent interested him more. When he approached and snuffled his chest and arm, Joseph shrank back.

"Sit, Cloud," Ned commanded.

Suspecting that Joseph's reticence had more to do with what had happened in town weeks before than with any real fear of Cloud, Allie knelt and called the wolf dog to her. She was certain the boy had been more frightened by his father's confrontation with Ned than by the dog. A nod from Ned freed Cloud to respond. When Allie wrapped her arms around his thick neck, the canine licked her face until she pulled away laughing. "Enough!"

Keeping one arm around the dog, Allie slipped the other around Joseph's waist, pulling his resisting body toward her. "You remember Cloud, don't you? I saw you pet him in town."

What she saw now was a mix of confusion and longing on the child's face. His father must have—wisely—forbidden him to touch animals he didn't know. And possibly, less wisely in her opinion, to stay away from Ned Harper, as well.

"Cloud thinks the two of you are friends," she said. "What do you think about that?" Joseph gave an almost imperceptible nod. Taking one of his hands in hers, Allie lifted it toward the dog. "Would it be okay if he sniffed you?"

In the moments that followed, Joseph got thoroughly sniffed, licked, nuzzled, and pawed. When it was over, his arms were tight around the dog's neck and he had a cheek-splitting grin on his face.

Still hefting the two squirming lambs, Ned grinned down at Joseph. "Like all his friends," he said, "you're a member of his pack now." When Ned turned his approving gaze on her, Allie willed her face not to flush. With limited success. "Let's put this new pen to the test," he said, shifting the weight of the sheep. "You boys do the honor of opening that gate. These lambs have gained ten pounds each since I've been standing here."

Timid again, Joseph stayed attached to Allie's side. When it became clear he was not going to participate, Albert unhooked the latch. Setting the lambs on the ground, Ned nudged one and then the other toward the opening with his knee. They dug in their hooves and became dead weight against his prodding. Like Joseph, they seemed unwilling to broach new territory.

"What should we do, Joseph?" Allie asked.

Joseph bent forward, placed two hands on the little ewe's rump, and gave her a firm shove into the pen. Albert did the same to the ram, then closed the gate. After giving the humans long, reproachful looks, the young sheep began to nibble the grass and were soon gamboling around their enclosure.

"Thank you, Joseph. You saved the day!" Allie said. "Besides not knowing how to get them to mind, how do you think we're doing so far?"

Joseph watched the weanlings frolic, then leaned a shoulder against the fence to test its sturdiness. It didn't budge, but wobbled some. Pointing to the variety of wild grasses growing in the enclosure, he managed an approving nod. "G . . . good . . . grass." Pushing on the railing again, he grimaced. "Ohhh . . . kay . . . fence."

Doc, Ned, and Norberto laughed, exchanged chagrined glances, but seemed disinclined to argue with their young critic.

With these successes, Joseph appeared to relax.

"Let's go play now!" Albert enthused, bouncing where he stood. When Joseph grew silent again and edged back toward Allie's side, her brother also became more subdued. "Do you want to see the kittens first?"

Joseph hesitated, but followed Albert to the barn. Just as they disappeared through the door, the whirlwind that was the youngest Hanovers hurtled into the yard. Whooping and hollering, Ian and Colum barreled into Doc, Allie, and Ned with a force that all but knocked them over. Hannah followed, carrying Angus. When she deposited the toddler on the ground, he catapulted himself at Ned, who swung the squealing child into the air, then settled him on his shoulders.

"I enjoy the privilege of being my youngest grandson's favorite," Doc said, "unless, of course, Ned Harper happens to be within reach."

Hannah smoothed the moss green satin of her dress—a hand-me-down from Allie's younger days. "Thank you for watching the terrible wee bairns, goodsister. I'll now go fetch my Dundee Cake from the wagon and enjoy the company of yon ladies. If I can remember how it's done, I may even engage in something called conversation."

With that, she turned on her heel and left them watching her try to manage her skirt while tucking escaped strands of red hair under her hat.

Balancing Angus in the crook of one arm, much like he had the lambs, Ned directed the 'terrible bairns' attention to the animals cavorting in the pen. As the boys engrossed themselves in the antics of creatures with energies much like their own, Allie saw Albert trudge from the barn alone, head down, hands jammed in his pockets.

"Where's Joseph?" she asked.

Not meeting her eyes, Albert glumly admitted, "In the barn."

"And why is it you're out here?"

"He doesn't want to play. He doesn't want to do anything."

Placing both hands on her brother's shoulders, Allie turned him and gave him a shove toward the barn. Following close behind him, she realized that a string of boys, men, chickens, and dogs followed her. Inside the small barn, beams of afternoon sun filtered in through high narrow windows. Motes of dust glimmered in the scant light and the aroma of hay, horses and leather filled the air. In the dimness, she saw Joseph's small form huddled in a corner. When she approached and offered her hand, he let her pull him wobbling into the light, his mouth twisted with the effort not to cry.

Although Hannah had prepared her young sons for their first meeting with Albert's new friend, the youngest Hanovers stared at Joseph with a mix of fear and fascination. Allie had forgotten how distressing his twisted limbs and contorted face would look to them. Colum clutched his grandfather's hand and backed up a step.

"Why won't you play with me?" Albert asked.

Joseph stared at his shoes.

"I thought you wanted to be my friend."

"I . . . do"

"Then why won't you play with me?"

"I . . . can't."

I should have understood sooner, Allie reproached herself. Albert had asked Joseph to *play*. She remembered what they all—including Joseph—had heard Mr. Findlay say about his son: "He can't play. It only shames him to be reminded he can't do like other boys."

A few hens wandered into the barn to peck at bits of grain beneath the straw, providing the inspiration for Allie's plan. Placing one hand on each boy's shoulder, she said, "The truth is Albert can't play either, at least not just yet. These poor chickens are looking for food. In all the excitement of building the fence and getting ready for guests," she gave her brother a stern look, "someone must have forgotten to do their chores."

When Albert started to protest—feeding the chickens was his responsibility and, as Allie knew, he had fed them that morning—her grip on his shoulder tightened, silencing him.

"Before Albert can play," she continued, "he has chores to do. If you wouldn't mind helping him, Joseph, it'll go quicker." Joseph's face fell again. Allie guessed chores must be another thing he'd been taught he 'couldn't do.' Handing each boy a pail of chicken feed, she said, "Albert will show you."

Hesitant at first, Joseph learned quickly it didn't matter how much he spasmed—feed was meant to be scattered. In minutes, he was casting it with authority. Colum stared at the twisted boy with jerking arms and tugged at his grandfather's sleeve. When Doc bent to listen, the boy whispered loudly, "Is he broken?"

"No," Doc said, loud enough for Joseph to hear. "He's not broken at all. His body just works differently than yours."

As the smaller children got accustomed to their uncle's odd new friend, they grew bored. Doc herded them back out to the pen to watch the more interesting lambs. To Allie's surprise, Ned stayed behind. Seating himself on a bale of hay, he leaned back and stretched his legs.

"About time I got to watch someone else work," he grumbled, making room for her. "Sit down, Boston. You've earned it, too."

Watching the boys do their chores, Allie settled next to Ned. They chatted about inconsequential things in the companionable manner they'd done since she was a child, but hadn't in the past two years. "How's the colt?" she asked.

"Fit and frisky and full of himself," Ned said with obvious satisfaction. "Smart as an outhouse mouse and he knows it."

"I don't think I ever thanked you for letting me be at his birth." An unexplainable shyness overtook her and she lowered her eyes. "I learned a lot."

He shook his head and frowned. "I learned a few things myself. Your brother says I can be stubborn and arrogant—a bad combination. He's right." His gaze met and held hers. "I s'pose I needed a lesson in getting out of the way when it's called for. Which it was that night."

How can looking into someone's eyes affect the rate of your heartbeat, she wondered. She had to look away so hers would slow.

As if sensing her disquiet—or completely unaware of it—she couldn't have said which it was—Ned turned his left palm up and pointed to a faded scar that ran from the mound of his thumb to his wrist. "Remember when Doc had you stitch me up?" he asked. "What were you then? Thirteen or so?"

"Twelve." Allie smiled at the memory. "Almost."

Every day after school, she'd hurried to her father's clinic. With willing patients, Doc allowed her to observe or assist in small ways. Most of the time, she handed him instruments or watched as he set bones, cleaned wounds, and, of course, sutured cuts. One day Ned had arrived with his hand wrapped in a bloody rag. His knife had slipped while he cleaned an elk hide and, try as he might, he couldn't stop the bleeding.

Doc had taken that opportunity to test Allie's devotion to the healing arts. While he examined the wound, he told her to prepare a suture needle. When she handed it to him, he handed it back. "With all the embroidery your mother has you do, I suspect your cross-stitch is better than mine.

Clean this cut, then let's see what you can do." Both she and Ned had gone pale. "That is, of course, if Mr. Harper's willing."

Ned had held him in a speechless stare, but finally said, "I'm willing, if she is."

"But what if I hurt him, Papa?"

"No need to worry about that," Doc said. "It's going to hurt no matter who does it."

Allie had passed her father's test. After that, she'd eagerly learned the intricacies of stitching all manner of wounds and become his chief suturer. By fourteen, she was adept at setting small fractures and assisting with more complex procedures.

Now, she and Ned admired her handiwork. The tiny, uniform stitches were barely visible.

"Prettiest scar I've ever had," he told her. His approval felt like a small sun pulsing in her abdomen. Then, he grew solemn. "What you just did with the boy," he said, nodding toward Joseph. "That was as much healing as stitchin' up a clumsy cowboy. More. Your father's right. You better go back East and learn everything there is to learn about bein' a doctor."

Although she appreciated the praise, his encouragement to leave town left her cold. "Doctoress."

"Doctoress Boston, it is."

When the boys finished feeding the chickens, Allie had them sweep the front of the barn where the fresh hay would be unloaded—another job that didn't require manual dexterity. Joseph seemed better able to control his limbs when they were being put to use.

Sweeping done, the specter of play arose again. Both boys stood awkward and silent, looking to her for direction. She found herself at a loss and beginning to panic, when Ned beckoned Albert and Joseph to him. "Allie's worked you both real hard and I know you're thinking you've earned a chance to play." With a nod in the direction of the wagon he'd backed up to the barn door earlier, he said, "But it looks like rain's coming soon and I could sure use some help getting that hay inside before it gets soaked."

Both boys eyed the overloaded cart. A knowing smile broadened across Albert's face—he'd helped with this task many times. "Sure!" He grabbed Joseph's arm and pulled him toward the wagon. "Come on, I'll show you how!"

Allie's throat went dry. The appalled look she gave Ned was lost on his retreating back as he hurried after them. Before she could demand to know what he could possibly be thinking by making such an impossible request of Joseph, he'd tossed both boys onto the mound of loose hay in the wagon and vaulted up behind them. Joseph sat where he landed, his face slack with shock. Ned and Albert stood on either side of him, grinning.

Helping Joseph to his feet, Ned asked, "Ready to work?" The boy's mouth hung open and his head lolled to one side. "On my count of three," Ned said. Albert nodded and they both bent at the waist, arms hanging in front of them. "One, two," he raised a brow at the other boy.

Allie watched a reluctant Joseph mimic their stance as best he could, his face a mask of resignation and dread.

"Three!"

Ned and Albert made shovels of their arms and scooped hay onto the barn floor. Joseph remained frozen. Ned moved behind him and helped him gather an armload and toss it out of the wagon. After a few assists, Ned stepped back. The uncertain boy looked over his shoulder at him, then scooped hay and tossed it out of the cart. Soon, all three were lofting armfuls of fodder onto the ground.

The wagon was more than half empty when the younger Hanovers caught sight of the work—which must have looked suspiciously like play to them—and came shrieking to the barn to join in. Doc lifted Ian and Colum into the wagon and handed Angus to Allie.

Straightening, Ned grimaced and made an exaggerated show of stretching his back, then stepped behind the children. Without a word from him, all the boys applied themselves to hurling armfuls of hay onto the barn floor. Soon, the wagon was empty and a deep pile of hay covered the ground. A gleam of anticipation shone in the eyes of all the Hanover children.

Albert spoke for the group. "Wagon's empty!"

"No, sir," Ned said, folding his arms across his chest. "Afraid it's not."

Four heads swung around. Four sets of eyes stared up at him in disbelief.

"I see a few sacks of potatoes that need unloading," he informed them.

Lifting Albert, he flung him onto the stack of hay—followed by Ian, then Colum, each streaming peals of laughter as they sailed through the air to land on either side of Albert. Without missing a beat, Ned hefted Joseph and tossed him next to the raucous boys. Joseph lay where he landed, eyes staring at the ceiling, no part of his body moving. Even his involuntary spasms had ceased. Afraid he'd been injured, Allie hurried toward him. She stopped short when she saw a smile spread across his face.

Ned swung down from the wagon and brushed hay from his clothes and hair as they all watched the boys clamor back into the cart to continue their game. Colum went first. With a determined look and chubby legs pumping, he dashed from the back of the wagon and jumped into the center of the haystack. As soon as his nephew rolled out of the way, Albert made the same run with arms spread shoulder high. Reaching the edge, he pushed off with his toes and launched himself into the hay, shouting, "I'm flying!"

Ian went next. Both arms straight over his head. "I'm diving!"

All eyes were on Joseph, who had awkwardly clambered back into the wagon. Hesitating only a moment, he lurched forward, propelling himself to make the leap. Mid-air, he shouted, "I'm . . . play . . . ing!"

Allie's throat tightened and she had to close her eyes against the stinging.

After a few more rounds of leaps and jumps, the boys took turns burying each other in the hay. The haystack would go still, the children silent, until the one who'd been covered popped up shrieking, pulling grotesque faces, and waving any assortment of limbs. Feigned terror and screams of laughter greeted each return from the dead.

Angus, who had been content to stand at Allie's feet and watch the older boys, turned to Ned and stretched pudgy arms up to him. "Ed!" Once lifted, he twisted and pointed to the haystack. "Me!"

The special smile only Angus could elicit softened Ned's features. For his part, Angus seemed to know, had always known, that Ned was the person—above his own mother, father, or grandfather—who could deny him nothing. Setting the delighted toddler in the midst of the heaving jumble of hay and boys, Ned told them, "Listen up, little men. You all watch out for this tadpole. Don't jump on him, don't sit on him, don't bury him so deep he can't breathe, and most of all," he leaned forward, "don't let him eat too much hay. If there's straw in his nappies tomorrow, his mama will make sure I'm the one who hears about it. Understand?"

After a round of solemn nods, Joseph was the first to pull a piece of straw from the baby's mouth. When Angus's face clouded, he showered him with a handful of hay, preventing the storm and drawing a chorus of laughter from all. Joseph's tow head lolled to one side and his eyes sought Ned's. The boy was rewarded with a tousling of his already disheveled hair.

At that moment, the light in the barn changed, altered by two figures framed in the doorway. The laughter stopped and all eyes turned to see Maude Mary and Sarah Sue Findlay standing arm in arm.

Sarah smiled at them all, but her gaze sought Allie's. With a slight widening of her eyes and an almost imperceptible tilt of her head in Ned's direction, she reminded Allie of the promise she'd wheedled from her of an introduction to him. The coming storm had made Ned anxious to get the hay inside the barn, but for Allie it wasn't the weather that had stolen the warmth and light from what had been a pleasant afternoon.

CHAPTER FIFTEEN

"Isn't she grand? Isn't she just a vision?" Maude Mary gushed, pulling the older girl into the barn. "That's what everyone keeps saying. 'Why Maude Mary your friend is so lovely—she is just a vision'!"

A vision doesn't even begin to describe her, Allie thought. Standing in a shaft of late afternoon sunlight, Sarah's golden hair haloed her face, her color heightened by a flush of excitement. And, Allie couldn't help but notice, the dress, which had hung straight on her own lanky frame, clung to the curves usually hidden beneath Sarah's shapeless Mother Hubbards. An acrid taste stung the back of Allie's throat. Mortified, she reproached herself. *I will not be jealous of this girl!*

But she was. If her own breath had caught at the sight of her, Allie imagined that Ned must be asphyxiated. Both he and her father stood transfixed. Even the children stopped their play to stare at the girls. The spell was broken when Sarah detached herself from Maude Mary's proprietary grip and walked straight toward Allie. Passing Ned and the boys without a glance, she also ignored Joseph, who stared at her from the haystack.

Taking both of Allie's hands in hers, she appeared to struggle to find words. "Just being invited to this ever-so-splendid house is like being in a fairy tale. When my Ma said there'd be a surprise for me, I thought maybe Mrs. Hanover is gonna borrow me a hat or pair of gloves for the day. But she says this dress, your dress," she lowered her eyes and smoothed the silk skirt, "is mine. That you're giving it to me. To keep." Tears glistened on her black lashes. "No one has ever done me this kind of kindness."

The words were sweet, but Allie sensed something sly in the smile that accompanied them. Sarah's next words validated the feeling. "Why, I feel like I'm Cinderella at the ball and you are my very own fairy godmother."

"It's you that make the dress look so beautiful," Allie said. Nothing in her wanted to be gracious, but she added, "You're not Cinderella, at all—you're the Princess."

And, I suppose, you want us all to know I'm just your frumpy fairy godmother.

Sarah squeezed Allie's hands, then released them. "I do feel like a princess, thanks to you. Now, all I need is to find my handsome prince." She smiled up at Doc, as if just noticing him. With a pretty curtsy, she offered him her gloved hand. "Sarah Findlay, sir."

Unaccustomed to such overt flirtation, Dr. William Hanover turned bright pink from his cheeks to the tops of his ears. Taking Sarah's hand, he made a deep bow. "Dr. Charles Hanover pleased to make your acquaintance, my . . . my lady."

Allie had never seen her father discomfited. When he caught her studying him with amusement, his ears turned even redder. Then, she became aware of Sarah's eyes on her. The girl's smile did not falter, but her brows lifted ever so slightly. The subtle reminder was not lost on Allie. She had to make good on her promise to introduce Sarah to the man who 'had made her pa heel.' There was no getting around it.

"And this," Allie said, trying to sound natural, "is our very dear friend, Ned Harper. He and my brother own the H & H Ranch, that's for Harper and Hanover, just outside town. They raise horses for the army. He's here today helping my father build the pen for the lambs we bought from your mother last week and to see to the hay and the . . ." She stopped speaking when she saw a corner of Ned's mouth twitch in suppressed amusement.

I am a babbling fool, she thought miserably.

Pulling off one work glove, Ned approached Sarah with an outstretched hand. "We almost met in town a few weeks ago," he said. "Sorry for the ruckus with your father."

Sarah drew a quick breath, as if taken by surprise at his presence. Gazing up at him from beneath lowered lashes, she took his work-roughened hand. "Pleased to meet you, Mr. Harper." Holding onto his hand, she added, "I've been hoping for a chance to apologize for Pa. He's a good man, I hope you know that, but a mama hen when it comes to our Joseph." Her eyes conveyed an intimacy that excluded everyone else in the barn. "Especially where wolf dogs are concerned. Once you get to know him, you'll see there's a lot more to like about him than you think. When you come to call out at our ranch, I know he'll be pleased to show off what he's done with the place."

The bold gleam in Sarah's eyes deepened Allie's wariness and darkened her opinion of the girl, but Ned's friendly expression didn't change as he extricated his hand. Before he could address her invitation, Maude Mary, who had stepped to Sarah's side unnoticed, spoke up. "We really must go back to the house this exact minute!" A frown line creased the girl's forehead, as she slipped her arm through Sarah's and pulled her toward the door. "Come along, Sarah Sue, Mama insists we join her to see the ladies depart and make our fond farewells."

"And we will." Sarah squelched the younger girl with a look and freed her arm. "First, I must make my 'fond' farewells to Dr. Hanover and Allie." She made a princess-like curtsy to them. "Thank you both so much for your hospitality." Turning toward the door, she hesitated, then turned back. "And, Mr. Harper, I'm countin' on you paying that visit to my pa real soon."

Ned's half-smile was noncommittal. "Appreciate the invite."

While the adults had been engaged in conversation, the boys—hidden in a layer of hay—had arranged themselves in a row. Hushing each other, they lay flat—Joseph's spasms notwithstanding—as Sarah and Maude Mary hurried toward the door.

Over her shoulder, Sarah tossed Allie an apologetic smile. "You've done so much already, I really hate to ask, but would you mind cleaning Joseph up some? Ma will be in a dither if she sees him covered in hay like that. We want to be on our way before the storm. Please and thank you!"

Too stunned to be outraged, Allie searched the tack equipment for something to use to groom all her charges before returning them to their mothers. With grim resolution she settled on a stiff-bristled dandy brush.

Ned grabbed a curry comb and applied himself to making Albert presentable.

After the children had been returned to their mothers and all the good-byes and thank yous said again and again, the guests had departed South Slope in haste. Wind gusted through the trees and the sky roiled dark and ominous. Lightning crackled in the distance, but so far no thunder could be heard.

With her skirt whipping around her ankles, Allie accompanied her father back out to the barn, clutching a bundle in her arms. Ned had secured the cow and lambs in their stalls and was trying to soothe the wind-skittered Hanover horses. Accustomed to exposure to all kinds of weather, his own horse stood placidly munching the leaves of a tree. In the fading light, Allie noted that the hay on the barn floor had been pitched into the loft and the floor swept clean.

"Well," Doc said to Ned, lifting his hat to scratch his sparse hair. "I came down here with a little speech all prepared to thank you for your hard work today. Now I have to revise it to include all this." A wave of his arm encompassed the orderly barn.

Ned held up a hand. "Thanks will do. I'm acquainted with your 'little speeches,' Doc. With night and that storm on their way, I'll ask you to save it for another time so I can be heading home before it hits."

"There is just one more thing I do need to ask of you."

Ned looked to Allie, who kept her face unreadable, then narrowed his eyes at Doc. "What now?" Despite his accusatory tone, there was no mistaking the affection he held for the older man. "I suppose you want me to whitewash that new fence before I go? "

"No, it's not that," Doc said slowly. "You know I wouldn't ask anything more of you if it were up to me. After all the work you've done today, the last thing I want to do is inconvenience you."

"Doc."

"It's Mrs. Hanover. She insists you stay for supper." He waited a beat, then added, "And since that would put you on the road at the worst of the storm, nothing will do but you must stay the night. She's already had the housemaid make up Will's old bed for you."

Ned's shoulders sagged and he bowed his head. For over a year, he'd politely deflected invitations to join them for supper. When he looked up, Allie was relieved to see a smile tug at the corners of his mouth. He's considering accepting, she thought, even if for no other reason than the discomfort of the ride back to his cabin in the rain.

Although he showed no sign of fatigue, Allie imagined the exertions of the day must catch up with him at some point. The accumulation of dirt and sweat certainly had. The muck of the morning's labors clung to his clothing and caked beneath his fingernails. Washing up for the noon meal had removed only the topmost layer of grime—and they all knew her mother would not tolerate an unkempt guest at her table for supper.

Ned rubbed a hand over more than a week's growth of beard. "I'm filthy, Doc, not fit to sit at her table."

Allie extended the bundle of Will's clean clothing to him, silencing his protest. Where her brother was tall and lanky, Ned was compact and muscular. The differences should even-out to a decent fit. Accepting the bundle, he said, "You both know what this means?"

Allie and Doc nodded as one.

With the bundle under one arm, Ned swung up onto Trickster and headed to the Grand Astor Hotel for a long, hot bath and a neat trim of his short beard.

Allie, who hadn't realized she'd been holding her breath, exhaled.

CHAPTER SIXTEEN

Accepting a tumbler of Old Forrester Bourbon, Ned settled into one of the well-padded chairs in Doc's study. His own Old Overholt's would have done the trick, but this fine whiskey did it without inflicting pain in the process. Doc eased into the matching maroon seat facing the blazing hearth. "The formula for this extraordinary libation was created by Dr. William Forrester, a physician in Louisville," he said. He held up his glass so the cut crystal caught the firelight and made it glow like a fist-sized topaz. "It's the first liquor sold in glass bottles and sealed so it can't be adulterated." With a chuckle, he showed Ned the label on the bottle, which was designed to resemble a physician's prescription. "Just in case you doubted its medicinal properties."

The smooth liquor melted down Ned's throat, warming his body without the harsh burn he was accustomed to. "I'd never argue with a doctor about the medicinal properties of anything."

"The witty and enlightened Voltaire might beg to differ." Doc leaned toward Ned to clink glasses. "He says, 'Doctors are men who prescribe medicines of which they know little, to cure diseases of which they know less, to human beings of whom they know nothing.' "

The men sipped the amber liquor in companionable silence. Behind them, Doc's mahogany desk filled the space in front of a wide window. At their feet, a thick Oriental rug covered the parquet floor. Ned closed his eyes and breathed in the rich aromas of wood, hearth fire, and old books. A comfort he'd almost forgotten.

He'd returned from the hotel and settled Trickster and Cloud in the barn just minutes before the storm struck. His sprint to the house had saved him from a drenching that would have required another change of clothing. Now, a strong wind drove rain and occasional volleys of hail against the study's windows. Ned was well aware he'd be out in the midst of that squall, if Doc hadn't insisted he stay. "I suppose I owe you thanks for saving Trickster from breaking a leg trying to pick his way up a muddy trail on a moonless night."

"In freezing rain."

Ned winced. "With a fool for a rider."

Doc raised his glass again. "Wise is the man who knows himself."

The long, hot soak in the hotel's tub had eased the aches from Ned's muscles and quieted his mind. At peace in a way he hadn't been for months, he eyed Doc over the rim of his tumbler. "I suppose I should be thanking you for the bath and shave, too." When he'd attempted to pay at the hotel, he'd been told the bill had been settled. "How'd you pull that off ?"

Doc raised a sly brow. "By being wily as an old collie, perhaps." At Ned's easy laugh, he explained, "I hoped the time would come when you'd agree to stay for supper againI knew it would require a day of working you to the bone to convince you to do it, and that Mrs. Hanover would require you to be presentable. The hotel had a standing order to take care of you, if you ever showed up." He studied Ned for a moment before adding quietly, "Glad you finally did."

"I am, too." He'd always found Doc easy to talk to, but hesitated to raise a topic he feared might cause him discomfort. "There's something I need to ask you. Just between us, for now."

Doc sighed. "And I had just been thinking this has been such a nice, simple day."

"I'll be leaving for a few days, in a couple of weeks or so." Ned shifted his shoulders, as if his shirt had gone too tight across his back. "I'd appreciate it if you'd tell Will—after I've left—there's been word of mustangs up north. Tell him I've gone with Heck and a few of his men to catch a few. I've been meaning to do it for awhile. Wild horses will add a lot to our breeding stock."

"I'm relieved to hear that's all it is," Doc said. "However, you understand, I must wonder what my son will do without you for a week."

"The work of three men, I s'pose."

They both laughed, then Doc directed a look of not entirely genial interest his way. "I'm curious as to why you don't want your *partner* to know about this enterprise before you go, or why you can't tell him yourself."

"If Will knows, he'll want to come along." Twisting the tumbler in his hands, he downed the contents before raising his eyes to Doc's. "I don't want him to come."

"That implies this venture of yours is either unsafe or illegal."

"It's legal." Returning the older man's gaze, he added, "Someone has to stay back to tend the stock we already have. Will has a family. The last time Heck and I went after mustangs things didn't go so well." He had a bullet hole in his hat to prove it. "Between you and me? I'm a lot more scared of what wee Hannah Hanover would do to me if anything happened to Will than I am of facing a herd of wild horses—or the unsavory element that hunt the honest men who catch'em. I can't look after Will and myself at the same time."

A knock on the door interrupted them, followed by Maude Mary's voice. "Supper's about to be served!"

When the men rose, Doc rested a hand on Ned's shoulder. "I do appreciate you looking out for my son's welfare. You're a good friend to this family, Ned, so I'll risk my son's ire to do as you wish. In return, I ask only that you direct some of that care toward yourself."

"Like I said, that's why I'm leaving Will at home."

While the others took their seats in the dining room, Maude Mary pulled Allie aside. "What does 'unsavory element' mean?" she whispered.

"Unsavory? Where did you . . ." As awareness dawned, Allie gave her sister a stern look. "Alice Maude Mary, you've been warned about listening at doorways."

"I wasn't listening!" she huffed, with the quick outrage of the guilty. "I just heard it. I thought you might be curious because it's about your precious Ned."

"My what?"

Maude Mary pressed her lips into a smug line. "He's going somewhere and he doesn't want Will to come along because of the 'unsavory element.' Whatever that is."

A mix of curiosity and concern tied a knot in Allie's stomach. Ned had been reckless in the past and now had even more reason to be so. "You can look that word up in the *Compendious* after supper."

Although Ned was accustomed to a few glasses of whiskey at the end of a day's hard work, he wasn't accustomed to the combined effect of strong spirits with fine wine and a substantial meal after a long, hot bath. In the hearth-glow of the dining room, he listened to the crackle of the fire and the cold rage of the storm outside and looked forward to the clean, dry bed awaiting him. A pleasant drowsiness dulled the voices around him, until Albert's chirp from across the table roused him from his stupor.

"Ned was just like Tom Sawyer today," he announced. An avid reader, the boy had memorized much of Mark Twain's writings. Like his father, he liked to quote his favorite authors. " 'Saturday morning was come and all the summer world was bright and fresh . . . then all the gladness left Tom,' " he recited. "Because Tom had to paint a whole 'continent of fence' and he sure didn't want to. So he made Ben think it was a game and Ben *paid* Tom to let him whitewash it. That's what Ned did to me and Joseph. Ned was s'posed to unload a whole continent of hay all by himself, cause Will went to play baseball. But all us boys did the work." He stopped for a breath. "Except Ned helped a little. And he didn't make us pay. And it wasn't really work, it was fun!"

Ned exchanged a quick smile with Allie. The memory of the crippled boy's beaming smile when he landed in the hay warmed Ned more than the claret.

Seated beside Ned, Maude Mary had remained silent. Now her words came fast and breathless. "I'm so very glad Albert finally has a little friend to play with, but, Sarah Sue Findlay is *my* true and dear friend and she was just the belle of the ball today. Mama gave her Allie's dress, but I picked her gloves and hat for her. Everyone made such a fuss about how pretty she looked, didn't they Mama?"

Before her mother could offer confirmation, the girl continued, "But isn't it just tragic her mother wouldn't let her take her dress home with her? 'Oh, Sarah, your Pa's not ready for this,' her mama said. 'Best leave it here and wear it if we're invited back.' I am just heartsick for her. But, they will be invited back, won't they, Mama? Why, Joseph is Albert's *only* friend. They have to come back, just for that, don't they?"

"They'll be back," Mrs. Hanover assured her, signaling the maid to bring in dessert. "We have our Benevolent Ladies' Gala in early September. Most of the town will attend. It will be the new schoolmarm's first time. "

Maude Mary's jaw dropped. Folding her arms across her chest, she glared at her mother. "Why is *she* coming? I don't want Miss Priscilla here. I don't even want to go back to that ridiculous school. Ever. "

Reaching for his wine, Ned was surprised at the tremor in his hand. With a pulse throbbing in his temple, he concentrated on steadying his glass.

Mrs. Hanover appeared as perplexed as her daughter was irate. "Why Alice Maude Mary, what ever has gotten into you? You've always loved school."

"I don't. Not anymore. I hate Miss Priscilla. She's bossy and boring, and I can do sums faster than she can. She doesn't know anything. We don't even have singing anymore and Millie Wilkins is her pet." Her face crumbled and tears glistened in her eyes. "I just want Miss Becky back!"

The room went silent.

Ned lowered his eyes. He laid his fork on the table and carefully aligned it with his knife. His chest rose and fell in slow, deliberate breaths.

As if suddenly aware of the statues seated around the table staring at her, Maude Mary gasped, covered her face with her hands, and began to cry. When she stood to flee, Ned caught her around the waist and eased her back into her chair. Tilting her chin up, he forced her to meet his gaze, the marks of grief etched around his eyes and mouth. He wiped the girl's tears with his thumb. "I miss her too, Maudie. Every day."

Albert materialized at Ned's side and laid a hand on his arm. "We didn't talk about Miss Becky dyin' 'cause we didn't want to . . . to hurt your feelings."

The room seemed to hold its breath, sharing the discomfort of its occupants.

Ned exhaled slowly and wrapped his other arm around Albert. The vise in his chest loosened as he understood that they all needed to talk about the loss that had broken their hearts. "It hurts more not to talk about her."

Wiping at her own tears, Allie said, "If that's the case, I have a memory of Miss Becky I'd like to tell." When Ned gave her a small nod, she said, "We kept it our secret because we didn't know whether Papa would be proud or scandalized."

Doc, who had just blown his nose into his napkin, said, "I can't wait to hear what either of you could have done that I would find scandalous."

Miss Becky, the Solace Springs teacher from the time Allie was twelve, had been a frequent supper guest at South Slope, before and after her marriage to Ned. "Well," Allie continued, "sometimes we would sneak into Papa's study and read his *Gray's Anatomy*. She'd help me figure out words I didn't understand or we'd look them up in the *Compendious*."

Doc chuckled. "So that's where you picked up all that Greek and Latin. I should have guessed."

Ned's glass was still half full, but in that moment, he didn't trust his ability to swallow.

"I sure wish she was here, too," Albert said. "My favorite memory is when Miss Becky took us to the mercantile to learn measurements and fractions. She gave everyone a penny and Mrs. Cuthbert let us each weigh our own candy!"

Apparently bolstered by Ned's assurance that he was glad to be talking about Becky, Maude Mary regained her composure. She stood up straight, shoulders back. Everyone knew Miss Becky had been a stickler for posture. "We have a map of the whole world on our wall at school. Miss Becky sent off for it—with a pin for each place most everyone in town's ancestors came from. She assigned us to visit as many families as we could to learn where their people came from. Most of the pins ended up in England and Europe."

Albert turned to Ned. "It's your turn."

Ned hesitated. He could only think of memories he couldn't share with them. With anyone. The scent of her dark hair, loose and soft, when he held her in his arms. The feel of her fingers, locked in his, binding them to one another. He forbade his thoughts to go further. Aware of all eyes on him, and wanting to assure them the boy hadn't wounded him with his innocent request, he thought for a long moment. Then another. Reaching for the glass of claret, he managed a swallow he hoped would open his constricted throat.

Seated at the head of the table next to him, Mrs. Hanover touched his hand. "Another time, my dear," she said, "if it's too distressing."

After a few heartbeats, he tried again. "Becky was the one who found Running Cloud. Out behind the schoolroom. He was a filthy, half-starved ball of matted fur. No one ever has figured out how that puppy got there.

"She cleaned him up and fed him goat's milk and mush until she was sure he'd live, then she brought him up to my place. Held him in the saddle in front of her the whole way up. It was the dead of winter and she hardly knew me. 'He's part wolf and part human and he doesn't belong in town,' she told me. 'He needs to be up here among his own kind.' Then, she handed him to me, got back on her horse, and said, 'His name's Running Cloud.' And rode off. I married her six months later."

After agreement all around that the stories made them each feel Becky was right here with them, the room grew quiet. The sadness that had ebbed began to flow back in. Maude Mary said softly, "I do like talking about her, but I just wish she could be here."

Albert grinned at Ned. "I know what Miss Becky would say to Maude Mary if she *was* here right now."

Ned managed a grin. "You do?"

With an emphatic nod, Albert put his hands on his hips. "She'd say: 'Miss Alice Maude Mary Hanover, you can put your boots in the oven and you can wish all you want, but they still won't be biscuits!' "

As Ned looked on, they all agreed that was exactly what Becky Harper would say. He understood their memories gave them comfort, like the fire that warmed the room on this stormy night. But life had taken back everything it had ever given him and left him only memories—cold ashes in a cold hearth, no comfort at all.

CHAPTER SEVENTEEN

Sheep bleated, the donkey brayed, and chickens cackled and strutted in the dirt yard. Just like they did every day. The morning after the Afternoon Tea, Sarah Findlay's spirits had plummeted. Wearing her drab Mother Hubbard, hair pulled back in a bun, she stood on the porch of the inelegant sheep ranch and surveyed her domain. No silk dresses, no exotic cakes and teas, no fawning admirers. Just this.

"Chores, Sarah," Ma called through the door. As if reading her mind, she added, "This isn't 'South Slope,' Missy, you know that. There's no servants here to do 'em for you."

I am Cinderella after the ball, Sarah thought despondently. Dressed in rags and worked to the bone. On legs that felt like lead, she trudged to the barn, where no rugged, blue-eyed prince awaited among the bales of hay. The aromas of the breakfast her mother was fixing followed her—small incentive to get her work done.

In a few minutes, she hurried back into the house. Pa had returned from his early morning check of the outer pastures and sat at the table with his coffee. Joseph slumped and spasmed across from him. Setting a plate of warm biscuits in the center of the table, her mother looked up in surprise.

Sarah entered the kitchen, pleased and perplexed. Biting her lower lip, she thought hard for a moment. "It's not my birthday today, is it, Ma?"

"Now, you know it's not! What are you up to, girl? You have morning chores to get to and your breakfast is almost ready." Turning back to the stove, she added, "I don't want no complaints about cold grits."

With a waggling arm, Joseph reached for a biscuit, wobbled it to his mouth, and took a bite. Crumbs crusted his chin and showered his shirt and the table. As always, he seemed detached from the interactions of his family, intent on the task at hand.

Sarah pulled out her chair and sat down, unable to think of an explanation for what she'd seen in the barn. "My chores are done, Ma."

With a plate of bacon and grits balanced in each hand, Ma frowned. "You just now stepped outside." She set the dishes in front of Joseph and Pa. "How in the world could they be done?"

Joseph chewed a piece of bacon.

"I couldn't tell you," Sarah said, reaching for a biscuit. "Someone did 'em and it sure wasn't me. The barn's swept and the chickens are fed." Just as she was beginning to imagine enchanted mice hard at work with tiny brooms, she saw her father lower his cup and glower at her. Defensive under his hard gaze, she lifted her chin. "It's true, Pa. Go see for yourself."

Joseph set a wobbly elbow on the table and rested his chin in his hand, shoulders moving, eyes agleam. His mouth turned up on one side. Sarah glanced at him, then did a double-take. "Joseph?" She stared at him in disbelief. "*You* did my chores?"

Equally taken aback, Pa looked from his daughter to his son, then to his wide-eyed wife. The tableau was still as a painting. All eyes turned to Joseph.

"No." The boy straightened his twisted body as much as he could. With a lopsided grin, he said, "I did . . . *my* . . . chores! Like Albert does. Miss . . . Allie and . . . Ned Harper . . . taught me."

Allie and Ned, Sarah thought, with a bad taste in the back of her throat. It still rankled that Miss La-di-dah had gotten to spend the whole day in the barn with him while she'd spent it with little Maude Mary and stuck up Mrs. Hanover's clucking hens.

Face red, Pa set his cup down. "What's Ned Harper got to do with all this?"

Her father's ire prompted Sarah to think quick. "He was over there yesterday, helping build a pen for the lambs. Ma told you Mrs. Hanover bought two of our lambs? Ned's a dear friend of their family . . ."

"A *dear* friend of the family?" Pa glowered at Ma. "Just listen to her. After one day at that Hanover place she's puttin' on airs." He turned to Joseph, who, Sarah noted, sat as still as he could manage. "Didn't I tell you to stay clear of that man and his wolf fiend?"

Stifling the urge to say too and make things worse, Sarah offered, "Joseph didn't do anything wrong, Pa. He was just playing with Albert."

Pa glared at his coffee for a bit. "How'd you get outside today, son?" he finally asked Joseph. His color had subsided, but his tone carried a reproach clearly meant for his wife and daughter. "Wasn't anyone lookin' after you this morning?"

Sarah saw that defeat dulled the shine that had momentarily brightened her brother's eyes. His chin quivered.

"Well, Joseph," Ma said, in a determined tone Sarah didn't recognize, "looks like they'll just have to be your chores from here on."

"Please, Pa," Sarah pressed. She relished the thought of being free of some of her lowly yard tasks. Like the lady she aspired to be. Joseph rolled his head to turn pleading eyes up at their father, who did not meet his gaze. "He can't get hurt tossing feed and sweeping the barn. It'll give me more time to catch up on my spinning."

Pa closed his eyes and raised his brows, as if displeased by an argument he heard in his own head. He stood and strode to the stove to refill his coffee cup. When he sat down, there was resignation, not approval, in the set of his shoulders. "Sarah Sue, did he do a good job?"

"Yes, Pa."

The tension in Joseph's face let go, freeing a broad grin.

"What harm can there be in it?" Ma coaxed. "Just look at him, Luke."

Shaking his head slowly, Pa's stern features softened. "I suppose we can give it a try." With a rare glint of humor, he warned, "But, Joseph Findlay, don't you let me catch you even thinkin' about shearing a sheep."

CHAPTER EIGHTEEN

Ned tried to remain patient with Albert tugging at his sleeve. Thursday mornings were slow at Kimble's Tack and Feed, which was why Ned had chosen this day to come. A rancher and his wrangler weighed the merits of different bridles and halters, while Mary Kimble and her son loaded sacks of grain into Ned's wagon in the yard behind the store. As luck would have it, Luke Findlay was the only other customer.

Behind the counter, a glass case displayed Mary's collection of leather martingales. One of her fine equine breast collars boasted tooled cabbage roses, another a silver heart within a heart, and her most prized: a hand-tooled, buck-stitched, painted portrait of a mare nuzzling a stallion—all works of art far too costly for most of the residents of Solace Springs. The locked case was the only item in the store not coated with grain dust.

"Ask him," Albert whispered.

"Mr. Findlay," Ned said, quelling his reluctance. More than a month had passed since their uncomfortable encounter in town. When the man glanced back over his shoulder with a frown, Ned forced warmth into his own smile. Albert stood to one side of him, Cloud on the other, both on high alert. "Ned Harper, we met a while back."

Findlay turned to face Ned, gave him and the dog a disdainful glance, then turned back to the harness he'd been examining. "I know who you are, Harper."

If Albert hadn't been standing there, full of expectations, Ned would have quit the store without another word and waited outside for his feed to be loaded. For the child's sake, he tried again. "We got off to a bad start. I'm sorry about that and hope we can set things right."

It had been Albert's idea and Ned was none too happy about it. With that jar of crickets he'd painstakingly collected clutched to his chest, the boy had looked up at him with such fierce pleading in his large brown eyes that Ned had no choice. And, he felt compelled to try on Joseph's behalf, as well. When they'd pulled the cart up around back, they'd found him sad-eyed and alone in Findlay's wagon, half-hidden in a small grove far behind the store. He'd lit up so at the sight of them that when Albert asked if Joseph could come along on their fishing trip, Ned had no choice but to agree. Seeing him come to life in the barn at South Slope the other day had lifted Ned's spirits and he knew it had helped Joseph.

"I'm taking Albert out to Crain's Pond Saturday morning," Ned said to Findlay's back. "We hoped you and Joseph might come along. The pond's so full of bluegill this time of year—everyone's sure to catch a few."

The six-acre pond was overcrowded with colorful, easy-to-catch trout—an ideal place for boys to learn their way around a fishing pole. Ned had been looking forward to a day in the shade of over-hanging trees, with Albert and the company of a few blue herons. He wanted to spend what time he could with the boy before summer ended.

"Probably more than a few!" Albert piped up.

For his sake, Ned forced enthusiasm into the invite. "Joseph had a fine time playing with Albert up at South Slope a couple of weeks ago."

"We didn't just play, Sir," Albert added. "Me and Joseph, we did chores, too. Ned made us unload the hay before he let us jump in it." Findlay's back stiffened and he swung around to face them, his expression as stony as his stance. Albert showed him the jar of insects. "I'll share my crickets with you both for bait. I caught them all myself."

Ned rested a hand on Albert's shoulder. "It'll do Joseph good to get outside and play and Albert would appreciate the company. There aren't many boys their age in town."

Findlay's mouth twisted. "Good for Joseph to get outside?" Cloud shifted uneasily at the menace in the man's tone. "Tell me somethin' Harper, where does a man like you get the gall to tell me what's good for my boy?"

A man like me? Ned breath slowed. The earthy aroma of sawdust and leather calmed him. His eyes held Luke's. *I'm telling you this because you don't seem able to figure it out for yourself. Your boy was spared. Joseph's desperate to live the life he was given and you won't let him.*

Don't say it, Ned cautioned himself, but anger—and something darker—sent wisdom fleeing. "When those boys were done workin', I tossed them all into the wagon like sacks of potatoes, then they took turns jumping into the hay. They played like that for hours." Certain Findlay had absorbed his meaning, he added, "I expect his mama was pickin' straw out of his ears for days."

Silence hung between them like a storm cloud. "Listen close, Mr. Harper," Findlay rasped. "It's not that we got off to a bad start." His expression matched the malice in his tone. "We didn't get off to any kind of start at all. And that's the way I intend it to stay. Why don't you just get your 'untamed' self back up to the hills with that demon dog of yours? Let decent folk go about their business without being bothered with your ideas of what's good for them."

Every instinct urged Ned to throttle the man, instead he made himself take a step back.

"Sorry to have troubled you, Mr. Findlay. It won't happen again."

Albert stared from one man to the other. When Findlay turned his back again, he spoke up. "Please, Sir, Joseph's my friend. I know he wants to come fishin'. Can't he, please?"

Findlay's turned back was a wall that couldn't be breached. With a hand on Albert's shoulder, Ned propelled him toward the back door. On the other side of the threshold, they found Joseph huddled against the wall, weeping.

Not caring what Findlay might say or do, Ned went down on one knee. "I'm sorry, Joseph," he said. "It just doesn't look like it'll work out this time."

The bereft child turned his wobbling head away, chin pressed to his shoulder. Standing, Ned braced for the assault of words or blows he half-hoped would come at him through the door. When it didn't, he and Albert walked the tearful boy back to his wagon and left him to wait for his father.

Several hours and two or three shots of Old Overholt's later, Ned sat on his porch and watched the sun sink behind the pines. The child's plight haunted him. That man's so damned scared his son might get hurt, he thought, he can't see he's the one doin' the hurting.

CHAPTER NINETEEN

With supplies for more than a week in his pack, and a loaded rifle secured in his saddle holster, Ned set out in search of mustangs. He'd forsworn using a gun for hunting, or carrying one in town, but out on the trail he'd be foolhardy to travel unarmed. He knew the violence men are capable of all too well. Riding northeast into the rising sun, he tugged the brim of his hat down to shield his eyes from the slanted rays of early morning.

Big-boned, big-bellied, big-hearted Hector Abernathy and three of his ranch hands rode at his side. When sixteen year-old Ned had shown up in Solace Springs looking for work after the war, the six-foot-six horse breeder had given him a straw-filled pallet in the barn and three meals a day in exchange for doing odd jobs around the place. For months, Ned's hands had shaken when he did anything other than tend horses, but when Heck saw how adept he was with the animals he moved him into the wranglers' bunkhouse and paid him fifty cents a day.

Although they rode beneath a cloudless sky, the ground was sodden from the previous night's rain. Now, the sun's warmth released scents of earth, rock, and wet vegetation. The mustangs had been spotted fifty miles north of Solace Springs, an easy two-day ride. Keeping their mounts to a slow trot on uneven terrain, the men urged them to an easy canter where the ground was more certain.

By mid-morning, the group had climbed to a higher elevation. As they walked the horses through a narrow, rock-strewn arroyo, the breeze stiffened and went from cool to cold, whipping at them from behind. With Trickster's reins in one hand, Ned fought to keep his battered hat on with the other. The black Stetson, faded and frayed, had served him well for many years. Aside from protection from sun and rain, he used it to dip water, fan campfires, and swat ornery livestock when need be.

Long white hair blowing in the wind, Heck and his mare ambled alongside Ned. The older man's body was as ramrod straight and strong as ever, but his weathered face—clean-shaven because his Ute wife, Red Moon, preferred it that way—showed every one of his seventy-three years. They walked in easy silence for over a mile before Heck spoke. "I remember that first time I brought you along to catch mustangs. More than ten years ago now. I was gonna get you used to ridin' and ropin' at the same time, then I was gonna show you how to gentle a wild horse. Maybe even let you walk one around the pen once or twice." Pale blue eyes sparkled in the narrow look he shot Ned. "But you had to go and spoil it all by catching yourself a mare that very first day. Then, without a by-your-leave or an if-I-might, you had the impudence to teach me a thing or three about handling those wild horses once we got 'em home."

Ned laughed. "Beginner's luck." Growing up on a ranch hadn't hurt either. He'd been eager—desperate—to earn his benefactor's approval. "The way you looked at me, I was sure as there are snakes in Virginia that I'd done something wrong."

"Hmmph." Heck's standard disavowal. "I'm still waiting for *that* day. Pertainin' to horses, that is."

Again, silence was their companion, neither man given to idle conversation. For Ned, the stillness was a conduit for memories of the circumstances that had brought him to Solace Springs. He'd been passing through town with no intention of settling there, no idea of where he was headed, and no money. A sixteen year-old war veteran. A few months after Heck had hired him, he'd taken him along on that first mustang hunt. Until then, Ned hadn't spoken about his past to his boss or anyone else. Never intended to. Heck had drawn him out the night they made camp. Hardly aware it was happening, he told Heck he'd been orphaned as a kid and raised—more or less—by three older brothers on a small horse ranch in western Kansas. "They meant well," Ned had said, sitting back against the trunk of a tree, "but, you might say, they were a little wild." His mouth quirked. "They could be forgetful when it came to their youngest brother. Suited me just fine."

A few town folk had made overtures to help the motherless brood, but the Harper brothers resisted. Ned learned self-reliance by necessity. He spent his time hunting, fishing, and working their small herd of horses—a good enough life, while it lasted.

"My brothers got restless. Nate, the oldest, mostly. He decided we had to see the world." The whiskey helped Ned put together more sentences than he had in all the time he'd worked for Heck. "Nate wanted us to have adventures. Get rich. He was sore he'd missed out on the big gold rush in California." Ned's insides had gone hollow with the telling, but his next words tasted of bile. "So he settled on the next best thing for us—joining the Union Army."

That's the place to end, Ned had reminded himself that night. Or tried to. A familiar heaviness had settled over him. He wanted nothing more than to slide beneath the blankets of his bedroll, but kept talking. "They were set on leaving me behind because I was too young."

Stop here.

"I fussed so much there was nothing for it, but they had to take me along."

Heck's kindly face had hardened. "They took you with? Into war? Fools!" He spat into the fire. "Why, you're scarce more than a boy now, you must have been a child."

"Fourteen." Ned lowered his eyes and stared into the dark liquid in his cup. A ragged shock of dark hair fell across his eyes. "Almost."

Broad shoulders sagging, Heck had reached for the large medicine pouch he kept with him at all times. Rummaging through it, he pulled out a sage smudge stick and a long feather Red Moon had given him. Ned sipped the rye whiskey. A harsh burn slid down his throat, igniting a flash of heat that shot back up his spine and into his chest. An unfamiliar sensation of well-being spread with it. "I wasn't the youngest to join up."

Ned's throat had always closed when he tried to talk about the war. That night was different. He wanted the words out of him and the whiskey made them slippery. Maybe the memories—shrapnel that tore at his insides—would follow.

"My brothers signed on as infantry—Ben got away with lying about his age." A shadow crossed his face, followed by the flicker of a smile. "Ben always got away with everything. I wanted to be a soldier, like them, more than anything. Boys who couldn't pass for old enough to fight could sign up as drummers and stay with the soldiers." He closed is eyes. He'd never had that much likker and he had to say he liked the feel of it. The letting go. Almost like falling asleep. "The army taught me to play the drums, what all the different drumbeats meant."

Ned tapped his knee. "Chow time." Ta-ta-Ta-ta-Ta-tah. "Formation." Tah-Tah-Tah, Tah-Tah-Tah. " Pay time." Tah-ti-ti, Tah-Tah-Tah-ti-ti. "Marches, of course." A *one*-two-three-four rhythm. "And . . . when to charge the enemy." *The enemy.* He hadn't wanted to remember that terrible cadence and went silent. "The drums were heavy."

"A drummer," Heck—who had never been to war—said. "Well, if beatin' on a heavy drum was the worst of it, I suppose that's not so bad for a boy."

Boy. Ned's gut twisted at the word. 'Boy' had not meant child in the army. There were no children in the army. His mouth went dry. But big, strong, kind old Heck was right there listening and the words spilled from

Ned like blood from a severed artery. "When we weren't drummin' we carried messages or waited on the officers or . . . we helped the medics."

Here he stopped again. Had to. He took another swallow and welcomed the burn, staring past the fire into the darkness. The rye failed to bring the feeling of well-being.

Don't say it. Don't think it. Stop.

"We held wounded men down while they sawed off . . . "

Heck's jaw went slack and he leaned forward.

Trying to silence the screams that still haunted him, Ned downed another gulp of whiskey. Drummers were tasked with disposing of the severed limbs. Bile rose in his throat as the stink of blood and feces came back to him.

His own face stricken in the flickering firelight, Heck refilled Ned's cup.

"We cleaned up the fields after the battles." Ned made himself keep talking. Spotsylvania was the worst. Two of his brothers died there. "Collected guns and ammo, whatever else we could find. Boots." His eyes went dark. "We carried bodies to the deadhouse 'til there was enough for a wagonload, then we buried them." Staring into middle-distance, he said, "Toward the end of the war, they gave us rifles and let us fight."

Gripping his cup with both hands, Ned still couldn't control the tremors. "Some of the younger boys . . . some were hardly taller than their guns. Nine-year-olds who . . ."

Ned had set down the cup and hidden his face in his hands. Children charging the enemy, running, trying to aim unwieldy weapons, slipping in each other's blood, falling, limbs shattered, faces gone. He rose unsteadily and stumbled behind a tree to vomit. No words Heck could have offered would have been of comfort. Ned was relieved he hadn't tried. Instead, the old man lit the sage smudge stick. When it smoldered, he waved the fragrant, healing smoke over the fire, Ned, and himself.

Recalling that night, Ned fingered the small, beaded medicine pouch that hung around his neck. Red Moon had made it for him soon after they returned home with the mustangs.

"For healing and protection," she had told him, showing him the contents. "The three sisters—corn, beans, and squash seeds, a piece of flint for grounding, a down feather from a snowy owl. Sage, sweetgrass, and cedar. And see, here's a totem for you." Bright onyx eyes shone in her somber face when she folded his fingers around the tiny carved horse. "Black Stallion says, 'I am from the Void where Answer lives. Ride on my back and know the power of entering the Darkness and finding the Light.' "

He'd opened the medicine pouch only once after that—to add locks of Becky's and his son's hair. Since their deaths, he'd come to know the Darkness well, but try as he might, he hadn't been able to find any Light.

Heck's booming baritone joggled Ned back from the troubled reveries of the past and made him smile.

"Oh, I do thank you, Great Spirit," the old rancher sang out, hefting himself back into the saddle, "that I am placed so well, that you have made my freedom so complete!" Lifting his hat, he pressed it to his heart and offered his version of the Cowboy's Prayer to the far heavens. Swaying on the back of his huge mare, he tilted his white head back to bellow, "I thank you, Great Spirit, that I'm no slave to whistle, clock, or bell!"

Ned settled his own hat tight on his head and stirruped onto Trickster. He shared Heck's gratitude for the wilderness. An endless azure sky arched overhead, the wind—sweetened with the scent of summer grasses—had gentled and the sun rested on his shoulders like the arm of an old friend.

Hat still over his heart, Heck continued the familiar poem. "Great Spirit, make me big and open as the plains, honest as the horse between my knees, clean as the wind that blows behind the rains, and free as the hawk that circles down the breeze."

The three ranch hands brought up the rear, grinning at each other.

"Let me be easy on the man that's down," Heck intoned, serious now, head bowed. "And, please, please, Great Spirit, let me be square and generous with all."

All the riders joined in for the next verse—Ned's voice the loudest. Throwing back his head in imitation of Heck, he hollered, "Cause I am careless sometimes, Lord, when I'm in town!"

Heck spat on the ground. That particular verse evoked dark memories, Ned knew. Mostly about him. He'd been a hard-working, sober youth when he was on the ranch, but his behavior in town had been another story. When he'd discovered the pleasures of bad women, good whiskey, and bar brawls, he'd tended to indulge to excess. Careless didn't come close to describing him in those days.

His vices had banished the screams and visions of mangled bodies for a few hours at a time. But had, on occasion, necessitated that Heck—in hopes of reforming his best, but decidedly wrong-headed young wrangler—lock Ned in the barn overnight. The sheriff had confined him to jail on others. Neither had had any impact on Ned's behavior. With an exaggerated sigh of relief, Heck put his broad-brimmed hat back on and tipped it to an older wiser Ned.

"Hold up!" Ned's raised hand and sharp command halted all the riders and left Heck holding Trickster's reins, as Ned swung down from his saddle and scuttled up the steep crag. With the agility of a Rocky Mountain goat, he balanced on a narrow ledge and bent to retrieve something the breeze lifted just beyond his reach. Making a treacherous forward lunge and flattening his body against the escarpment, he grabbed for an object that fluttered to his feet. He straightened to examined his prize, then lifted his gaze to scan the plateau. His shoulders went taut. Motionless, he stared into the distance, then scrambled back down and handed a foot-long brownish feather to Heck.

"Golden Eagle," Heck pronounced, holding the light brown plume, mottled with chevron-like white bars, flat across both palms. He'd named his ranch for the magnificent bird. A gust of wind ruffled the tufts of down at the base. "Flight feather, I'm thinkin'. Probably from an adult." Raising his eyes to Ned's, he said, "*Sacred* Golden Eagle. From the heights of the clouds, it's Eagle who flies closest to the realm of Spirit."

Ned knew the feather would please Heck. After ten years, Ned's medicine bag was the same four-inch by four-inch pouch Red Moon had made for him. Over more than forty years, Heck's pouch had grown, replaced by larger and larger deerskin bags. He told Ned he'd learned much from his Indian wife that made more sense to him than the teachings of the white world. The bag he now carried hung from a thick leather strap across his chest and measured more than a foot square and a few inches thick. An inveterate collector, he'd filled the sack with objects he believed held spiritual significance. Smudge sticks and an abalone shell. Feathers of every ilk—crow for skill and cunning, hawk for strength, dove for kindness, and falcon for soul healing. Owl, raven, wren. And, of course, wild turkey for fertility. Red Moon had given him five fine daughters, and he swore the turkey feather was responsible. He'd picked up scores of stones whose colors or shapes caught his fancy, as well as bird and mice skulls, mountain lion claws, hawk and vulture talons. Small animal bones. Bear scat. Fragrant herbs.

But, Ned knew, he'd never found an eagle feather.

Heck gazed upward, as if searching for the venerated bird, then lowered his eyes to Ned's. "All Spirit's gifts come with tests and trials."

When Heck tried to give him the feather, Ned raised both hands, and stepped back, shaking his head. "Great Spirit just had me fetch it for you. He knows your legs aren't what they used to be." Ned squinted into the distance. "And that 'trial' you're so excited about? It just might be headin' this way. Up on that ledge, I caught sight of six riders a few miles back. I'd wager they're tailing us."

Tucking the feather into his medicine pouch, Heck said, "I'll keep this for now." Lines tightened around the rancher's mouth. "What makes you think they mean trouble?"

"They've made sure to stay clear of our sight and hearing. That doesn't strike me as friendly."

In truth, Ned was more worried than he let on. Mustangs were valuable and difficult to catch. Honest ranchers would 've joined up with Heck's crew, glad to combine efforts. Poachers—the 'unsavory element' Ned had mentioned to Doc—didn't have the skill or fortitude to round up the wild horses themselves. They let others do the work, then lay in wait to steal the animals they caught. Three years earlier, he and Heck had had a run-in with a gang of rustlers that led to bloodshed. The frayed notch in Ned's hat was a reminder of a bullet that had come uncomfortably close to its mark.

"If they're up to no good, they won't try anything 'til we've caught the horses," Heck said, rubbing his thumb against his chin. "Let's see what happens when we make camp. They've got a night and a day to meet up with us if they've a mind to."

Every instinct told Ned the men were thieves. Hunting had sharpened his senses and his intuition. He had an acute awareness of what it meant to be both predator and prey. With a lightness he didn't feel, he said, "Sure, they're probably hangin' back because they're shy."

The next day, the fine weather held. Taking advantage of crags, Ned climbed as high as he could to survey what lay ahead. And who followed behind. The interlopers kept their distance, apparently confident they remained undetected. With each report from Ned, Heck and the other men grew more wary.

Just before sunset, from atop an outcropping of huge boulders bordering a stream and a thicket of trees, Ned caught sight of the mustangs. Serene and beautiful, they grazed just miles away. He always found these forays bittersweet—heartbreaking and exhilarating. He fought the impulse to tell Heck he hadn't seen any horses, that the stories had been wrong, that they should turn around and head home. Let the wild creatures live the lives they'd been born to live.

But, when he descended, he nodded toward the northeast. "Band of about thirty, a few miles north. We'll make camp here, so we don't spook 'em." In answer to Heck's unasked question, he said, "Two miles back, just behind that last stand of trees. You're right. They'll stay put 'til we've got the mustangs."

That night, after a supper of hardtack, pemmican, and rye whiskey, Ned signaled to Heck that he wanted a word with him. They walked in silence to the stream where their loosely-tethered mounts grazed and drank at their pleasure. Trickster, the only horse saddled, whickered at their approach. As he thought about what he wanted to say, Ned stroked his horse's neck.

"If you brought me down here to check on the horses," Heck said, arms folded across his chest, "I'm satisfied they're tethered just fine. If you've got something else on your mind, I'd appreciate it if you'd quit ponderin' and spit it out. I'm an old man's been in the saddle for too long, for too many days, with you jabberin' on and on about horse thieves on our tail. My usually genial demeanor is wearin' thin."

"Can any of your men shoot straight enough to hit what they're aiming at?"

Heck snorted a laugh. As a youth, Ned had worked, eaten, and shared a bunkhouse with these same wranglers for over three years. "You know them as well as I do. Maybe better. Hell, they practically raised you. They're able ranch hands, but as gunmen go I'm sorry to say they probably couldn't hit a bull in the backside with a bass fiddle." His eyes lingered on the bullet hole in Ned's hat. "I don't expect they'll be any more use in a gunfight than the ones we had with us last time. Why d'ye ask?"

Untying the rifle from his saddle, Ned handed it to Heck. For what he had in mind, he'd be safer unarmed. He also figured it would probably be safer not to answer Heck's question at this particular time.

With a wary glance at the rifle and a nod in the direction of the saddled horse, Heck raised a bushy white eyebrow. "You goin' somewhere?"

"Figured I'd call on our neighbors down the way."

Heck's chest puffed out and his shoulders lifted making him appear even larger than he was. "You're fixin' to 'call on' a devilish pack of horse thieves?" In a low growl, he asked, "What in the goddamned hell are you thinkin'?"

Climbing into the saddle, Ned steadied Trick. "I'm thinkin' I'll invite them to join up with us to catch those mustangs."

Heck grabbed the horse's bridle. "Invite 'em?"

"Well, or try to persuade them."

"Alone?" He gave Ned a scathing look. "Unarmed?"

What Ned didn't say was that there's no one more persuasive than a man who has nothing to lose. "That's right."

Heck opened his mouth, then closed it. "I know there's no stopping you once you get something in your head. No matter how calf-brained it might be." After studying Ned hard in the deepening twilight, he surrendered the bridle. "Who is it exactly who's aiming to 'invite' those reprobates—Ned Harper or," his mouth thinned to a severe line, "that Seven fellow?"

"Heck," Ned protested, feigning an injured frown, "that was a long time ago."

In his younger, brawling days, the ranch hands had given Ned a nickname. Heck had overheard them refer to him as 'Seven' and made them spill what it meant. One of the hands told the boss, "We call him Seven 'cause that there boy can kick seven colors of shit out of just about any man in Miss Birdie's place."

Heck had strongly disapproved of the behavior, the nickname, and Ned's visits to the disreputable Tanglefoot Saloon. But the rancher's displeasure—like the nights Ned had spent locked in the barn or in jail—had not reformed him. Now, worry pulled at the corners of the big man's mouth. "I expect you've got it worked out as to just how you're gonna buddy up to your new friends without getting your head blown off."

"I do." *More or less.*

"So," Heck said, pulling the eagle feather from is pouch, "you'll humor an old man and take this with you?"

Ned's eyes went from the feather to Heck's stern face. Resigned, he accepted the totem and slipped it under his shirt.

"Go then." After mumbling something under his breath that Ned assumed to be addressed to the Great Spirit, Heck added, "Just be damn sure you come back."

They both understood that might not happen. One of them worried. The other did not.

CHAPTER TWENTY

A quarter mile from the poachers' camp, Ned tied Trick to a tree and made a hunter's slow, silent approach, guided by their voices. He stayed far enough away from their hobbled horses to prevent anxious neighs from signaling his arrival. Shielded by the darkness of a moonless night, he remained invisible until he stepped into the circle of light cast by their campfire. Grunts of surprise greeted him. Men leapt to their feet and grabbed their weapons, followed by the rapid clicking of six rifles cocked and aimed at his head and chest.

With an amiable smile, Ned held up both hands. The glare of the fire blinded him to their faces. "Ned Harper. H & H Ranch, Solace Springs."

A voice snarled from the other side of the fire, "What do you want here, Ned-fucking-Harper?"

"To start with, I'd be obliged if you'd lower your guns." His raised hands were steady, his tone matter-of-fact. "I'm unarmed and alone and don't aim to trouble you."

"Jeb, Nix, frisk this scalawag real good, then go take a look-see."

The cold metal of a gun barrel pressed into his neck and his right arm was wrenched behind his back. Hot breath hissed in his ear. "Stay still, Ned Harper of the H & H Ranch, and this won't hurt hardly a bit."

Another man, big and rank as a bear, searched his body. Meaty hands, rough and intrusive, pawed up and down his sides and between his legs.

When he flinched, his arm was twisted at an angle meant to tear it from its socket. Clenching his teeth, the part of him that had been named Seven fought the instinct to pull free and unleash a fury of fists and feet on the brutes. Stopping him was the certainty that they would kill him if he did, and he'd fail in his mission to thwart them from attacking Heck and the others.

With a jolt of alarm, he remembered the hunting knife strapped to his ankle, but the cheroot-smoking miscreants manhandling him didn't have the sense to check his boots. Ned knew the ordeal was over when the larger man blew a cloud of foul smoke in his face and punched him in the gut, doubling him over. The other twisted his arm higher, then released him with a shove that sent him sprawling toward the campfire. Righting himself, he didn't draw a breath until the two men—and the miasma of cheap cigar and sour breath that clung to them—shoved past him. The others—a scraggly-bearded, scrofulous crew—lowered themselves onto logs or small boulders and laid their rifles across their knees. Even at a distance, their tattered clothing reeked of sweat, cheap whiskey, and homelessness. Fire-lit eyes gleamed with the watchfulness of animals assessing their quarry.

"What do you want?" the crusty voice repeated.

Straightening his hat, Ned brushed off his clothes. Only a slight jerk of one shoulder betrayed his irritation. "I'm up here with another rancher and a few of his men, looking for mustangs. We made camp a couple of miles north of here." As his eyes grew accustomed to the glare and darkness, he identified the source of the gruff voice—a fat, balding fellow with a graying beard to the middle of his chest. "You know all that, of course, 'cause you've been doggin' us for two days."

One man chortled, but was quickly hushed when the others shot him harsh glances.

The man Ned assumed to be their boss took a swig from a clear jar and wiped his mouth with the back of his hand. "Go on."

"We've sighted a herd up ahead." Ned sensed a quickening of interest, although he knew they couldn't be surprised to hear it. "We intend to take no more than five. There's plenty for everyone—no need for trouble."

Silence confirmed what he already knew. Rustlers. "You're welcome to join up with us." This time, a chorus of guffaws came unrestrained. When it stopped, Ned continued the pretense of persuasion. "A dozen men working together can get the job done in half the time."

Hard glares, expressive as raised rifles, drew a bead on him.

"I see," Ned said slowly. The danger he'd evoked sent a fiery shock coursing through him. He savored the sensation. "You're not ranchers. So, you must be *businessmen* out to collect yourselves a few horses to sell." Looking around the campsite, he shook his head. "But, it looks like you're missing the gear you'll need. All I see is . . . guns. No lassos. No harnesses." He waited, giving them time to explain their lack of equipment, then made the offer he knew they'd refuse. "If you're interested in working with us, we'll outfit you and show you how it's done."

The men shifted position, fingers edging toward the triggers of their weapons.

"If you're honest horse traders," Ned said, "be at our camp at sun-up." Another surge of heat and energy thrummed through his veins—an old, familiar readiness for violence. The thought of mustangs in the hands of these men sickened him. "You know where to find us."

Gaze fixed on the man he'd been speaking to, he said, "If it so happens you *are* thieves looking to steal what we round up, we won't be so friendly." His demeanor remained calm, but steel flashed behind his eyes. Taunting them now. Heck would disapprove of this lack of regard for his own life. "I do feel obliged to tell you three of our men served under Hiram Berdan in the First Regiment of Sharpshooters—the 'Devil's Den.' Maybe you've heard of them?" Most men had. The regiment was famous for the record number of Confederate soldiers they'd killed using breech-loading weapons that fired eight to ten rounds a minute. The marksmen were reputed to be accurate at 600 yards from a prone position. "They're sentimental types. Still carry those army-issue Sharps carbines everywhere they go."

Boots crunching on dry leaves announced the return of Jeb and Nix. Ned studied them as they neared. Jeb, huge, slack-jawed and empty-eyed. Nix, a sneering, ferret-faced scoundrel. He would remember them.

With new wariness, the leader queried, "What'd you find out there?"

"Horse tied up yonder—fine Morgan stallion," the one called Nix reported, leering at Ned. "I'd sure like to have me one of them myself someday." He tossed the butt of his cheroot to the ground. "Nothin' else interesting."

The reference to Trick caused Ned's fists to bunch, but he acknowledged the louts' return with a nod. Seven Colors of Shit stirred in his belly and marked the man as his enemy: Nix. Average height, average weight, cheroot in one hand, clear jar of moonshine the other. An almost affable mask hiding a malevolent soul.

His message delivered, Ned took a few steps to leave, then swung back to face them. "Hope to see you boys in the morning. There'll be coffee and grits. Bacon, if you get there early enough."

Ambling away from the campsite, he braced for the bullet in the back he more than half expected. His life had come to mean almost nothing to him, so if one of those black-hearted fools wanted to take it, they could have it with his thanks.

On the way back to his own camp, Ned pondered what he would and would not say to Heck about his visit with the rustlers. Enough to keep the everyone alert, not enough to alarm them. Without a word to anyone, he decided to stand watch through the night. When dawn grayed the horizon, he slipped the eagle feather back into Heck's medicine bag.

That morning, he and Heck returned to the campsite and found no sign of the horse thieves. Horse tracks showed they'd headed back in the opposite direction.

"Well, hell," Heck told Ned, poking the cold ashes of their fire with the toe of his boot and scratching the back of his neck. "Can't say I'm too surprised. You never have been any good at making new friends."

When they came upon the mustangs later that day, Ned and Heck and his men kept their distance to observe the wild horses dotting the grassy plateau—a shifting palette of blacks, browns and sorrels. Some meandered, grazing or drinking at the water hole, some stood in one place, asleep on their feet. Spindly-legged foals huddled near their mothers. Ned noted three watchful stallions guarding the perimeter of the band—an indication a few small harems had joined together for strength. He identified one boss mare, the true leader of any feral herd. He and Heck agreed to leave the stallions and boss mare alone, for the protection of the remaining mustangs.

By afternoon, Ned had chosen the horses he wanted—a spirited brown colt and a lithe sorrel filly. He guessed both to be just under three years-old and close to fifteen hands tall, almost the same size as Trickster. Wild and uneducated, they would require much work—and even more patience—but Ned felt certain it would be well worth the effort. Watching them gallop across the plain for the pure joy of it, an odd sensation welled up in his chest. It took him a few moments to recognize the unfamiliar feeling for what it was: pleasure.

The following day he caught his filly. He spent that evening letting her get used to the sight and smell of him with Heck's mares nearby to comfort her. To accustom her to his voice, he spoke of some of the strange new things she would soon encounter. "There'll be fences, I'm sorry to say. And stables, dogs, and children. Bits, bridles, saddles and the like."

He realized his words sounded like an apology. Which they were.

When the other men turned in, he sat on the ground a few feet away from the filly and told her all about how he'd met Becky Saunders. In the morning, the horse let him stroke her forehead.

"This one," he told Heck, "is about as sweet as a June breeze in a hayfield."

For Ned, the next days provided an idyll of riding and roping across sun-blessed prairie, chasing creatures too splendid to be of this world. Chilly nights around the campfire were warmed by the camaraderie of good men sharing food, whiskey, and stories. Over the next few days, they caught another mare and Ned's colt. The young male proved to be more than a handful, but Trickster, a gentle, albeit stern, disciplinarian, helped Ned teach him some rudimentary manners.

"This one," he told Heck, his eyes bright with admiration and a dawning awareness of what he'd gotten himself into, "is wild as a West Texas wind."

He named the filly Sugarplum and the colt Trouble.

Heading home the same way they'd come, they took it slow to allow the mustangs to adjust to captivity in familiar surroundings. At every opportunity, Ned climbed as high as he could to scan the vast landscape, but found no sign of the rustlers. Apparently his bluff had paid off, without having to call on Seven Colors of Shit. Ned supposed he should share that success with Red Moon. She'd been the only one to understand that nineteen-year-old Ned Harper had been tottering on the razor's edge. He remembered the day many years ago when she'd pulled him back from certain self-destruction.

On that Sunday morning, after enjoying a particularly wild Saturday night at the Tanglefoot, something had awakened him in the bunkhouse. Too early. Scant sunlight pierced his hung-over eyes, his raw knuckles stung, and when he licked his cracked lips he tasted dry blood. Sensing someone standing over him, he'd groaned and pulled the covers over his head.

"Go away," he'd muttered, turning toward the wall.

"Get up, Badger."

His still-drunk mind had registered her presence. Red Moon. He rolled back over and squinted up at her through the eye that wasn't swollen shut from the previous night's brawl.

She held out a cup of steaming coffee. "Drink this."

Even in his addled state he knew not to defy Red Moon, though he couldn't figure why she seemed so angry with him. Pushing up on one rubbery elbow, he'd taken the tin mug and sipped the strongest, most bitter coffee he'd ever tasted.

"Get dressed and come outside."

Pulling on his clothing, Ned had been aware there was no part of his body that didn't hurt. The thought made him smile. He stumbled through the door and stood beside Red Moon who waited in front of the bunkhouse.

Holding out her hand, she said, "Give me your pouch."

He'd pulled the small medicine bag over his head and handed it to her. His stomach clenched as awareness of the depth of her displeasure sobered him. He—Seven—must have gone too far the night before, but he barely remembered what he'd done. Whatever his offense, Red Moon evidently found him unworthy to wear the sacred pouch. Despair welled up inside of him. He'd never really believed he deserved it, had known the day would come when she would figure that out, too.

"I'm sorry," he whispered, still not sure what he was apologizing for. Bowing his head, he squeezed his eyes shut against the burn of sunlight and tears.

"Look at me, Ned."

He couldn't.

She waited until he raised his head. When he'd blinked his eyes clear, he forced himself to face her.

"Badger is vicious," she told him. Opening her clenched fist, she showed him a large, yellowed tooth and a claw an inch-and-a-half long. "Quick to anger, and quicker to pounce. The thought of facing Badger makes other animals run. Everyone knows his hissing fangs and terrible claws can tear less aggressive opponents to shreds."

Ned tried to hold her gaze, and again failed.

Fragments of the previous night came back to him. He'd fought and won. But fought brutally. Viciously. Not the good-natured brawling between men who would be friends the next day. Nausea forced him to lean back against the bunkhouse wall. That morning, he experienced the hot flush of shame for the first time in his life.

"I'm sorry . . ."

"Sorry means nothing if you're not willing to change. You must understand your anger for what it is. Aggression is not the same as strength. Find your true strength." She dropped the tooth in his deerskin pouch and gave it back to him, then opened his hand and closed it over the badger claw. Her black eyes offered no reprieve. "Otherwise," she said, "you are an ugly animal that no one can befriend."

She'd left him standing alone in front of the bunkhouse with the badger claw in his hand. He'd attached it to his hatband as a reminder of her warning and, from that day on, followed Will Hanover's lead. He drank in moderation, swore off the Tanglefoot, and exited the more respectable Tongue Oil Saloon before the fighting started. Mostly.

The ride back to Solace Springs with the mustangs was uneventful, except for a small incident with the colt. Ned had made progress with both his young horses. Sugarplum allowed him to stroke her forehead and neck. She stood politely while he walked around her running his hands up and down her sleek flanks and legs, brushing off dirt and pulling out burrs, always talking to her in a quiet voice.

Trouble proved more standoffish. When the colt finally allowed him to touch his forehead, Ned assumed he'd been given permission to stroke his neck and get acquainted. Nothing in the horse's demeanor alerted him that wasn't so. No swishing tail, no flattened ears. Without warning, powerful jaws clamped down on his wrist. The crushing bite didn't break the skin, but left his forearm badly bruised.

Greenhorn mistake. He blamed himself for the mishap, not the horse.

After making Ned prove he could open and close all the fingers of his right hand, Heck opined, "Seems to me it was an act of friendship that young'un didn't break your arm."

CHAPTER TWENTY-ONE

Riding toward the sanctuary of the H & H Ranch, Allie and Albert agreed they should count themselves lucky to have escaped South Slope with their lives.

"But what's wrong with her?" Albert asked plaintively. Ordinarily generous of spirit, it was clear to Allie her brother's patience had been tried past its limit.

For over a week, Maude Mary had been more shrill, quarrelsome, and ill-tempered than ever. She declared each member of the household insufferable. The maids were rude and lazy, Allie conceited, Albert a hooligan, and her parents annoying beyond endurance. Dash, she announced, deserved nothing better than to be taken to the woods and left with all the other horrid, untamed beasts that resided there. And, she had squalled, someone must stuff a sock in the mouths of those horrid lambs to stop their bleating—this very minute!—or she would see to it herself that they were Irish stew by morning.

Only the kittens, who wisely stayed hidden in the darkest rafters in the barn, were spared her wrath. In the tearful aftermath of one of her tirades, Maude Mary admitted she found her own company unbearable.

Alice Maude Mary Hanover had flowered.

After mercilessly haranguing Allie for not warning her about the cramping and The Mess, she had wailed to her bemused mother: "Every month?

No! No! No! I changed my mind! I don't care about ugly long skirts and ridiculous put-up hair. I don't want to be a maiden!"

Urging her father's mare to quicken her trot, Allie rode ahead and looked back over her shoulder at Albert. "Women's trouble," she called out, before kneeing Hippocrates to a canter.

She was not about to elaborate on such things to an eight-year-old boy.

Hands on hips, Allie and Hannah exchanged identical, rueful frowns as they surveyed the pitiful vegetable patch they'd spent the morning weeding. And weeding. And weeding.

"They'll be back by tomorrow," Hannah said glumly, pushing back the damp copper hair that fell across her forehead.

Unable to find honest words of reassurance, Allie nodded.

Shrunken peas straggled on their frame, the harvested onions, carrots, turnips, potatoes, and leeks lay limp and half the size they should have been. "No matter what I do, everything just dwindles," Hannah lamented. Two bushel baskets full of the languishing vegetables added mute testimony to her observation.

Allie offered what consolation she could for the disappointing crop. "They'll be fine when they're cooked."

"Och, I suppose," Hannah sighed. "Too bad I can't just make a big batch of weed soup."

Allie knew Hannah composted as diligently as she did everything. Leftover vegetables and yard scraps went into the bin, along with copious amounts of aged, crumbly horse manure.

Shading her eyes, she looked up at Allie. "Martha Findlay's got the same clayey soil, same merciless sun, and the same drowning rain, but her plants thrive. Look at that poor, wee leek. D'ye not see how it's accusing me of failing it?"

"I'm sure it appreciates how hard you try."

Clearly not dwindling, Hannah's healthy young sons cavorted under the trees, while the ranch dogs—intent on their morning naps—did their best to ignore them. Peals of childish laughter, punctuated by shouts of outrage and an occasional bark, accompanied the birdsong and buzz of insects.

"I just dinna ken why . . ." Hannah stared at her disappointing garden, then her freckled face brightened. "Mrs. Findlay did tell me her secret at yer mum's Tea! I'd forgotten. She went on and on about manure, of all things. Something about how many stomachs an animal has."

Hannah's russet brows furrowed beneath the brim of her sunbonnet. "I told her I use horse manure because we have so much of it. She said horses have only one stomach, so most of the weed seeds pass right through and get planted and fertilized all over again." She directed a wheedling grin up at Allie. "Goodsister, I recall ye now have a pair of bonny lambs at South Slope Ranch. Mrs. Findlay said sheep have enough stomachs to digest the weeds. If it's not too much to ask, I'd be ever so grateful if ye'd be kind enough to save their dung for me."

Wrapping an arm around Hannah's petite shoulders, Allie said, "I would do anything for you and you know it. Even that. Now, can we please go inside and talk about Guid whatever-you-call it?"

With a quick laugh, Hannah wiped her hands on her apron. "Aye! Please let's do. I canna bear to look at those sad turnips for one more minute." She tilted her head in the direction of her hardy sons. "At least I can feed my wee bairns properly, can't I ?"

Sensing the proximity of food, the boys paraded noisily into the house. With a lunch of meat-filled pasties in each grubby hand, they squealed their way back outside to tease the dogs with their bounty.

Allie had come to the H & H Ranch in part to escape Maude Mary and in part to help with the weeding. But, the true lure was to help plan the much-anticipated Guid Nychburris—'Good Neighbor'—Gathering that Hannah and Will held every Midsummer Night. The annual festivities were always what Hannah called 'a jiggery-pokery' of Scottish festivals mashed together: Guid Nychburris, the Highland Games, with its caber-throwing. haggis-tossing, and tug o' war, and the pagan Fire Festival of Litha. The next night at the Frolic, townfolk and visitors would come for more food and drink and to dance the quadrille to the music of an accordion, fiddle, and banjo.

Allie knew the Scottish festivities had a deeper meaning for Hannah and her family. When Will first brought her home to meet the Hanovers, Hannah had regaled young Allie, Maude Mary, and Albert with stories of her family's heartbreaking migration from Scotland after the deadly Battle of Culloden.

"The Brahan Seer predicted it, ye ken, long before it happened," she always began in a hushed voice, like her Grandda Fergus had. "He prophesied: 'The moor, before many generations have passed, shall be stained with the best blood in Scotland. I willna live to see the day and I am glad of that.' "

When her own children came along she'd gather them round to listen.

"After the fall of Culloden, the English hunted down the Highlanders who had survived. Those they didna kill were imprisoned, or transported to the Colonies, leaving their poor families to fend for themselves. My great Grandda Malcomb joined thousands of Scots who came to America and settled along the Cape Fear River in North Carolina. He knew if he didna leave Scotland right then he'd be either a dead man or . . ." Hannah would purse her lips and narrow her eyes. "a *murderer.* Ye ken?"

For the most part, she would tell them, the Scots kept to themselves and preserved the language, customs, and clothing they'd been forbidden in Scotland. "Some slaves raised on their plantations in North Carolina spoke with Scottish accents," Hannah would say, in a lighter tone. "Some even had a bit of the Gaelic!"

Now, Hannah sat back in her chair thinking out loud. "My da will make the haggis." Both girls grimaced at the thought of what was to them a noxious concoction of offal cooked and served in a sheep's stomach. "Ned promised a haunch of venison to roast. I'll make pasties and rumbledethumps. Mam will bake bushels of bannocks."

A batch of chicken and leek soup bubbled on Hannah's stove as they spoke. Allie inhaled, savoring the aroma. "Of course, your folks will stay with us again," she said. "They can use our kitchen and Mrs. Olney and Miranda will help make the food."

Doc eagerly anticipated the visits as an opportunity to bring out his finest single-malt Scotch whiskey to share with Eoghann 'Hugh' MacGregor—a man who knew how to appreciate it. Her father told Allie that drinking with a large, red-haired Scot wearing a kilt and sporran gave the aged liquor even more flavor.

The first time he and Hugh had shared a 'wee taste,' Doc said Hugh had swirled the amber liquid in his glass and held it up to the light. "*Slinte mhath,*" the Scot had toasted in Gaelic: to your health. Then he'd taken a long sip. "Och, Dr. Hanover," he'd sighed. "Whiskey may or may no cure the common cold, but I ken it fails more agreeably than most other remedies."

Looking around the kitchen as if wary of spies, Allie lowered her voice "This is supposed to be a surprise, so don't tell your da or grandda, not even Will." Leaning forward, she whispered the secret. "My father has ordered several casks of something called '80 shilling ale' from Fort Collins. He seems overly pleased with himself for some reason."

Pressing her hand to her throat, Hannah rolled her eyes. "Och! The lads will be thanking him—until the next morning. The lasses, maybe no. 'Eighty schilling' means 'wee heavy' and 'wee heavy' means verra, verra strong ale." With a laugh, she added, "Your da has a fair bit of the chancer in him, aye? That's mischief, lassie. My mam wouldna allow a wee drop of that stuff in her house. But my da will surely say, 'Yer a long time deid, Dr. Hanover, so ye might as well live whilst ye can.' "

As much as she enjoyed Hannah's company, Allie's eyes had sought the door several times. Albert, who had been missing his older brother, had hurried up to the far paddock to help him mend fences. "Will my brothers be down soon?"

Making a long-suffering face, Hannah nodded. "They're supposed to be seeing to yon fences, but if Will has a baseball with him—and ye can bet he does—he'll be tossing it to any man or beast that'll toss it back. The laddies will be down when it occurs to them they're hungry." Handing Allie a plate with a bannock and a meat pie, she said, "That'll be any time now."

"And Ned?" Allie asked. She took a bite and chewed the savory pastry slowly.

"Ned? Och, he's not here. Hasn't been for over a week. Did yer da not tell ye? He's gone off hunting wild horses with wee Hector Abernathy and left Will behind to mind the ranch."

Allie felt a drop in her good spirits as Hannah continued, "That scunner didn't even tell Will he'd be going. Yer poor da was the one gave him the news after he'd gone, and the one took the blistering. I haven't heard the end of it yet and Will says Ned willna either. But when the lad shows up with a few fine mustangs in tow, you'll see—everything will be forgiven. No matter how hard he tries, your brother canna hold a hard feeling toward Ned." Biting into her oat cake, she swallowed before adding, "For my part, I'm grateful he left my bairns' da out of it. The last time Ned went off with Hector, he came back with a bullet hole in his hat."

Lifting a bannock half-way to her mouth, Allie set it down. She'd heard the story of the bullet hole before. What caught her off guard was the pinch of disappointment that she wouldn't see Ned today. Trying to dismiss the feeling, she found Hannah studying her. "Och, lassie. So that's how it is with ye."

"How what is?"

Holding Allie in an amused gaze, softened by affection, Hannah said, "Ned Harper's a braw and bonny lad who's always had too easy a way with a searching look. Ye ken? Why, if he'd turned those lovely eyes my way back in the day, I can't say I wouldna have been tempted to look back. Before I'd won *mo chridhe* Will Hanover's heart, that is."

Hannah's incorrect assumption took Allie by surprise. She told herself it was being misunderstood that brought the warmth to her cheeks. Hannah, who was right about most things, was wrong about this. "That is not at all how 'it is' with me." Allie protested. "Ned is a friend and nothing more."

"I'm glad to hear it." With a sigh, Hannah laid a hand on Allie's. "The truth is, lassie, he isna ready." Her voice went soft with emotion. Becky had been her dearest friend, Will Ned's. For months after his wife and child's death, they had been the only people he would let near. "He may never be."

Allie thought of the long night she'd spent at his side, helping him birth Josie's foal and of the emotional supper at South Slope when they'd all shared memories of Becky. Both times, she'd seen the depths of his still raw sorrow. Of course, she had strong feelings for Ned, Hannah wasn't wrong about that. But what she felt for him was simply deep compassion.

"My heart does ache for his losses," she said. "But I certainly have no silly notions of anything else."

Patting Allie's hand, Hannah withdrew her own. "Of course ye wouldna have any such thing. The last word I'd ever be caught using to describe Miss Alexandrina Victoria Hanover is silly. Overly serious, if anything." Hannah always had a knack for knowing when enough said was enough said. "So, now, I need yer very unsilly opinion on something very serious for Guid Nychburris." She sat back with a mock-solemn expression. "D'ye ken we should have the bairns play 'What's the time, Mr. Wolf' or 'Plainy-clappy' or both?"

"Both," Allie said, relieved at the change of subject. "And 'Lazy Stick,' too. And," she added, "I do believe we must have our patient and fun-loving Maude Mary mind the children while they play."

At the alarming images Allie's suggestion conjured, they laughed so hard they sputtered crumbs of bannock and didn't notice Ned in the doorway. Angus perched on his shoulders, while the other boys clustered around his legs, quiet as cats. Lips pressed tight, they all appeared to have swallowed the same canary. Colum, known to have difficulty keeping a secret, covered his mouth with both hands.

Eyes bright as the children's, Ned said, "Mistress Hanover, we'd like to invite you to come outside and meet your two newest bairns." Turning to leave, he added over his shoulder, "You, too, Miss Boston."

CHAPTER TWENTY-TWO

Once she convinced her racing heart that Ned hadn't overheard her and Hannah talking about him—and had gotten over her affront at being an afterthought—Allie was able to exhale. Will and Albert had come down from the pasture and they all stood a few yards back from the corral fence admiring the young mustangs who were acquainting themselves with their new home.

At first, Will was standoffish with Ned, pulling a disgruntled face. But, as Hannah had predicted, as soon as he saw the mustangs all rancor left him. Gazing at the dusty and dirt-encrusted horses with unkempt manes and scruffy tails, Will punched Ned's shoulder. "Just look at those beauties!"

To Allie, Ned appeared as disheveled and trail worn as the horses. Drawing the children farther back from the corral's fence, he knelt to be at eye level with them. He wrapped one arm around Angus and Colum to contain them, the other around Ian, and gathered them close. Albert faced him.

"Listen here, boys. There's something I need you to understand and," he paused and made sure they were all paying attention, "remember. Those horses are wild." Voice stern, he held them tight as they tried to squirm toward the corral. "They've never known what it is to be penned in and they sure don't have any reason to like or trust us. Any of us. Yet. I'm the first person they ever met and look what I did—caught'em and took them away from everything they know." The boys quieted, their faces solemn. "These horses have never seen a dog, either. So we've got to keep all the dogs away for now. They're just the same as wolves to them. Maybe worse. You wild pups," Ned jostled them for emphasis, "are not to go any closer to those horses than we are right now, without me or your da right beside you."

Will hunkered down in front of them. "Understood?"

Big-eyed and silent, all four boys bobbed their heads.

Releasing them, Ned stood and brushed the dirt off his knees. The children stepped back a pace as if to demonstrate their understanding of his instructions and got nods of approval from him and their father. The colt and filly roamed the corral, nibbled at the hay, and drank from the trough. Shying at every move the humans made, they put as much distance between them as possible.

"Penning a mare with 'em ought to quiet their nerves," Ned said.

Will nodded. "Which one?"

"I was thinkin' Mollie. She's steady and patient."

"She's the one, then," Will agreed.

Kicking dirt off one boot with the other, Will removed his hat and smoothed back his hair. He looked sideways at Ned, started to speak, then stopped. Allie's curiosity piqued. Her suddenly fidgety older brother hadn't known a reticent moment in his entire life.

Finally, he spoke. "Ned."

"Will?"

"There's something I've been meaning to talk to you about." When he hesitated again, Albert gave him an encouraging nod. Ned looked from the boy to the man with a puzzled expression. Will drew a longish breath and exhaled sharply. "It's Zeke. He asked me if I would see if you might be willing to . . ."

Before Will could complete the sentence, Angus tugged urgently on Ned's hand demanding his attention. "Orse!" Angus demanded, pointing to the corral. "Up! Me!"

Ned scooped him up in the crook of his left arm and balanced the child on his hip. When he turned so the baby could watch the horses, Allie glimpsed the deep-purple bruise encircling Ned's right forearm. Without thinking, she lifted Angus from his arms and set the protesting child on the ground. She no longer saw Ned Harper. What she saw was a severe contusion that might be the sign of a more serious injury.

Ned gaped from Allie to the now howling child on the ground, then back to Allie.

"What happened to your arm?" she asked, as Hannah soothed the boy.

"Trouble," Ned told her, with a half smile.

"What kind of trouble?"

"Horse trouble," he said. "The colt thought I was being a little too forward, so he bit me to teach me some manners. His name is Trouble."

Bit. Alarm pricked the back of Allie's neck. A horse bite could carry the risk of dangerous infection. *In wounds, there are miasmata causing disease if entering the body.* As she'd learned from watching her father with his patients, she kept her expression and voice interested, but neutral. "Did he break the skin?"

"No, he did not." Ned didn't hide his irritation at the fuss. "And he didn't break any bones either, if you're thinking of asking. Heck made sure of that."

"That's good," Allie said. "Mind if I have a look?" Before he could refuse, she took his arm and rolled up his sleeve. "My father would say I was irresponsible if I didn't make sure Heck's diagnosis was correct."

She took the slight twitch of his shoulders as permission.

"Pretty," she said. His arm looked worse than she'd feared. Blotched in shades of purple so dark it was almost black and bordered by a bilious green-yellow, his forearm was swollen from below the wrist to near his elbow. The red-black area where the horse's teeth had clamped and left their mark indicated a deep hemorrhage. She ran her fingers over the bones. Ned's sharp intake of breath told her he was in more pain than he was likely to admit.

"No deformities," she murmured, giving him a reassuring smile. "Dr. Abernathy was right—no broken bones." When she bent his hand back slightly, he winced and glared at her. "Hurt much?"

"Not 'til you started messing with it."

His sarcasm didn't trouble her. She was intent on recalling the procedure to evaluate this kind of injury. Her father would want to hear every step she took, everything she observed, and what she made of what she found. "I'm going to apply pressure to each fingertip and to the muscles and tendons in your forearm to look for any weakness of the joint," she told Ned. "This might hurt a little."

Will, Hannah, and the boys stood to one side, watching.

Ned's eyes were as intent on her, as hers on him. When she bent his hand back, his mouth tightened. "A little?"

Curling and uncurling his fingers, she paid close attention to fingers two through five. She'd seen the power of a horse's jaw before and would not underestimate the damage it could do. *Possible crushing injury to the flexor tendon without laceration or detachment from the bone.*

"The bite most likely injured the tendon," she said, the self-consciousness she often felt in Ned's presence replaced by a sense of purpose. "I don't think it's too serious, but your wrist should be splinted."

Withdrawing his hand, he rolled down his sleeve. "Not necessary."

"It is if you don't want to risk more damage." She'd also learned how to deal with recalcitrant wranglers from watching Doc. In her work in New York, Lydia Brennan dealt almost exclusively with the health and hygiene of women and children. It struck Allie that she herself was getting a broader education treating cowboys and baseball players. "The pain," she told Ned, "is telling you that you shouldn't be moving it."

"You are lookin' a wee bit peeley-walley, if ye ask me," Hannah offered.

Allie smiled. "Everything I need is in Hippocrates' saddle-bags."

"Better?" Allie asked Ned.

With Hannah's kitchen table as a make-shift clinic, Allie had splinted his arm while the others watched. Ned stared at his bound wrist with barely-concealed displeasure. "I can't say it isn't." Braced between padded leather splints, fastened by a row of linen ties, his right forearm and hand had been immobilized. "How am I supposed to get anything done like this?" He cast an accusing glance at Allie. "I'm as useless as a button on a hat."

Allie was certain the arm in question had been extremely tender—useless—for days. Any bump or movement would have caused him pain. For Hannah's curious boys, who crowded closer to get a look, she hoped the ugly injury served as a timely illustration of the dangers of getting too close to untamed horses.

Allie lowered her brows at Ned. Fatigue and a week's dark stubble shadowed his face. "Just how much were you able to get done before I did you this terrible disservice?"

Silent, Ned glowered at the splint.

"Well, aren't ye the wee crabbit," Hannah scolded, resting an affectionate hand on his shoulder. "Ye should be thanking the lass, not girning at her."

"He's just grumpy," Allie told her, "because he had a thorn in his paw."

Ned narrowed his eyes at her. "A thorn? In my paw?"

Hiding a smile, Allie studied her handiwork. "I just need to check the distal pulses and I'll be done." She found strong beats at both ends of the splint indicating she hadn't made it too tight. As the tautness in his shoulders eased and the color returned to his face, she felt free to tease him. "Hasn't anyone ever told you the fable of Androcles and the Lion?"

"No," he grumbled. Lifting his arm off the kitchen table, he lowered it to his lap. "My brothers weren't the type to tell bedtime stories."

With the benevolence one would bestow upon an over-tired child, Allie began, "Once upon time, Androcles, the slave, came upon a fierce lion moaning and groaning in the forest." Rolling up the remaining linen, she packed it along with the rest of her medical supplies back into the saddlebag. "The poor beast had a huge thorn stuck in its paw. Even though the slave feared for his own life, he did the lion a kindness and pulled it out. The lion was so grateful, he let Androcles go unharmed." After securing the bag, she gave Ned a mildly reproachful look. "The moral of the story is: Don't bite the people who try to help you."

Bowing his head, Ned appeared to be engaged in an internal dialogue he did not find pleasing. When he looked up, his expression was sheepish. "Sorry," he said. "Everyone. And, thanks, Boston. Doctor . . . Doctoress . . . Boston. My arm does feel better." He feigned a wounded look that encompassed them all. "And, I wasn't moaning and groaning."

His eyes lingered on hers with what she took to be approval or something else she couldn't name. Flushing at his praise, Allie wondered if that was what Hannah meant by "an easy way with a searching look."

Ned swiveled to face Hannah. "Now that you've improved my manners, *lassie,* a bowl of that soup and a few bannocks might improve my 'crabbit' mood." Reaching for a bannock, he chewed with obvious satisfaction. "Haven't had a hot meal in over a week and have to say I'm about as hungry as . . ."

Rolling his eyes, Albert chimed in, "Two bears in a cave!"

Allie saw the quick smile Hannah and Will exchanged. She knew it had been a long time since Ned had joined in their light-hearted banter. He's coming back to us, she thought. But hoped it wasn't a ruse. She believed he'd become adept at showing them what they wanted to see and hiding what might trouble them. His moods had seesawed between light and dark over the months since Becky's death and still, Allie had to admit, darkness seemed to prevail.

"When we've been out on the trail for a week or so," Ned said, "Heck always tells us, 'After a few days of hardtack and pemmican, pemmican and hardtack is a welcome change.' "

"Och, please come help me serve the cock-a-leekie," Hannah said to Allie. "Else we may have to suffer more of the scunner's jabbering."

Ned turned to Will. "What was that you were sayin' about Zeke wanting you to ask me something?"

"Nothing important," he mumbled between mouthfuls. "It can wait."

The odd tension in her brother's tone caught Allie's attention. Even the children quieted to watch their father and Ned.

"It seemed important enough an hour ago," Ned said.

"A lot's happened in an hour."

"Will." Ned turned to Hannah with mock gravity. "I can see this isn't gonna be pretty. Maybe you'd best send the children to bed."

Before the boys could protest, Will, who never stammered, set down his spoon and stammered, "It's just this. Zeke and the boys, you know, the Sluggers, and Doc and Albert, too . . . well all of us . . . we're just wondering if you might be willing to think about—just think about—playing on the baseball team." Allie understood Will's reticence. A quick glance at Hannah confirmed she had the same reaction. Will said, "Look, we really need a good hurler and everyone agrees you could be the one."

Ned set down his spoon. "A hurler? You want me to play baseball?"

"I told them it was a bad idea."

"With you and Zeke and your Solace Springs Sluggers."

Will's face went dismal. "I told them you wouldn't be interested."

"Me? Not interested in spending the good part of a day throwing a little brown ball across a canvas bag as hard as I can hoping no one will hit it?

Or swinging a stick at one someone's throwing one at me?" Ned appeared incredulous. "With two new mustangs waitin' to be gentled?"

"I knew it was a mistake, but I told them I'd ask." Will finally met his gaze directly. "I'm really sorry."

"Sorry? You oughta be. You oughta be downright apologetic." Ned leaned back in the chair, making a show of deliberating. "S'pose I'd be willin' to give it a try," he said slowly. "Just to get rid of that hang-dog look you and Zeke and Doc get whenever you see me." With a wink to Allie, he added, "Whenever Doc Boston gives me the go-ahead, that is."

Will exhaled noisily, then pulled the baseball cap and red plaid bandana he'd had in his back pocket and slapped it on the table in front of Ned. "Welcome to the Solace Springs Sluggers."

CHAPTER TWENTY-THREE

As Norberto drove the wagon closer to the Winnicott place, Allie slipped a hand into her pocket and felt for the small pouch that held the treasure she'd brought for Clare. Potential treasure, she reminded herself, fearful she might have over-promised. Other than abstinence, nothing could be guaranteed to prevent conception, not even a womb veil. When the hovel came into sight, what she saw soured her anticipation.

Ephraim slumped in the broken wooden chair in front of the shack, head lolling on his chest, an empty whiskey bottle at his feet. The sound of the cart and horses hadn't roused him. Silent, scrawny, and hollow-eyed, the children waited for the wagon to stop before they approached. Etta balanced the baby on one hip and clutched the fingers of the toddler in her free hand. Caleb squirmed half-hidden behind her. Clare was nowhere to be seen.

Climbing down from the cart, Allie was aware of the children's eyes fixed on her pockets. "Hello, Etta. Caleb." Smiling at them, she pulled the hidden treats from her pocket. "Yellow or red?"

"Red, please," Etta whispered, without the smile that usually accompanied those words. "For me and Caleb." Dirty face drawn, she darted an anxious glance in the direction of their sleeping father.

After placing a candy in Etta and Caleb's grimy hands, she gave the babies Zwieback rusks. From another pocket, she extracted a pink ribbon. "For you, sweet Etta, for being such a help to your mama."

"Thank you, Miss." Etta lifted anguished eyes to hers, but didn't take the ribbon. "Mama's inside." In a mannerism much like her mother's, she bit the corner of her lip. "She don't smile no more and she don't hardly talk to me. I try to keep up with the sweepin' and with washin' the little ones like you said to, but they run away and make my daddy holler."

Pulling a pin from her pocket, Allie fastened the ribbon to Etta's bedraggled smock and tucked the girl's hair behind her ears. Ephraim snored loudly from his seat.

"Let's go inside and see if this pretty gewgaw cheers your mama up." Allie lifted two sacks of provisions from the cart, refusing Norberto's offer of assistance. The girl's uneasiness alerted her that something was amiss and she preferred to go inside alone. "If the ribbon doesn't do it," she told Etta, "I suspect the ham, flour and potatoes might!"

Inside the dreary cabin, Allie's chest tightened at the sight of Clare stiff-backed at the table, hands clenched in her lap, staring straight ahead. Scant light from the lone window blurred rather than brightened the room.

Etta approached her mother and laid a small hand on her arm. "Miss Allie's here, Mama," she said, her pinched face solemn. "She give us red candy and a fine ribbon for my dress."

Clare covered her daughter's hand with hers, but didn't look at the girl.

"I thanked her real nice."

Clare withdrew her hand and folded it back in her lap, head bowed.

Standing with a heavy sack in each arm, Allie hesitated. Crumbs were imbedded in grease on the filthy table. "Etta," she said, "will you bring me a wet cloth?"

Etta turned in a circle looking around the room, then hurried to fetch a rag dirtier than the table from below the three-legged stove. She dipped it into the barrel of drinking water before Allie realized what she was doing. "I'll clean it, Miss," Etta said, scrubbing the wood with all her strength. "See? Mama says I'm a good cleaner. Ain't that so, Mama?"

When Clare stayed still and silent, Allie cupped the child's chin and smiled at her. "Of course, it is! Your mama has told me so many times what a help you are to her. That's why I brought you that ribbon."

Setting the sacks on the still grimy table, Allie pulled out the ham and cornmeal. Clare had not moved or raised her eyes.

"Oh, Mama! Look what Miss Allie brung!" Etta pointed at the meat. "When Daddy wakes up I'll ask him will he please make us a fire and then I'll fry up that ham quick-smart for you and the babies."

"I've been so looking forward to our visit, Clare," Allie said carefully. With the children's eyes following her every move, she set sugar, corn meal, coffee, and hard cheese in paraffin on the table. Hannah had sent meat pasties and her ubiquitous vinegar pie. "Etta has the sweetest manners. And," Allie ruffled Caleb's unkempt hair. "I do believe this young man just might be warming up to me."

Clare's response was a slight lifting of her chin.

From the other sack, Allie withdrew a candle and lit it. Nothing had changed. The flea and lice-infested straw filling in the new mattresses had not been changed, the ammonia odor of urine still reeked from the unswept dirt floor, and the stench from the privy had worsened. She'd warned Clare of the dangers more than once and each time had been assured Ephraim would see to it "first chance he got."

Nothing is ever right in this woeful place, Allie thought, but today something is very, very wrong. Handing each child a pasty, she sent them outside.

"Don't worry, Mama," Etta said, over her shoulder. "I'll mind the little ones don't wake daddy or get drown in the stream."

When the children had gone, Clare remained silent. Kneeling at her side, Allie took her cold hands. "Clare," she said, hoping that what she had brought might ease her distress. The womb veil would provide some protection from pregnancy without interfering with what Clare said Ephraim had called his "God-given rights as her God-damned lawful husband" in a drunken tantrum. "I've brought you what we talked about."

Flat eyes fixed in middle-distance, Clare pulled her hands free from Allie's, balled them into fists, and pressed them against her belly.

"It's too late." Her lips barely moved. "You're too late."

CHAPTER TWENTY-FOUR

Ned dreamt he'd lost Becky.

In his nightmare, she was alive, he just couldn't find her.

In his dream, he'd been so caught up working with the young mustangs at the H&H that he hadn't gone home in days. Hadn't thought of Becky in days. Had gone to the Tongue Oil to unwind. Sipping a whiskey, it occurred to him Becky was alone up at the cabin. Waiting. Likely furious with him. Her anger always burned hot, but cooled just as fast. When he apologized, she'd forgive him quick as a hiccup. His body hummed in anticipation of the tender passion he knew would follow and he hurried out of the saloon. But the night had gone black and thick and he couldn't find his way home. When he finally reached the cabin, he found the porch steps crumbing in disrepair, the door ajar, and the hearth cold. Becky wasn't there.

Now, awake in mid-morning sunshine, Ned stood on the bank of a stream, buffeted by the soothing breezes that always accompany water rushing over rocks. He and Becky had come to this place every year to pick early berries. In the dappled shade of cottonwoods edging the bouldery brook, he tried to surrender to the serenity of his surroundings. He heard the birdsong, babbling water, and soughing of wind through the trees, saw purple primroses and the blue and white bells of columbine blossoming between grey stones, breathed in the green scent of moss, woods, and water.

There were memories here, but nothing eased the crushing sorrow the dream had evoked.

Amid the hum of bees manic with their bounty, he spent the morning picking wild raspberries as a distraction. His hands were bloody from his battles with the brambles, but he'd gathered enough to dry for the batch of pemmican he'd make to trade at Cuthbert's.

Reluctant to return to his empty homestead, he lingered near the meadow. At the line of sycamores bordering the stream, he watched a plump black-breasted bird peck out a niche for a nest in the soft bark of a tree and met the predatory gaze of a hawk perched on a higher branch.

Upstream, he noted a beaver dam and lodge. Where there are beavers, he thought, there'll be trappers. Recalling the man buying a bear trap at Cuthbert's, he rested a hand on Cloud's head. Best keep the dog close while he searched out the vile contraptions and sprang them with branches.

He'd gathered a few fallen limbs and was about to set out, when a flurry of birds lifted from the trees and the chittering of insects ceased. Cloud froze, ears pricked, hackles bristling. A difficult morning was about to go from bad to worse, Ned thought. Just as he recognized the lilting voices and peels of childish laughter, Cloud bounded away, barking a welcome. He saw Albert drop his basket and slow to allow for Joseph's ungainly gait and watched them cross the glade shrieking greetings to the dog. Allie followed with a picnic hamper over one arm. As the boys and dog cavorted around her, she lifted her gaze to search the trees. When she caught sight of Ned, the delight in her smile drew him into the sunlight. If his bruised spirit could tolerate the company of anyone, it would be these three.

"So, what exactly *is* pemmican?" Allie asked, handing Ned a slab of cheese and the last of the bread from her picnic basket. He explained pemmican was the reason he'd come berry picking. Sitting in the shade of a sycamore,

Allie drew her knees up and encircled them with her arms. Ned stretched out on his side, propped on an elbow.

Having eaten in haste, the boys had run off to fill their baskets and themselves with more raspberries. Determined to keep the darkness in his heart from his eyes or voice, Ned gave Allie a sidelong glance and forced a glimmer of humor into his smile. "I don't expect you'd find it on the menu at South Slope."

"What are you implying, sir?" She arched a brow in mock offense. "We have a very diverse menu."

"I doubt it's 'diverse' enough to include pemmican."

Rummaging in the pouch tied to his belt, he pulled out a small, brownish lump and held it out to her. When Becky was alive, they'd made the dried meat to trade for provisions at Cuthbert's. "Dried venison pounded to powder, mixed with deer fat and dried berries, made into bars." He grinned at her grimace. "It lasts a good long time. Trappers and seamen survive on it when there's nothing else to eat. They cook it in a stew with whatever they can find, or fry it. Or eat it raw. It's seen me through some hungry times."

"I see."

"Seein' won't tell you much, Boston."

Thirty yards away, Joseph and Albert strolled in and out of the bushes near the stream, their cheerful voices buoyant on the breeze. Cloud lounged in the shade near enough to supervise.

Accepting the bit Ned offered, Allie studied it in the palm of her hand, and rolled it between her fingers. "People eat this?"

He broke off a larger piece and demonstrated. "Times I would've starved without it."

Pinching off a tiny bit, she sniffed it, placed it in her mouth, and chewed. "Not bad, really. Just . . . odd."

"It's our own recipe. Becky's really. Horace labels it 'Cuthbert's Finest' and sells it to trappers who pay more than they should. Becky didn't care about that, she was just proud people liked it. It was one of his best-selling items. Still is." Ned's smile faded. He hesitated, surprised at how hard it was to talk about such a small thing. The dream had opened a hole in his spirit that he was determined to keep hidden. "But there's a reason for that."

A line creased the space between Allie's eyes. "Go on."

"It's our . . . it's Becky's . . . secret ingredient makes it special." Staring over Allie's shoulder into the sunlight and shadow dappling the meadow, he remembered how much Becky had delighted in the intrigue.

"Special," Allie echoed, widening her eyes. "And *secret*. I do know how much Becky loved secrets." Watching him as if he were a wild thing about to bolt, she spoke in the tone Ned himself would use to calm skittish horses. "Mrs. Olney has lots of recipes with 'secret' ingredients. Most of the time," she looked around, leaned forward, and confided, "it's butter."

The unfamiliar sound of his own laughter startled Ned.

"Ours is salt pork," he told her. At first, he'd resisted the new addition out of loyalty to Red Moon, who'd taught him to prepare pemmican the way the Indians did. When he tasted the first batch, Ned knew Becky had been right. "The trappers tell Horace they've never had pemmican so tasty. They come from all over to buy 'Cuthbert's Finest.' He gives us . . . me . . . a good enough price." The memory cost him, but he managed a smile. "Because of Becky's idea, I can't make enough to keep him stocked."

"Well, I won't tell a soul." Allie took another bite and grimaced. "I can't say I care much for pemmican, but I do like having a new secret with Becky." A breeze whispered through the sycamores. She cupped her ear, as if to listen. "I do believe I hear Becky saying 'this one's not quite so scandalous as *Gray's Anatomy*, but it'll do.' "

It'll do, Ned thought. It'll have to. He might have smiled at Allie, meant to, but couldn't be sure he had. Couldn't be sure of much of anything anymore. A familiar heaviness settled in his limbs. Shake it off, Ned told himself.

Cloud trotting at their side, the boys reappeared, laughing and stumbling, berries spilling out of their topsy-turvy baskets. They plunked down beside Ned and Allie with fingers and lips stained red—Albert with the sleepy, satisfied look of a boy sated by sun and sweet berries; Joseph tousled and flushed, bright-eyed, Ned guessed, with newfound freedom.

"I can't help but wonder if those baskets will ever stay full," Allie lamented. She cupped a handful of berries and handed them to Ned, then took another for herself. Nibbling the fruit, she told the boys, "Remember, we need enough for two big, plump pies. One for the Hanovers and one for the Findlays." Tilting her head toward Ned, she whispered, "Maybe someone will take pity on poor Mr. Harper and see he gets a small slice of one."

Joseph placed a berry in his mouth and sucked the flavor from it. "My sister will . . . make . . . him a whole one. Sarah's . . . sweet . . . on him."

Before Ned could decipher the change in Allie's expression, a cottontail bounded across the far side of the meadow, then hesitated as a shadow darkened the ground. A red-tail hawk—a pinprick in the sky seconds before—swooped down and pierced its neck with hooked talons. The rabbit screamed, then went limp as the hawk soared skyward, its prey dangling from its claws.

Albert and Joseph both knew enough of the ways of nature not to be shocked, but witnessing the sudden display of brutality left them wide-eyed. "Poor rabbit!" Albert swallowed hard, watching predator and prey shrink again to a speck in the sky. "How'd that hawk see him from way up there?"

Equally distressed, Joseph turned to Ned. "He . . . was safe . . . under the bushes."

He'd been little more than a youth when Red Moon had explained the cottontail's plight to him. A cautionary tale. "Indians say Rabbit is the Fear Caller."

"Fear Caller?" Albert echoed. Both children shot Ned identical quizzical looks.

"Hawk has keen eyesight—he can spot what he's hunting from high up," Ned said. "But Rabbit's so afraid of getting caught that his fear is very loud. It calls out to the things he's most afraid of, 'Here I am, Hawk!'"

Though Allie made a good effort to appear light-hearted, she seemed somber in a way Ned hadn't known her to be before. He feared his own dark mood had affected her and was determined to lift it. Standing, he suggested they get back to the work they'd come to do. "Else we'll be pickin' berries by moonlight."

As they strolled between the stream bank and the meadow, he told Allie and the boys other things Red Moon had taught him. "Little green gooseberries are always the earliest to ripen. They're tart at first." He pointed some out and made a face. "Indians use the juice for fevers."

When he'd first come to work for Heck, Red Moon had shared bits and pieces of Indian lore with him—a boy almost mute with the traumas of war and loss. She'd asked no questions, offered no observations, just told him what she knew about nature. Her smooth, slow words had soothed him and kept him by her side.

"Elk berries are shaped like hearts," Ned said.

Joseph slipped a hand in his. "Can we . . . see . . . some?"

"They don't grow in these parts." The child's small hand was an unexpected comfort. "We'd have to go higher into the mountains to find 'em."

Ned and the old Indian woman had walked for hours—or ridden for days—while she showed him the plants and wildlife in and around Solace Springs. He'd come to believe it was her spirit animal—Snowy Owl—that told her when he was having a particularly dark time—the nights he feared to sleep, the days his hands shook even when he tended the horses.

"And, then there are the muh-ko-tam-ins." Ned added, with a slow smile. "You have to stay up wind of those berries. Utes say if the stink of a person reaches them, their taste'll be spoiled."

"Stink!" the boys shouted in unison.

Albert hooted, "*Mucky* tay mins?"

"Mucky? . . . Mucky muck . . . ee!" Joseph held his nose.

Both children collapsed to the ground in the throes of their laughter. When the hilarity spent itself, they stood and brushed dirt and leaves off each other, still given to bursts of giggles and an occasional hiccup from Albert.

With a the-nonsense-is-over look, Allie handed them their baskets and pointed toward the serious business of the berry bushes. "At least two pies worth."

Holding them back with a hand on each boy's shoulder, Ned hunkered down in front of them, remembering he hadn't sprung the beaver traps as he'd intended. Gaze stern, he said, "There might be traps out there, especially by the creek. Watch every step you take. Use your wolf senses. All of them. A wolf sees everything, hears everything, and smells everything." Both boys nodded, mirroring his solemnity. "Same goes for finding berries. There's another kind I didn't tell you about nearby—see if you can spot it."

When they nodded again, he let them go. Joseph lurching, Albert steady at his side. At the cluster of berry brambles, they turned in opposite directions bellowing challenges at each other.

"I bet I find it first!" Albert hollered, scampering away.

Joseph shouted over his shoulder, staggering into the bushes. "I . . . will!"

Peering into Ned's basket, Allie said, "You're as bad as those children—you've eaten as many as you've picked."

He considered protesting, but laughed instead. The worried crease had smoothed from Allie's forehead and he intended to keep it that way. They strolled in companionable silence until they reached an untouched berry patch. From there, Ned could see Albert's brown head bob up and down among a cluster of bushes and Joseph's yellow hair among others. Watching them, he recalled his unpleasant encounters with Joseph's father. "I can't help but wonder how you convinced Luke Findlay to let you bring Joseph out here all by himself."

The mid-day sun burnished Allie's brown hair and brought out the gold in her flashing eyes. It occurred to Ned she was growing into a fine-looking young woman.

"First of all," she said, hands on her hips, "you must have noticed he's not out here 'by himself.' He's here with Albert, who is here with *me*."

"I didn't mean . . ."

Arms folded, lips tight, her eyes locked on his.

"I just meant Luke's awfully protective of Joseph," Ned said.

"Your point?"

Seeing the laughter in her eyes, he hung his head. "My point is I'm an idiot."

Unfolding her arms, Allie smiled at him. "I'm glad we found something we can agree on. Since you asked, it was Martha Findlay who did the convincing. She gave him a smarting look and said, 'It's berry picking, Luke. What harm can come of that?' He just stood up, snarled something, and went back to his sheep."

"Heck says there's only two things a man need be afraid of. Findlay must have known it, too. One's being left afoot." Ned paused for effect. "The other's a good woman."

He took the blush that deepened the color of Allie's cheeks as a sign of the afternoon warmth. Pinching fruit off the bush with as little additional damage to his scratched hands as possible, he noted that the light conversation seemed to have brightened her mood. His, he was surprised to realize, as well. "Speaking of Rabbit and fears and such," he said in a teasing tone, "I'm just curious—if it's okay to ask—what you might be afraid of?"

"Me?" Allie flushed deeper. "Oh. I don't know. Too many things to name." She lowered her eyes and frowned at what Ned assumed to be visions of spiders or rattlesnakes or other disconcerting possibilities. "But I guess what really scares me most . . ."

She stopped mid-sentence, her words cut off as shrieks of pain and terror pierced the air.

Joseph! Almost blind with panic, Ned raced toward the screams, Allie at his heels. *I didn't spring the traps.*

The cries stopped abruptly. In the ensuing silence, the boys emerged from the bushes. Albert, an arm around Joseph's shoulders, pulled him along. Red-faced and snuffling, the lurching boy cradled one hand against his chest.

"Bee sting," Albert explained, with a shrug. "He's never had one before."

Bee sting. Not a beaver trap. Relief flooded through Ned like a shot of Old Overholt's Straight. Two shots.

"It . . . hurts," Joseph whimpered. He'd stopped crying, but tears left white tracks on his cheeks and his chin still quivered.

"Let me take a quick look," Allie said. The stinger was clearly visible and Joseph's hand showed no signs of an allergic reaction. One arm wrapped around his shoulders, she said, "Why, Joseph, those bees just got alarmed because they saw you were finding all the sweetest berries!" Before he could protest, she grasped the stinger between her thumb and forefinger and pulled it out, careful not to burst the tiny venom sac. "Now, the best part." Taking his other hand, she led him toward the stream. "Mud."

Ned, Albert and Cloud followed them. Kneeling by the bank, Allie scooped a handful of mud and daubed it on Joseph's hand. "It'll feel better soon."

In a few moments, he grinned. "Better."

Allie had come to the meadow heavy-hearted and knew Ned had noticed. His efforts to cheer her with light banter and Indian lore had touched her, but couldn't change the fact that she'd let Clare Winnicott, who had relied on her, down. Doc had ordered the womb veil, which had taken a few weeks to arrive, but Allie had been so caught up in the excitement of planning the Gathering that she hadn't brought it to Clare as soon as it arrived.

Pulling a stinger from a child's hand did nothing to change that.

"There you go," Allie told Joseph. Standing, she wiped her muddy hands on her skirt, then put one on each boy's back, and gave them a gentle shove toward the berry bushes. "Now, fill those baskets and let's see which of you can find that other bush Ned says is there."

When the boys had run off again, Ned gave her a rueful grin. "Findlay's gonna find a way to blame that bee sting on me. Just you wait."

She knew there was as much truth as jest in his words. It was clear to everyone that Luke Findlay harbored animosity toward Ned. "I'll be sure to set him straight. I wish he could understand that every boy gets hurt sometimes. Bumps, bruises, cuts, stings. Horse bites. You men seem to think your wounds are badges of courage for your magnificent feats of derring-do." Eyeing his braceless wrist, she gave him a hard look. "How long?"

He lifted a shoulder. "A week . . . or so."

"I told Hannah you'd have it off by the next morning." Her eyes narrowed. "A week?"

"Or so."

At her quick laugh, Ned's dark blue eyes met hers, stirring a sensation that started in her chest and traveled to more alarming parts of her body. Will that look change if I tell him what I truly fear? she wondered. *I'm afraid of failing to help. Of letting down those who rely on me.* "I suppose," she said, finally answering his question, "what I've always been most afraid of is that my mother will send me off to Boston to be a debutante."

"So, what exactly is a debutante?

Making their way back toward the meadow, they strolled in the shade of the sycamores and cottonwoods. Ned had thought he needed solitude to shake the disquiet of his dream, but realized it was this easy companionship that had done it.

Allie broke the silence. "So, in the spirit of curiosity, it's my turn to ask you what you're afraid of." When he didn't respond, she said, "Let me guess." She closed her eyes, as if in deep thought. "I bet you're going to say you're not scared of anything."

"Something like that." He couldn't tell her that if he could hold his wife and infant son in his arms, just once more, he might not be so afraid to go on living without them. Instead, he raised his hand and pointed at the scar on his palm. "I used to be afraid of getting stitched up by a twelve-year-old girl, but I got over that."

The late-afternoon angle of the sun elongated the shadows cast by the trees, signaling the bees it was time to return to their hives. Ned was untying Trickster, while Allie packed the picnic basket in preparation for the walk back to town, when they heard the urgent shout.

"Here!" This time Joseph's shriek was triumphant. Cloud bounded across the meadow toward the sound. "I . . . I . . . found it!"

They all hurried to where the boy stood beside a six foot tall shrub. An impossibly broad grin stretched across his face.

"That's the one!" Ned confirmed. The boy's elation gladdened him. Today he's living the life his father's so afraid to let him live, he thought. "Utes call these 'big berries.' They're choke cherries—wild plums. Indians make a red dye from the roots and use the twigs and bark to brew a tea to cure sore throats." Pulling off four reddish-yellow, crabapple-sized fruits, he handed one to each of them. "They're not ripe yet, but when they are the skins'll be bitter and the fruit sweet as honey." He grasped the boy's shoulders. "You've got keen senses, Joseph and you know how to use them.

That's strong Wolf Medicine." Eyes fixed on Ned's, Joseph's glowed with pride. His clawed hand rested on Cloud's huge head.

CHAPTER TWENTY-FIVE

Ma had turned a basketful of berries into a into a big, flaky pie that they ate hot out of the oven with cream on top, Joseph remembered with pleasure. Everyone said it was the best they'd ever had, even Pa. Everyone was happy.

Then, Joseph had said the part about wolf medicine. Even now, that was the part of the memory that still soured his stomach.

"Ned Harper says what?" His father had wheeled around and glared at him. "You listen to me, boy. Wolves are beasts. They prey on the weak and unguarded. One day I'll show you a lamb that's been got by a wolf and you'll see for yourself. You stay away from Harper." Pa's mouth had gone twisted and ugly. "That wolf of his, too."

Joseph knew that was why Pa wouldn't let him go fishing with Ned and Albert. Or go watch the baseball practice. Joseph tried to not let himself think about that because it made a hot, sick feeling in his chest. As he did most days, he was sitting outside under the poplar tree in the big cushioned chair Pa had made for him watching everyone else work. Today, more than ever, it felt like a cage.

Ma was weeding, Sarah was spinning on the porch, and Pa was chopping wood. Everyone had some job to do, except him. Even the sheep dogs had earned their rest herding the flocks. He had not and it shamed Joseph to just sit. Sliding off the chair, he lurched across the yard to his mother's side.

On her knees in the garden, she looked up in surprise. "What is it, Joseph? Something wrong?"

"Ma. I can help . . . you pull weeds."

She directed a wary sideways glance at his father. Pa was concentrating on the wood, his red face gleaming with sweat. Joseph knew Ma was torn. She understood how much he longed to have things to do and how it worried his father when he tried to do them. "Pa means well," she was always telling him and his sister. "He just doesn't want to see any harm come to you."

Joseph knew Sarah felt as trapped as he did. Her body was whole and did what she wanted it to do, but even so, Pa refused to let her have the life other girls her age had. Joseph could almost see the chain he imagined kept her moored to the spinning wheel. It was longer than his, but stretched only as far as the gate of their property.

"P . . . please, Ma."

Pa hefted an armful of kindling and carried it around to the other side of the barn to stack. With a furtive glance in that direction, Ma motioned for Joseph to kneel next to her. "See here?" she said, grasping a small, spiky-looking plant at the base. "This is a weed. Show me first, when you find one, just to be sure. Then, pull it out hard, by the roots."

Joseph pointed a waggling finger at a scraggly green plant. At her nod, he wrapped the fingers of both hands around it. Pulling, he fell it pop and come free, roots and all. He briefly lost his balance, but was quick to right himself. The satisfaction of accomplishment surged through him.

"Just the ones like that," Ma cautioned him.

He was concentrating on another weed when the donkey in the near paddock began to bray and the agitated sheep to bleat—which set the dogs to barking. His head snapped up and swiveled around to see who was coming. When the dainty green and gold surrey turned the bend, his heart leapt. Albert sat on the back bench waving both arms at him.

"Ma!" he exclaimed, wobbling to his feet.

Making himself as tall as he could, he rocked from side to side, waving back. He was smiling so hard, his face hurt. Memories of the days in the barn and berry picking were Joseph's only respite from captivity.

Ma stood, brushed dirt from her skirt, and tidied her hair. With a guarded expression, she watched the visitors approach. Pa, alerted by the commotion of the nervous animals, strode out from behind the barn and waited with his arms akimbo.

Pa's face is a door that no one can open, Joseph thought.

When the two young women—Miss Allie and young Mrs. Hanover—and Albert climbed out of the surrey and ambled toward them, Joseph saw Ma find her strained smile—the one she wore in town—to welcome them. He wanted to run to Miss Allie and throw his arms around her waist and climb into the surrey with her and Albert and ride right back to South Slope where he would tell his friends how well they were doing caring for their lambs. Then, Ned Harper would come with Running Cloud and Joseph would throw his arms around the huge wolf dog's neck and he would remember him and lick his face all over and lean against him, panting to be petted. And Ned Harper would say, "Seems Cloud's decided you're part of his pack, Joseph."

When Sarah saw who had arrived, she ran down the steps and stood with her mother and Joseph, her face alight.

"What brings you young ladies all the way out here?" Ma asked.

Sarah gave her a sharp look. "Ma!"

"Oh, my," Ma said, pressing both hands to her cheeks. "You're right, Sarah Sue. I must surely have misplaced my manners." Pa had swung around to face them, his posture no more welcoming than it had been before. Her back to him, she waved the girls up to the porch. "Why, you girls come right inside and let me give you a glass of milk. Or do you prefer buttermilk? And some gingerbread. Then you can tell me why you've done us the pleasure of this visit."

Following them into the house, Pa stopped in the doorway. Ma brought out a tray of cookies and milk and served them to the girls at the table and to Joseph and Albert who sat on the settle. When his friend reached for a cookie, Joseph did the same. To him, their laughter felt like soap bubbles tickling his insides.

Holding her home-made basket on her lap, Mrs. Hannah Hanover—small and pretty as a fairy—was the first to speak. "Thank you for yer hospitality, Mrs. Findlay. This is some of the finest gingerbread I've had since I left my Mam's house."

"And thank you, right back. It's my Ma's receipt. My young'uns—and their Pa," she looked at him with lips pressed tight, almost turned up at the corners, "they just can't get their fill." In a tight, cheery voice she said, "Now, Luke, inside or out, you make up your mind. If you're stayin', come take a seat and I'll pour you coffee. If not, get on with your choppin'."

A shiver of anxiety made Joseph's hand shake more than usual, almost dropping the cookie. He'd never heard Ma take that tone with his father. Whatever Pa felt, he kept it walled away behind his stony face, strode to the table, and pulled out a chair. Sarah sat beside him, hands folded in her lap. Her eyes darted from Ma and Pa to the visitors.

Setting a steaming mug in front of Pa, Ma stood behind him. All three stared across the table at Miss Allie and Mrs. Hanover.

"Since you're new to town," Miss Allie said, "we came to give you a personal invitation to Hannah and Will's annual Guid Nychburris Gathering. That means 'Good Neighbor' in Scottish."

"Gaelic," Mrs. Hanover corrected.

Joseph didn't know any of the strange words, but he liked the sound of them. The only word that mattered to him was 'invitation.' A butterfly of hope flitted around his heart.

"It's in two weeks, and we hope you'll all come." Miss Allie said. "It's a two-day Gathering for folk from town and families from all over to get together for food, drink, and dancing. There'll be a day of Highland games, then a square dance Frolic at night."

Albert sat up straight. He elbowed Joseph in the ribs, eliciting another explosion of giggles. "There's always a bonfire the first night and Uncle Hamish sings Scottish songs and Uncle Aidan drums on his bodhrans and Hugh MacGregor plays his bagpipes!" His eyes gleamed. "Sometimes people just get up and start dancing. You don't even have to know how, you just jump around to the music. Then, Hannah's Grandda Fergus takes us children to the barn and tells us Scotch stories until we fall asleep on the hay."

Joseph imagined himself next to Albert, with little Angus snuggled between them, listening to the tales. He would make sure the tot didn't eat any straw, so Ned Harper wouldn't get scolded the next day.

"I saw those fine collies outside," Mrs. Hanover said. "Some folk come just for the herding trials. You can enter yer dogs and see how they do against the others. They'll have eight minutes each to fetch four sheep from a hundred yards up the hill, get them in and out of two pens, then separate one out from the others."

Joseph's heart beat slow and heavy. Pa was always going on about how smart and fast his dogs were. Maybe he would want to show them off.

Mrs. Hanover directed a smile toward Sarah. "Every year the town votes on a Cornet and a Cornet's Lass. Ye may have seen the ballot jars at the mercantile and other places. The Lass and the Cornet lead the horses and clans in the sunrise rideout."

"Even if we had the time for such things, they wouldn't interest us." With a loud scrape of wood on wood, Pa pushed back his chair and stood. "We appreciate the invite," he said, "but we don't care to mix with strangers."

Joseph felt the world and everything in it dissolve like spent soap bubbles.

Miss Allie and Mrs. Hanover exchanged a bewildered look. "But Mr. Findlay," Miss Allie said. "Sarah was chosen to be the Cornet's Lass."

Once, feigning sleep, Joseph had overheard Ma tell Pa how Sarah always attracted attention in town. Modestly dressed, of course, Sarah kept her eyes down when Ma was watching. But Ma had caught her sliding glances toward the young men who always hovered nearby. She said they tripped over each other and their own feet to win the privilege of assisting Sarah and her in loading their purchases into the wagon.

Hands on hips, he repeated, "We appreciate the invite, but we'll not be going."

At her father's refusal of the invitation, Sarah rose abruptly and stood beside him with her hands balled at her sides. The pretty flush of excitement had dissolved leaving her face mottled. Joseph saw fire and ice in the eyes she fixed on their father.

Speaking slowly, she uttered one word at a time. "Pa, I have been chosen. Chosen. By the whole town." With her shoulders set in defiance, Joseph noted the resemblance between his father and sister. "At least, *I* should be allowed to go." Her chin trembled. "Please, Pa."

Joseph knew that to be challenged so directly by his headstrong daughter was an affront Pa had never suffered before this moment. He shot an aggrieved look at Ma. After a long moment, he said gruffly, "I'll need to think this through." He turned to Miss Allie. "Who'll be looking out for her there, if I give my say?"

"My parents and my older brother and Hannah and her brothers and I will be with her every minute," Miss Allie promised. "She can stay with us the night before."

Reaching into her basket, Mrs. Hanover pulled out a long scarf of purple, blue, and red plaid with thin black lines running though it. "I hope you willna mind, sir, but I looked up yer family name in my Grandda's book of the clans. Findlay is a sept of Clan Farquharson. These are your tartan colors and the motto on your crest is 'Fidelity and Fortitude.' I was going to make a rosette sash for Sarah to wear when she leads the rideout as the Cornet's Lass."

"Fidelity and Fortitude." Pa nodded and his face softened. "You're sayin' we're Scots?"

"Aye. There've been Scots in America since before the 1600s. Many people dinna ken where their ancestors come from. Most just assume they're English. The unlucky ones are."

Miss Allie added, "Give Hannah half a chance and she'll find Scot blood in just about anyone."

"My Da is a Master Draper and keeps a shop in New Edenton," Mrs. Hanover said. "People come from miles to buy his wares. They say, 'If you canna find it at MacGregor's, you probably dunna need it anyhow.' But what gives Da the most pleasure is seeing that any Scot who wants one has the tartan of his own clan. At no cost at all." She hesitated for a moment, but Miss Allie gave her a small nod. "If ye will, Mr. Findlay, I'd be pleased to send word and Da will bring one for you, and a sash for your missus, and a wee tartan for Joseph to wear to Guid Nychburris."

Joseph saw his father's face change. Pa's jaw worked and a mix of emotions dulled his eyes. *He's going to say no. To everything.* Joseph bit his cheeks to keep from crying.

Glancing from Sarah to Ma, Pa expelled a long breath. To Mrs. Hanover, he said, "That's a kind offer, but we won't be needing tartans. Joseph and I won't be going to your Gathering. You Hanover's have been kind to us, especially to Joseph, and I do appreciate it, but I won't bring my boy into a crowd of strangers to be gawked at and pitied. Joseph and I will keep our own company that night."

Sarah stood at his side, still as a portrait, as Joseph realized her name hadn't been included in the stay-at-homes.

"Sarah Sue can go," Pa said. "Martha will come along to keep an eye on her. I trust you all to keep your word to keep Sarah out of harm's way. Including any of her own making."

Sarah threw her arms around her father's neck, then stepped back quickly. His ears turned red and a deep blush crept up from his neck. Joseph had never seen them exchange affection.

"Ma!" She hugged her mother so vigorously she almost knocked her over. "Do you believe it? I'm . . . going to be the . . . the . . .?"

Mrs. Hanover and Miss Allie said, "The Cornet's Lass!"

And, Joseph thought, I am the pitied and gawked at.

Allie's voice penetrated Joseph's misery.

"Mr. Findlay," she was saying, "please think about coming and bringing Joseph. I was his age when we came here from Boston and I know what it's like when no one knows you or quite what to make of you."

The look he leveled at Miss Allie held no fire, only ice. "We keep to ourselves, Miss Hanover, so as not to trouble folk with havin' to figure out 'what to make of us.' "

"Luke!" Ma whirled on him. "Don't you go getting all bulled up. I'm sure the girl means no offense." When she turned to Miss Allie, her voice faltered. "It's just most folk don't understand about Joseph. You saw for yourself in town. Children . . . and others . . . have been cruel to him. To us."

"I know that," Miss Allie said. "And I'm sorry for it. But I'm certain if you give people a chance to know him, most will see Joseph's more *like* other boys than he is different."

"You're a smart young lady, Miss Hanover," Pa said. "I do believe you mean well." Gripping his coffee mug with both hands, he stared into it. "What you don't understand is that people don't bother to 'get to know' Joseph. They take one look at him and make up their minds. Then, they look away."

The heat from Joseph's suppressed tears failed to melt the ice encasing his heart.

It didn't bother him so much that they talked about him like he wasn't there, that happened all the time. What made his insides dry up was understanding that he'd never escape the cage of Pa's fear.

CHAPTER TWENTY-SIX

Doc and Albert arrived at Elysian Field earlier than usual to watch the Sluggers' practice game, as had many of the players. Like those men, they were excited and edgy. Games against nearby towns had been disappointing, mostly due to the lack of a competent pitcher. This practice promised to be different. Still, no one knew what to expect from their newest teammate, who had not yet arrived.

Will and Zeke's conversation stopped mid-sentence several times as their anxious gazes searched the trail from town. Ned Harper had agreed to be their hurler and they had great hopes as to the strength and accuracy of his pitching arm due to his prowess with a bow and arrow. Despite his longstanding reputation as a man of his word, wagers had been laid as to whether or not Ned would show up. The 'nots' outnumbered the 'woulds' three to one.

Resting a hand on his youngest son's shoulder, Doc Hanover told him how much President Abraham Lincoln had loved the game of baseball. Like the other men, Doc's eyes were fixed on the path, but talking while he waited soothed his nerves. He had abstained from the betting.

"With all the cares that great man carried, Mr. Lincoln made time for the game," he reminded Albert. They stood in the late morning shadow of one of the silver maple trees that edged the meadow. "Just south of the White

House, in the area they call The Ellipsis, the President had them construct a baseball field. Called it the 'White Lot.' "

"I know about the White Lot, Papa. You already told me."

"Sometimes," Doc went on, "to shed his burdens for a while, and you know he had many, the President would go out there to watch the young men play. Sometimes he'd join them. Those that had the good fortune to witness it said Lincoln would take a turn at bat, then stride around the bases with those long coattails of his flying behind him."

"And you already told me how folks say Mr. Lincoln was playing baseball when he heard the Republican Convention in Chicago wanted him for President." The boy imitated the deep baritone of a grown man, "He said, 'I'm glad to hear they're coming, but they'll have to wait a few minutes 'til I get my turn at bat.' "

One of Doc's most prized possessions was a framed 1860 Currier and Ives cartoon displayed in his study. Abe Lincoln stood on home plate with a bat resting on his shoulder as his three defeated rivals looked on. The caption read, "You must have a good bat and strike a fair ball to make a clean score and home run." The words Equal Rights and Free Territory were scrawled on the bat.

"And," Albert added, staring in the same direction as his father, "you don't need to worry about Ned. He said he'd be here and he will. "

Doc chuckled, gratified by his son's confidence. Not a man to be easily flustered, Doc had always taken pride in his ability to deal with critical matters—illness, injury, birth, death, maiming, mayhem, and worse—with a steady hand and heartbeat. So it interested him to observe himself unsettled about Ned Harper's first baseball practice.

Of course, there were reasons for his concern. The shared worry that Ned might not appear wasn't entirely unfounded. Too raw to tolerate either kindness or conflict for many months, he'd kept to his cabin, his dog, and the H&H horses for the most part. Doc feared what he sensed in Ned. He'd seen it before and knew it to be a threat as dangerous as the most virulent disease. Disinterest. Detachment. Melancholia. Life had hurt him and Ned had turned his back on life. And yet, Doc held onto the hopeful thought, he had agreed to come play baseball.

"He's here!" Albert hooted, as Ned emerged from the wooded path. He approached the group of waiting players and submitted to their handshakes and claps on the back with a pained, but not altogether displeased smile. "Ned's here!"

Mid-afternoon sun heavy on his back, hands jammed in his pockets, Ned had trudged through the trees and high grass on the hills behind Commerce Street to get to the baseball field. He'd left his horse at the livery, so he wouldn't be tempted to turn Trickster around and ride back up to the cabin at a gallop, now he chewed on the question as to why he'd agreed to play in the first place. Thinking back to that day at Hannah's table, he recalled he'd felt good teasing back and forth with Will—something they hadn't done in too long—and that he'd lost track of what it was they'd actually been talking about. He'd said yes to joining the Sluggers because he knew Will expected him to say no. Now he was stuck with it.

All the enthusiasm thrust upon him by Doc, Albert, Reverend Carstairs, and the players increased his ambivalence. He wished he'd fled when he could and, yet, was glad he hadn't. Elysian Field was a pretty place—a golden, short-grass meadow bordered by the greens and blues of spruce, ash, and silver maple trees. Bases set ninety feet apart formed a diamond in its center. Runners had worn paths in the grass between each base. A barrel of ail waited at third base where any player who got that far could take a dipper.

Grinning fit to split his face, Zeke slapped Ned on the back a third time and handed him the brown ball and a red plaid bow-tie that matched his own. The team had no uniforms and presented as what they were—a rag-tag bunch of ranchers and merchants. Hannah had sewn them all red or blue bow-ties from scraps of tartan wool to give them a semblance of cohesion. For practice games, the Sluggers divided into two sides, one red, the other blue.

With a nod toward the waiting batter, Zeke said, "Show us what you've got, Cowboy. Will says you haven't played before, but don't worry about that. I'm your catcher, just aim where I show you and you'll do fine. Pretend I'm a big, buck deer."

Ned felt a twinge of conscience about saying he hadn't played before. In his banter with Will he'd implied he hadn't played baseball as a boy because the orphaned Harper brothers hadn't had time for such games. That was true, as far as it went.

Zeke took his place behind home plate with the Reverend, still in his clerical collar, umpiring behind him. Striding to the pitcher's mound, Ned displayed more confidence than he felt. Once there, he wrapped his fingers around the horsehide sphere and tapped it against his palm. The ball weighed heavy in his hand, familiar and unfamiliar in his grasp. His heart thudded, not so much from nerves, as from the unexpected and unwelcome memories the feel of the ball brought back. Intruding images blurred his vision. Blinking them away, he lifted his cap and wiped sweat from his forehead. He rotated his shoulder, but his back and neck wouldn't relax. To loosen his arm, he lobbed a few wobbly pitches across the plate into the catcher's waiting hands.

Drawing a deep breath and exhaling slowly, Ned signaled the first batter to step to the plate. He sensed every eye upon him, bright with hope and sharp with expectations. Zeke mimed a hunter drawing a bow, then crouched behind the plate. He punched his fist into his hand to indicate where Ned should aim. The batter smoothed his drooping mustache, adjusted his blue plaid bowtie, and leaned forward waggling the bat shoulder high. Ned studied him, then raised his arm, reared back on one foot, and threw as hard and straight as he could. The ball went so high and wide that Zeke had to shove the Reverend out of the way with one hand and leap to catch it with the other.

Ned's next pitch was low and inside causing the batter to scissor his paunchy body and jump back to avoid getting hit. The next was over his head, the one after that behind him.

"Dammit, Cowboy," Zeke groused. With a glare that he divided between Ned and the Reverend, he dug six cents out of his pocket and handed it to the preacher.

After turning his back on the plate to settle his nerves, Ned delivered a mediocre pitch straight down the middle. The batter swung hard and nicked a piece of it, lofting a pop fly easily caught by the second-baseman. After three more pitches as wild as his first two, the alarmed look Zeke shot Will steadied Ned. Holding the ball close to his chest with both hands, he focused on the exact spot he wanted it to go, wound up, and reared back to throw. This time he drilled the pitch toward the plate. The hiss of the ball hurtling toward the catcher made Ned smile.

His smile broadened when the striker swung with all his strength and missed. Zeke—accustomed to the gentler lobs of his teammates—grinned and swore, rubbing his stinging hand against his thigh. "Dammit, Cowboy," he exclaimed with admiration as he pulled more change from his pocket. "Now, that was worth the six damned cents!"

"Twelve," the Reverend corrected him, holding out his hand.

After two more swings and misses, the disgruntled striker spat and made his way back to the bench. The next batter took his stance, bat ready, eyes fixed on Ned. After two roundhouse swings that missed the ball that whizzed by, he walloped the next in a clothesline drive to right field and sped to first base.

At the crack of the bat hitting the ball, Ned froze.

His heart all but stopped with fear. The sound of horsehide colliding with wood hurtled him back in time. Paralyzed, he waited for the approach of gunfire. When none came, he swallowed the bile that rose in his throat. What he hadn't mentioned to Will was that in the army soldiers—and drummer boys—had played baseball to while away the hours of boredom and anxiety between skirmishes. On sunny, languid days, just like this one, they played at being as carefree as they'd been before the war.

This isn't Spotsylvania, Ned told himself, desperate to shake off the spell. Not a battle. This is Solace Springs. Solace Springs, Colorado Territory. This is a baseball game.

Generals had instructed commanding officers to encourage baseball in their camps to improve morale. "The game promotes good health and keeps the mind off the war," they were told. Every encampment and most Companies kept a baseball pattern from which they made their own balls. Ned had learned to wind yarn around a walnut, cut the horsehide to fit around it tightly, and to sew it up to make an acceptable baseball. Soldiers cut oak limbs to carve into bats. The physical activity eased tension and, Ned had discovered, was more fun than playing cards, the only other diversion available. Cheers and laughter replaced the sounds of battle on bloodless fields, but many a game had been cut short by the gut-loosening staccato of advancing rifle fire. Sometimes, cannons thundered in the distance and acrid smoke roiled the air. Sometimes, the ground shook with chaos, terror, and death.

When his vision cleared, Ned saw Doc take a step toward him. Waving him away, he turned toward the right fielder and caught the ball he chucked to him. Shake it off, he told himself. This is Solace Springs. That's Zeke Foster gawking at you and all he's afraid of is that you won't hurl the ball hard enough.

From that moment, Ned willed away the past. His pitches burned toward the plate fast, ferocious, and more accurate. He struck out most batters and allowed insignificant hits to others. Playing baseball just might turn out to be all right, he thought. And he hadn't even thrown his skew ball yet.

He'd save that until Will came to bat. In the army, he'd learned to throw an elusive pitch by placing his fingers on the ball in such a way that it arched and dipped, instead of going straight. Some called it an illusion, slight of hand that baffled batters and had them flailing at pitches they thought were doing one thing until, at the last moment, they did another. Illusion or not, the ball almost always got swung at and missed.

The Sluggers and their new hurler played until it was too dark to see. Each team member demanded a turn—and then another—to try their bat against the impossible curving pitch and hone their skills at hitting fast balls they barely saw coming.

Exhausted and satisfied from the day's exertions—and the jollification that followed at the Tongue Oil Saloon— Ned returned to his cabin late that night and poured himself a cup of whiskey. He'd done what Will had asked of him and the Sluggers would be a better team for it. Just as baseball had served as a distraction during the war, it would be a diversion now and help pass the time until autumn.

With Cloud at his feet, he relaxed into one of the wicker chairs on the porch and looked out at the dense and endless woods that sloped in every direction. The shadow play of clouds backlit by the moon gave the trees shape and substance in the darkness. Soon enough autumn would strip them bare, then ice and snow would clothe them for winter.

He'd worked it all out in his mind and attained a kind of peace within himself. By mid-October, he'd have finished the cabin, bought his up-proved land outright and deeded it to Will, schooled the young mustangs, Trouble and Sugarplum, as best he could, and seen the Sluggers through their much anticipated game against the Fountain City Nine. He thought of a few other things he'd need to see to. He'd prepare a winter's worth of pemmican for Horace Cuthbert, give the finest doeskin he'd ever tanned to Red Moon, and finish all the odds and ends that needed doing around the homestead.

Closing his eyes, he pictured Becky standing in a green and gold meadow with her dark hair loose and Benjamin nestled in her arms, both bright-eyed and smiling in the sun, sweet as ever.

Why wait? he asked himself, sipping his whiskey. Fall was just the time to take that long walk into the woods.

CHAPTER TWENTY-SEVEN

Excitement in Solace Springs spread as quick as white-topped weeds in anticipation of Hannah and Will Hanover's annual Scottish *ceilidh*—celebration—of Guid Nychburris. Some folks looked forward to the singing and dancing and stories, some to the shared food and free-flowing ale, others to the Highland Games and sheep dog trials. Some folks looked forward to the singing and dancing and stories, some to the shared food and free-flowing ale, others to the Highland Games and dog trials.

People had been arriving for days. Those that had no relations nearby set up camp on the outskirts of the H & H Ranch. Glowing cook-fires dotted the twilight like giant fireflies, while the aroma of woodsmoke and roasting meats flavored the evening breeze.

At dusk on the eve of the Gathering, Ned rode back from escorting the H & H livestock to the upper pastures—away from the coming commotion—relieved to be finished with the last job he'd been called upon to do. From a hill overlooking the house and stable, he saw Will, along with Hannah's younger brothers Hamish and Aidan, arrange bales of hay around a large, dirt circle they'd raked smooth in readiness for the dancing. Slowing Trickster to a walk, he watched the men disappear into the stable to make a quiet place for sleepy children to listen to Grandda Fergus's tales.

Try as he might, Ned couldn't shake the dread that knotted his insides. He had to face Hannah and knew she wouldn't like what he had to say. When he reached the cleared circle, he set his horse free to graze and took a seat on one of the bales. Cicadas rasped their shrill one-note song and green lightning bugs twinkled between nearby branches. By this time tomorrow, the serenity of the place would be disrupted by scores of visitors eager to join in the Gathering and the Frolic to follow on the next night. That thought hardened Ned's resolve. Head bowed, he leaned forward, hands clasped tight in front of him.

When Hannah sat down next to him, he greeted her with a strained smile. The brim of his hat cast his eyes in shadow. Looking straight ahead, he kept his focus on a stand of trees in the distance. "I can't."

"Aye, ye can," she told him firmly, locking her fingers in his. "It's time, Ned. It's been almost two years."

Last summer, several months after Becky died, he'd stayed away from the Gathering. Will had assured him Hannah understood. It was no different for Ned this year, but all the excuses he thought of tasted like lies. The truth, he decided, was the only thing that couldn't be argued with. "I don't want to."

"And why is that?"

He blinked at her ruthlessness.

Because I don't want to stand in the glow of a bonfire without my arms wrapped around her. I don't want to look for her flying dark hair and laughing eyes and just see other girls swinging on the arms of other men.

Eyes on his boots, he thought, I don't want to be here. Anywhere . . . without her. And then realized he'd said the words out loud

When Hannah's long silence drew his gaze back to her, he saw she'd paled. Her small hand gripped his with such strength his fingers ached. "Ye don't want to *be here*? What are ye sayin', Ned?" She stared into his eyes and, he was certain, saw everything. "Yer surely not tellin' me ye have thoughts to . . . ?" She drew back and shook her head. "No. Ye must not. Ye must never even think such a thing." Anguish flattened her features. "*Mo charaid*, have yer friends all failed ye so badly?"

Her expression sank teeth into his soul. He knew then that he was trapped in a life he didn't want as surely as if he'd stepped into one of those cruel contraptions Horace sold in his store. Hannah had made him understand that if he walked into the woods and never came out—as everything in him wanted to do—his friends would more than grieve. They would blame themselves.

Though the loss of hope left him hollow, he manufactured the teasing grin he knew would reassure her. "Well, aren't you the gloomy Scot," he said. "I'm just sayin' I don't like the idea of showing up at this shindig of yours."

"Yer sure that's it?"

"Sure as a goose goes barefoot." The effort to deceive her cost him.

"I'm going to believe ye because I must."

"Good."

She squeezed his hands and released them. "Last year I kent it was too soon and didna press, did I? Now it's time and I *will* push ye. And shove. And kick, if I have to—on Becky's behalf. Ye know what she'd say about you sulking up in that cabin all by yourself when everyone else is down here dancing."

He shot Hannah a warning look.

"She'd tell ye this: 'It's been long enough, Ned Harper, now stop going about lookin' like someone licked all the red off your candy and get on with livin'!' "

The air left his lungs. She had mimicked Becky's tone, and words, and inflection. Flawlessly. When he could breathe, he said, "That was low, Hannah." He was surprised to find himself fighting a smile. "Even for you."

"So ye'll come."

He grimaced and shook his head. "I'll think about it."

She stood, wrapped her plaid shawl tighter around her shoulders, then sat down again. "There is something else."

The compassion in her eyes and the gentleness of her smile terrified him. "There better not be."

"I'll be riding Angel in the procession," she said. "Like I did last year, and like Becky did all the years before. You and Trickster must be at our side."

Neither his face nor his body gave away how hard the unexpected blow hit him. Hannah seemed intent on making his already impossible life more difficult. Flattening his hands on the hay at his sides, he steadied himself. *Angel.* Three days after Becky's death, he'd taken her golden palomino mare to Hannah, certain it was what Becky would have wanted. He hadn't dismounted from Trickster and hadn't said a word when he handed her the reins.

Swinging his black stallion around, he'd ridden off. No one had seen him for weeks after that.

Hannah rested a hand on his shoulder. When he didn't shrug it off, she left it there.

"Becky taught that sweet horse to love to show off in a parade," she reminded him. "She trained Angel to prance and hold her head high and toss that white mane of hers. Ye know better than anyone they'd both be heartbroken if her Angel had to watch the rideout from a pasture."

Ned kept his eyes fixed on the darkening horizon.

"We'll ride tall and proud," Hannah said, "right behind the Cornet and Cornet's Lass. Me and bonnie Angel prancing in the middle, you and Will on your braw stallions strutting along on either side of us." Her voice was little more than a whisper. "If we don't do it, Ned, all our hearts will stay in pieces and our dear Becky will be grievin' harder for us than we are for her."

As usual, Hannah was right. He understood then that his life would be about enduring traps he couldn't seem to free himself from. "I'll think about it."

"There's something else." Hannah gave no indication she saw the tensing of his shoulders as he braced himself for yet another blow. "If I haven't yet convinced ye to come, this is sure to do it."

Before he could protest that he'd heard about as much as he could take, the mischief in her eyes stopped him.

"Those casks ye see lined up by the side of the house?" She raised a russet brow in that direction. "They were sent over by Doc. He doesna ken what he's done."

Ned stared at the innocent-appearing barrels. "Ale?"

"Not just ale, laddie." Leaning forward, she murmured in his ear, "Wee heavy ale. Eighty-shilling ale."

Ned knew exactly what poor, unsuspecting Doc had done. Distracted from his anguish, he let a slow smile make its way to his eyes. "For that," he said, feigning surrender, "I'll come."

After Hannah disappeared into the house, he lingered on the bale of hay to watch day merge into night. The sun lost, the moon found. Stars too far out of reach to matter. Dusk blurs everything, he thought.

He'd do what he could to make peace with living in the twilight that had become his life.

The Findlays were divided in their feelings about the Gathering. Sarah and Martha flew about their tasks flushed with excitement, hardly able to breathe with the anticipation of spending the night at South Slope, dining in the formal dining room—served by servants!—and by all that would follow the next day for the chosen Cornet's Lass. They'd agreed it wouldn't do to let on about the teal silk dress, fearing it might give Pa reason to change his mind.

Even from her lofty cloud of fantasy, Sarah felt a pang of compassion for her bereft, earthbound brother who so wanted to go, but was to be kept at home to protect him from the cruelty of strangers.

When the women climbed into the buckboard, Pa watched them ride away in flat-eyed silence.

Joseph had taken to his bed before sunset and lay facing the wall.

CHAPTER TWENTY-EIGHT

Balefires—wild and pagan—blazed against the blackness of the night, one in the center of the yard and others dotting hillsides in the distance. The first night of the Gathering, a group of Scots arrived from as far as Edenton. Along with Doc and Will Hanover, Ned joined the knot of men clustered around the fire sipping whiskey—an easy group that would require nothing more of him than that he raise his glass to their toasts. Rounds of "Slinte Mhath!" and "Pour me another wee dram!" accompanied the crackle of burning mountain ash branches.

Although not a Scot himself, Doc had a keen appreciation for the culture. Ned wasn't surprised when the doctor, a man of science in a field where exact measurements were crucial, asked a rare direct question of Hugh MacGregor. "Just how much liquor is actually in a dram?"

After a chorus of hearty laughs died down, Hannah's father chuckled, "Och, laddie! How much is a dram?" Lifting his glass, he turned it to catch the flicker of firelight in its golden contents. "A dram, my friend, is always the size of the heart of the man who's pouring it."

The keening of a single bagpipe being tuned and the rhythmic thrum-thrump of Aidan testing his drum drew everyone to the bonfire. Talk and laughter quieted, then ceased.

Hamish MacGregor lifted his voice in a heart-wrenching Scottish ballad about war, betrayal, love, and longing:

There shall I visit the place of my birth
They'll give me a welcome the warmest on earth
So loving and kind, full of music and mirth
The sweet-sounding language of home.
There shall I gaze on the mountains again.
On the fields, and the hills, and the birds in the glen
With people of courage beyond human ken!
In the haunts of the deer I will roam.

Many eyes shone with tears, as the Scots joined in the soulful chorus:

Hail to the mountains with summits of blue!
To the glens with their meadows of sunshine and dew,
To the women and men ever constant and true,
Ever ready to welcome me home!

Hamish's sweet tenor, the plaintive wail of Hugh's bagpipes, and the solemn heartbeat of Aidan's bodhrans, resonated with Ned's heavy spirit. Moving away from the others, Ned leaned against the outer wall of the stable, a solitary shadow in the shadows, sipping the 'wee heavy ale' that numbed his grief. Two years ago he'd stood behind Becky with his arms wrapped around her, her head resting on his chest. Content that night in a way he'd never believed possible, Ned had been certain he'd never be alone again.

Even though he knew he should move back toward the light and warmth and join his friends—Will, Hannah, and Allie, with Sarah Findlay at her side stood together near the fire—his legs wouldn't obey him. As the bagpipe moaned the first poignant notes of the next ballad, Ned saw Hannah's eyes widen and her hand go to her throat. Her stricken gaze found his. "I'm sorry . . ." she mouthed to him.

At first, Ned was perplexed by her distress. Soon, he understood.

"How full of sorrow am I . . . Oh," sang Hamish, his clear voice rising and falling like waves lapping at a desolate shore. "Oh, I would follow thee. Oh." From a previous Gathering, Ned recognized the words of *Allain Duinn*—the haunting lament of a young woman whose lover has been lost at sea and who will soon perish herself from a broken heart: "Oh! I . . . would follow thee . . . Oh . . ."

As much as the words and melody tore at his heart, they also eased it. Becky, Ned thought with an inward smile and a keen awareness of her presence, you were always a tease when you had something important to say.

He remembered a time she had done just that a few years ago.

Ned had always risen before dawn to build a fire in the cabin's hearth, and was glad to do it. Becky hated going from the warmth of their feather bed to the toe-numbing cold of winter mornings. Most days, she snuggled into the warm spot he left and pulled the comforter up to her chin to watch him. Making a show of shivering and rubbing his hands together, he would slide back under the covers and warm himself with her body. So, when he'd awakened one morning to find her standing barefoot in the center of the dark and freezing room in her flannel nightdress, frowning and biting the corner of her lip, he'd sat up alarmed.

"Becky?"

Lifting her hand, she made a gesture indicating their snug home was the source of her displeasure. "I just don't know what we're going to do."

Although she'd never said so, or even hinted at it, Ned had feared the day might come when Becky would no longer be content to live up in the hills away from everything. She had assured him that their simple life suited her. The serenity of trees and brooks, the solitude of their cozy cabin. One evening, as they sat side by side on the porch watching the setting sun paint the clouds, she had taken his hand and laced her fingers through his.

"Thank you for all this, Ned Harper." Then, as if concerned he might shy from the emotion in her eyes, she'd added, "I'm about as happy as a tick on a fat dog up here with you and my National Excelsior Stove."

In the year since their marriage, she'd made the arduous ride to and from the school house in all kinds of weather without complaint. She and her palomino mare had found—or, Ned suspected—devised their own shortcut through the woods, ignoring his protests regarding their safety.

On that icy morning, she'd repeated, "I just don't know what we're going to do."

Certain what he'd feared had come to pass, he said, "You know I can't see living in town." He had made sure she understood that before he'd asked her to share his life. "But if you want to move closer, I'll build you and that stove of yours a place down in the foothills where my land meets up with Will's."

"Don't be silly!" She slipped into bed beside him and gently pushed him back against the pillows. "I don't want to live anyplace but right here. Ever." Laying her head in the hollow of his shoulder, she tucked her cold feet under his legs. He wrapped his arms around her and breathed in the scents of lavender oil, Castile soap, and woodsmoke in hair. In a sleepy voice, she murmured, "I just can't think where we're going to put the cradle."

Everything in him—blood, heart, breath—went still.

When he didn't respond, she raised up on one elbow and studied his face, eyes shining. "It's okay, isn't it?" she'd asked. "About our baby? You're pleased, aren't you?"

After a moment, he'd managed a nod, his throat too thick to speak.

"I thought you might be," she said.

First, she'd kissed his lips, then the tear at the corner of his eye.

CHAPTER TWENTY-NINE

The morning after the first night of the Gathering, Ned rose in the dark and donned his battered Stetson and boots. Having refused repeated offers of a kilt, he draped the blue, black, and red tartan Hugh MacGregor had gifted him years ago over his cotton shirt. He'd never given a thought to the origins of his family name and been surprised when Hannah informed him Harper was Scottish and a sept within Clan Buchannan. Everyone had agreed the motto on his crest suited him. Sauvis et Fortis: Pleasant and Strong.

Despite his assurance to Hannah, he contemplated escape as he and Trickster trotted up to take their places alongside her and Angel—Becky's Angel—at the rideout. The sight of the mare golden in the dawn light made his eyes burn. As his resolution began to falter, the pretty palomino pranced closer, bumped his knee, and gave him a long, knowing look.

When the horse lifted her graceful neck and tossed her creamy mane, his heart eased. He could hear Becky say, "See, Ned? Angel understands. If you love me, you must live."

I understand, Ned thought. But understanding doesn't make it so.

Despite his misgivings, Ned had to admit that the rideout, which began at sunrise, was as always a colorful affair.

Hannah had told him that it was with fierce pride, the Scots donned their once forbidden kilts and tartans and attached plaid flashes to their white Highland hose. In her annual telling of the events that had driven Malcomb MacGregor to bring his family away from Scotland, Hannah's tone always turned defiant when she explained the Dress Act of 1746. "After Culloden, 'twas decreed 'any person caught wearing the plaid, kilt, trews, or shoulder belts, tartans or parti-colored stuffs, would be imprisoned for six months for the first offense, and on second conviction be transported for seven years.' And," she would pause here, as her grandda had done, to let the outrage sink in, "speaking the Gaelic? That could get ye hanged by the neck until dead!"

On this morning, some riders sat their horses, some walked. Bagpipes tuned softly, then swelled with the rousing call of pipes and drums to ride-out. Resplendent in formal Highland regalia, Hugh MacGregor stood on a small platform near the front and called out the clans as they passed.

"Are the Fosters here?"

Zeke, the proud Coronet with his lovely Lass at his side, rode forward' "We're here!"

"Are the MacGregors here?"

"Aye!" Hannah and her brothers shouted, marching their mounts to the fore, with Hamish waving a banner emblazoned with their clan crest—a lion's head, crowned—and their motto: Royal is my Race. "The MacGregors are here!"

"Are the Harpers of clan Buchanan here?"

Ned raised an arm high over his head and Trickster stepped forward, snorting and shaking his black mane. "The Harpers are here!"

Hugh called the Galbraith's, MacCrains, Hoggs, Hopes, and Campbells to raise their voices and banners and join the procession. The Adairs, Olliphants, and Sinclairs followed, bellowing their "Ayes!"

In the hoarse roar of a Highland chieftain, Hugh called the clan bringing up the rear: "Are the Abernathys here?"

Ned couldn't help but smile at the answering call. Wearing their red, green, and purple tartans—along with their feathers and medicine bags—Heck, Red Moon, their five daughters and assorted sons-in-law and grandchildren advanced their pinto horses to join the others. Amid hoots, ululations, and Indian war cries Heck and his family rode forward. "The Abernathys are here!"

Heck had been dumbfounded when Hannah informed him that, according to her book of clans, the Abernathys were Scots. The old rancher and his family had embraced this unexpected addition to their heritage with gusto.

They did however alter the clan motto from 'Christo Salus' to 'Great Spirit Salus.'

Plaid tartan furled around his shoulders, Hugh raised his arm straight up, then dropped it, signaling the rideout to commence. Carrying the beribboned standard and leading the way was the proud Cornet, Zeke Foster. The dapper barber sat tall in the saddle wearing his Sunday suit and felt derby hat. His collar-length brown hair was parted in the middle and doorknocker whiskers—a meticulous chin beard that encircled his mouth to join a full moustache—framed his wide grin.

After many years of disappointment, he'd finally been elected Cornet—with the help of several rounds of stiff drinks bought by Ned and Will and most of the baseball team who then proceeded to stuff the ballot box at the saloon. At his side rode Sarah Findlay, the lovely Cornet's Lass luminous in her teal silk dress, with a rosette tartan pinned at the shoulder, and a tiara of summer flowers. Despite Zeke's oft proclaimed adoration for her, Ned was irritated to see that Sarah's reactions to him were perfunctory. Her gaze searched among the other riders and, to Ned's further dismay, brightened only when it found him. The first time he caught her looking at his way, he lifted the brim of his hat. After that, he took no notice of her.

When Hannah had come to Solace Springs as Will's new bride, she'd held the first of her annual Scottish Gatherings. She'd explained to Ned and her new family that her notion of a rideout—which had originated in Scotland in lawless and battle-strewn times to identify property boundaries and discourage thieving—was a condensed version of the time-honored Selkirk Common Riding. Every year, the Cornet's Chase began uphill and ended at a tent where Maggie MacGregor and Jane Hanover served the riders curds and cream—soordook—for refreshment. Restored, they continued to trot around the outer perimeter of the ranch, until they arrived at the second stop—the Sneeshin or Scottish Snuffing.

Traditionally, snuff was dispensed by the town Song Singer on these occasions. At the H&H, the riders were met by Hamish, who offered them a pinch from his father's old horned mull which was carved in the shape of a chambered nautilus. High-toast snuff—definitively Scottish—was believed to cure such ills as toothache, catarrh, and naughty breath.

Lustily singing one of the twenty-four rousing verses from *Teribus,* Hamish greeted each group of riders with a different stanza. To his sister and her friends he sang:

> Down they threw their bows and arrows,
> Drew their swords like veteran heroes,
> Charged their foes with native valor,
> Routed them and took their colors!

Neither Ned, Will, nor Hannah had ever developed a liking for snuff, but at the Gatherings they engaged in the ritual to humor Hugh. After snorting a pinch of the acrid ground tobacco leaves and stems, Hannah—as always—shuddered and blew her nose into her sleeve, Will paled and broke into a sweat, and, eyes watering, Ned sneezed and rasped irritably, "My head's buzzin' like a blue-assed fly.!"

Every year the friends agreed they would not partake again, and every year—as Becky, who adamantly refused to join in, had predicted—they always did.

At the third and final stop, still before breakfast, Doc served the riders generous cups of rum and milk to fortify them for the Highland Games. Ned was grateful he'd taken Hugh's definition of a dram to heart.

When the rideout was over, the Games began.

Heck Abernathy's son-in-law, Two Trees—named for the powerful legs he'd been born with—always drew the largest crowd. Bronze skin shining in the noonday sun, he had won every Caber Toss contest since the first time he entered. The Indian—who defeated burly Scots outweighing him by half, sometimes more—just had a knack for lifting a shaved Scot's Pine trunk twice his height and heaving it farther than any other man there.

Ned's sport at the Games was the Hammer Throw. After returning from the rideout, he visited the food tables and ale kegs and was about to head to the meadow where the event would take place following the Caber Toss. Instead, he found himself engaged in a heated dispute with Doc—surrounded by several members of the Solace Springs Sluggers—about the wisdom of risking injury to his pitching arm. He was baffled to discover there seemed to be some confusion about the ownership of the arm in question. Ned was convinced it was his; the Sluggers believed it belonged to their hurler, thus making it the property of the baseball team. Ned's pitching had exceeded their expectations of his value to them. With their hopes of defeating the Fountain City Nine riding on that arm, and the man attached to it, the Sluggers felt compelled to protect it.

"I wouldn't do it if I didn't think it was safe," Ned assured them.

Squinting into the noon sunshine, Doc—the team's self-proclaimed Number One Crank—fixed Ned with a pleading gaze. "You thinking something is safe doesn't give me much reassurance."

Hannah had introduced Ned to the Hammer Throw years ago. "It goes back centuries to when King Edward I of England forbade Scots to possess any kind of weapon during the Wars of Scottish Independence," she'd explained. "But, the canny Highlanders found a secret way to do their military training, to build up their strength, and hone their skills. They practiced throwing a sixteen-pound metal ball, attached to a four-foot long stick, as far as they could."

"There is no danger," Ned insisted to Doc with a mix of amusement and budding exasperation. He'd found something to enjoy about the day and was looking forward to the competition. "It's all about speed and balance."

He'd easily mastered the throwing motion that involved two overhead swings from a stationary position, then three or four rotations of his body using a heel-toe movement of the foot, while swinging the hammer overhead. The ball moved in a circular path, increasing in velocity with each turn, until he released it. Safe and simple. He'd thrown the hammer dozens of times without mishap, occasionally winning the competition.

Hoping for support, Ned turned to Will, who would be competing against him in the Throw. "Ned's right," his rival concurred with an amicable grin. "Not much danger he'll hurt his arm. More likely, he'll sprain an ankle."

Despite his best efforts, Zeke could not keep Sarah all to himself. Maude Mary hovered at her side most of the day, her self-proclaimed lady-in-waiting. The barber left his comely, if somewhat dour, Lass ensconced in a chair he'd borrowed from Mrs. Hanover's parlor, beneath the shade of a tree while he hurried to the kitchen to beg sweets and savories for her. When he returned, plate piled high, he found her surrounded by a half-dozen young men who plied her with tongue-tied compliments along with cups of cider, spruce beer, or buttermilk.

Zeke almost came to blows with a fellow he heard tell Sarah, "If you were a flower, Miss Sarah, I would surely pick you."

At sunset, the ceilidh drew to a close. Many of the older Scots packed up their plaids and sheep dogs and set out for home. A new undercurrent of excitement thrummed through the air. More town folk and visitors arrived to join in the Frolic to come. They brought food to share and left their side-arms and spurs at the gate.

A circle of lanterns strung between posts illuminated the make-shift dance floor and the animated panorama of people of all ages waiting for the first lively quadrille to begin. The swirl of skirts, the exchange of shy smiles, the decorous touches of hands and elbows, set Allie's heart racing with anticipation. For an instant, she felt Becky must be among them, her foot already tapping to the music. The light-hearted notion quickly turned to stone in her chest. She wondered what it must cost Ned to be here. The lump in her own throat told her. Searching the growing crowd, she saw him standing just outside the cleared dance circle.

Emboldened by the tin cup of spruce beer in her hand—and the unaccustomed daring a few sips had bestowed—Allie approached him. The afternoon they'd spent berry-picking, which should have made her more at ease in his presence, had, in fact, had the opposite effect. It troubled her that she could not fathom why. As the musicians tuned their fiddles, banjoes, and mouth organs, she watched the play of lantern light on his face and tried to read his expression. Closed and guarded summed it up. To settle her shyness, she took a deeper swallow of the mild beer.

When she reached his side, Ned ducked his head in greeting and his expression brightened. With a raised brow, he teased. "Spruce beer, Boston?"

Lifting her cup in a toast, she grinned and took another sip. She hadn't participated in the rideout, but had watched from the sidelines. She'd seen the effort it had taken Ned to join Hannah and Will—and Angel—by the too-straight set of his shoulders, the tightness of his jaw.

Doc had taught her that a statement might encourage more openness than a question and that stating the obvious might unlock closed off emotions. Or not. "It must be hard for you to be here."

He finished what was left in his cup—not spruce beer, she was certain. "It was," he admitted. "Hannah scolded me out of it."

Allie sighed, she'd been the recipient of many such scoldings herself. "My goodsister does have the knack for that." At that Sunday supper at South Slope, Ned had assured her and her family he wanted people to talk about Becky, to remember her. She decided to take him at his word, no matter the risk. This," she lifted her hand in a gesture encompassing the festivities, "this all reminds me of Becky. I suppose it always will . . ." Her voice faltered and she sensed Ned had gone still and alert in a way that made her question the wisdom of continuing. "I'm sorry."

He gave her a slow, solemn smile. "Don't ever be sorry for talking about Becky."

"You're sure?" She waited for his nod before saying, "Then, tell me if I remember this right. You hardly knew Miss Becky Saunders the year you bought one of Hugh MacGregor's awful haggises at the Gathering and dared her to eat it." His silence, and the odd expression that accompanied it, caused Allie's insides to shrink. "I'm sorry."

"There you go again, bein' sorry for no reason." He angled his shoulder to face her. "You really remember that?"

"Of course I do." The bit of light that had appeared in his eyes was a beacon that led her to continue. "I was thirteen-years-old and Miss Becky's prize pupil, if I must remind you. I knew she'd never back down from a challenge." Allie had never tried the delicacy herself. A traditional staple of Scottish gatherings—haggis was not much appreciated by the general public. Hannah's father always prepared two and donated them to the

Ladies Benevolent Society bake sale to raffle. Every year, the novelty evoked hilarity, grimaces of disgust, and fetched a good price.

Allie had watched her beloved young schoolmarm eat—at Ned's amused urging—a hearty portion of the haggis—a dish made of sheep's heart, lungs, and liver, mixed with oatmeal, suet, spices, salt and stock, encased in the sheep's stomach, then boiled. Becky had washed the offal down with several cups of spruce beer and then demanded Ned find her a cup of geneva to settle her stomach.

"Did you not know that about her?" she asked.

"That she loved a dare? Not back then," Ned admitted. "I do now."

"You also already know that Becky and I shared a few secrets." Allie hoped what she was about to reveal would cheer him, keep the warmth in his eyes. "This one isn't quite as scandalous as sneaking into my father's study to read *Gray's Anatomy* or as tasty as her secret ingredient to add to pemmican, but I do believe I might know something you may not."

For a moment, Allie feared she'd gone too far. Ned seemed to draw inward, until a twitch played at the corner of his mouth. "You've got my attention, Boston."

At that Gathering years ago, she'd witnessed Ned and Becky discover each other. Close to Maude Mary's age at the time, Allie had marked curiosity about such matters. "Did you ever wonder what it was about you that got *her* attention?"

Ned's brow furrowed. "I always thought it was the haggis."

"It was not the haggis."

"Boston."

A tightening around his eyes told her this conversation had become more than light-hearted banter for him. She understood that a gift from Becky had been left in her safe-keeping, unopened. With a pang of sadness, Allie felt the weight of the responsibility she carried.

Ned's eyes locked on hers.

"That night, Hannah caught Becky watching you at the dance and teased her," Allie said. "You know how Hannah can be." He didn't nod or blink. "Of course, neither of them knew or cared one bit that I was right there, hanging on their every word. Hannah told Becky, 'Wee Ned Harper is a braw and canty lad and he surely does draw the eye, does he not?' Becky gave her a look. You know that look. Then, she tossed her head and said, 'He does, maybe, but it's not those nice shoulders or pretty eyes I'm looking at.' "

Allie paused, flustered by her own words. She hoped the flickers of lantern light hid the warmth she was certain reddened her cheeks. Encouraged by a crinkling at the corner of the eyes in question, she continued. "Becky told Hannah: 'What draws my eye to Mr. Harper is that kerchief tied on his arm.' "

Ned laughed. Hard and long.

Will had told Allie that much to everyone's surprise, most of all his own, Ned had discovered he loved to dance. After Red Moon shamed him into giving up hard drinking and brawling, he'd found little to entertain him in sleepy Solace Springs. As restlessness and boredom were about to seduce him back to his old vices, Will had begged him and Zeke to come to a Frolic in a neighboring town. With much reluctance, Ned had agreed to go to one only if Will and Zeke agreed they could leave early. They'd 'bowed to their partners, promenaded south, and swung their pretty girls round and round' for most of the night. After that, once a month, sometimes more, the three young men rode for hours or days to attend a dance, 'kick up some dust,' and meet girls.

"The kerchief?" Ned echoed.

"The blue one."

Those friendly barn dances offered little opportunity for misadventure. Fighting was forbidden, for the most part, and guns and spurs had to be surrendered at the door. Ned developed a passion for the quadrille, Will had told Allie. And the mazurka. And the polka. And, under the right circumstances, the waltz. When the music began, Ned was often the first to take the floor. There were times when there were ten men to every girl at a Frolic, so a fellow willing to take the woman's part and dance with other men 'heifer-branded' himself by tying a kerchief to one arm. Ned never lacked for partners.

For a moment, he stared into his empty cup. "I didn't know that."

"I thought you'd want to. It's . . ."

"It's Becky." Ned's fingers went to the dark blue scarf tied just above his elbow. Raising his eyes to Allie's, he smiled. "Thanks for telling me."

A surge of warmth suffused her body. She didn't know if her heart was beating too fast or if it had stopped entirely. Or why. Taking a half step back, she chided herself for her silliness. What she had seen in his eyes was nothing more than gratitude for giving him something new to treasure about Becky. That was all he could feel, as Hannah had warned her, all he might ever be able to feel. What Allie felt for him was surely nothing more than sympathy.

At that moment, Sarah Findlay appeared between them.

Allie had observed the Cornet's Lass encircled by a group of admirers. Zeke—glum and steadfast—stood anchored at her side with adoring Maude Mary at her elbow being schooled in the art of coquetry. It appeared Sarah had deserted the men to cross the dance floor with Allie's sister hurrying after her.

"The music's about to begin, Mr. Harper," Sarah said, tilting her head just so to look up at him from beneath lowered lashes. "And I just cannot decide who I should give my first dance to."

Allie felt Ned stiffen at her side. Ignoring Sarah, his gaze riveted on something across the circle. Following his line of sight, Allie saw nothing unusual. In the next instant, she watched his back disappear as he strode through the waiting dancers.

Smoothing the folds of her dress, Sarah bit her lip. With a bewildered expression, she turned to Allie. "Do you suppose he's gone to ask someone else to dance?"

Stirred by her own exchange with Ned, Allie was adrift in a sea of emotions—none of which she had any intention of sharing with Sarah. And, she was certain Ned's abrupt departure had nothing to do with choosing a dance partner. Something he'd seen had spooked him and Allie knew Ned to be a man who was not easily spooked. A feather of fear brushed the back of her neck.

To answer Sarah's question, she said, "Not with that look on his face, I hope."

CHAPTER THIRTY

Malice.

Ned hadn't put a name to what he'd sensed all evening until that moment. Since dusk, he'd felt eyes on him. Shadows had moved just outside his awareness, lurking among the dozens of visitors who'd come to join in the festivities. He recognized most of the guests, but, as always, there were a few strangers. Listening to Allie, half his attention had been directed toward her, the rest toward searching for those evasive eyes. When she revealed Becky's reaction to his kerchiefed arm, he'd lost his concentration.

The Findlay girl's arrival had snapped him back to the present. When he glanced across the circle to the knot of men the young woman had abandoned, an itch of recognition told him he'd identified the source of the animosity—a man of average height, average weight, cheroot in one hand, and a mason jar of moonshine in the other.

Chagrin replaced apprehension. Ned strode across the circle to confront the unwelcome face. Sarah's newest admirer stood shoulder to shoulder with Zeke. "Pretty girl, I'll warrant you that," Ned heard him say. "But you boys all know you can't tell much about a chicken pot pie 'til you cut into the crust."

The interloper joined in the laughter that followed his jest, his own chortles louder than the others. Fists clenched at his sides, Zeke did not take part in the mirth. As Ned approached, he shot the barber a sympathetic look. The Findlay girl was clearly heartbreak waiting to happen.

Ned now knew for certain who had been dogging him. Nix. The scrofulous rustler who had manhandled him on the mustang hunt was almost unrecognizable. His hair and beard were neatly trimmed, his clothes and boots new. It was obvious he'd come into some money. Ned flinched inwardly, as he speculated on the source of that wealth.

"Ned Harper," Nix greeted him with a genial grin. Touching a finger to the brim of his spotless new Stetson, he dropped the cheroot and extended his hand, which Ned ignored. "Just the damned feller I've been askin' about. And here he is," the man said. His eyes were red-rimmed, watery, and untrustworthy, his words slurred. "Ned Harper of this here fine H & H Ranch." Despite Ned's stony response, he grabbed his hand and shook it. "Why, it's Nix, old friend. Nix Hooley. Jeb's here, too. You remember him, I'm sure. Big feller?" Ned remembered rough, intrusive hands and foul breath. "He's around here somewheres, prob'ly partaking of the fine food and ale and," Nix's smile twisted to a taunt, "them lively young ladies you kind folks are providin'. Can't say the last time I had the pleasure of female company."

A rustler come to take part in the festivities at a horse ranch, Ned thought. The man was fearless or foolish—or both. Keeping his own face unreadable, he assessed the risks Nix might present. He and his gang had made a craven retreat when Ned had threatened them with sharpshooters among his own men.

"Last time I saw you," Ned said, scrutinizing him from hat to boots, "you were lookin' too poor to paint and too proud to whitewash."

Drawing back, Nix leered at him. The cold caginess in his eyes belied any pretext of amicability. "Why, Harper," he countered, "even a blind ole squirrel can find hisself an acorn now and then."

"Zeke," Ned said, not unlocking his gaze from Nix's. He recalled the lout's interest in Trickster. "We'd best keep an eye on our *acorns*. Tell Will to set a couple of guards on the horses. Armed."

"Damned right I will," the barber snarled, shouldering past Nix.

"Now see here," Nix protested. "That ain't necessary. Me and Jeb, we mean no trouble. When we heard tell of a shindig at the H&H in Solace Springs, I said to Jeb, 'Why, we know them folks, Jeb. I'll bet that's Ned Harper's spread, I said, you recall the nice feller offered to help us catch wild horses up yonder? Offered us coffee and biscuits."

"Bacon, too," Ned said. "If you showed up to help round up those mustangs."

Filling the mason jar from a flask he pulled from his hip pocket, the rustler took a swallow, grimaced, and wiped his mouth on his sleeve. "We got called away sudden-like and couldn't take you up on that kindness. Didn't thank you proper neither, and that's been eatin' at me. That's partly why we're here, Jeb and me. Why, I made it a point to remember the name of your spread."

The rich, reedy vibrato of an accordion tuning up cut through Nix's speech.

The familiar music, the circle of lantern light, the scent and blaze of bale fires against the star-scattered sky, shook Ned's concentration. He quickly settled himself and focused on his assessment of Nix Hooley. A nuisance for sure, but with guards posted on the horses, not likely to pose much of a threat.

A fiddle and banjo joined the squeeze box to play the opening strains of a quadrille and announce the arrival of the caller.

At the sight of couples taking their places on the make-shift dance floor, Nix smirked. "Why Harper," he said, "we just come down here for the dancin' like everybody else."

A scorpion with its tail behind its back waiting to strike, Ned thought. But, escorting Nix and Jeb off the ranch would likely cause an unpleasant ruckus, at best. This was Hannah's night and he wouldn't see it spoiled. "And just like everyone else, you're welcome here," Ned said. "Until you're not."

Before Nix could respond, Ned found himself entrapped by wiry arms that encircled him from behind and held him tight. Stumbling back a step, he regained his balance. Without looking, he knew who had locked him in that embrace—Ollie Oxter, the elderly dance caller and town undertaker. Disengaging himself from the tiny old man, Ned pulled him around to face him. "Ollie," he said, and was promptly hugged from the front.

The dance caller, two years older than dirt by his own reckoning, beamed up at Ned, tears streaming down his wrinkled cheeks. Nix observed the scene with a bemused expression and a deep quaff of moonshine.

"Dear boy," Ollie said, grasping Ned by both shoulders. The undertaker had taken Becky's death hard. "We all missed ye both so last year. The Frolics weren't the same without you and yer . . . our . . . darling."

Glad of a reason to remove himself from Nix, Ned guided Ollie toward the platform where he would direct the dancers through their paces. "They're waiting for you," he said, assisting the frail old man up the two steps.

Ollie straightened his shoulders and smoothed his sparse whiskers. Enthusiastic applause greeted him from the audience. The caller slicked back the few strands of wispy white hair on the top of his head and raised a hand to silence the instruments. At dances, he was jovial, at funerals solemn. His somber demeanor worried Ned that he might have forgotten which he was at.

"Dear Ones," Ollie intoned, raising his still resonant voice. "Let us join hands and take a moment to remember those beloved souls no longer here with us." Laughter stopped, voices hushed. He gestured to the accordion and fiddle players who exchanged nods and began an inharmonious, but nonetheless moving, rendition of *Amazing Grace*.

When it was over, Ollie clapped his hands over his head to the rhythm of the quadrille. The band took their cue and dance music filled the night.

"Ladies and gents, let's raise enough merriment so our dear departed can hear us all the way in Heaven!" Slapping an elbow and then a thigh to the lively beat, he began his patter. "Call your dogs and grab your gun," he sang out. "Let's start dancin' and have some fun!"

Relieved to be free to lose himself in the crowd, Ned cringed when he heard Ollie call his name. The old man gave him a broad wink. "Go find you a pretty young thing and lead the first quadrille!"

Amid a chorus of encouraging cheers and claps in rhythm to the music, Ned resigned himself to a fate he could not escape. Sensing all eyes on him, he made his way across the dirt circle to where Allie, Sarah, and Maude Mary watched from beneath the lanterns. He strode past them, cut through a cluster of onlookers and, with a flourish, offered his hand to Hector Abernathy. The portly old rancher gave a courtly bow to Red Moon, then took Ned's kerchiefed arm and let himself be escorted to the dance floor.

Accompanied by more cheers, with the addition of hearty chuckles, Ned extended his left hand, palm down, in front of Heck, who grasped it in his own left hand. Ned placed his other behind his right hip, just so, and Heck covered it with his right hand. A dozen other couples assembled in groups of four to do the same. The music stopped. The clearing grew silent with anticipation. When Ollie winked at the band, accordion, banjo, and fiddle struck up a lively melody.

"Now," Ollie's voice rose above the music. "Tighten up them bellybands and loosen up them traces, all join hands and we're off to the races. Circle left!" He clapped out the rhythm. "Big foot up, little foot down, make that big foot jar the ground!"

At first, Ned floundered, awkward and lead-footed. Memories of being here with Becky, the appearance of a pair of ruthless rustlers, and a cup or two of wee heavy ale conspired to disorient him. The music was too fast.

Too loud. The lanterns too bright. The crush of moving bodies jostled him. And Heck's huge hands in his were just plain wrong.

"Promenade, go side-by-side, like a knock-kneed groom and a bow-legged bride!"

Promenade? Ned's mind went blank. Luckily, what Heck lacked in grace, he made up for with enthusiasm. He swung Ned to the left to walk counter-clockwise round the circle. When they reached their home position, he lifted his arm and twirled Ned with an unpolished flourish.

"Allemande left with your left hand grand, bow to your partner and there you stand!"

Soon the familiar words and movements became automatic for Ned. He and Heck exchanged a bow, linked arms with other dancers, and pranced around the square. The four-four beat soothed Ned into mindless surrender. He found himself able to smile.

"Up the river and 'round the bend, all join hands we're gone again!"

Ned glimpsed Allie on the arm of strapping Hamish MacGregor. She blushed and smiled when the young man bent his head of wild red hair to whisper something to her. Glad to see it, Ned told himself. She's a special girl, always has been.

In the neighboring square of couples, Aidan MacGregor—dark as his older brother was fair—awkwardly led Maude Mary, who appeared to have her own ideas on the matter. She swished her long skirt in the stylized 'skirtwork' of square dances whether called for or not.

"Promenade two and promenade four, keep that calico off the floor!"

Then, the hairs on the back of Ned's neck bristled. Sarah Findlay swung around the closest square with Nix Hooley's hand in hers and his other arm tight around her waist. Her eyes were locked on his, offering a look of sweet seduction to a man who clearly needed no encouragement. When Nix caught Ned watching them, he lifted his chin and shot him a feral grin.

"Ducks in the mill pond, geese in the clover," Ollie chanted. "Hide that pretty girl 'cause I'm comin' over!"

As Ned linked arms with other dancers and pulled himself in, out, and around the circle, he saw Sarah succumbing—flushed and smiling—to the rustler's roguish charm. Clearly oblivious to the man's true nature, it seemed enough for her that Nix played the part of admirer to her naïve and misguided temptress. A bad combination, Ned thought.

Ollie, agile as ever, demonstrated the footwork to go with his next call. "Promenade on a heel an' toe, like a barefoot boy on frozen snow!"

Ned was well aware of the slippery slope the young woman had set her dainty feet upon. He believed himself to be the reason Nix Hooley and Jeb—wherever the other scoundrel might be—were in their midst. In his mind, that made the girl his responsibility.

Despite the good-natured atmosphere of the Frolic, Ned became aware that something decidedly ill-natured had begun to stir within him. Something aggressive and eager. Badger-like.

His brother Ben's words—always uttered with glee in his eyes and dread in his voice—came to him: "I've got a real good feeling something bad's gonna happen . . ."

CHAPTER THIRTY-ONE

Aware his willing, albeit portly, partner had become red-faced and sweating, Ned felt relief on both their counts when Ollie made the calls that ended the first set of quadrilles.

"Stop where you are and don't be blue, the music's quit and I will, too!" A brief break allowed the dancers and musicians to find refreshment. And new partners. "Ladies to your seats and gents all foller. Thank the fiddler," he winked and tapped his cheek, "and kiss the caller!"

Ned lead Heck to one of the casks and drew them both a cup of ale. After a few swallows, the old rancher placed a beefy hand on his shoulder. "Thanks for the dance, darlin', but it's time for me and Red Moon to head home and for you to find yourself a proper partner. If I know old Ollie, he's fixin' to make the next dance a waltz, so that old codger can find himself a little lady to traipse around the floor with him." His flushed face grew somber. "You do the same, Ned."

"I intend to."

But not for the reasons Heck had implied. After Ned's initial stupefaction had worn off, following Ollie's directions had come easy enough. His body remembered the steps, the turns, when to link arms, and when to let go. With every turn of his head, he kept track of Nix's whereabouts. He'd watched him deliver a miffed-looking Sarah back to Zeke, then slide himself between Allie and Hamish. With growing consternation, Ned saw him take the girl's hand, hold it to his heart, and turn a beseeching look to her partner. Hamish nodded a grudging assent.

When the first strains of the waltz summoned dancers back to the circle, the horse thief bent his knee to Allie and led her to the far side of the dance floor. Ned noted Nix Hooley seemed to take a particular fancy to girls he had seen at Ned's side. A troubling thought. The rustlers had come to the H & H looking for more than a pleasant quadrille. They had mischief, or worse, on their minds, Ned was certain. He was not about to let Allie get caught in the midst of it. As he took a step toward the dance floor to cut in and put an end to Nix's foolery, a rough hand on his arm stopped him, half spinning him around.

Wrenching free, Ned found himself looking at the uncharacteristically fierce face of his closest friend. "Just when were you figuring on telling me why you think it's necessary to post armed guards on the horses?" Will demanded.

Making a show of smoothing his shirt sleeve, Ned nodded toward the dancers. "I had it in mind to fill you in as soon as I rescued your sister from one of the rustlers I ran into when I was hunting mustangs with Heck. Two showed up here."

"Rustlers? Here?" Will glared at Ned as the words sank in. "With my sister?"

"She's dancin' with one right now," he said lightly. "I'm keeping an eye on them. I know how you tend to fret, so I didn't want to . . ."

"My sister's dancing with a horse thief? Here on my property?" Staring at Allie and her partner, Will drew a deep breath and exhaled slowly. "What in the name of holy hell are you talkin' about?"

"I told you how a handful of rustlers dogged me and Heck up north. I told you how I warned'em off and they let us be." With dark pleasure, Ned recalled convincing Nix and his gang that he was riding with men who had served in Hiram Berdan's legendary Regiment of Sharpshooters. "They say they came here for the dancin'. I've got my doubts, but as long as the horses are guarded, there's nothing to worry about. Even for you." A twinge of something he couldn't name caught Ned off guard. "I'll look out for Allie."

In fact, Ned hadn't taken his eyes off Allie throughout his conversation with her brother. He supposed he was feeling protective. Grateful for the kindness she'd done by telling him about Becky and his heifer-brand kerchief. Allie'd always had a knack for doing that, he thought. Like pulling out the bee stinger and knowing just what to say to Joseph. Ned was relieved to see her disengage herself from Nix as soon as the waltz ended. Her grim face and flashing eyes told him she'd taken quick stock of the man's character.

Will lifted his hat and ran a hand through his hair. "We've got rustlers on the property, my sister's dancing with one, and you're telling me there's nothing to worry about." He appraised Ned, then asked, "Just how much of Doc's wee heavy ale have you had tonight?"

"Not enough to give you cause to ask."

Rubbing the back of his neck, Will frowned. "I'll have a word with Tucker T."

"Not necessary," Ned said. "He's come out here tonight to enjoy himself like everyone else. No need to trouble him about something that's not gonna happen."

Sheriff Tucker T. Stapleton, affable, unflappable, and soft around the middle, kept the peace in Solace Springs with the force of his iron will. When he took the job fifteen years ago, he'd made it known that disorderly conduct upset his digestion and that he would not be tolerating either one. Years ago, he'd locked Ned in a cell on the nights Seven Colors of Shit got out of control.

"You and Tucker T. go entertain those good women of yours." With what he assured himself was relief, Ned noted that Allie was once again in the trustworthy company of handsome, young Hamish MacGregor. "I've got the rest handled."

"I'm not sure whether I should be worried or relieved to hear you say that."

As much as Nix's presence irked Ned, Jeb's absence troubled him more. Anxious to continue his search, he told Will, "What you should be doin' is dancing with your wife."

As if to make Ned's point, the music started up. Ollie clapped his hands and tapped one foot to the beat. "She likes whiskey, I like rum, that's where all the trouble begun!"

Ned watched Will pull Hannah into the panorama of swirling bodies. Less to his liking, he saw that Nix had reclaimed an all-too-willing Sarah Findlay from an irate Zeke and was about to escort her to the center of the circle. With doting eyes locked on hers, the horse thief whispered something, draped an arm around her waist, and clasped her hand in the Sweetheart's Wrap. With his other hand, he pulled the flask from his back pocket, took a swallow, and offered it to the girl. Lantern light glinted on the tin as she raised it to her lips.

Before either of them realized what was happening, Ned appeared between them, seized the flask, took a sip, and grimaced. Moonshine ignited a blaze from the back of his throat to his gut. "Not fit for a lady," he gasped, emptying the flask onto the ground. Turning his gaze on Sarah, he added, "Neither is the likker.

"This young lady promised me a dance," Ned said to Nix. "If I don't take her up on it right now, I expect I won't get another chance. You never know what can happen on a night like this, so pardon my cutting in.." He took the hand Sarah had freed from Nix's grasp. "If it suits you, Miss Findlay."

"Of course it suits me." With a slight lift of one pretty shoulder, she dismissed the rustler who stiffened at the rebuff. "Why, Mr. Harper," she murmured, lacing her fingers through his. "*You* suit me just fine. I've been in a pout since you said you'd come to call and haven't."

Taking her elbow, Ned guided Sarah toward a group of dancers in need of a couple to complete their square. They took their places beside Allie and Hamish just as Ollie sang out, "Left allemande and right hand grand, promenade to beat the band!"

Ned had been aware only of his need to caution Sarah to be wary of Nix Hooley. But the nearness of her body soon awakened other long-suppressed needs. And the shame that came with them. He felt, more than saw, her full lips and fair, flushed skin. Eyes that made promises. Wisps of golden hair curling at the nape of her neck. A breast brushed his arm when he swung her. He fought the urge to draw her closer. From that moment, he made certain only their hands and arms touched, that he kept a distance between himself and her teal silk gown, and that he concentrated on the rustlers. He searched the crowd for Jeb, although he hardly remembered what the man looked like.

When Ned linked arms briefly with Allie in an allemande, he was baffled that her smile seemed too bright and she didn't quite meet his eyes. He couldn't think what he might have done to offend her, but it seemed he'd done something. That concern was overshadowed by a more disquieting one: Nix had found a new partner. Maude Mary seemed so enchanted to find herself on the arm of a mysterious—and considerably older stranger—that she'd forgotten her skirtwork entirely.

When the dance ended, Ned looped Sarah's arm through his and strolled to where Nix chatted with Maude Mary. Nix's pale eyes flashed and his lip curled. "Again, Harper?" Trading the snarl for a forced smile, he said, "Damn! Soon as I find me a sweet little lady, seems you show up to spoil my fun. And hers." His angry gaze scrutinized Sarah from head to toe, lingering on the parts of her that seemed to interest him most. Then he scowled and added, "For now."

"Your mama wants you, Maudie. Now," Ned told her. "Right now. She needs to talk to you about how sweet little thirteen-year-old girls," he turned cold eyes on Nix, "choose their dance partners."

Flushing to the roots of her newly-coiffed hair, Maude Mary raised a defiant chin. "My mother doesn't tell me who I can dance with . . ."

Ned grasped the girl's elbow and steered her —still protesting—toward the sidelines where Mrs. Hanover received them with a questioning look. "You best keep your eye on this one, ma'am," Ned told her irritably. "I can't keep track of all your young'uns."

"You embarrassed her," Sarah chided him, as they left mother and daughter in mutual states of high dudgeon.

"I meant to," he snapped. "Had to."

"Had to?"

"There are a few things I have to say to you, too."

Ned led her away from the lanterns and music to a more secluded spot—still visible enough to be proper. Leaning back against the rough wood of the stable wall, Sarah raised a smiling face to his while he explained that the man she and Maude Mary and Allie had been entertaining on the dance floor was a known horse thief who shouldn't be trusted.

"Just because he can't be trusted to know an allemande from a do-si-do," she said, "doesn't make him a bad man."

"Allie had the sense to figure out what he is and know to steer clear of him. You need to do the same."

Sarah bristled. "Miss La-Di-Dah Hanover has too much sense for her own good."

"That moonshine likker he tried to give you? A few swallows would've made you drunk as a hillbilly at a rooster fight," Ned said. "If it didn't kill you first."

"Oooh," she murmured, a smile bowing her lips. Hands behind her, she arched her back, lifting her chin and breasts. "You make him sound dangerous."

"He is." Irritated by her flippancy and flirtatiousness, the words came out harsher than Ned intended. "It's best you stay as far from him as you can."

Tilting her head, she gave him a seductive smile and laid her hand on his chest. "It's so dear of you to say that, but you've got no cause to be jealous of Nix Hooley."

He started to correct her, then understood she'd told him the best way to reach her. "I knew you'd understand."

"Course I do." Her grasp tightened on a fold of his shirt and she pulled him closer.

When their bodies touched, lust surged through him, unbidden and unwelcome. He disentangled her fingers and stepped back, his face a careful blank. "I've got livestock to see to."

"Course you do." Standing on her toes, she pressed her lips to his, then shoved him away. "Don't be gone long, Ned Harper. Pa says I get myself in trouble when I'm bored and this party would be fearful boring without you."

Appalled his body had responded to the ploys of a young woman he didn't even like, Ned was shaken by the heart-sinking sense he'd betrayed Becky. He turned to leave, then remembered his duties and swung back. "Find Allie. You'll stay out of trouble if you just stick close to her."

"I'll be sure to do just that." Confident she'd do as he said, Ned strode away in search of one of the elusive horse thieves. Sarah waited until he was out of sight before setting out to find the other.

Ned felt the need of air and the space to breathe it. Sarah Findlay had ignited desire in him that left him hollow with guilt. Nix had gotten under his skin, as well. He's more nuisance than threat, Ned thought, but he knew the danger of underestimating men like him. The horses were secure, he'd seen to that, so Nix and Jeb could do no damage there. Still, until he found Jeb, he wouldn't be able to shake the uneasiness that still plagued him.

Certain it was unnecessary, he checked the stable. The children had been lulled to sleep by Grandda Fergus's recounting of Scottish folk tales. Some appropriate for young ones, some not. The old man always began with benign stories of faeries and kelpies, but when no other adult was present, Fergus was known to sneak in a few tales about the Dogs of Darkness, the Monster of Glamis, and, of course, the fearsome half-man, half-rotting horse Nuckelavee—the essence of evil.

In a chair fashioned of two bales of hay, Martha Findlay watched over her charges and knitted in the light of a single lantern. When Ned appeared, she greeted him with a quick smile. Albert and his nephews, with a dozen or so other small bodies, curled together on beds of loose hay beneath an assortment of colorful wool tartans. Some slept still as stones, some twitched and murmured. Moans, whimpers, and an occasional yelp identified those battling the Nuckelavee in their dreams. It saddened Ned that Joseph wasn't among them.

From the stable, Ned hiked down the slope, circled the ranch house, and scouted the surrounding groves and thickets. Satisfied no one lurked nearby, he poked his head inside the brightly-lit house, bustling with women arranging platters of food. Making his way up the hill to the paddocks where the horses had been corralled, Ned watched the crescent moon rise higher, obscured behind amassing clouds. When he reached the upper pastures, nickering horses and bored guards greeted him.

"Nope, no rustlers, Harper. No visitors of any kind. None at all," one of the sentries assured him in an accusatory tone. The men had been pulled away from the festivities to keep an eye on the horses. "Lonely as a duck in the desert up here."

"It's a comfort we can hear the music," the other added. "At least some of it."

His companion sighed deeper than necessary. "I s'pose all the food's gone. Ale, too."

"Bet the girls have all headed home. Pretty ones, that is."

With a promise that the food and girls were still there, Ned assured them he'd send replacements and made his way down the slope. Strains of fiddle music wafted up to meet him. He stopped to watch the dancers below spin like multi-colored pinwheels in a breeze, but saw no sign of Jeb anywhere.

Ollie's voice carried up to him. "I got a wife who's lean and tall, sleeps in the kitchen with her feet in the hall!"

The rhymes and music, the balmy night, did nothing to lessen his uneasiness. The only thing that'll settle me tonight, Ned thought, is to lay eyes on a man I'd hoped to never see again.

CHAPTER THIRTY-TWO

"Hullo, Harper." Jeb stepped out from the shadows behind the bales of hay encircling the dance floor. "Much obliged for all the hospitality. By that I mean the food. Brung my own jar of 'shine."

Jeb knew he possessed none of the practiced, if spotty, refinement of Nix Hooley—nor wanted it. He'd cleaned himself up some, because Nix said he had to. His new clothes chafed, and Nix's bossiness did rankle, but Jeb had to admit, he'd proven himself right about most things.

As broad at the belly as he was at the shoulder, heavy-browed, and scraggly-haired, Jeb hadn't come to the Frolic to dance. Ladies didn't take to him like they did to Nix. Nix was the coyote that dogged the herd until he found the easiest targets and cut them away from the rest. Jeb's job was to watch and wait and claim what was there for the taking. Horses, money, a certain kind of girl.

The pickings had proven slim at the well-guarded H&H Ranch, so he'd comforted himself with moonshine and hearty portions of the hot dishes served up by the local ladies. His beard, not trimmed fancy like Nix's, dripped with grease from the roast venison he'd devoured. Eyes fixed on Ned Harper, he rubbed his hand over his whiskers and licked his thumb.

As planned, Nix had provided the distraction, taunting Harper with his attention to the ladies he liked, while Jeb had scouted the house, stable, and outbuildings. People were everywhere. Watching, maybe. He hadn't seen much worth taking anyhow.

It was almost time to collect what Nix had promised him, so Jeb had shown himself to Harper. "Take away the mystery now," Nix had instructed him, taking a long drag on his cheroot, "so the damned varmint'll stop looking for you and let down his guard."

That's what he and Nix always did. Worked every time. One way or another.

Relieved as he was to know the whereabouts of the elusive horse thief, Ned had to suppress some amusement when they met. Seeing Jeb in the light of the lanterns, Ned quickly realized the huge man was as oafish as he was dimwitted. Further dulled by the moonshine and wee heavy ale he'd been drinking all night, he had the blank, long-suffering look of a beast of burden who expects to be punished for failings he cannot comprehend. Where Ned had expected to sense violence, he sensed only hunger.

"Glad to hear you're enjoyin' yourself," Ned said. But, he reminded himself, hungry beasts, no matter how dull they seem, are the most dangerous. "Jeb, is it?"

"Jeb Thurow."

Ollie's calls rose and fell in rhythm with the music from the makeshift stage. "All jump up and never come down, swing your pretty girl round and round!"

The rustler stared over Ned's shoulder, his stolid gaze scanning the grounds. "When d'ye suppose the wimmin'll be layin' out the cakes and such?"

With a thin frown, Allie searched the faces of the dancers yet again. Still no sign of Sarah. Or Ned.

Looking over her head, Hamish did the same. "Are ye that worried about Sarah, then?"

"No. Not really. I believe she's with Ned." Her throat was not so dry she couldn't swallow. "So, of course, she's perfectly safe. I just haven't seen either of them since they . . . for a while."

It seemed to Allie that Sarah had made sure to catch her eye when Ned pulled her around to the side of the stable. The girl had let him lead her right into the kind of trouble Allie and Hannah had assured her parents they would make sure she did not find. Allie told herself that was why she felt so irritated. But she knew what irked her was that Hannah—who was never wrong about anything—had been wrong about Ned 'not being ready.' He was clearly all too ready for Sarah Findlay. Not that it should matter to Allie.

"If ye ken she's with Harper, why the troubled brow?" Hamish asked.

No matter how much she tried to will it away, the image of Ned kissing Sarah plagued her. "I promised her pa I'd keep an eye on her."

"A mighty task, if ye ask me. But don't fash yerself, lass. Every man here's been doin' it for ye all night."

"That's what worries me."

Hamish chuckled, but Allie couldn't share his amusement. Let it go, she told herself. They should be none of your concern. Are none of your concern. At that moment, she caught sight of Ned's back half hidden among the people watching the dancers, his shoulders taut as he faced a bearish man Allie had never seen.

Relief washed through her. Then, her heart went small with apprehension—Sarah was nowhere to be seen.

Before Ned could assure Jeb Thurow that the ladies would soon set out the cakes, Allie strode to his side. "I thought Sarah was with you."

"Not me. I've been making rounds." Her icy tone baffled him, causing him to wonder again what he'd done to offend her. "Haven't seen her in some time." Sarah Findlay—and Allie Hanover, for that matter—were the least of his worries. He had Jeb in his sights, but had lost track of Nix. "She's here somewhere. Not one to be alone for long, I'd bet."

"That's exactly why I promised her folks I'd keep an eye on her. Mrs. Findlay says Sarah has a way of falling in with the wrong sort." Leveling a hard look at Ned, she added, "The last person I saw her with was *you*."

Ned rubbed a spot between his brows that suddenly felt sore. Before he could speak, Allie had disappeared in a swirl of calico.

"Wimmen," Jeb sympathized.

Uncapping his flask of moonshine, he offered it to Ned, who politely refused. With that, the man downed a long swallow, wiped his mouth with the back of his hand, and lumbered back into the shadows.

Hands on his hips, Ollie flapped his elbows, and crowed, "The little banty rooster told the little banty hen, meet you 'round the corner at half past ten!"

Allie scanned the dancers linking arms and circling each other. Instead of enjoying Hamish's company, as she should be, she was wasting what might have been an enjoyable evening minding Sarah. Or failing at minding Sarah. Who was obviously intent on doing just as she pleased, where she pleased, and with whom she pleased. Allie turned her attention to the guests chatting beneath the lanterns, or milling about sipping ale and spruce beer. Although she thought it unlikely, she crossed the yard and went down to the house to see if the girl had gone to help the ladies with the last of their food preparations.

"Alexandrina, there you are," her mother exclaimed, thrusting a tray of sticky gingerbread at her. "Make yourself useful. Take this up and send your sister and Sarah down immediately. Please and thank you. I'm afraid Maude Mary is getting notions about Aidan MacGregor—just to try my patience, mind you. Sarah is sure to be in cahoots with her. Hurry now!"

Allie carried the still-warm pastries up to a table near the front of the stable and was quickly engulfed by a swarm of hungry guests. She'd been relieved to learn Sarah and Maude Mary were together—and that their disappearance likely had to do with entrapping Aidan—until she saw him and Hamish watching the dancers.

His back to her, Allie saw Ned bend to refill his cup with the exotic and dangerous 'wee small ale.' When he turned and tried to catch her eye, she ignored him. The fist clutching her heart tightened. He had kissed Sarah. Why that troubled her, she couldn't fathom, but her will to locate the girls faded. She wanted silence and solitude and to be free of all of them. The only place she might hope to find that on this night would be out by Hannah's forlorn vegetable garden behind the stable.

Walking along the side of the wooden building, she left lantern light, laughter, and conversation behind. The shadows welcomed her, matched her mood. Then, she heard stirrings in the stillness, sounds she couldn't identify. Farm animals, she supposed. When she rounded the corner, she stopped and stared at what she could not comprehend. Maude Mary perched ramrod straight and motionless on a bale of hay, hands clenched in her lap, staring straight ahead. The burly, unkempt man Ned had been talking to sat beside her with his heavy arm draped over her shoulders. He stroked her now-loose hair. A few yards away, the dark silhouette of a man's body pinned Sarah's squirming form to the wall. His one hand covered her mouth, the other fumbled beneath her skirts. Nix Hooley.

It was all wrong. Terribly. Wrong. Allie knew she had to do something, but had no idea what. "Maude Mary!" she heard herself say in a loud, stern voice. "Come here, right now. Mama wants you down at the house."

Her sister pulled free, ran to Allie, and threw herself into her arms. The startled brute stared after her, but made no move to stop her. Heart pounding, mouth dry with rage and fear, Allie lifted her sister's chin. "Did he hurt you, Maudie?"

"No . . ." Maude Mary buried her face in Allie's chest and drew a shuddering breath. "No." Her whole body shook. "He just wanted . . ." she raised horror-stricken eyes to Allie's, her whisper a suppressed scream, "to touch my hair."

Struggling against her captor, Sarah whimpered. Her eyes bulged above the hand silencing her. Hooley's head turned. He acknowledged Allie with a leering grin, then ground his hips harder against Sarah. Clutching Maude Mary, Allie meant to scream for him to stop, to scream for help, but her voice died in her throat. She knew she and her sister should run, but fear shackled her where she stood.

A blur charged past them like a maddened bull Allie had once seen released from a chute at a Wild West show. Ned yanked Nix off Sarah with one arm and shoved her to the side with the other. Slamming her assailant to the wall with his forearm crushing his windpipe, he delivered a savage knee jab to his groin. Nix's eyes bulged, his face went blotchy purple, and his body sagged. Grabbing a fistful of his hair, Ned slammed his head back against the wall and unleashed a torrent of blows to his ribs and gut, kneed him again, then flung him to the ground where he writhed and vomited. Straddling the helpless man, Ned pummeled his face and head, each punch more ferocious than the last.

Detached from the sickening sight and sounds of bone turning flesh to pulp, Allie wondered how a person's eyes could go as black as Ned's had. How an appealing face could turn so ugly.

Detachment turned to horror. The bear-like man on the hay lurched slowly to his feet. He'd watched in stunned silence while his friend was assaulted. Now, his stupefied face came alive with dawning awareness. Bellowing like a beast, he propelled his bulk toward Ned.

Until that moment, Allie had never known true terror. Her scream, high and feral, brought Ned to his feet. The other man stood half a head taller than him, outweighed and outreached him. Tightening her arms around Maude Mary, Allie willed her own knees not to buckle. We must run, she thought, still immobilized. Sarah huddled on the ground, knees drawn up, trying to cover her exposed breasts with her torn gown.

The lout advanced on Ned, swinging cudgel-like arms. Ned lunged at him, ducked one blow and was knocked sideways by a battering ram fist that smashed into his ribs, doubling him over. Recovering his balance, he charged, head-butting the brute full force in the face. The man stumbled backward, hands raised to his bloody nose. Eyes that had been dull ignited with lunatic light. He reared back and rushed Ned, straight-arming him into the wall.

Ned's body went slack and Allie feared he'd been knocked unconscious. His opponent grunted and let down his guard as Ned slumped. In that instant, Ned charged again. He swung a crippling kick to his leg, followed by an onslaught of blows to his gut. With a pitiful scream, Maude Mary's attacker collapsed to the ground, grabbing his knee. Stomping the injured limb, Ned silenced the man's whimpers with a kick to the side of his head.

The girls' attackers sprawled on the ground. Pulling a hunting knife from his boot, Ned stood over Nix, who had begun to show signs of recovery. He aimed the point at him. Teeth bared, he kicked him in the ribs. "Move," Ned rasped, "and I'll geld you."

With the gleaming knife, Ned gestured toward a loop of thick twine hanging from a hook on the side of the stable and planted his boot on Nix's neck. Breathing hard, he told Allie, "Get the rope."

She stared at Ned, almost as frightened of him as of the other men. His face was ashen and sweaty, his mouth a twisted scar. Letting go of Maude Mary, Allie did as he told her.

Increasing the pressure of his boot, Ned grabbed the rope, cut four lengths, and held two out to Allie. "Tie his hands and feet. Quick." To Nix, he said, "Don't even breathe, you dog."

This is Ned, Allie told herself, trying to slow her own breathing. Ned. He's protecting us. She took the thick twine, wrapped it around Nix's wrists and ankles, and double-knotted it. Ned's eyes stayed fixed on the other man, who lay grunting a few feet away.

Maude Mary, arms wrapped tight around herself, watched wild-eyed.

Dropping to one knee, Ned pressed the tip of the knife into the flesh behind Nix's ear, drawing a bead of black blood. His mouth a thin, hard line, he handed Allie the knife. "Hold this here—like this—while I truss up the other one."

Stomach churning, Allie grasped the hilt of the knife. She dropped to her knees and pressed it to Nix's throat. His alcohol and vomit breath gagged her. Ned's hand covered hers until it stopped trembling. "Good girl. Don't let up."

After he'd bound the big man, Ned straightened slowly and wiped sweat from beneath his eyes. He drew a shallow breath and pressed a hand to ribs Allie knew must be badly bruised or broken. Wincing, he exhaled, "Get Sarah's ma and the Sheriff."

Unable to speak, Allie nodded and turned to leave. She grasped Maude Mary's icy hand, desperate to pull her away from the horrid scene.

"Noooo . . ." Sarah wailed, still huddled on the ground. "Please, Allie, no! My pa . . . they'll tell my pa. If he finds out he'll . . . he'll . . ."

"Sarah," Ned snapped, his voice harsh with weariness and disgust, "we can't just let these devils go."

She covered her face, rocking. "Please . . . please, please, don't tell . . ."

Going to the hysterical girl, Allie knelt beside her. She had no doubt Luke Findlay would punish his daughter severely for what had occurred. Blame her. Stroking disheveled hair back from Sarah's tear-streaked face, she said, "Don't worry. Everything will be all right. I know what to do."

"There's nothing you can do," Sarah sobbed. "You don't know my pa. No one can know what happened. Please. Not my ma. Not your ma. No one. It's all ruined." Pulling her hands free of Allie's, she tugged helplessly at the tattered dress and whispered, "I ruined everything."

"This is not your fault. None of it." Allie wrapped her arms around Sarah's shoulders and held her close. "Nothing is ruined. No one needs to know." She released the shaking girl and sat back. With a steady hand, she ripped the bodice of her own dress and shift, exposing her pale breasts.

Ned stared, blinked, then quickly looked away.

"Maudie, take Sarah down to the house. Use the back door. Don't let anyone see you." Allie's voice was even. "Tell Hannah what happened. She'll fix Sarah's dress. Then go tell the Sheriff what happened. *To me.* Understand, Maudie? *To me.*"

With grim determination and no thought to the repercussions she might unleash upon herself, she added, "Neither of you were here."

CHAPTER THIRTY-THREE

Allie had no sense of how much time had passed between when Maude Mary and Sarah ran for the house and when her brother and Sheriff Stapleton arrived. Her mind, it seemed, had gone somewhere else. When the men appeared, she was surprised to find herself weeping and pulling Ned's blood-spattered vest across her partially-bare breasts. She huddled against him, his arm around her shoulders, and wanted nothing more than to disappear.

A few town folk had followed when Will and the sheriff made a hasty exit from the dance. Allie saw the small crowd turn the corner of the stable and pull up short. Ladies with hands pressed to their mouths and gents with tight scowls stood a few yards back eyeing the hog-tied men who had obviously caused the commotion. And staring at Allie.

Will pulled her away from Ned and into his own embrace. "What happened?" Before she could speak, he held her at arms length. His anxious eyes didn't linger on the obvious indecencies inflicted upon her, but held steady on hers. "You're okay?" She felt his body shaking when he pulled her close again. "They didn't . . .?"

"No." Shuddering, she buried her head in her brother's chest. Nothing had been done to her. Still, Allie felt shattered by what she'd witnessed, by what might have happened to her sister and Sarah. What might have happened to Ned. By what she had seen he was capable of doing. "Ned got here before anything . . . happened."

Will's body tensed against hers. The look he directed at Ned lanced razor sharp. "You said you had this handled, said you didn't need any help." His tone was heavy with suppressed rage. "You put guards on the damned *horses*!"

"I thought that'd be enough." Ned raised stricken eyes to meet Will's. "I'm sorry."

"Sorry? You damned cocky son-of-a . . ." Will glanced down at Allie and stopped. After another tense moment, he tried for the lop-sided grin that Allie knew had ended most of his disputes with Ned since they were youths. This time, it failed. Through clenched teeth, he rasped, "Do you have any idea what could have happened here? " He stopped and swallowed hard. Allie knew his anger at Ned rarely lasted longer than moments. She hoped when Will exhaled that would be so. It wasn't. Lips still tight, and not meeting Ned's eyes, he muttered, "I thought I could count on you."

Head bowed, Ned's shoulders slumped as if he could neither dodge nor absorb this blow from his friend.

Then, to Allie's relief, a grudging half-smile tugged at the corner of her brother's mouth. "At least Seven gave these louts a good dose of what for."

Fists on his broad hips, the sheriff continued to survey the scene. Tucker T. Stapleton massaged his chin, lifted his hat, and scratched his head. First, he addressed himself to the gawkers. "Go on back to the party, folks. Can't you hear Ollie calling you? Nothing more to see here."

With urgent whispers and backward glances, they did as they were told. Ollie's voice beckoned from a distance. "Swing with Mary, swing with Grace, allemande left with old Prune Face!"

When the onlookers had gone, the sheriff went to Allie, her arms still tight around her brother's waist, eyes closed, head on his shoulder. "Miss Hanover, are you hurt?"

She opened her eyes, but couldn't meet his. Pulling Ned's vest tighter, she shook her head. "No, sir. I'm just . . . just . . ."

"She's shaken up," Will said. "But, she's all right."

The sheriff studied her face, then nodded. His gruff voice gentled to say, "Well, I'm glad for that." Then he swung around and turned his piercing glare on Ned. "But, dad-blast it, Harper." Everyone knew that Tucker T. Stapleton never took kindly to the peace of his town being disturbed and that Ned Harper had done so too many times in the past. "I don't like what I see here, son. Not one bit. Appears you've raised all kinds of heck on these morons. Or should I say, Seven Colors," a glance at Will included him in his ire, "of You-Know-What has gone and agitated my dyspepsia. It's fixin' to burn a hole in my gut." Frowning, he pressed a hand to his middle and raised a riled brow at Ned. "I s'pose you're gonna tell me it was necessary."

"It was."

Allie had heard the tales that back in Ned's brawling days, Tucker T. had locked him in a sour-smelling jail cell—more than once—with threats of keeping him there until the circuit judge came through. It had taken Ned years to get back in the Sheriff's good graces.

"There were two of 'em, Tuck," Ned said. After another gimlet glare from the older man, he corrected himself. "Sheriff. I had to make sure these bastards stayed down."

"S'pose you did," Tuck sighed. Lifting his hat, he smoothed back his still thick hair, then set it back on his head. When he'd adjusted the slant of the brim just so, he added, "You could at least have done me the courtesy of working up more of a sweat doin' it."

At the arrival of the lawman, Nix had begun to rouse from his stupor and struggle against his restraints. Lifting his battered head from the ground, he spat blood. "Ya got it all wrong, Sheriff," he muttered, "We didn't do nothing to them girls. They come with us willingly."

Allie cringed as Ned let loose another volley of kicks to the man's kidneys, leaving him speechless with his cheek pressed to the dirt and defeat in his eyes. The other man lay curled on one side, still clutching his knee.

"Gosh-all-fish-hooks, Harper," the sheriff barked. "That's about enough of that." Tucker T. had always been an inveterate cusser, but his pious wife forbade profanity of any kind. In her presence, he was permitted only an occasional "Bosh!" He'd had to come up with language sufficient to vent his many frustrations. "I thought you'd put all that nonsense behind you."

"I did, too."

"All right, then. Let's just clean up this mess you've made, Harper, and get this pair of nackle-faced fools loaded into that hay wagon. You've seen to it neither one's fit to sit a horse." He gave Ned a look that Allie was surprised to see held as much approval as disapproval. "I'll accompany them to what I'm sure they'll welcome as the comfort and safety of their jail cells." A flicker of regret passed across his weathered features. "I s'pose I'm done dancin' for the night." Turning to Allie, his face and tone softened again. "Miss Hanover, I'd appreciate it if you'd stop by the jail tomorrow so I can take your statement."

Allie blanched. It was one thing to allow a lie to be believed, quite another to make a statement to the Sheriff about it, or—worse—put her hand on a Bible and swear to it in court.

"No call for that," Ned said, before Allie could speak. She was relieved that save for the hollowness around his eyes his features had returned to normal. "She's been through enough. You can see for yourself what happened here. If you can't, I'll give you your statement. No need to make her come to the jail and relive it all." To Will he said, "You see to your sister. I'll see to the rest."

The sheriff sighed deeply. "I'd had it in my mind you were quit makin' my job such a dad gum trial, Harper. I see that's not to be so." He told Will,

"Go on then. Take your sister home. But I do have a few questions for your friend here."

When Allie and Will had gone, Ned fetched a pair of horses from the paddock and hitched them to the wagon. Sickened by what he'd done, what he'd let himself do to Nix and Jeb, he worked in silence. When the cart was ready, he and the sheriff hefted their bound prisoners—moaning and groaning, some of it justified, some not—into the wagon.

Tucker T. started to climb onto the bench, then stepped down. "Harper, I'm still difficulted on two counts. First, what does that there reprobate mean by 'they and them'?"

Glancing at Nix, who had a sneer on his swollen, bloody face and seemed eager to explain what had really occurred, Ned put aside his remorse. There would be time and Old Overholt's to deal with that later. Now, he had to make certain Nix didn't spoil Allie's efforts to protect Sarah.

"What exactly are these randy bastards facin' from the judge?" Ned asked the sheriff.

Tucker T. hooked his thumbs into his belt. "Well, the penalty for rape is hanging by the neck until dead. For attempting it? Thirty-nine lashes give or take a few stripes, for each offense."

The sneer faded, taking what was left of the color from Nix's face with it.

"So, exactly how many girls was it you put your filthy hands on?" Ned shot him his iciest glare. "Go on. Tell the Sheriff."

Nix took a moment to mull the matter, then muttered. "Just the one."

A wily man himself, Tucker T. sighed with the resignation of one who knows he doesn't really want to know the truth.

"I'm not criticizing, hear?" he told Ned, grasping his shoulder. "I'd allow you did what you thought had to be done under the circumstances. And what you did is close enough to reasonable to suit me. I have to say I'm half glad you got it out of your system."

Ned tensed, resisting the urge to shrug off the sheriff's hand.

"I'm just sayin'—and this is where that second thing that's bothering me comes in—I do expect this to be the last we see of that so-called 'Seven' feller. Ever." Tucker T. climbed into the wagon and adjusted his hat, eyes straight ahead. "You take my meaning?"

Aware he'd gone too far, had vented rage and pain he could no longer contain in the worst possible way, self-loathing sickened Ned. He had relished the brutal beatings he'd unleashed upon Nix and Jeb, savored every blow and kick. Only the horror on Allie's face had stopped him from doing worse.

Now, remembering Red Moon's words from all those years ago, his insides caved. "You must learn to hold the reins of your anger," she had chided him, stone-faced. "Otherwise, you are nothing more than an ugly animal no one can befriend."

Trapped in a life he couldn't live, Ned knew he was turning into the beast Red Moon had warned him he might become. As much as he longed to walk into the woods and be done with it, his promise to Hannah chained him here. He couldn't live his life, but to spare his friends he couldn't end it.

Eyes not meeting the sheriff's, he muttered, "I take your meaning."

CHAPTER THIRTY-FOUR

Ma was not a woman given to smugness or lengthy chatter, but on this morning Joseph sensed she couldn't help herself.

"Can you imagine," she gushed to Pa, setting his coffee down in front of him. "Miss Allie—our very own Alexandrina Victoria Hanover—getting herself into such a fix! No one can reckon whether she actually went with those men of low character or was just plain foolish enough to wander off behind the stable by herself in the dark of night. It was all the talk she'd been dancing with one of them all evening. Now he's in jail and she's well . . . tarnished . . . as they say." Ma seemed to be trying not to smile, but she did. "Terrible thing. I always thought she was such a nice girl."

Joseph didn't understand what his mother was hinting at, only that Miss Allie was in some sort of trouble. He also sensed something had befallen his sister. Sarah was pale and small and silent. She didn't reach for a hot biscuit and when Ma put one on her plate, she stared at it like she didn't know what it was for.

"Why, if it hadn't been for that Ned Harper," Ma went on, "I can't begin to imagine what might have happened to the poor girl."

When Pa snorted derisively at mention of Ned Harper, Sarah pursed her lips. Her cheeks flamed, but her eyes stayed dull. Something had happened to Miss Allie and Ned had saved her. Joseph watched his sister with increasing curiosity and burning envy. He should have been there with them.

"They're saying Mr. Harper came along just in the nick of time," Ma went on. "If you know what I mean. The girl's ruined, no matter what." She sat down and savored her coffee like she'd never had better. "Our Sarah was truly the Belle of the Ball at that Frolic. The Cornet's Lass. You remember, Luke, the whole town voted for her to be the Cornet's Lass. You'd have been all puffed up to see her lead the parade! I must say she comported her self just like the lady we raised her to be. Still, I must say that quiet-seeming Allie Hanover is a revelation. And not a good one, at that." As if catching herself being small-minded, she added quickly, "Why, it's just what everyone's saying."

"Allie *is* a nice girl," Sarah said, her voice as flat as her expression. She slid narrowed eyes at Pa. "And you've no call to think bad of Ned."

Pa bristled. "Don't you be telling me what I've cause to think or not think, girl."

"I hear he beat those horrible men to a bloody pulp," Ma said. "Course, I can't be the one to say if that's a good or bad thing."

"Sorry, Pa. I didn't mean to sass," Sarah said, in the tone Joseph knew meant she wanted something. "Zeke's asked me to come out to watch the baseball team on Sunday. May I go with him?"

Pa chewed his biscuit. "That barber fellow?"

"The Cornet, Luke," Ma said. "You know who he is. He was voted by the town, just like Sarah." Her eyes brightened. "Zeke Foster's as fine a young man as there is. Runs his own business and all. He just dotes on Sarah. Oh my!" she stood abruptly and refilled Luke's cup, set down the pot, and nervously smoothed her skirt. "In all the excitement, I didn't think to tell either of you—he asked if he might come call on her." At her husband's stiffening, she added, "He means to ask your permission himself, of course."

"May I go, Pa? To the baseball practice. "

From Albert, Joseph had learned Ned Harper was the Sluggers' hurler, that he'd be there dazzling the batters with a mysterious pitch that almost no one could hit. Or, as Albert had said, even see. He wanted to be there with Albert—who had described it all to him—and see the wondrous world that was the baseball field, to see the men swing mighty clubs that launched a ball into the heavens, to see them leap and dive and lunge to catch the ones that hugged the earth. To be part of the crowd that gasped and cheered. To be part of something.

Heart running faster than his legs ever could, Joseph entreated his father. "Can . . . I go, too? Please, Pa . . . please."

Pa stood, palms flattened on the table, and leaned toward Sarah. "You see what you're stirring up here, girl? What do you think'll happen if I let your brother go out there with the boys that'll be at that game? Boys who've got nothin' better to do than look for trouble?"

"Nothing will happen, Pa. They'll be there to watch the game, not him. Besides, Albert will be there, he'll stick with Joseph and I'll look out for him, too."

Emboldened by Sarah's support, Joseph lurched to his feet. He wanted to say what he wished he'd said when his father had refused to let him go to the Gathering. Or fishing. Or when he hadn't understood about wolf medicine.

Scared as he was, the words had a will of their own. "I . . . I don't care . . . what anyone says . . . or does . . . Pa. I . . . want to go." At his father's stunned expression, he lifted his trembling chin. "You never let me . . . be . . . like other boys."

Pa recoiled. To Joseph, his father's flinch felt like a slap. In the silence that followed, time slowed. Joseph saw his mother's jaw drop and her hands twist in the folds of her apron. Sarah tilted her head and stared at him. His father's face went hard, then crumbled in on itself.

"You're not like other boys, son," Pa said. "It's time you understand what that means and stop wishing for what can't be."

Wishing, Joseph thought. He's going to tell me wishes are less than spit in the palm of my hand. Ned Harper thinks I can be like other boys.

He let me work with him. He tossed me like a sack of potatoes, just like he tossed Albert.

"From the day you were born," Pa's voice was thick and rough, like it pained him to talk. "I swore I'd protect you from any harm I could. That's what I intend to do." He lowered himself heavily into his chair. "That's all I can do."

Not meeting his eyes, Ma whispered, "Luke, please. He needs to go beyond our gate sometimes. The boy needs to look at something more than what he sees here every day."

Pa clasped his hands so tight around his mug his knuckles turned white.

"You're not going to that baseball game, son." Setting his mouth, he said, "You want to get outside our gate, you can come with me when I go to the tack and feed and sit out in the wagon behind the store. You'll see the same old trees, birds, carts, and horses you see in your own yard."

Joseph collapsed inside of himself. The cage had gotten smaller since he'd come to understand not everyone lived in cages and—his heart ached with the thought—that his father was his jailer, not his protector.

Not looking at Joseph, Pa sighed. "Sarah Sue, I'll think on what you asked. I do reckon it's time you found yourself a husband. I can't protect everyone from their own foolishness."

CHAPTER THIRTY-FIVE

On the morning after the Frolic, Allie sat stiff-backed in the delicate Queen Anne chair in her mother's morning room. She sensed Maude Mary listening, a huddled presence on the third step down from the top of the staircase. Her thoughts went to the night before when her younger sister had crept into bed with her and wept in her arms.

"I don't know why I went with that horrid creature," she'd sobbed, shaking so hard Allie had to wrap her arms tight around her. "Why I let him touch me . . . touch my hair. I should've known . . . better."

"You couldn't, Maudie. You mustn't blame yourself, not for one single, solitary part of one single second." Allie stroked the girl's hair, still horror stricken herself at what they had witnessed. The despicable men, the violence. The madness that had possessed Ned. Her heart constricted. What might have happened if he hadn't appeared and released that darkness on those monsters. His darkness.

"They picked you because they knew you were too young to understand what they intended." Sarah should have known, Allie thought. Still, she had no regrets for what she'd done to shield the girl from the wrath of her father. Hannah, level-headed and steady-handed, had repaired the teal dress and calmed the shaken girls enough so Sarah could return to South Slope and change into the clothes she'd worn there. So she could pretend all was well, while Mrs. Findlay eyed Allie with an expression of sympathy, soured with distaste. A look Allie would find mirrored on the faces of many of the townfolk over the next weeks.

With a gentle finger, Allie had tilted her sister's tear-streaked face up to meet her gaze. "And, Miss Maudie, remember this: No one—no one—can ever know that you and Sarah were at the stable. Ever. You understand why."

Maude Mary had nodded. When her weeping subsided, she'd whispered, "But what will Mama do to you?"

There are many possible answers to that, Allie had thought. To ease her troubled sister, she'd chuckled softly. "Our mother will undoubtedly sentence me to a Debutante Ball in Boston which I will be required to attend wearing the ruffled pink taffeta ball gown she wore at her own Coming Out. With her plumed aigrette in my hair, of course."

Smiling at the images, Maude Mary had slipped into an exhausted sleep.

Allie had not.

Now, in the lemony light of midmorning, their mother, her face splotched with the high color of ire, glowered from the sofa. Doc stood behind her with one hand on the back of the couch, his expression unreadable. Not even the pot of tea steeping on the mosaic table could add cheer to the tense atmosphere. With its hard back and cushioned seat, the Queen Anne chair had always been Allie's least favorite piece of furniture in the entire house. She'd never been able to find a comfortable position in what she and Will had dubbed the Scolding Chair and had to stifle the urge to fidget.

Long ago, she'd realized her mother's frame of mind could infuse the bright and pretty room with whatever mood she happened to be in at the time. Today, Allie mused to calm herself, we have the sharp tang of anger, a hint of righteous indignation, and a strong note of parental disappointment. All to be expected and, she had to admit, all well-deserved. But what heightened her apprehension was the trace of triumph she sensed permeating everything else.

"I will not ask what you could possibly have been thinking because, of course, you clearly had not," Mrs. Hanover began. Her plump features had withered, shrinking her eyes and mouth to tight circles. Last night, when she'd learned of the events at the Frolic, she hadn't inquired about Allie's well-being nor asked a single question.

Allie had felt her father tremble when he'd held her close and made her repeat again and again that she had not been harmed. Finally satisfied with her answers, he'd stepped back and said, "We'll discuss this in the morning."

"I have come to expect you to be somewhat irregular in your ideas," her mother went on, "but it never occurred to me to be concerned for your sense of decency." She rose and walked to the open French doors. With her back to Allie, she said, "You've proven me wrong about that, I'm saddened to say. I am stricken, Alexandrina, and shamed beyond enduring by my daughter's wantonness. I—this family—have always enjoyed the highest regard in our small community. Your shocking behavior has deprived us of our good name."

Allie understood her parents' distress. She'd known the moment she ripped her dress there would be consequences, but was certain she and her family would not be destroyed by them as Sarah most certainly would have been. With genuine contrition, she cast her eyes down. "I am truly so very sorry."

Pressing her back into the polished wood of the uncomfortable chair, she awaited her sentence. She hadn't been joking when she told Maude Mary what she expected it to be. Their mother was an opportunist. Allie knew full well that this unfortunate incident afforded her the chance she'd thus far been denied.

"If there ever had been anything to discuss before, there is most assuredly nothing now." Mrs. Hanover turned partway, so she now spoke in profile. "There is nothing for it, Alexandrina, but that you must go away from here. To Boston. I've written to Aunt Hope and expect to hear she'll receive you this autumn. You will have your Bud Year, culminating in your presentation to society at your Debutante Ball. This is not meant to be a punishment, though I imagine you'll disagree." She completed the turn to face Allie. "Your behavior has clearly demonstrated you have been sullied by the foul influences of this place. Boston will counter that."

Sullied. Absorbing the blow she had known was coming, Allie still couldn't help but shudder inwardly. My 'Bud Year,' she thought bitterly. My mother cares little and knows me less—except, of course, in understanding how to hurt me most. Banishment to big, dirty, teeming Boston and the inane life of a debutante would do just that.

Allie knew all to well what she would endure there. Her mother had regaled her since childhood with the delights of a girl's introduction to society: Months of music and dancing classes at Papanti's exclusive Academy, horseback riding lessons two afternoons a week on the Fenway—to master the absurdity of the English saddle, despite the fact that Allie was already adept in the more practical and comfortable Western style—and long, long Saturday evening cotillions on the arms of over-eager Harvard sophomores.

A frivolous season of afternoon teas and nightly dances, dinners, theater, and parties with other 'buds' awaited her. She would attend scores of Debutante Balls at scores of opulent houses decorated with smilax and floral vines and roses and lilies. Elegant rooms would be cleared for dancing, with antique chairs lined up against the walls for chaperones. Champagne and sherbet would be served by bored waiters standing behind linen-draped counters. And, she would stand in endless receiving lines greeting proper men from proper families with proper incomes. Like the suffocating stays and corsets she'd be forced to wear, the thought stifled her ability to breathe.

Her mother's voice rasped on. "Aunt Hope will try . . . and isn't it unthinkable that she should have to *try* . . . to restore your respectability and find you a suitable husband. One who is unaware of your indiscretion."

Aunt Hope. Allie brightened at the thought of the irreverent old lady who had once whispered to her, "Have no fear, child. You are stronger and smarter than your mother and always will be."

As if sensing Allie had seized on a comforting thought, her mother quashed it. "I, of course, will accompany you."

Out of the corner of her eye, Allie noted that Maude Mary had silently crept down to the landing where she could peer through the banister posts. Straightening her shoulders, Allie folded her hands in her lap and steadied herself. "That won't be necessary, Mother." The gaze she directed at her was unfaltering. "I'm not going to Boston."

In the stunned silence that followed, Mrs. Hanover darkened, a storm about to strike. "Alexandrina Victoria, I warn you—do not provoke me."

"I understand it's best I leave Solace Springs for a time," Allie said, edging into what she knew would be dangerous territory. "I've applied to medical schools in Iowa and New York and expect to be accepted by one or both. Lydia assures me the work I've done with Papa has afforded me rare preparation and that the case studies I've included in my petitions should help my chances of acceptance."

Doc met her eyes and a small smile played at the corners of his mouth. He had told her more than once she knew as much about horse bites, bullet wounds, ax mishaps, and snake bites as she needed to know. There was nothing more for her to learn in Solace Springs. Emboldened by what she took to be his approval, she added, "I prefer Iowa because as a 'regular' medical college that accepts men and women, it offers a more comprehensive education. After I complete my studies, I intend to return here to practice."

Aghast, Mrs. Hanover turned to her husband. "Charles, what do you say to your daughter's defiance? Or are you complicit in this absurdity?"

Her father, who had been silent and unreadable, came to stand at her mother's side. Allie feared he might, despite all his encouragement for her to attend medical college, see her future from her mother's perspective. A finger of ice pressed into the small of Allie's back.

"My darling," Doc said, slipping his arm around his wife's waist. "I say our beloved daughter has demonstrated an uncanny ability to turn what was a disastrous lapse in judgment," he paused and frowned at Allie, "into a decision about her future that we can—and should—applaud." As he pulled his wife closer, Allie saw her outrage soften. "The only thing that might be considered absurd in any of this," he said, grinning down at her, "is that you entertained the notion that our daughter would consent to wear pink taffeta and put an aigrette in her hair."

CHAPTER THIRTY-SIX

Struggling to order his drunken thoughts, Ned tried again to figure how it was he found himself stumbling out of the Tanglefoot Saloon so late that the moon had begun to dissolve into the murk between dark and dawn. Cheap whiskey and disgust churned in his gut. The soul-sullying place had once fostered his youthful debaucheries and cheered him on during his most brutal brawls.

Miss Birdie's whores had nurtured other things. He supposed he'd come tonight to seek comfort in a place as defiled as his spirit. In the weeks that followed his attack on Nix and Jeb, Ned had kept to himself. He left the cabin only to work with Trouble and Sugarplum at the H&H and to hurl for the Sluggers. The horses expected nothing more from him than a steady hand and a quiet voice; the baseball team needed only his curve ball.

Convinced Red Moon's dire warning about Badger had been proven correct, he was certain everyone he cared for would be better off without him. With increasing frequency, a voice in his mind insisted that, like a brainsick calf, he needed to be put down.

Steadying himself against Trickster before making another clumsy attempt to swing up into the saddle, Ned was too lost in sodden self-loathing to notice the small shape charging toward him in the darkness until the child barreled into him. The ragged little girl staggered back, righted herself, then stood in front of him, chin tucked to her chest, eyes on her bare feet.

When he comprehended the situation, it sobered him some. *A child. Alone. In the dead of night. At the degenerate Tanglefoot.* Hunkering down on one shaky knee, he put himself at eye level with the waif. Her flushed face knotted with the effort to hold back tears.

"Hey, little miss," he said, in the tone he'd use to soothe any skitterish animal. "I'm Ned Harper. What's your name?"

When she raised her head, the eyes that met his were as wide and white as a terrified mare's. Wrapping an arm around her, he pulled her closer. "What's got you so upset? Maybe I can help."

"My Mama," she whispered, raising her eyes. "Please, mister, I'm Etta Ruth Winnicott and I need my daddy quick-smart. He comes here to pull the tiger's tail and my mama is crying and there's blood in the bed."

Ned stood, shaken by the image of a woman lying in a blood-soaked bed, his face almost too wooden to speak. "What's your daddy's name?"

"Mr. Ephraim Winnicott."

"Wait here."

Stumbling through the swinging doors, Ned was assaulted by the rough language, ribald laughter, and chime and clink of tobacco hitting spittoons. The place stank of filthy sawdust, sour sweat, and the sickly-sweetness of cheap perfume. Angling between patrons and prostitutes, he pushed his way to the saloon's gambling room. At each of three oval tables that all but filled the faro parlor, six men faced the banker with piles of chips stacked or spilled on the green baize in front of them. Avid-eyed onlookers hovered at their backs.

"Ephraim Winnicott!" Ned bellowed, above the din. "Eph . . . raim Winnicott!"

Heads turned at the interruption.

Intent on the game at the center table, a lanky young man with stringy blond hair glanced over his shoulder. Ned recognized him from the baseball practices—a lazy player who could be good with a bat when he had a mind to.

"That's me, to whoever's askin'." Returning his attention to the faro bank, Ephraim flattened his hands on the table. "But as you can see, friend, I'm havin' a fine run of luck right about now, so whatever you want is gonna have to wait a spell. A long spell, I hope."

Grasping the back of Ephraim's chair, Ned wrenched it away from the table, almost toppling him out of it. The men standing behind stepped back to make room for a brawl. "Your child's outside crying and your wife's at home bleeding," Ned spat. "You will come with me." Snatching the hat from Ephraim's head, he swept his chips into it. "Now."

"My wife?" Ephraim gaped at him. "Clarie? Clarie's bleeding?" Understanding drained the color from his face. He grabbed his hat back and followed Ned from the saloon.

Etta flung herself at her father. "Daddy, it's Mama," she whimpered into his neck. "It's Mama, she's . . ."

"I know, Chipmunk." Ephraim stroked her matted hair, staring grim-faced and helpless at Ned. "It'll be fine, Etta. Don't you worry. Your mama's gonna be just fine."

"Go to your wife." Ned knew all too well what Ephraim would find there. Calling on strength he didn't feel, he swung into the saddle. "I'll get Doc Hanover."

"He knows us. Miss Allie does, too," Ephraim babbled. "She calls on Clarie. Just tell them it's the Winnicott place up the slope. They'll know where. You can see it from here." He pointed in the direction of the shanty, but made no move to go there. Slack-jawed, he turned back to Ned. "What should I do? I don't know what to do."

"Go home, Ephraim," Ned said. "Doc'll be there, soon as he can."

Turning Trickster, Ned spurred him to a gallop until he pulled up at South Slope. He'd made that same crazed ride down Commerce Street before. Still drunk and mad with fear for the young woman in the bloody bed, he vaulted up the porch steps and pummeled the Hanovers' door until a sleepy maid opened it.

He'd pounded that door before. Would have broken it down, if he could. Steadying himself with one arm against the door jamb, he rasped, "I need Doc."

Sinking to the top step, he sat with elbows on his knees, palms pressed to his eyes, trying to push back memories he couldn't bear. When Doc appeared, Ned didn't stand or turn to face him. "Clare Winnicott's bleeding."

The weight of Doc's hand on his shoulder was meant to comfort, Ned knew, so he tried not to wrench free of it.

A single oil lamp haloed a small, cold circle of light in Doc's study. Although it was past midnight and a summer squall battered the mullioned windows, no fire warmed the hearth. Allie and he had ridden off to Clare Winnicott before dawn that morning and the servants knew when the doctor went on a call, there was no telling when he might return.

Slumped in the large Chesterfield chair, Doc said, "I've seen it before, blast my eyes. And will likely see it again. And so will you. Women so desperate to end a pregnancy they'll grasp at any means available."

Standing at her father's side, Allie faced the window, arms tight across her chest. Wind-maddened branches slapped at the glass, but it wasn't the weather that chilled her. Her father was not a man given to profanities and she added his distress to the list of failures she blamed upon herself.

"Clare Winnicott will survive, my dear. Or she will not." Doc rubbed a hand wearily across his eyes. "We've done everything we can, now we must get what sleep we can, then watch and wait."

Allie nodded, an automatic response to words she only half heard above the clamor in her head. *My fault, all my fault. I could have . . . should have . . . prevented this.*

Heeding Ned's urgent message, Doc had awakened Allie, and they'd hurried to the shanty early that morning. They'd found Clare bleeding, thrashing in pain, and wracked with fever. The stench of blood, foul secretions, and infection thickened the air in the cramped room. Ephraim knelt by her sweat-soaked pallet trying to comfort her. Huddled in a corner, Etta did her best to soothe the younger children.

While Doc spoke reassurances to Clare and prepared to examine her, Allie had pulled Ephraim from his wife's side. Waiting until his eyes focused on hers, she told him. "You must take the little ones to a neighbor."

"A neighbor?" He'd blinked in confusion. "We don't know no neighbors. I can't think what to do, Miss." His pleading eyes searched her face. "Clarie would be the one to know about such, not me."

"The children need to go someplace for a short time," Allie pressed. "It's too upsetting for them to be here now."

Clasping his hands behind his head, Ephraim squeezed his eyes shut. When Clare cried out as Doc touched her distended belly, he flinched and the children sobbed louder. "I s'pose . . . I s'pose I could take 'em to the whores . . . the girls . . . at the Tanglefoot," he mumbled. "Clarie won't like it, but it'll have to do. Leastways 'til it's time for the ladies to go back to work."

Before Allie could inform him the saloon most certainly wouldn't do—even though she had no other solution in mind—Etta slipped her small hand into hers and tugged.

"I know a neighbor, Miss," she said. "Old Nanny Lou up the hill. Her knees hurt her, so me and the little ones pull carrots from her garden and wash 'em in the creek and she calls us her bunnies and let's us munch one each." The girl stared at her delirious mother, then, up at her father. "I want to take the babies to Nanny's house, Daddy." Releasing Allie's hand, she took his. "I'll show you the way."

When Ephraim and the children had gone, Doc told Allie, "Extensive vaginal bleeding, foul-smelling discharge, severe abdominal pain. High fever, chills."

"A miscarriage gone septic?"

"No," Clare had moaned, grasping Doc's hand and pulling him closer. "No. I . . . *I* did it. A turkey feather . . . God forgive me . . . from Miss Birdie's hat." Her breathing more labored, she whimpered, "The girls at the Tanglefoot say they do it all the time."

Every part of Allie went cold. If I had brought the womb veil when it arrived, she thought, this wouldn't be happening.

"I understand, my dear," Doc told Clare, stroking damp hair back from her forehead. "You did what you believed must be done. God has forgiven you and you must forgive yourself." Slipping an arm behind her shoulders, he raised her head. "Now, *you* must forgive *me* for the bitterness of this laudanum. Swallow it and your pain will ease."

Allie struggled for composure. *My fault if those children are left motherless.*

Clare sipped, gagged, then turned her face away from the noxious glass of red-brown liquid. But even that small amount brought relief and in a moment she grimaced and finished what remained. When her eyes closed and her tortured features relaxed, Doc turned to Allie.

In the teaching voice she knew often masked his own emotions, her father said, "Septic abortion, then. Self-inflicted. Different in cause, but similar in effect to any miscarriage gone bad. Pay close attention, Allie. As Hippocrates said, 'Life is so short, and the craft so long to learn.' "

Allie had read advertisements in periodicals selling potions, pills, and powders with cloaked promises to cause miscarriage. "French Periodical

Pills: Warranted to Have the Desired Effect in All Cases." Abortion was illegal, so the ads spoke euphemistically of "unblocking an obstructed womb" or "curing the problem of suppression of the courses." All, Doc had explained, carried the risk of sepsis, infertility, or death. "I'm sorry to say," he said now, "you'll see this many times, in one form or another, as you practice our craft. So, it's time for you to learn the use of the curette."

While he cleaned out Clare's womb, he asked Allie to name the three layers of the uterus.

Seared to the core by guilt and failure, she found some relief in the simple anatomy exercise. "Inner lining, endometrium," she said. Her astute father always knew how to calm her nerves. "Middle muscular layer, myometrium. Outer, perimetrium."

"Good. Now for the practical." He gestured for Allie to take the handle of the sharp-looped curette. After a moment's disbelief, she willed her shaking hands to be steady and inserted the instrument. "Feel the size and shape of the uterus," Doc instructed. "Scrape only the surface of the endometrium to remove any remaining fetal tissue. Work quickly, but take care not to perforate or nick the organ."

When she found no more excess tissue, Allie relinquished the curette to her father. "I believe I'm done."

Doc made a few cursory scrapes and nodded. "Yes, I do believe you are, my dear. Well done."

They'd spent the rest of that anxious day and much of the night at the shanty in what Doc called "watchful waiting." Clare didn't improve, but she didn't worsen. When Ephraim returned from Nanny Lou's, they kept him busy learning to give Clare regular doses of laudanum and to keep her as hydrated as possible with water he was firmly directed to fetch from far upstream of the privy. When he'd mastered those tasks, Allie sent him to South Slope with a note requesting a large pot of hearty beef broth for the patient and stew, milk, and sticky black ginger bread for the children.

When they'd done what they could for Clare and settled Ephraim's nerves as much as possible, they rode home just before midnight, promising to return in the morning.

Exhausted, yet certain she would not sleep, Allie joined her father in what she'd always known to be the sanctuary of his study. Tonight she found no comfort there. Neither he nor she spoke for many moments.

"It's in the hands of the Almighty," Doc finally said, rising slowly from the chair behind his desk. "Go to bed, my dear. Morning will be here sooner than either of us wish."

"Yes, Papa." If I look at him, I'll cry, Allie thought. And I will not cry.

"What is it, child?"

She managed to hold back her tears, but the words she hadn't wanted to say rose in her throat and forced their way out. "It's my fault, Papa. I promised to help her. I had the womb veil and I didn't bring it in time." She surrendered to the safe circle of his arms until she could breathe, then pulled away. "I am stupid and selfish and irresponsible. If I'd done what I promised, she wouldn't have turned to the whores and their horrid feathers. How can I tell Lydia I failed my patient because I was more concerned about Hannah's silly Gathering than about a woman in my care? You taught me the Physicians' Oath is to 'do no harm,' but I've harmed Clare in the worst possible way. She may die because of my negligence."

Doc sighed and guided her to one of chairs facing the hearth.

"I see you've been introduced to the physician's constant companion: Regret." He sat in the facing chair, pulled the stopper from a decanter of amber fluid, and poured a finger of whiskey into each of a pair of glasses. "He hovers around awaiting any opportunity to remind us of our lack of omnipotence." Wrapping Allie's icy fingers around a tumbler, he added, "As I told our poor Clare Winnicott, the potion may be bitter, but it will lessen your pain. Sip slowly."

The first taste of whiskey she'd ever had burned her throat, but sent a warm flow of well-being through her chest. As promised, it eased the ache in her heart. Some. And not for long.

"Dearest girl," Doc said, easing himself into the chair facing her. He set his glass on the small table between them and took her hands in his. "Do you not understand that your patient was already with child at the time you offered her the womb veil?" He made Allie hold his gaze. "You mustn't blame yourself. If you intend to do the work you are meant to do, you must learn this: There will always be tragedies beyond your control. You can only do that which is within your limited power to lessen them."

"She used a feather, Papa. She maimed herself, killed her baby, with a . . . a . . . turkey feather."

Taking a generous sip of his own whiskey, Doc indicated Allie should do the same.

"The harsh truth is the fetus was at least three months gestation. You could not have offered her a means to end her pregnancy. You did not cause this, Allie, and you, nor I, nor any physician could have prevented it."

The whiskey turned sour in her stomach. "In that case, what could I have done for her?" Regret, the nemesis her father had spoken of, mocked her. The thought of going to medical school became a lump of lead in her heart.

"Often, we cannot prevent suffering, but when called upon, we must try." Doc held her gaze with eyes she now understood to be wearied by the anguish of others. "Sometimes the best a physician can do is to ease pain where we find it. We must learn to be satisfied with that."

But what if I can't, she thought, dizzied by doubt. I'm unfit and unworthy and can't be trusted to 'do no harm.' Doubt hardened to certainty. Mother was right, it is absurd for me to imagine myself going to medical school. Maybe it *is* best to let her and Aunt Hope plan my life. I seem to be making a fine mess of it on my own.

With that, her decision was made.

CHAPTER THIRTY-SEVEN

Stumbling upon little Etta and being thrust into Clare Winnicott's tragic plight had plumbed the depths of Ned's misery. That night, his soul began its walk into the woods. Sleepless, he wrestled with the dilemma of how to end himself in a way that wouldn't cause his friends to feel they'd failed him. Night after night, he ransacked every dark alley and refuse heap of his mind for a solution.

Finally, it had come to him—the way out. With a clear plan, his spirits lifted. He and Cloud lounged on the porch absorbing the early morning sun. After savoring a cup of strong black coffee, Ned studied the baseball cap in his hands, fingering the edges. Hurler for the Solace Springs Sluggers. The thought made him chuckle. Becky would be amused, too. Leaning back, he breathed in the scent of sun-baked pine and—for the first time in weeks—looked forward to the afternoon baseball practice.

Slapping the cap on his head, he swung up on Trickster and made his way downhill toward the aptly named Elysian Field. Baseball. Completing the tasks he'd set for himself would get him through the days until autumn. He now knew he needn't distress his friends by walking off into the woods and disappearing without a trace. He'd figured a way to leave them that would cause neither guilt nor grief.

"Have a seat." Doc said, setting the papers he'd been reading on his desk. With a gesture toward the reclining treatment chair in the center of his clinic, he raised a brow at Ned. "I hope I shouldn't be concerned to see you here."

"Not at all," Ned replied with an uneasy laugh, eyeing the large contraption. He'd had his share of less-than-pleasant experiences in Doc's chair, including getting stitched up by Allie when she'd been hardly more than a child. He wrinkled his nose at the odor of carbolic, chlorine, and charcoal that hung in the air. "I'm fine as snuff."

The clinic—two rooms at the rear of the Bank of Solace Springs—reminded Ned of Zeke's barber shop, only bigger. And with shelves of books. And cabinets full of ointments, potions, powders, and liquids. Knives, probes, saws, forceps, clamps, and other instruments he'd never asked the name or purpose of, and never would, decorated the walls. A massive, antique Chinese desk that commanded a quarter of the office.

"Have a seat," Doc repeated more firmly, pointing to the chair. "Since your encounter with those miscreants at the Frolic, I've noticed you favoring your arm when you pitch." Though they'd never spoken of it, Ned knew that what Doc believed had happened to Allie that night still distressed him. "We certainly can't risk arm trouble with the game against the formidable Fountain City Nine coming up in little more than a month. Let me take a quick look."

"That's not why I'm here."

"I'll be the judge of that."

Surrendering to Doc and the chair, Ned rolled up his sleeve and offered the arm Trouble had bitten months ago. While Doc prodded his forearm and bent his wrist and fingers every which way, he dug his heels into the leather foot rest and managed not to flinch. The thrashing he'd given Nix and Jeb had cost him. "I'm here because there's something I want to ask you."

"After I've determined whether or not you're fit to pitch." When the examination was complete, Doc rolled his chair back. "In my opinion as a physician, you should avoid any strenuous use of that arm. As the Slugger's most ardent booster, I'll just say you should rest it as much as you can, then give us everything you've got at the game with Fountain City." Doc leaned back. "Now, ask away."

Ned swung out of the examination chair and settled into the ornate seat next to Doc's desk. A calm had settled over him since he'd figured out how to end his life without troubling his friends. Part of his plan was to prepare them for his exit. Doc would be the easiest, so Ned thought to tell him first. Practice of a sort.

After studying the detailed depictions of warriors in battle carved into the desk's drawers and panels, Ned said, "I've been thinkin' you ought to come out and have a drink or two with me at the Tongue Oil." At the perturbed look on the older man's face, he added, "I'm talking about takin' you across the street to the tame old Tongue Oil, Doc, not down to the devil's doorstep. By that I mean we won't be goin' anywhere near the Tanglefoot."

He knew the staid doctor disapproved of the goings on at the town's most disreputable drinking establishments, and of the many kinds of trouble a younger Ned had gotten himself into at most of them. Tongue's girls were respectable, mostly, and darts was the only game of chance available. Brawls did break out on occasion, Ned had to admit, but on Saturday nights. Mostly.

"And, why is it, exactly," Doc, who rarely asked questions, inquired, "you think I ought to accompany you to that establishment?"

"In all the years you've lived out here, you've never once set foot in a genuine saloon or had yourself a single shot of rotgut whiskey." Ned grinned at him. "It's about time you let down and enjoyed yourself."

Doc pondered the invitation with a show of gravity that failed to mask his interest. "I must say I don't much like the sound of 'rotgut.' If I'm going to ingest something you suggest will damage my viscera, I'd like to know exactly . . ."

"Doc, rotgut's rotgut. Just like it sounds. Cheap whiskey . . . cut with a little something extra."

"Ned Harper, you know me to be a man of science and science requires exactitude. 'A little something extra' tells me nothing."

Ned quelled his impatience. "Could be turpentine," he offered. "Or ammonia or gunpowder. Maybe a pinch of cayenne pepper. I do believe Tongue favors gunpowder."

Deciding on full disclosure before luring his cautious friend out of his cozy study with every intention of getting him soundly drunk, he added, "Some folks call it 'coffin varnish.' "

"Coffin varnish." Doc grimaced and shook his head. "I suspect I may regret this, but a man of science shouldn't pass up an opportunity to broaden his knowledge of the greater world, gun powder condiments notwithstanding." He leveled a hard look at Ned. "And we will *not* mention this . . . research . . . to Mrs. Hanover."

"I surely won't."

Ned felt confident that drunk or sober Doc would understand his need to leave Solace Springs and find his plan to do so believable. And, he hoped, after a few glasses of strong whiskey, the man of science would be less apt to ask his questions that weren't questions.

Their visit to the Tongue Oil Saloon a few nights later turned out just as he'd hoped. Doc had given his blessing to the plan. Nonetheless, Ned knew getting Will and Hannah to do the same wouldn't be as easy.

Will listened in silence, mouth downturned, eyes burning through Ned. "New Zealand."

"Yep."

"No, mo charaid," Hannah whispered, her eyes bright with tears. "Ye canna leave us. What will we do without ye?"

"I'm sure you'll find another scunner to torment with your vinegar pies," Ned said. "Now won't ye, Lass?"

Hannah's face remained solemn. "Ye really feel it's what ye must do?"

"I do." He deceived them with the truth—he had no doubt what he'd decided to do must be done. Empty now, he felt nothing. "I haven't seen my brother since the War."

"And what of your cabin? What of Cloud and Trickster?"

"I'll buy my homestead and leave it in your keeping. Trickster," he hoped they didn't notice the catch in his voice, "Trickster, too. Cloud'll come with me to New Zealand." Another lie. "He can sail leashed." He planned to take the dog with him into the woods just outside of Morrison, a few stagecoach stops from Solace Springs. Half wild, Cloud would survive in the winter wilderness. Find or make a pack of his own. Thrive there, Ned told himself. Or not. Darkness enveloped him. I can't be here, he reminded himself. Don't let them see that.

"Think of the gold I'll bring back!" Ned poked Will's arm. At about the time gold had run out in California, it had been discovered in New Zealand. "You'll see, I'll be back someday with saddlebags full of it and buy up all the land for miles. If you stop giving me those black looks, I might even consider partnering up with you again."

Hannah wept and Will scowled, but both agreed it would be good for him to get away from Solace Springs. For a while.

It took more than a week before he could force himself to make the ride out to Heck and Red Moon at the Golden Eagle Ranch.

Ned hadn't seen them since the Gathering, hadn't been out to their place in almost two years, so when Red Moon caught sight of him leaning against her kitchen door jamb, framed in the silver light of dawn, she gave a small yelp.

Heck looked up from his coffee with a startled look, but his expression quickly changed to pleasure. "Now I surely do understand what's meant by a fellow 'darkening your doorway!' "

Head down, Ned said, "I was hopin' I might trade a day's work for supper." The same words he'd muttered when he'd appeared at the ranch ten years ago, hat in shaking hand, as unable then to meet their eyes or return their smiles as if the kind old couple had been a pair of grizzlies.

Heck laughed. "Sure, son." The elderly rancher echoed the words he'd replied at the time. "That might be arranged—long as we can agree on just what constitutes a day's work."

"And," no longer the frightened boy he'd been back then, Ned nodded toward the steaming pots hanging over the hearth fire, "if we can agree supper includes elk and cornmeal patties, a big bowl of that stew I smell, and as many slices of fry bread as I can eat."

"You'd best come inside, then." The old rancher lifted his bulk from the chair and extended his hand. It struck Ned he had aged in the few months since he'd seen him last. His long white hair had thinned and there was a slight stoop to his shoulders. "Appears," Heck continued, "we have us a bit of parleyin' to do before you can start mucking out stalls."

Sauntering into the warmth of the familiar kitchen, Ned removed his hat and took the seat at the table that had been his for the three years he'd worked for Heck—and anytime he'd visited since. Mixed aromas of breakfast and the supper Red Moon was cooking for the ranch hands reminded him he hadn't eaten since some time the day before. "I wouldn't object," he added, "if our deal includes a cup of that coffee. Before I start work, of course."

"You drive a harder bargain than you did back then. You showed up here looking like you didn't have a day's worth of work in you." Heck chuckled again and shook his head. "Why, back then you'd have settled for a slice of stale bread and a cup of cold chicory."

"And been glad to have it," Ned agreed. Heck and Red Moon had taken him in and stood by him when he'd faltered as a youth. As difficult as he knew this visit would be, he'd gotten himself here and meant to accomplish what he'd come to do. He owed them that. And more.

"That chair has been empty too long, Son of My Heart." Red Moon, straight and slim as ever, stood behind Ned with one hand on his shoulder, the other resting on the top of his head—a gesture so familiar and forgotten at the same time, that it stopped his breath. "But since you're here, he. . . " she tilted her chin at Heck, ". . . will be happy to know I'll cook corn and pumpkin pudding today."

From just past sun-up until dusk, Ned toiled as hard as he ever had mucking stalls, mending fences, and reminiscing with Heck and the ranch hands as they worked. Sitting at Red Moon's table for supper, they all ribbed him about playing baseball, passionately detailed the progress they'd made with the mustangs, and joked about the scalawags Ned had beaten senseless at the Frolic. All agreed it had taken a lot of gumption for those horse thieves to show up at the H&H. Ignoring Heck's stony frown, the men congratulated him on the triumphant reappearance of Seven Colors of Shit after all these years.

Late into the evening, conversation dwindled and the workers excused themselves to their bunkhouse. Ned knew the time had come to say what needed to be said, but waited for the odd sensation that overtook him to pass.

"I finally got a letter from my brother, Nate," he began slowly, gripping his refilled coffee mug. His hands had gone cold, but the heat that warmed his fingers kept them from trembling. As a man who valued honesty in himself and others, it pained him to tell a deliberate untruth to anyone, most of all Heck and Red Moon. The letter had come five or six years ago and been crumpled into the fire as soon as he'd read it. "After the war, he headed down to New Zealand to hunt for gold. Nothin' else would do but for him to cross that damned ocean."

Making his eyes lie was even harder, but Ned managed to convey pleasure he didn't feel. "He says he wound up at a place called Gabriel's Gulch. Says it's nothing short of paradise and there's still plenty of gold to be had. Says after so many years in this dusty little town, I'm probably wanting some adventure, too."

Here, a bogus grin. "He wants me to hop on a steamship and come find him there." Ned remembered the letter he'd read and reread before throwing it in the fire. "He might be somewhere up along the Wakamarina River, or maybe in the foothills of the Longwoods. Or, he says, he just might be in the town of Hokitika or Okarito. Somewhere on the west coast of New Zealand. Nate couldn't say for sure where he'd be prospecting next—he'll go wherever the gold leads him. Says he's sure I'll be able to track him down wherever he is."

After the war, the idea of a long steamship voyage across vast oceans to a strange land had drained what was left of Ned's spirit. No matter how hard his brother pressed him to come along, nor how much he didn't want to be left alone, Ned hadn't been able to bring himself to go with Nate. It wasn't that he hated him for taking them to war. That would come later. But, after burying Ben and Thomas at Spotsylvania, the idea of going anywhere with his surviving brother had worsened Ned's cold sweats and nightmares.

Nate lusted after excitement, riches, and loose, exotic women. What fifteen-year-old Ned longed for was the comfort of hay and horses and solid ground. When he finally told his brother that all he wanted was to go home and work the family ranch again—on his own if he had to—Nate confessed the ranch was gone. Sold for half the pittance it had been worth, just enough to pay their ways east to join the Union Army. That was when what might pass for hatred had set in.

Ned had accepted his share of what little was left of the proceeds from the ranch and they'd gone their separate ways—his brother to work passage across the sea on a mail ship, Ned to wander west until he wound up at Heck's kitchen door—where he'd found safety, succor, and Red Moon.

Now, he felt the old Indian woman's gaze bore through him. "Are you going away from here," she asked, her face impassive, "to that place?"

That place. A chill slid down Ned's spine.

"I'm considerin' it," he told her, solemn because he knew she wouldn't believe his smile. He met her gaze and hid nothing. No point in trying. "I need to get away from here. For a while, at least. Maybe longer."

Still and empty-eyed as a carved totem, Red Moon listened.

She knows.

"For a while then," Heck said heartily, slapping a hand on the table. Red Moon flinched. She stood behind him, fingers tight on his shoulders, eyes flat. "Go on then, get it out of your system. Find some gold. Find a lot of gold," he told Ned. "Then come on back here when you're ready. You don't want to be away from that fine little ranch of yours too long. Will's a good man, but he doesn't know horses like you do." Slanting mischievous eyes back over his shoulder at Red Moon, he covered her hand with his. "Maybe I'll join him, Darlin'. Just for a while, like he said. Every man needs an adventure now and again. I expect Hokamarina or Wakarita or some such should do just fine."

Ned took Red Moon's stillness as the displeasure he'd expected and was relieved it wasn't more. He'd spoken the truth—at least partly. She'd seen through it.

Heck poured them both a generous dram of whiskey. "To New Zealand!"

After more talk and a few more drinks, Ned declined the offer to spend the night in his old bunk. Though drained by the effort of deception, he felt relieved. As he'd done with Will and Hannah and Doc, he'd laid the groundwork for his leaving. He'd let them put him on the stage to Morrison to catch a train to Denver. Maybe even let them throw him a send-off of sorts. Let them believe he was on his way east to work his passage to Nate and New Zealand on a mail ship.

Red Moon knows and it doesn't change anything.

After Ned rode off, Heck dozed by the fire while Red Moon tidied the kitchen. "I do believe Ned's himself again, Darlin'," he said, when he roused. "Least ways, he's not lookin' glum as Job's turkey anymore."

Red Moon turned to him and patted the moisture from the corners of her eyes with the hem of her apron. "No, Bear Blinded by Hope, he's worse than we feared."

Heck stiffened at her words. "But what about all that talk about New Zealand and gold? Findin' that rascal brother of his? There was life in his face when he said he was thinkin' of an adventure." When he saw that his words hadn't comforted her, he added softly, "Don't worry so, Mother, he'll come back."

"I'm afraid that might not be so," she said. "Where others are deceived, one with Owl medicine sees and knows what is truly there. Whether we want to or not." She shook her head. "Our son has befriended the Warrior in White Robes, who now walks at his side. I saw it in his face. That's who he was smiling at, not us. The Warrior carries his burdens now."

Heck's bushy white brows lifted over troubled eyes. "You're sure, Darlin'?"

"I have proof." Pressing a hand to her chest, she sat heavily in the chair next to him. Tears found their way into the lines at the corners of her mouth. "He told me the secret ingredient to Becky's pemmican."

"Pemmican," Heck sighed. He wrapped an arm around her shoulders and pulled her close. "What can we do for him, then?"

"Nothing," Red Moon whispered, shrunken by sorrow. "If what I saw is true, he's lost to us. All we can do for him now is mourn."

She had come to the cabin uninvited, so Allie supposed it was her own fault she found Ned half naked.

"Hello!" she called out, quickly swinging down from her saddle. Flushed with embarrassment and the odd sensations that flooded her body, she kept her eyes lowered and hurried toward the shelter of the covered porch. For that moment, she forgot what had brought her here. Collecting herself, she called out again, "I'll set Hannah's basket right by the door."

When she'd rounded the bend that lead to his cabin, she'd caught sight of Ned crouched on the roof engrossed in hammering shingles. Shirtless in the mid-afternoon sun, his brown arms and shoulders glistened with sweat and a tumble of dark hair hid his face. As startled as she, he had straightened at her greeting, taken a step back, and almost lost his balance. With the hammer dangling in one hand, he'd shaded his eyes with the other. "Boston?"

"Yes! Yes . . . it's me." *What was I thinking? What am I doing here?* She'd almost turned back twice before letting Hippocrates make her way up the wagon trail. Struggling for calm, she reminded herself—I'm leaving town. I've come to say goodbye to a friend. A lifelong friend. "I'll . . . I'll just wait right here. On the porch."

When she heard the creak of the ladder and the soft thud as he skipped the last rungs and dropped to the ground, she seated herself in one of the wicker rockers and fixed her gaze on the farthest pines. She'd come with a heavy heart on several counts, but sitting in this chair—Becky's chair—reminded her there were hurts more tender than her own.

She hadn't seen Ned since the Frolic. The violence of that night still troubled her, but it had been the brutality she'd witnessed in Ned—what Allie understood to be unfettered rage and pain—that had made her stomach cave.

Now, buttoning his shirt, Ned appeared from the side of the cabin and loped up the wooden steps. He lowered himself into the rocker next to her and gave her an easy smile. "You came all the way up here to bring me Hannah's basket?"

"Yes." The color that had warmed her cheeks fled, leaving her cold. She studied the lacework of the far trees. "I mean, no. Well, not just for that." Meeting his gaze, she said, "I came because I have something to tell you."

Lifting his hat, he pushed damp hair back from his forehead, then turned to her. "Sounds serious."

Under his scrutiny—albeit teasing—her scant courage dissolved. She'd planned to amuse him with a description of the dreary debutante life that awaited her back East, determined not to mention medical college nor the reasons she'd decided not to go. His dark blue gaze threatened her resolve. "It is serious," she countered lightly, fighting the urge to tell him all, "but not in a bad way."

He arched a brow. "If you're here to tell me Luke Findlay gave Zeke permission to court Sarah, I already know. Baseball players are bigger gossips than a corral full of mares."

With a laugh, she relaxed. "It's not as serious as *that*."

Still, the words she needed eluded her.

In her lengthening silence, Ned slumped down in his seat, stretched his legs out, and tilted the brim of his hat to shade his face, as if preparing to nap.

"I'm going back East in the fall."

"Glad to hear it," he said, sitting up with a broad grin. "When you come back I'll be proud to call you 'Doctoress Boston.' "

"No. It'll just be 'Boston.'" The smile she fought for faltered. "I'm going East to become a debutante. Like you said about Rabbit, it seems I've called the thing I'm most afraid of to me."

Drawing back, he gaped at her, all playfulness gone. "Why?"

I can't tell him I've shamed my family and my mother is exiling me. I can't explain that I'm not fit for medical school because my negligence almost killed Clare Winnicott. I can't say I have nightmares about turkey feathers.

"My mother thinks it's for the best." Her words sounded as vacant and false as she felt. Lifting her chin, she forced resolve into her tone. "Believe it or not, I happen to agree."

"I *don't* believe it," he said. Sitting back hard, he narrowed his eyes at her. "I don't think you do either." The bravado she'd counted on to get her through this visit deserted her. When she said nothing, Ned pressed, "And Doc? What does he say?"

Her father had reasoned with her about her skills and passion, reminded her of Regret—the physician's constant companion—told her she would encounter countless tragedies in her work. If she'd made a mistake with Clare Winnicott, he hoped it would be the first of many because that would mean she had gone on to help numerous others. Ultimately, he'd pleaded with her to take time to let her feelings settle before making a disastrous decision.

"He agrees it's my choice to make."

Ned's mouth tightened. "Does this have anything to do with what you did for Sarah?"

In the days that had followed the Frolic, Allie could have found many reasons to rue her actions, but had not. The repercussions she'd given no thought to when she'd ripped her bodice had fallen upon her sure and swift—stares and whispers in town, grief and disapproval at home. She bore them all in silence and apologized only once to her parents for the poor judgment that had disgraced them all.

Tangled emotions tightened her throat. "It's not that." Ned's grim expression mirrored the feelings she didn't want to own. "I would be leaving in any case."

"Then go. But go to college, Boston. Be a doctor. That's what you're meant to do."

His disappointment in her added kindling to her own. "I came up here," she said, "because I wanted to tell you myself."

"That you're goin' East to be a *debutante?*"

"Yes."

When the silence grew so heavy Allie feared it would crush them, Ned turned to her again. "Since you were a little girl, the only thing you ever wanted was to be a doctor." She saw hurt in his eyes and knew it to be pain at her surrendering her dream. "This just doesn't make any sense."

Numb now, she could be stoic to make it easier for them both. Still, she had to look away. "It makes sense to me."

He drew a slow breath. On the exhale, he said, "I hope you change your mind."

Having told him what she'd come to tell him, Allie waited for what she'd come to hear.

A different hurt engulfed her. She hadn't been entirely truthful with him, or with herself. Delivering Hannah's basket and informing Ned of her plans were not the only reasons for her visit. After Doc and he had enjoyed their night of carousing at the Tongue Oil Saloon, her father had been heartened. The next morning, he told Allie that Ned seemed to have shaken off his despondency. "He's made up his mind to follow his brother to New Zealand to prospect for gold." Doc had looked over his spectacle rims and smiled at her. "I do believe it's a sign of the rekindling of his spirit."

Careful of her own expression, Allie had said, "I'm sure it is."

That, of course, had nothing to do with her decision to accept her banishment to Boston. Nor, she insisted to herself, did it have anything to do with her tears. For reasons she couldn't name, she had needed Ned to tell her himself that he would be leaving Solace Springs.

Keeping her eyes on the far trees, she gave him what she considered ample time. When he said nothing of his own plans—proof, she was certain, of her insignificance to him—she stood and bid him a stiff goodbye.

She knows, Ned thought, watching Allie ride off after the awkwardness that had followed their conversation. Of course, she knows. He remained on the porch, elbows on his knees, head bowed. Doc would have told her about New Zealand. She wanted me to tell her myself, but I didn't. Couldn't.

He stood and almost called her back, but couldn't do that either. Couldn't bring himself to lie to her. New Zealand was, aside from all else, a monumental lie. It's best the way it happened, he tried to convince himself. Allie would've seen beyond the trickery of his plan and taken it upon herself to make him answer for it.

Believing he was beyond feeling pain, he was surprised that the realization hurt the back of his throat and stung his eyes.

All this leave-taking left him more resolute than ever that it was nearly time to actually take his leave.

CHAPTER THIRTY-EIGHT

With her siblings straggling behind her, Etta walked alongside Allie toward the shanty. "Miss, I was just wonderin' would you tell me when my mama's gonna get well?"

Allie was hard-pressed to answer the child. The girl's words and emotions echoed her own. She visited every day and found Clare the same each time. "Your mama's mending, but she was very sick and it can take a long time to get better from something like that."

"She's not cryin' and moanin' no more, but she don't talk a lick." Etta's big eyes and brave chin tilted up toward Allie. "She don't even look at us. What happened to her eyes, Miss? Don't they work no more?"

In contrast to the girl's heartbreaking astuteness, Allie knew her answer to be inane, but how could she explain to the child the emptiness in her mother's eyes? "I'm sure they'll get better when the rest of her does."

Clare's body had recovered from the self-induced abortion, but her mind had not.

Following several anxious days and nights of fever, Doc had pronounced their patient free of infection: "A miraculous recovery after all she's endured," he told Allie, who was certain his hesitation in saying the rest was reluctance to inflame her guilt. "However," he'd added, "she may not be able to bear more children, should she ever wish to do so."

My fault, Allie thought, but didn't say it aloud. Doc would only argue with her again.

For weeks, Clare had lain mute and stuporous on a straw pallet facing the wall of the shanty. When asked to sit or stand or eat, she obeyed. She sipped broth, accepted bites of solid food, and often murmured to herself, her fingers making incomprehensible gestures in the air.

Better fed than they had been in some time, thanks to the generosity of the Ladies Benevolent Society, the children were starving nonetheless, though not from hunger. Their mother had abandoned them. Though she was in the same room and they could see and touch her, she didn't speak or open her arms to them. When they crawled into bed to nestle against the curve of her body, Allie had seen tears slip from Clare's eyes, but—arms stiff at her sides, she made no move to cuddle them.

Entering the airless hovel, Allie built a fire in the stove with wood Norberto had chopped and gave the children Hannah's pasties to tide them over until Mrs. Olney's hearty stew warmed. Clare showed no sign she was aware of Allie's presence. While the children ate, Allie crouched next to her. "Good morning, Clare. I've given the children mutton stew and have broth heating for you. Mrs. Olney made both, so I can assure you they're well-fortified with butter!"

Expecting no response, and getting none, she slipped an arm under Clare's back and raised her to a sitting position. It took no effort, the woman weighed next to nothing. Beneath her, the bedclothes were befouled with urine and feces. "Will you sit in the chair while I put fresh linens on your bed?"

And brush your hair and wash your face and change your shift.

With Clare staring into middle distance, Allie helped her to a chair at the table. She sat, as always, with her head drooping, hands limp in her lap. Stupor, mutism, waxy flexibility, and automatic obedience. Allie reviewed the disturbing symptoms again. After she'd described Clare's state to him, Doc had come to the shanty to see for himself.

"I'm sorry, my dear," he'd told Allie after his visit. From a pile of papers on his desk, he'd given her a monograph by German psychiatrist Karl Ludwig Kahlbaum that listed the signs she had observed in Clare. The learned doctor labeled them 'catatonia,' but Allie was unconvinced. Despite Etta's fears, she'd noticed that Clare's downcast eyes were often alive with emotion. A severe psychiatric disorder, she wondered, or simply unbearable despair?

Etta perked up at the sight of her mother out of bed and hurried to the stove to ladle broth into a bowl. With a conspiratorial grin at Allie, she thickened it with stew. Spilling only a little, she soft-stepped to the table and set it in front of Clare. "Mmm, Mama, don't it smell fine? I'll spoon you up some so you can taste it. I know you'll say, 'Why Etta Ruth, that's fine soup, I think I'll have me another.' And, I'll say, 'Why sure, Mama, I'll just spoon you up some more."

Etta had solved the problem of her mother's silence by cheerfully carrying on both sides of a conversation. The younger children watched as their sister cajoled their mother to take sips of the concoction she lifted to her lips.

In a fugue of her own remorse, Allie hardly noticed the dirt and pestilence anymore. She exchanged the soiled linens for the clean ones she'd borrowed from South Slope and prayed the maids wouldn't notice them missing. Or complain to Jane Hanover of the filthy additions to their laundry. While water heated on the stove—sponge baths for all was Allie's plan—she swept the dirt floor. A Sisyphean task, Doc would say, one doomed never to be complete. And, no matter how vigorously Allie swept the floor, or scrubbed bodies that would not relinquish their filth, or tried to draw Clare from her emotional morass, no matter how many flea bites or lice nits she found on herself, nothing diminished her self-blame.

At the berry-picking and again at his cabin, she'd confessed to Ned her dread of being forced to go East to be a debutante. She'd made the jest to hide her true fear. The terror that lives within me, she had been unwilling to tell him, has always been of failing those who rely on me.

And, in Clare Winnicott, she thought, I have surely called that to me.

Depleted at the end of yet another excruciating day at the Winnicotts', Allie drove the cart slowly along Commerce Street. Her clothes reeked from the odors of the shanty. The small of her back ached and her ankles and calves itched with new bites. She would have to bathe and wash her hair with lye soap, or maybe even New England Rum, as soon as she got home. But, as always, it was her mind that caused her the most distress. Naming her fear had only made it more intolerable. Helplessness. She would not—could not—accept that beyond keeping her and the children clean and fed there was nothing more she could do for Clare.

When Doc had reminded her of the state institution for 'deteriorated women,' she'd experienced true anger at him for the first time in her life. Turning her back until she could face him without spewing fire, she'd said, with deadly calm, "Clare Winnicott will never, ever see the inside of a lunatic asylum as long as I am alive to prevent it."

From that day on, Allie vowed she would not allow herself to be frozen in fear, waiting for Hawk's talons to seize her. She spent part of every waking hour crafting, then discarding, one futile plan after another. When her resolve faltered, she forced herself to recall the horrors she'd read patients suffered at the Colorado State Hospital.

She had tried everything she could think of to bring the young woman out of her stupor. She'd helped her outside to sit in the sun, walked her to the creek to put her feet in the icy water and watch the children play, taken her and the children for long wagon rides through town or into the countryside. All to no avail. Silent and expressionless, Clare always returned to her bed.

Rain had fallen throughout most of the afternoon and the muddy road was rutted with new and deeper potholes. Allie let the horse pick its way along to avoid the worst of them. When she passed the tack and feed store, the sun pushed through the lingering clouds and made mirrors of the puddles. The familiar sights and sounds and smells of the busy street cheered her. South Slope, the town, the surrounding fields and forests and ranches, were all home to her. A deep sense of well-being eased her disquiet. Home always had the power to soothe her--no matter how vexatious her mother could be, or trying her siblings, or all-knowing her father.

And then it came to her. She knew just what had to be done for Clare.

Ephraim stared slack-jawed at Allie, jammed his hands in his armpits, and hugged himself. Rocking back and forth on his heels, he blinked up at the sky. "I just couldn't figure what to do myself, Miss." His voice was thick. "So I thank you for worryin' on our behalf. I been scared as a sinner in a cyclone all these weeks." He covered his face with his hands when Allie told him what she believed could help Clare recover. "But what you're tellin' me I got to do? I just don't know, Miss." He shook his head and rubbed tears from his cheeks, then looked down at her. "You're sure that's the one and only way?"

They stood at the edge of the shaded creek, fifty feet up from the shanty. The stink of the untended privy fouled what should have been a stream-sweetened breeze. Below them, Etta—out of earshot—bossed the younger children at play on the narrow bank. Their mother languished in the shack.

"I am."

Once Allie had determined what she believed might help Clare—and she knew it to be more might than would—her next dilemma had been how to present it to Ephraim. The success of her idea sat squarely on his broad, if unreliable, shoulders. She didn't doubt the man's love for his wife and children, but questioned his ability to see the plan through. It would require sacrifices she wasn't certain he'd be willing to make.

Ephraim stared at his children, chewed his lip, then looked back to Allie. "You're probably right," he muttered. "I can see it for myself, what's happening to Clarie. She's . . . she's just lettin' go." His anguished eyes filled with tears again. "But why, Miss? I know she's sick over what she done, but why don't she want to stay with her live babies? With me?"

"It's not she doesn't want to, Ephraim," Allie forbade tears to fill her own eyes. Clare, already fragile, had crumbled under the weight of her circumstances. "She just can't."

Slump-shouldered, he dragged his fingers through his straggly hair and shook his head again. "I just don't see how I can do what you're askin'."

"I know it sounds difficult." He's a weak, selfish man being asked to do something he doesn't want to do, Allie told herself, and I must convince him to do it anyway. "You're a smart, strong man, Ephraim, but you simply can't take care of her yourself. Few men could. And neither of you can take care of the children. Clare's life here is making her worse." She looked up at him with all the sympathy she could muster. "She needs to go home. To her family, to people who can look after her."

His jaw worked. Eyes averted, he blurted, "But what about *me*? We come all this way so's I could make something of myself. I've almost got that tiger by the tail, I'll pull it soon enough. We'll have everything we need then. If I go back home now, they'll all say I . . ."

"Clare is dying."

He glared outright. "She ain't. Doc said so. She's got no fever, no festerin'."

"Her spirit is dying, Ephraim. You can see for yourself, she's almost gone. You must take her and the children to Nebraska. Take her home to her mama before it's too late."

After a moment, he surrendered. Apprehension replaced the anger in his eyes. "But how? How am I gonna do it? How am I gonna get them there?" He hung his head. "You know better than anyone. We got no wagon, no horses, no money for supplies."

Though she hadn't been able to prevent Clare's desperate act, Allie was hopeful she'd found a way to ease her suffering. As Doc had said, sometimes that's the best a physician can do.

Giving Ephraim a reassuring smile, she told him, "Let me look into that."

"Mother," Allie said when she returned to South Slope, "I need your help."

CHAPTER THIRTY-NINE

The pemmican he brought to the mercantile was the largest batch Ned had ever made and he'd taken care to make sure it was the best.

Horace Cuthbert looked askance from Ned to the ten-pound sack on the counter. "Where in blazes do you expect me to store all this?"

"Wherever you see fit, Horace."

Ned attributed the shopkeeper's ill-humor to the weather—which he expected would be at its worst in the middle innings of the baseball game that afternoon. In advance of an approaching storm, the air hung hot and heavy inside and out. Cloud lay panting on the floor, stretched to his full length with all four legs stuck straight out. He'd wedged himself between a pickle barrel and the back wall, the coolest place in the store.

The store was busier than usual, packed with people who'd come to town to watch the Sluggers play against Fountain City. Throughout the summer, excitement had grown over the sport and the crowd had increased with every contest.

"All right, then," Horace said, wiping sweat from his face with his sleeve. "I suppose the trappers'll be stocking up for winter soon enough." He raised a bushy brow. "How do you want it?"

"Whiskey and coffee," Ned said. "The rest in cash."

He had enough other provisions to last until he tanned a few more hides to trade for what he'd need to get him through to late fall. And, he could count on Hannah's baskets of pasties and vinegar pie. As he accomplished each task he'd set himself in preparation for his departure, Ned's frame of mind improved. He didn't dwell on the past or worry about the future. Strong emotion of any kind had left him and he couldn't say he missed it.

Turning to exit the store, he heard his name in a conversation among a small group of men. "Harper'll give' em what for with that whatchamacallit pitch he throws." One caught his eye and winked at him. "Neddie-boy'll have' em scratchin' their you-know-whats trying to figure how he turns that ball into a puff of smoke!"

Another approached and slapped him on the back. "Tell us, son, how d'ye do it? Do you hide that wicked pitch up your sleeve? In yer back pocket?"

Joining in their laughter, Ned cordially refused to reveal his secret, then made a quick escape. Once outside, he exhaled. He stowed his whiskey and coffee in Trickster's saddlebags and left him tied in the shade behind the mercantile. The stallion had acquired a taste for the leaves and berries of a particular hawthorn tree that grew there and Ned knew he'd be happier foraging than at the crowded baseball field.

With Cloud trotting beside him, he headed down the plank sidewalk of Commerce Street and mused on his strategy for the game. He'd keep his mysterious curveball in reserve for the more adept hitters. His hurling skills had sharpened significantly, which gave his teammates gleeful confidence in their ability to win the long-anticipated contest against their rivals, the formidable Fountain City Nine.

To Ned, the big game was the last task on his list of things to do. The outcome didn't concern him one way or the other. Absorbed in reviewing the mechanics of how to throw an unhittable 'puff of smoke,' he came within feet of Allie and Luke Findlay before he noticed them. Or puzzled at the fact they stood together outside the tack and feed Store. Or realized both appeared to be agitated. Cloud barked a friendly greeting to Allie, held Findlay in a warning stare, then settled on his haunches at Ned's side.

Ned hadn't seen Allie since the day she'd come to his cabin, so he hoped her distressed expression had nothing to do with him. He regretted the awkwardness—his fault, he knew, he should have told her himself he was leaving—but had done nothing to make it right. Noting the medical bag she carried, he assumed she'd be filling in for Doc, as she did whenever he was called away from town.

With a finger to his hat brim, Ned nodded to both of them. "Boston," he said, hoping the smile he gave her would be welcome. "Findlay," he added, with less warmth.

Casting a quick glance at Findlay, whose mouth was frozen in a grim line, she set the satchel on the ground. "Joseph's wandered off and we can't find him. He was waiting in Mr. Findlay's wagon behind the store and now he's gone."

Alarm broke through Ned's numbness. From the first time he'd seen the boy, his heart had opened to him. The tack and feed and its outbuildings covered a large lot that backed onto the woods. Huge bales of hay, mountains of sacks of grain, and an arsenal of farm equipment offered all kinds of hiding places to a child, none of them safe. "You've checked the yard and barns?"

"Course we have," Findlay snapped. "And we've searched up and down the street and in the stores. He's not there."

"There are still a few more places we need to look," Allie said. "The livery, the church, the . . ."

Without waiting to be asked, Ned said, "I'll check the woods."

Findlay glared at him. "If my son's gotten it into his head to go out there. . ." His face reddened as he tilted his chin in the direction of the trees. "I lay it square at your feet, Harper. You're the one filled his head with wild ideas about wolf senses and whatnot." An answering growl rumbled in Cloud's chest until Ned lay a hand on his head. Ignoring the dog, Findlay went on, "My boy's hardly stepped beyond his own gate. And never alone.

Now he's wandering around somewhere—maybe even out in those damned woods—because of you."

Ned absorbed the words as if they were the blow they were intended to be. "If he's out there, I'll find him."

When Ned and Cloud disappeared behind the building, Mr. Findlay shook his head and turned to her. "Fool," he spat. "He's wasting his time. Joseph won't be in the woods. Even if he had a mind to, there's no way he could get that far."

You don't know your son, and that's a pity for both of you, Allie thought. "Mr. Findlay," she said, choosing her words and tone with care. "I do believe Joseph's capable of going a lot farther than you may think. In many ways." She didn't begrudge the man his outburst, he was clearly beside himself with worry. "I'm sure he's all right. Running off is a rite of passage for most boys his age."

Still searching the street in both directions, he swung around. "You keep telling me what 'most boys' do, Miss Hanover, but you keep forgetting that Joseph isn't like 'most boys.' "

"When he came to play at our house, I watched him romp and roughhouse with Albert and our nephews. I wish you'd let yourself consider the possibility that he's more *like* other children than he is different."

Albert, who had begun the walk to Elysian Field with Allie, had abandoned her to join a pack of older boys who had conjured up a bat and ball. She hadn't noticed he'd caught up with her or that he'd been listening.

"Did Joseph run away?" Albert looked from one adult to the other. "Don't worry about that, Mr. Findlay. I ran off to the woods myself once, too."

With a jolt, Allie realized this was not the time for Luke Findlay to hear this particular story. "Albert," she said, her smile tight as she grasped her brother's shoulders and turned him toward the street, "please run down to the mercantile and . . ."

Grinning at the recollection, Albert pressed on with his tale. "I fell down a gulley and Ned found me and climbed down and got me out. He carried me all the way home."

". . . ask if anyone there has seen Joseph . . ."

Resisting her gentle push, Albert planted his feet and looked back over his shoulder to finish his account. "My arm got busted, but my father fixed it and I'm good as new. Isn't that so, Allie?"

"Yes, it is." She couldn't quite meet Findlay's eyes. "Now, please go ask at the mercantile if anyone's seen Joseph."

Albert swung around and raced down the street.

With the first sign of warmth Allie had seen in him, Findlay gave her a commiserative smile. "So, Harper had your brother wanting to be a wolf, too?"

"Oh, no," she said, "that wasn't it." Remembering her parents consternation, she hesitated, wondering how to best put it. She settled on the simple truth. "Albert wanted to be a Ute."

Findlay chuckled, but his amusement faded fast. Despite her talk of rites of passage, the longer the boy was missing, the more Allie's own apprehension grew. "Why don't you and I walk toward the baseball field?" she said. "Joseph told Albert he wanted to see it someday. We can check a few places along the way. Is there anywhere else you think he might have gone?"

Findlay studied his boots. His jaw tightened as he fought an emotion Allie couldn't decipher. "He told me he wanted to go to school. When I told him that wasn't possible," he stopped and stared down the street, "Joseph asked if I'd at least take him to see the school house."

Aware he'd allowed her a glimpse of a part of him he kept well-guarded, Allie slipped her arm through his. "Then let's go there and have a look. It's on our way."

It wouldn't occur to her until much later that Luke Findlay, like Rabbit, and like herself, had called out to his worst fear and it had found him.

CHAPTER FORTY

Despite his halting gait, Joseph imagined himself flying through a magical maze of trees in his very own world. Everything here belonged to him—the breeze cooling his cheeks, the thick carpet of leaves beneath his feet, the gray castles of clouds towering in the distance.

He savored the thought that the next time he saw Albert, he'd have an adventure of his own to share. "The bucket gave me the idea right when Pa drove the wagon away from our place," he'd tell his friend. It wasn't that he was mad at Pa for making him wait in the wagon again or not letting him go to the baseball game or fishing with Ned and Albert. Or to the Gathering. Not exactly. It was more that a sour feeling toward his father had crept into his restlessness.

When they'd gotten to town, Pa told him to settle himself for a wait. "I've got doings at the mercantile and at the tack and feed that'll take me an hour or more," he'd said.

At first, the familiar words had made Joseph's chest heavy. The cart was just another one of Pa's cages. Then, the sour feeling rose up in his throat and he knew the only thing for it was that he had to escape. He had to show Pa he could do things like other boys so Pa would, finally, let him do those things. Glancing at the bucket, he decided to head straight to the berry bushes, fill it up, and get back to the cart before Pa got there. When he'd show him the berries, Pa'd say, "I always knew you could do anything you put your mind to, son."

Joseph set out full of energy, but it wasn't long before the aches in his legs made him stumble so much he had to rest. Catching his breath, he sank down on a fallen log and began to worry. Mostly about the time. He didn't remember it taking so long to walk through the trees to the meadow when he'd come with Allie and Albert. The woods behind the mercantile looked just like these, but all woods look the same. Picking up the bucket, he was only a little uneasy—not scared—when he set off again.

"I told myself, just find the creek," he'd tell Albert. "That'll lead you straight to the berries. Use your wolf senses. Remember what Ned Harper told us? 'If you listen, you'll hear the stream before you see it. Some days, you can even smell the water.' "

Joseph listened for the sound of rushing water. He closed his eyes and tried to find the scent of moss, mud, and wet stones. Trudging through trees that seemed to grow taller and closer together with every step, he reached a rocky incline. Nothing looked familiar. "I didn't know which way to go," he'd confide to Albert. "Then, I heard the stream with my wolf senses."

Slipping and sliding in loose leaves, he grabbed at exposed roots and plants to pull himself up the knoll. Almost at the top, he feared his wolf senses had failed him and he wouldn't find the rivulet. Then, he heard the shush-shushing of water rushing over rocks and pushed himself the last few yards to the crest of the hill. Standing there, legs and arms shaking from the effort, he saw the tree-lined stream—his stream—bubbling along, just as he remembered it.

Clutching the bucket tight to his chest, he scooted down the slope on his backside. When he reached the muddy bank, he felt uncertain again. "But not scared," he'd assure Albert. The creek was narrow and shallow. Maybe just a foot or two deep and not even as far across as from his porch to the barn. Not as wide as he remembered it from when Miss Allie put mud on his bee sting.

Shading his eyes, he looked upstream, then downstream. This side of the creek bank was blocked by a mound of twigs and branches, the other appeared clear of obstacles.

"That's when I knew I had to cross it," he'd report.

Gazing across the moving water, fear tap-tapped in Joseph's chest. Envisioning Albert's admiration made it go away. Some. At his first cautious steps, the shockingly cold water swirled around his ankles and made them ache so much he thought he'd have to turn back. Then the wonder of it hit him. He was standing in the current of a creek. By himself. He stared down at the mosaic of shiny, multi-colored rocks. Leaves and twigs raced each other over his shoes. Sparkling eddies circled his legs. With the handle of the bucket over his useless arm, he took a few more steps and played tug-of-war with the icy current. Shin-deep, he leaned forward to grab at protruding rocks to pull himself across with his good hand.

When he was close to the shore, the current turned mean. It dragged his legs out from under him and pushed him to his hands and knees. "You might think I got swept away," he'd say to Albert, after he showed him his bruises. "I was wet all over, but me and the bucket made it."

Colder than cold, knees and hands battered, clothes torn and wet through, he followed the bank upstream. Although one leg still dragged, the exertion seemed to make his body obey in ways it never had. Delight at the icy squishiness of his sodden shoes and socks made him forget everything else. Use your wolf senses like Ned Harper told you, he reminded himself. Listen for the bees. Your bees.

He's heading to the berry bushes, Ned decided. If his pa couldn't find him in the yard or barn— and he was certain Findlay had searched at least as thoroughly as he himself would—Joseph must have set off into the woods. Shouldn't take long to track him down and bring him back to town.

A lesser worry occurred to him: No matter the reason, Zeke would be mad as seven hornets if Ned was late to the game—which he was likely to be. He cringed at the thought of how much his lateness would cost the barber in swearing money.

"Joseph!" He watched for a tousled head of straw-colored hair to come lurching toward him. Exuberant in his element, Cloud darted in and out of trees, raced ahead, then circled back to Ned. "We're lookin' for a boy," he chided the dog, "not chasin' squirrels. Pay attention."

The terrain was rough and uneven. Loose rock, decaying leaves, and raised tree roots troubled him on Joseph's behalf. Even for someone sure-footed, it would be easy to twist an ankle, or worse. After a quarter of an hour of searching, Ned had to admit the boy had gotten farther than he thought he would. Uneasiness prickled the back of his neck.

"Joseph," he shouted with more urgency. "It's Ned and Cloud!"

When he reached the incline, he stopped to consider if Joseph would have—could have— scaled it, or would have turned back, or gone another way. No, he wouldn't turn around. If he got this far, he'd be determined to go all the way. At the top, Ned saw no sign of him in either direction, but on the slope he saw a disruption in the leaves about as wide as a boy's rump sliding down the hill. And, with a touch of uneasiness, he noticed the unmistakable scent of the coming storm.

Ozone, Doc called it.

Although school was out for the summer, the classroom, as always, was unlocked. Allie crossed the threshold unprepared for the surge of emotions she felt entering the place that had defined so much of her childhood. All was as she remembered, only smaller.

"This is it," she told Luke Findlay, breathing in the aroma of books, wood, chalk dust, and decades of children. The sight of Becky's map of the world centered on one wall made her want to smile and weep at the same time. Findlay hesitated in the doorway, then entered.

"Joseph!" he called out. When he got no answer, he checked beneath the eight rectangular tables and in the coat closet. All expression gone from his face, he muttered. "He's not here."

The school occupied a chamber at the rear of the first floor of the Grand Astor Hotel, which had been optimistically intended to serve as a space to hold meetings or socialize. The elegant room sported walnut paneling, a broad, brick fireplace with a carved mantelpiece, and bay windows draped in thick green velvet. When it became evident most guests chose to do their business—and socializing—at the Tongue Oil Saloon, Mrs. Hanover had prevailed upon the hotel owner to allocate the rarely-used room to the Solace Springs Common School.

After the fine Persian rugs had been rolled up and stored in the attic, the children, with their wet wool and muddy shoes, moved in. When Miss Becky Saunders came to teach six years ago, she had cajoled the owner into building bookshelves—walnut like the paneling, of course—on both sides of the fireplace. And to donate enough tables, chairs, and lamps to accommodate the two dozen or so students of all ages attending at any given time. And to provide firewood for the entire winter. And cake and cocoa from the hotel's kitchen on holidays. And birthdays.

Despite her awareness of Findlay's urgency to find his son, Allie couldn't resist the draw of the bookshelves. Becky's bookshelves. She ran her fingers over titles that had broadened her world. Reading, spelling, penmanship, and history. Arithmetic, science, and geography. Two entire shelves of novels.

And *Sander's School Speaker.* Her heart ached at the sight of it. *A Comprehensive Course of Instruction in the Principles of Oratory.* The book was illustrated with drawings to demonstrate facial expressions and gestures to communicate such things as an indignant appeal, rapturous delight, joyful surprise, and aversion to an object. Becky would act one out, then call on students to offer their own interpretations. These inevitably led to shrieks of hilarity and occasional wet drawers.

When her emotions settled, Allie turned to Findlay. "This place," she said, "these books, they'll give Joseph a view of the world he doesn't have to run away to see."

Ned and Cloud scrambled down the embankment to the same sights Joseph had seen. On this side of the creek, a good-sized beaver lodge, half on land, half on water, blocked the way. On the other, the bank was clear. A beaver dam of rocks, twigs, and branches spanned the stream, creating a pond to protect the lodge. A chill, not caused by the wind, went through Ned. Where there are beavers, he thought, there will be traps.

Here, or near here, Joseph had crossed the stream. Ned's chest tightened. "Joseph!"

Cloud bounded across, gamboling between exposed rocks like one of Albert's lambs. Ned followed with more care to his footing. The leg-numbing cold, the drag of the current, the slipperiness of the stream bed increased his fear for Joseph's safety. With Cloud just behind and to his side, he followed the bank downstream toward the berry bushes.

At the baseball field, Zeke approached them with a bat resting on his shoulder and a wide smile.

"Hello, Mr. Findlay." He extended his hand to the man and touched his cap to Allie. As he gazed across the field, a besotted grin broadened across his face. "Sarah's just over yonder lookin' pretty," he told her father. With a nod at Allie's satchel, he said, "Appears you'll be the one doctoring the Sluggers today, if need be."

"Have you seen Joseph?" Findlay blurted.

"Can't say as I have." Zeke studied their worried faces. "Somethin' wrong?"

Findlay exhaled sharply. "He's wandered off, seems he's playing hide-and-seek with me. Don't bother Sarah about it. He'll turn up."

"Course he will. They always do." Zeke turned his attention to Allie. "More important, have you seen Harper? He should've been here an hour ago warming up. That damned cowboy best not be playin' hide-and-seek with *me*. The Sluggers need him. Or should I say we need that damned arm of his." He looked up and scowled at the sky. "Unless that . . . storm spoils everything."

Allie gave him her brightest smile. "I'm sure he and his arm will turn up soon, as well."

"Joseph!"

Ned shouted for him every few yards. A sharp breeze slapped at his clothing and warned of the storm's approach. He'd gone more than a quarter mile before it occurred to him the boy might have headed in the opposite direction. Swinging around to double back, he saw his dog chest-deep in the stream, intent on something only he could see.

"Cloud, to me!"

Obedient as the dog was, Ned had learned he was deaf to any command when he'd been called to hunt or fish. Without either hope or expectation, he tried again. "Now!"

There was nothing Ned could do but resign himself to wait.

After a few snaps at the water, the dog had his catch flapping in his mouth. Chest puffed with pride, he raised his head to show off his prize. When he had consumed it, he trotted to Ned's side and they resumed their search.

Concerned about the delay, Ned imagined the frustration and colorful language his absence would be causing Zeke. I'd best offer to pay back some of his swearing money, he decided.

Tired, sore, and discouraged, Joseph grew more fretful with every step. He couldn't find the bees or the berries and he'd dropped the bucket to save himself the extra weight. Pa would be all bulled up about that and about him not waiting in the cart. The sun hid behind a wall of dark clouds and the wind picked up. Shivering with cold, he couldn't make his teeth quit chattering. He was hungry. And very, very lost.

This isn't the story I want to tell Albert, he thought glumly.

His wobbling legs couldn't take any more. Despondent, he sank to the ground and slumped against a mossy tree trunk. He'd come so far he couldn't remember the way back. How could he tell Albert there were just too many trees, too many hills, that all looked the same? He couldn't even figure which direction he should follow the stream.

The burbling water laughed at him.

Buried deep in dismal thoughts, he no longer felt the breeze or heard the forest sounds. All he heard were his father's words. Pa's right. I'm not like other boys. Can't do like other boys. Never will. Albert wouldn't be out here lost and trying not to cry about it.

In a world he now knew wasn't his, Joseph closed his eyes and surrendered to the mercy of exhausted sleep.

At first, he thought he was dreaming. But, when he opened his eyes, he knew that the odd and wonderful sensation of a dog's wet tongue licking his fingers and Ned Harper's hand on his shoulder were real.

Sitting on the damp ground next to Joseph, their backs against the tree, Ned gazed up at the tarnished sky through a canopy of deep green leaves. The air was rich with the scents of pine, moss, leaf mold, and loam. And ozone. Filtered through branches stirred by the wind, what light there was fluttered before it reached them. Bird song came in lulls and bursts.

Ned was at peace. He'd found Joseph safe and would have him back to his pa within the hour. He himself would soon be throwing his curve ball at the Fountain Valley Nine, if the game didn't get called off on account of the rain. The bunched muscles between his shoulder blades relaxed. Then, a thought undid his serenity—the boy is spent and soaking wet and the storm is coming.

"I guess I'm about as cold as a toad," Ned announced, reluctantly sitting up straight. "We'd best be on our way back." That being said, he couldn't get himself to stir and settled back against the tree. "Nothing more peaceful than the woods this time of day. 'Specially right before a rain."

Cloud did not appear to share his tranquil mood. On guard, he settled at their feet. At every rustle in the undergrowth, the dog's head whipped around and his ears pricked up. Ned breathed in the calming scents of the flora, the wolf dog alerted to those of the fauna.

Pulling a small hide pouch of pemmican from his pocket, Ned tore off a piece and offered it to Joseph. "This'll hold you 'til you're sitting at your ma's table."

The boy hesitated, then popped it in his mouth. Chewing the dried meat, he studied Cloud, then reached a palsied hand forward to stroke his head. "Is he . . . really a wolf?"

"Part wolf, mostly dog."

"Pa says wolves . . . are bad." He withdrew his hand and sat back.

Ned wasn't surprised Findlay had cautioned Joseph to be wary of Cloud. And of him, he guessed. "Your pa's right. Wild wolves can be dangerous, 'specially if they're hurt or starving. Or if their pack's threatened. They're protective of their own." With a rueful smile, he added, "A lot like your pa."

Joseph's eyes widened, then he chortled. "Don't let Pa . . . hear you say . . . *he's* like a wolf!"

"Nope," Ned shook his head. "I certainly won't do that. Only thing your pa wants to hear from me is that you're safe." Standing, he brushed dirt and debris from his clothes and frowned up at the sky. "Let's beat that storm to town. Think you can show me how you got here?"

"Sure!" Joseph struggled to his feet and looked around at the trees scattered in every direction. "Well . . . maybe."

When Ned dropped to one knee and motioned for him to climb onto his back, the boy took a step away. His chin dropped. "I . . . I can . . . walk."

Straightening, Ned said, "I know you can." He resigned himself to a long, slow trek back to town and likely tardiness to the game. Pride in Joseph's resolvemade him grin and raise his hands in mock surrender. "Lead the way."

"Prettiest building in town," Allie said, as she and Findlay approached the Greek Revival church that presided over a quiet side street atop a small rise. The whitewashed structure boasted a two-stage tower topped by a belfry, steeple, and weather vane visible from every part of town. A chill wind tore at her skirts and set the blade whirling against the darkening sky.

Findlay gave her a wry look. "My wife and daughter would say it's your place, South Slope, fits that description."

"My mother certainly would be pleased to hear that, South Slope is her creation. It's lovely, I suppose, but quite . . . you might say, *ornate*. In some places, houses like it are called 'Painted Ladies.' My mother insists since ours is grey and white it's 'refined.' " Climbing the steps to the entrance, she stopped to admire the church's front. "I especially like these tall, sash windows in the flanking bays and the round-arched openings."

I'm babbling, she chided herself. He doesn't care about façades or pilasters or pedimented gables. Truth be told, neither did she. But with no expectation and little hope they'd find Joseph hiding behind the altar or asleep in a pew, she wanted to keep his father distracted until Ned returned the boy to him.

Like the school room, the church was never locked. Making the requisite search of the empty chapel and back rooms, they found no one. Reverend Carstairs had evidently already gone to the baseball field to perform his duties as umpire and profanity monitor.

"I didn't really expect we'd find Joseph here," Findlay said. With a puzzled expression, he raised his eyes and studied the frescoed walls and ceiling. "Can't say I've ever seen anything quite like this."

"Yes," Allie agreed. She felt a familiar mix of pride and embarrassment. "Most people haven't." Her mother had commissioned an itinerant artist to create the trompe-l'oeil depiction of a domed ceiling and to paint the walls in such a way as to give the illusion of a much larger choir space. Mrs.

Hanover had been impressed by a church she'd seen in New England and nothing would do but that Solace Springs have similar art.

"I'm glad to have had the chance to see it," Findlay said. He'd removed his hat when they entered and now gripped it so tightly his knuckles shone white. Clearing his throat, he added, "Haven't been inside a church in a long time. Not since . . ." His voice trailed off, then came back gruff. "Let's head back to the tack and feed. Joseph should be there by now. Harper seemed to think he'd have no trouble finding him."

Allie offered up a small, fervent prayer that it would be so. "Try not to worry too much, Mr. Findlay. Ned knows those woods better than anyone in town."

Findlay's mouth pulled down and Allie couldn't miss the scorn in his voice. "He's a friend of yours?"

"Yes, since I was a child. Well, actually, he's my older brother's closest friend and they used to let me tag along. Sometimes. They own the H&H Ranch together." The disdain in his tone had rankled, causing her to add, "My family thinks the world of Ned."

"I don't see it, but seems everyone 'thinks the world' of Ned Harper. You, your family, most of the town folk, the baseball team. Even my own children," Findlay shook his head. "I suppose I should be obliged to him for takin' the time to look for my boy." After some hesitation, he added, "But, tell me something, Miss Hanover. Just what kind of man goes around wearing badger claws and Indian amulets and keeps a wolf at his side?"

Heat surged through Allie. "He's a good man who tries to live in harmony with all creation." Weighing her next words, she said, "I do believe Ned understands you and Joseph better than most people do."

"Understands me?" Findlay stiffened and glared at her. "I almost lost my wife and my son at his birth. Joseph was left . . . as he is. What can a man like Harper possibly understand about things like that?"

Without responding to his question, she said, "We can go out the back way. There's a shortcut into town through the churchyard."

"See there?" Ned laid a hand on Joseph's shoulder and pointed up the stream. They'd made decent progress and would soon be at a place where they could cross. "That pile of twigs and rocks, is a beaver dam." He spoke softly so as not to disturb the animals. "Look a little past it and you'll see their lodge, half in the water and half on the bank. Looks like a teepee made of leaves and branches."

A crooked smile spread across Joseph's face. "I see it!"

"Six or so beaver might live in that one. There's an air hole at the top—on a cold day, you can see their breath come out of it. The Indians call them 'Little People' because they build those houses and live in families."

Though the boy made no complaints, Ned could see he was dog-tired. It showed in his slowing pace and the increased effort it took him to lurch and stumble along the uneven ground. Concern for the boy won out over urgency to get him home and himself to the baseball game. "Let's sit awhile and watch for beaver."

Ned lowered himself to the loamy bank and Joseph awkwardly did the same. Cloud hunkered between them. They sat in companionable silence for several minutes.

"Where are they?" Joseph asked, peering upstream.

"Maybe out getting some supper. With their big, strong teeth, they can gnaw down a tree in a few hours and bring it home in pieces. Beaver build with wood, but they eat leaves, twigs, and bark." Red Moon had taught Ned the ways of Beaver when he was a youth. Looking back, he figured she'd just been trying to instill the importance of hard work and family in him.

"They like cottonwood and willow best. Look real hard. See those yellow water lilies floating near the lodge? They'll roll those lily pads up just like cheroots to eat' em. "

"Why . . . do they build dams?"

"Dams make a calmer pond in the stream. And, to protect their lodges."

"Who are they . . . afraid of?"

Ned knew boys well enough to know that one question would lead to another. And another. As much as he enjoyed satisfying Joseph's curiosity, it would take time they didn't have to explain the lives of beaver. He hoped the short rest had restored Joseph enough to continue on for a while. Rising, Ned held out a hand. "Tell you what. If you do me a couple favors, I'll tell you everything I know about those critters while we walk."

Joseph let him pull him to his feet and cocked his head to listen.

"First, when we cross this creek, it'll be easier for me if you ride on my back. I know you did it yourself, and you could again, but the water's at least knee-deep and the current's stronger up ahead. If I'm watchin' you—and you know I have to, I'd do the same with Albert—it'll take us a lot longer. And, you know this is true, your pa'll be a whole lot happier with both of us if I don't bring you back sopping wet."

After pondering the request, Joseph nodded.

"Second favor. While we're walking near the stream, I need you and Cloud to stick close to me. There may be beaver traps in the water or on the bank. Use your wolf senses to be on the lookout."

"Okay."

Grateful the boy was agreeable, Ned let himself relax. They'd cross the creek just up ahead, then make their way through the forest into town. As promised, Joseph stayed close. The same couldn't be said for Cloud.

Nearing the beaver dam, Ned again pointed to the lodge. "When beaver build their homes, they hollow out a room, sometimes two, where they eat, sleep, and birth their kits. They make beddings out of grasses and wood chips." With a sideways grin, he said, "I s'pose they do about everything people do, except build a fire to keep warm." Stopping just short of the dam, he shouted, "Cloud, to me!" When the dog came bounding out of the woods, Ned went down on one knee and said to Joseph, "Climb on now and we'll cross here. But I'm relying on you to tell me which way to go when we're on the other side."

Joseph did as he was told, wrapping his arms around Ned's neck. Locking the boy's legs tight to his body with his arms, he stepped into the knee-deep creek. He shuddered at the bite of frigid water, then gritted his teeth and slogged among the protruding rocks toward the opposite bank. Cloud appeared oblivious to both the cold and wet as he frolicked back and forth in the stream.

Partly to keep his word to Joseph, and partly to distract himself from the gnawing cold, Ned said, "Beaver's enemies are trappers after their pelts, bear—who like the way they taste—smelly and greasy—and other beaver, who might take a shine to the fine lodge they've built and want to take it over."

"I still don't . . . see any."

"They probably hear us splashin'."

The creek was so clear Ned could see the hard sandstone bottom and so slick he could gain little purchase with his deerskin boots. He bent to grab a jutting boulder and used it to pull himself and his passenger through a particularly tumultuous spot in the current. The effort made it hard to catch his breath. "Or, they may be underwater. They build at least two canals . . . that lead from their lodge into the creek . . . and go underground to get to their trees." He tightened his jaw against his chattering teeth. "All we may see of them is ripples in the water."

Stumbling again, Ned almost lost his footing. He righted himself, readjusted Joseph's weight, and planted his own feet to steady himself while he took several deep breaths. "Their eyesight's so poor that with you up on my back they just might take us for a bear and hide 'til we're gone."

Taking a another stride, he grabbed for the knuckle of a small boulder to pull them to the bank. Arms wide, Joseph raised them above his head. "I'm . . . a bear!"

When they were on solid ground, Joseph squirmed on Ned's shoulders. "Put . . . me down. Please."

Setting the boy on his feet, Ned stretched the kinks out of his back and legs. He let Joseph take the lead. Wind whipped them both. The boy struggled through the willow brush and up the hillock, using his already scraped knees and elbows to drag himself to the top. At the crest, he said, with what Ned took to be as much doubt as hope, "This looks like . . . where I came before. Maybe."

Steel gray clouds glowered down at them. Harmless enough for now, Ned thought, but those at the horizon are black as the devil's riding boots. Ahead of him, Joseph lurched through tangles of trees. At first, Cloud followed the boy with Ned bringing up the rear. Then, the dog's behavior became erratic. Bounding out of sight, he hurtled back to them in fits and starts, barking with manic urgency. Nose high, he bayed at the sky, and darted off again. Ned attributed his excitement to the overabundance of creature scents in the forest.

Looking back, he would regret not heeding the dog's warning.

Allie unlatched the wrought iron gate and led Findlay into the cemetery behind the church. On sunny days, scattered trees offered oases of shade. Flowers planted in front of some headstones dotted the burial ground with clusters of color. Today, wind tore at the blossoms, sprinkling petals like confetti throughout the churchyard in advance of the rain.

She and Findlay walked in silence along a path that meandered among an acre of tombstones. Most were plain slabs with names and dates, some more elaborate. Sculpted shrouds of mourning draped a few. Several had cameos etched with likenesses of those who had passed, statues of angels or cherubs adorned others. One had been carved to resemble a tree stump with leaves vining around it.

Stopping at a marker carved to look like an open book, Allie drew a penny from her pocket, touched it to her lips, then set it on top of the stone. "For remembrance," she murmured.

Findlay, clearly irritated by the delay, waited at her side.

"I thought you should see this one," she told him.

It took him a moment to understand that she meant him to read the inscription.

Rebecca Harper

August 18, 1849 November 8, 1872

Benjamin Thomas Harper

November 8, 1872 November 8, 1872

Where your heart is, there will be your treasure.

"Ned wanted them together," Allie said. "The baby in his mother's arms."

She remembered the terrible day of the funeral. Everything had been the color of ashes—sky, ground, mourners' clothing—all shades of black and grey. Not unlike today. Ned had stared into the open grave, his face pale and impassive as the tombstones. Will stood on one side of him, Hannah on the other, her arm linked through his. Allie recalled feeling grateful for Hannah's bright red hair, the only spot of color.

Ned endured the eulogy, waited for Reverend Carstairs to finish the last prayer—Psalm 61, Verse 2. "From the end of the earth, I call to you when my heart is faint. Lead me to the rock that is higher than I." Then, he'd turned his back and walked away. Will would have followed, but Hannah laid a cautioning hand on his arm.

The eyes Findlay raised to Allie's were anything but indifferent. "I didn't know."

"You couldn't," she said softly. "You once told me people don't take time to get to know Joseph. They just look at him, then they look away."

Still staring at the slab, Findlay rubbed a hand over his face. "I did the same to Harper."

Taking two pennies from his pocket, he placed them on the stone. "God keep you both," he whispered. "And him."

CHAPTER FORTY-ONE

Flat on his back in forest duff and leaf litter, Ned knew his leg was broken before he hit the ground. At his howl of rage and pain, Joseph spun around and gaped at him.

With surreal clarity, Ned understood he'd stepped in a trap—bear trap, by its size and weight. Jagged, two-inch teeth bit through his boot, skin, and bone. For seconds, he'd felt nothing, but when the pain hit, it blinded him. Instinct told him to run or crawl or writhe away from his attacker, but movement made what was only excruciating become unendurable.

Willing himself to lie still, he drew a short, shallow breath, then another. His heart raced high and desperate, sweat stung his eyes. Chained to a tree with thirty pounds of steel clamped above his ankle, he pushed up on one rubbery elbow and tried for a sitting position. Stifling a cry at the agony that exploded in his leg, his vision darkened again. Consciousness faded to grey.

Don't pass out.

Supporting himself on one arm, he reached for the upper jaw of the trap. He knew he didn't have the strength or leverage to spring it, but had to try. The effort cost him. Cloud whined and nuzzled his neck, growling and snapping at the trap. Joseph's frightened whimpers brought Ned to his senses. Willing himself away from the grey place, he forced his eyes to focus.

Think.

"Joseph." His voice sounded papery in his own ears. "Don't be afraid. Come here."

The boy edged toward him, eyes fixed on the trap. "Does it hurt?"

Through clenched teeth, he hissed, "Yes."

Before his arm could collapse, he lay back down. He wanted to wipe the sweat from his eyes, but couldn't think how to do it. Cloud ceased barking and turned his attention to the tree. Stretched to his full length with forepaws on the trunk, his entire body quivered. Frenzied, he howled and jumped at a spot about seven feet above the ground. His agitation forced Ned to look up. What he saw froze the breath in his chest—a beaver carcass nailed to the tree.

Bait to lure a bear to the trap.

Panic cleared his head. If Cloud smelled the beaver, bears would, too. The ruckus and bared fangs of a large barking dog might deter a bear, but not if food was involved. Or cubs nearby.

The boy can't be here.

When he pushed himself up again, a red-hot wire twisted from his foot to his hip. When he could speak, he commanded Cloud, "Down."

Ignoring Ned, the dog clawed at the trunk and continued his frantic yowling.

"Now!"

Cloud dropped to all fours.

"Sit."

With a reproachful look at his master, he obeyed.

Ned's eyes fixed on the bear bait.

Get Joseph away from here. Anywhere but here.

He slowed his breathing and fought for calm. The desperation of his plight and the danger it brought to the child knotted his insides. He fought for every word. "I need your help."

When Joseph's eyes went to the trap, Ned's followed. His deerskin boot was dark with blood. Too much blood.

Don't pass out.

The muscles in his calf spasmed. Gritting his teeth, he dug his fingers into the dirt to keep his grip on consciousness. When the mind-killing seizure eased, he rasped, "Go back to town."

Gaping at him, Joseph took a tottering step closer. "By . . . myself?"

A groan more than a word. "Now."

"I can't."

Aware he need only close his eyes to escape to the grey place, Ned willed his voice to stay strong. "Go back the way you came." If Joseph left now, right now, he'd have daylight. Maybe beat the storm. His thoughts eddied like leaves and twigs around a rock in the stream. "Take Cloud."

"You come, too."

Ned shook his head, too weary to argue. Cold sweat ran down his back and prickled under his eyes. The trap meant bear sightings. Recent sightings.

The boy edged closer. "I'll . . . help . . . you."

"No," Ned growled, glaring through pain-squinted eyes. He was deliberately cruel. "You can't help me standing here whining. Go." The wind picked up and the stink of the rotting animal sickened him. Warm blood pooled in his boot, between his toes. Shivering with the icy fever of weakness and pain, he couldn't be sure if he thought the words or said them aloud. "Get your pa and Miss Allie."

"I can't."

"Bring them here."

Clearly tormented, Joseph stared into the woods, at the trap, at Ned's bloody boot. Chin trembling, tears slipped down his cheeks. Then, at last, he raised terrified eyes to Ned's. "I'll go." He stood tall and set his shoulders. "I'll get you help."

Ned exhaled. With a few hours of daylight left, the boy would probably be safe walking through the woods. Safer than here with the bear bait. As Joseph turned to go, Ned signaled Cloud to follow. Whimpering, the dog looked from the boy's retreating back to his injured master.

"Go, Cloud."

On this, the dog kept his own counsel. Choosing disobedience over desertion, he settled at Ned's side, chin on his paws. Joseph stared at them for only a moment, then began his halting trek back through the woods. When he was out of sight, Ned was finally free to surrender to the grey place.

But, try as he might, he couldn't find it.

Getting out of the woods is harder than getting in, Joseph thought. A lot harder. Ned Harper had told him to go straight to town, but there was no telling which way straight was. The trees were all mixed up. Everything looked familiar and everything looked strange. Brown and green and green and brown. Leaves and twigs and rocks and roots. All the same. "But," he'd tell Albert when he saw him, "I didn't care. I had to help Ned Harper."

He understood Ned's situation to be bad. His heart pounded when he thought of the horrible trap and the bloody boot. Joseph had watched Pa stun and slaughter sheep and knew being bled was what killed them. Stumbling along as quick as he could, he pushed forward. Or hoped he did.

I'll tell Albert: "I used my wolf senses to find the way to town. I made my eyes big to look ahead for buildings or chimney smoke. I perked up my ears and listened for people talking and horses neighing and carts crunching. I put my nose up in the air and closed my eyes and sniffed for hearth fires and food cooking." And Albert'll say, "You did just what a wolf would do."

As time went on and the sky blackened with gathering clouds, Joseph's resolve faltered along with his body. His clothes were wet and torn, his feet rubbed raw. He feared he might be going sideways or in circles. His heavy legs grew even clumsier—he could hardly drag one foot in front of the other. And, he wouldn't tell Albert this, he'd begun to doubt his wolf senses. He couldn't see or smell or hear anything of town.

In his haste, he tripped over roots and slipped on leaf mold. His scraped knees and palms smarted worse than a bee sting. A tiny stream, just a few feet wide, appeared off to one side. This is wrong, he thought, with a jolt of despair and trudged doggedly in the opposite direction. Once, when he fell, he hit his head so hard on a log he couldn't move. Rolling onto his back, he lay on the damp ground with tears in his eyes and a big bump throbbing on his forehead. He watched the clouds build rows of beaver dams and lodges in the sky. Then he remembered Ned Harper was hurt and that he was the only one who knew where he was. Struggling to his feet, he stumbled on.

"I knew I should've gotten to town by then," he'd tell Albert. It seemed he'd been plodding for hours. "But I didn't give up."

Which wasn't entirely true. Cold and tired, every limb aching, Joseph longed to sink back against a tree and go to sleep and have Ned Harper and Cloud find him and wake him up from this terrible dream. He wanted his mother. He even wanted his sister. When he came upon the wrong little brook again, something inside him caved. Certain he'd never find his way to Pa or back to Ned, he slouched on a stump, covered his face with his freezing hands, and sobbed.

He wouldn't tell Albert that part because that was exactly when he realized everything was going to be all right.

"I heard Cloud barking." Joseph looked up to see the silver wolf dog silhouetted among the trees, watching him from a distance. "I tried to go to him, but he just barked and trotted ahead. He wanted me to follow him. I knew he'd lead me to town, because that's what Ned Harper wanted him to do."

The woods thinned and he came upon some structures. Half hidden in the shadows, Cloud woofed and wagged his tail. Elated at first, Joseph hurried toward the buildings, but soon realized he'd never seen them before—clapboard houses scattered on the hillside behind the main street. He smelled smoke from chimneys and food from kitchens. It was supper time, twilight. A thread of lightning sparked, then, many moments later a faint clap of thunder mumbled in the distance.

Sliding down the slope, Joseph saw the backs of stores. But they were stores he'd never been to. The tack and feed yard with its bales of hay wasn't here. He got a bad taste in the back of his throat at the thought this might not even be the right town.

Joseph's belly hurt and his body tingled in a bad way. He comforted himself with the thought that Albert would understand. He'd say, "Joseph, I know just how you felt. I feel the same way every time I get lost."

But Albert couldn't really understand how he felt. Albert had never left Ned Harper alone in the woods counting on him for help. Shoved backward by a gust of wind, Joseph struggled to stay upright and wobbled down a crooked alley that opened onto a big street. A wooden sidewalk stretched forever in either direction, lined with buildings on either side. The street was almost empty. Loading supplies into his wagon, a man hugged his coat and held his hat against the wind. His horses rolled their eyes, stamped their feet, and tossed their heads, edgy in the unsettled weather. A particularly spiteful gust tore at Joseph's jacket.

Everyone wants to get home before the storm, he thought. His insides twisted up. Ned Harper would be alone in the woods in the rain and wind and thunder and lightning if Joseph didn't bring help soon. Signs above doorways or painted on buildings told him nothing because he couldn't read them. He felt a dart of anger at Pa who wouldn't let him go to school.

"Every thing you need to know you can learn at home, son," Pa said every time Joseph begged to go. "Here no one can bother you."

But Pa was wrong. It hurt worse not to be able to read than to be teased. If he could read, he'd be able to find the sign that said Tack and Feed. Looking up and down the street, he found nothing to guide him. Back doors and storage yards were all he knew of Solace Springs. The twisty feeling got worse. Tripping along the uneven boardwalk, Joseph could tell what some shops were by what was in the window or by ducking his head inside. Most were locked.

Swinging doors opened to a room with three men standing at a bar. The few people who passed him on the street took no notice of him. The idea of asking for help terrified Joseph. He'd never talked to a single person he didn't know—or even looked into their eyes—until Miss Allie and Ned Harper. Pa or Ma or Sarah always spoke for him.

When he came to a tall window, its contents startled all the urgency out of him. Transfixed, he stared at a leathery-looking man standing in a box that just fit him. Joseph wanted to run or close his eyes, but couldn't do either. He'd seen dead animals, but never a dead person.

That was when the oldest and smallest man he'd ever seen stepped out of the doorway and joined him in to admire the corpse. The tiny man planted his feet against the wind and folded thin arms across the chest of his black suit. "One of my best mummifications, if I do say so myself," he murmured. Giving Joseph a sideways look, he added, "I see yer a young man appreciates artistry when ye have the good fortune to come upon it."

Silenced by shyness, Joseph dropped his eyes to his own muddy shoes.

"Ollie Oxter, here." The hand the man offered was frail and wizened, but his voice was vibrant. Wind fluttered his fine white hair like wisps of smoke. "Funeral director and embalmer extra-ordinaire. Town's best and only dance caller, too." He winked at Joseph and his face crinkled into a kindly smile. "What's yer name, sprout?"

Joseph lifted his gaze only a few inches to be eye to eye with the undertaker. "Joseph Findlay. Sir."

"Well, Joseph Findlay, I don't warrant yer in need of my professional services at the moment, now are ye?"

Joseph answered with a small shake of his head.

Raising his eyes to the sky, Ollie grimaced. "Black and blustery day for a soul to be out and about all on his own." The old man's face softened with concern. "Are yer folks nearby?"

Standing still, Joseph realized how terribly tired and cold and wet he was. He felt like a rag toy without its stuffing. "I'm looking for . . . my pa."

The undertaker raised a brow that appeared to have more hair than the top of his head. "Misplaced him, eh?" he said, with a knowing nod. "I've always been of the mind the best way to search for something lost is to go back to the place ye saw it last."

"Tack . . . and . . . feed." Tears spilled from Joseph's eyes. "I . . . can't find it."

"Well, then, I'm pleased to say there's some comfort to be had, after all." Ollie patted Joseph's arm and offered him a black silk handkerchief. "I know for a fact the store yer looking for is right where ye left it." He linked his spindly arm through Joseph's. "Lest this devilish wind catch us both and transport us to parts unknown, I'd be pleased to walk with ye."

The band that had tightened around Joseph's chest loosened as he proceeded down the street anchored to his new friend. Ollie Oxter will take me to Pa and Miss Allie, he thought, and I'll take them to Ned Harper.

The wind must have blown away the fog, Ned mused. That's why he couldn't find his way to the grey place. It didn't matter much anymore, the pain in his leg had settled into a crushing ache. Tolerable, if he didn't move. Last time he looked, blood had darkened his pant leg and the ground beneath it to his knee.

Pressed to Ned's side, Cloud's thick body radiated enough heat to keep the worst of the cold at bay. Head high, eyes and ears alert, the dog's breathing was rapid and even. Ned's had become ragged and required effort.

An owl hooted overhead. Dusk, Ned thought, more night than day. The scent of ozone permeated the misty air. Soon the storm would blacken the woods, blow away all tracks, and stymie searchers. He hoped the boy had found his way to his pa and Allie, but had no expectation Joseph would be able to lead them back to him. They wouldn't find him until morning, at best. That didn't matter, either.

The beaver carcass ripened in the tree above him.

It occurred to Ned he might die in the woods, as he'd planned for months. Shock, loss of blood, a wet, cold night and, of course, the likelihood of a bear attack would probably take him. A death no one could question. A death no one could fault him for, or themselves.

Just let go.

CHAPTER FORTY-TWO

Shivering on a bale of hay, Allie had to admit something was most certainly wrong. When she and Luke Findlay returned to the tack and feed from the cemetery, they'd found Mary Kimble shuttering her windows—as anxious as everyone still in town to be home before the storm made muddy rivers of the roads. No, she told Findlay, she'd seen no sign of Ned or Joseph.

The only thing that made sense to Allie was that Ned hadn't found the child. That thought opened the door to possibilities so frightening she would not allow them to enter her mind. Findlay paced the length of the hay-strewn storage yard, stopped to peer into the woods, then resumed pacing. Striding to his wagon, he searched it yet again. Finding the cart still empty, he trudged back, shoulders sagging. "I'm going to look for him." He stared at the line of trees. "It's been too long."

Although she agreed, Allie said, "Give them a little more time. If you go off now and Joseph comes back, we'll be out there looking for you." Tucking wind-whipped strands of hair behind her ears, she hugged herself for warmth. Ned wouldn't keep the boy out in this weather a moment longer than necessary. "I'm sure they'll be back soon."

Findlay looked unconvinced. To Allie's surprise, he removed his canvas jacket and wrapped it around her shoulders. Slipping her arms through the sleeves, she pulled it tight. "Thank you."

“Thank you for helping me look for Joseph.” His eyes remained fixed on the trees. “And for sticking with me while we wait for Harper to bring him.”

“Of course.” She smiled up at him. “Joseph has a way of winning the hearts of just about anyone who gets to know him.”

Looking away, he said, “I owe Harper an apology.” His jaw twitched. “And you. I judged him without taking the time to know him.” He leveled a troubled gaze at her. “I hope you won’t do the same to me, Miss Hanover.”

“Oh, Mr. Findlay, I would never judge you.” Her protest felt empty because she had done just that on more than one occasion.

He stood silent, engrossed in the trees. When he spoke, his voice was thick. “I don’t talk about this.” He cleared his throat. “After Joseph was born, I almost lost him a second time.” Crossing his arms tight across his chest, he rocked slightly, as if soothing an invisible pain. “I knew something wasn’t right when he was a month or so old. Martha said no, no, he was fine. Said all babies are different.” He was silent for so long, Allie thought he’d said all he meant to say. His next words were a whisper. “But I knew.”

The lines in his weathered face deepened. “I finally convinced her. It broke her heart when she came to see what I’d seen all along. We took him all the way to Denver. Doctors there told us our boy would never walk. Never talk. Never learn. That was their word. Never.” His mouth puckered. “They had an uncommon fondness for it, if you ask me.” Silent again, he closed his eyes, drew a long breath, and exhaled. “They told us we should put him in an asylum for the feeble-minded and forget him.”

“I’m so sorry.”

Lowering himself to sit beside her on the bale of hay, he stared straight ahead. “One of those damned doctors took me aside. Put his hand on my shoulder and told me ‘Women aren’t strong when it comes to giving up their babies.’ ” He lifted his shoulder, as if to shrug off that haunting hand. “Said I needed to help my wife understand giving our baby up was for the best. Said I should be strong and do ‘the right thing.’ So, I thanked him for his help and told him we wouldn't be putting Joseph in any asylum, that we'd be taking our son home with us."

Shifting his body, he faced Allie. "I held Joseph in my arms that whole night and I promised him I'd never let anyone or anything hurt him ever again."

In ways she couldn't have before, Allie understood the depth of Findlay's bitterness and the fear beneath it, the hardness around his eyes, and his fierce protectiveness of his son. She shared his rage at the doctors—doctors!—who had taken an oath to do no harm. Compassion replaced whatever judgment she had harbored toward him.

"You protected him when he needed it most," she said. But Findlay had fashioned an asylum of his own to shelter Joseph from the dangers of the world and it had walled him away from life's pleasures, as well. "Joseph wouldn't have survived without your strength. You've raised a boy who *can* walk and talk and learn. Please," she laid a hand on his arm, "let him do those things. Don't let the promise you made do what you wouldn't allow those doctors to do to him."

Before Findlay could respond, something caught his eye. Allie followed his line of sight. The whole time they'd been waiting, she'd pictured Ned striding out of the woods with Joseph on his shoulders, both grinning. Making sense of what she saw now took a few seconds. Joseph, face dirty and tear-streaked, leaves and debris stuck to his straw-colored hair and wet, tattered clothing, shuffled toward them hand in hand with the town's ancient undertaker.

When he saw his father, the boy pulled away from Ollie and shambled toward him as fast as he could. Findlay ran to his son, scooped him up, and held him close. Joseph clung to him, then wriggled free and dropped to the ground. Almost weak with relief, Allie watched for Ned to come around the side of the building. He'd be sheepish and full of apologies for Joseph's disheveled appearance and the search taking so long.

"I did it, Pa," Joseph said, his breath and words coming in fits and starts. "I had to find the way back. It's . . ." A haunted look took over the eyes he turned up to them. "It's . . ."

"Take a deep breath, son." Findlay hunkered down and pushed matted hair back from Joseph's face. He took in the whole of Joseph's battered appearance with horror. Frowning, he ran his hands over the boy's arms and down the sides of his body, as if certain he'd find broken bones and gaping wounds.

Pulling away from his father's hands, Joseph stumbled back a step. "It's not me, Pa! It's Ned . . . Harper. He's hurt. Bad. Bleeding."

Allie's throat went dry. "Bleeding?"

"Bear trap."

B*ear trap*. Mind-numbing panic seized Allie, then the physician's calm took over. She pressed her trembling hands to her skirt to still them. *Trauma, fractures, blood loss, shock*. "Where is he, Joseph? Can you tell me?"

"I can . . . take you."

"No, son," Findlay said firmly. "You cannot." Hands on hips, he turned to Allie. "He's been through enough. Look at him. I'm taking him home."

"I need to help Ned Harper." Joseph grasped Allie's hand and lifted his chin toward his father. "We have to . . . go now!"

"Please, Mr. Findlay." A kaleidoscope of ugly images, one worst than the last, spun through Allie's mind. "He says Ned's badly hurt." The light was fading. As it was, they'd be searching in the dark, maybe in the rain. "It could take all night to find him without Joseph. Even if I do, I can't spring a bear trap myself. Or get him back to town. You must come, too. Please."

"I'm the only one. . . knows the way, Pa." Joseph raised his eyes to old Ollie's. "I know just where I left him."

Findlay looked from his son to Allie, then nodded grudging assent.

Noting that relief at his father's approval vied with something darker in the boy's expression, Allie asked, "Are you sure you're up to this?"

Joseph nodded, but didn't meet her eyes.

Unconvinced, but taking him at his word because there was no time to do anything else, Allie turned to the undertaker. "Ollie, go see if Zeke's back at his shop. Or at the Tongue Oil? We need his help, too. Please hurry!"

"I'll fetch him right quick, Miss Hanover." Hurrying as much as his old bones would allow, he stopped and swung back. "I got water and blankets and lanterns at the parlor, I'll fetch them, too. Don't ye fret, we'll see our Ned home safe."

Allie retrieved her satchel from the bale of hay. *We'll see him home safe.* Fighting the cutting wind, she ticked off what she'd need to stabilize Ned until they got him to town: splints, tourniquet, bandages, carbolic, laudanum. She'd packed them all to tend to the baseball players possible injuries. Her knees slackened with the realization her father was days away. On her own, she'd never treated wounds as severe as what she imagined hours in a bear trap could inflict. It seemed hours since Ollie had gone for Zeke and every interminable minute endangered Ned further.

Her dire musings were forgotten when she caught sight of Joseph's hunched shoulders and distraught face. His father hunkered in front of him, looking equally distressed.

At Allie's approach, Findlay stood. "He won't say what's wrong."

When she wrapped an arm around the boy's shoulders, he sagged against her and sobs shook his body. "Don't worry, Joseph. Ned'll be all right. He's hurt, but thanks to you, we'll bring him home and help him." Her words only served to make the child cry harder, which increased Allie's apprehension for Ned three-fold. Holding him at arms length, she forced herself to ignore the ice forming around her heart. "Joseph, when you left him was he talking? Moving?"

The boy's face knotted with misery, but he nodded. Stifling a sob, he turned away. "It's all . . . my fault. If I hadn't gone into the woods . . . he wouldn't be hurt."

The boy's confession allowed Allie enough relief to force a solemn smile. "Joseph Findlay you are Ned's friend, are you not?"

He sniffled and nodded. Raindrops dotted the sleeve of his jacket.

"Good. So, I'm going to let you in on something only his closest friends know." She saw Luke Findlay listening, as well. With feigned reluctance, she told them, "Ned doesn't much care for people to know this about him." Bending closer to Joseph, she lowered her voice. "It so happens, that if there's a log to trip over, a hole to fall into, a roof to fall off of, or a trap to get caught in, Ned Harper will be the one to do it." Truth be told, he'd had his share of accidents, but was anything but clumsy. "So, please don't take any credit for his current misadventure."

Ignoring the rain that had begun to pelt them in earnest, she added, "I would very, very much appreciate it if you'd not let on I told you that."

Joseph wiped away tears and snot with his sleeve. "I won't."

Baseball cap still on his head, Zeke hurried into the hay yard, frowning. "A goddamned bear trap? How in the hell did Harper, of all people . . . ?"

Allie's sharp look silenced the barber before he could dispute the mythology she had just created for Joseph's benefit. When she explained what had happened and what needed to be done—what she needed Zeke to do—he closed his eyes and swallowed hard. "Allie," he whispered through thin, pale lips, "you know I can't do that."

"Zeke Foster, I know you can and you will. You will pull yourself together and do what your papa taught you to do. For Ned." She ignored his beseeching look and quelled the added uneasiness it evoked in her. His father had been the town's bonesetter since before it was a town. "Understood?"

Zeke didn't meet her eyes, but his tight-lipped nod was good enough for her.

Moments later, Ollie trundled into the yard breathing hard. Toting a stack of blankets, he had a lantern hanging from each arm and a canteen hooked on his thumb. Allie gave the old man a grateful smile, then laid a hand on Joseph's shoulder. "Ready to take us to Ned?"

At that moment the storm, which had introduced itself so politely, released a vicious downpour, sending them running for the shelter of an overhang. When Allie pressed her satchel to her chest and headed out into the torrent, Findlay pulled her back. "We've got to wait for a break in this squall."

"No!" Fear almost stopped her breath. "We can't. Please! It's been too long already."

"I don't like leaving Harper out there any more than you do," Findlay said, raising an arm to shield them both from a maelstrom of flying hay and debris. "But, we'll never find him in this."

As if to prove his point, a powerful gust ripped a board from the overhang and flung it into the yard. A cold fist closed around Allie's heart. "He's waiting for us. He'll . . ."

Zeke put a hand on her elbow. "Findlay's right, Allie. We won't do Ned a lick of good wanderin' blind in the damned woods."

Lowering her head, Allie hoped the rain obscured her tears

CHAPTER FORTY-THREE

Cloud's icy muzzle prodded the side of Ned's neck, nudging him from his stupor. A sudden downpour and the whoo-whooing of an owl brought him to his senses. His mouth and throat had gone dry and his eyes felt glued shut. Not asleep, but not quite awake, he had to admit he was confused. Couldn't figure why he'd chosen such an inhospitable spot to camp for the night. Sharp sticks and jagged rocks bruised his back. One side of his body was stiff with cold, the other, pressed against Cloud, less so. Like a pond freezing inward from its edge, ice crept toward his core.

No point staying here, he thought. The rain had gotten heavier and would only get worse. When he tried to sit up, the agony in his leg reminded him not to move and that he was waiting for something. *Something.* He just couldn't think what.

Growling, Cloud sprang to his feet and straddled Ned. Shielded him. Every inch of the dog's body trembled. The coarse hair on his broad shoulders bristled. Then, snarling and barking, he raised his muzzle to the sky and loosed a crescendo of howls. No longer confused, Ned recognized the noise that had alerted Cloud. It wasn't the creak of tree limbs snapping in the wind. He'd heard the ominous sound before—three hundred pounds of bear lumbering through the woods, breaking low branches, crushing undergrowth, quickening its pace at the smell of beaver. The sound flooded Ned with alarm.

Cloud leapt between him and the approaching danger, lunging back and forth and sideways, his yowls growing more and more shrill. In the vacuum that terror sometimes creates, Ned thought of what Red Moon had said on the subject of what to do when, not if, he met a bear in the woods: "If it's black, stay back. If it's brown, hit the ground."

He'd had the occasion to take her advice on a few hunting trips.

Now, already flat on the ground, chained to a tree and unable to move, he had no choice in the matter. His own fate was sealed, but Cloud's wasn't. If Ned could get him to back off and stay quiet, the dog might stand a chance of surviving. Struggling to one elbow, Ned pointed to a spot yards away. The movement cost him. "Cloud, sit."

The big dog shuddered, standing his ground.

"Sit," he managed through clenched teeth. "Now."

With a staccato of aggrieved barks, he berated Ned for his poor judgment, but slunk backward and sank to his haunches. The din grew louder and closer. If it were a lone bear, the approach would be almost silent. The noise meant more than one, likely a she bear and her as yet undisciplined cub.

"Quiet," Ned breathed.

Growling under his own breath, Cloud's eyes went feral.

"Down."

Any strength he had left dissolved by fear, Ned collapsed back to the ground. Just as the quivering dog lowered himself to his belly, chin on his paws, the bears appeared. A big, brown sow trailed by two husky cubs.

Focused on the beaver carcass, the bear plodded past him, lowered a perfunctory glance at him and Cloud, then planted huge hind feet less than a yard from Ned's head. The odor of her rank, wet fur gagged him. Staying back, the cubs watched their mother stand upright and stretch to swat at the carcass nailed to the tree. Snagging the rotting meat, she tore it loose. When it fell to the ground, she dropped to all fours and batted it to the cubs, then swung her massive head around and fixed black eyes on Ned. He knew then she meant to take him for herself.

After months of searching for a way to die, death had found him. While Ned waited for the world to end, the beast lowered her head close to his. Cloud whimpered. Time stopped. All sounds ceased.

Just let go.

I can't.

A heartbeat later, another thought left him shattered. *Can't or won't?*

Though he had no answer to his own question, and told himself it no longer mattered, something in him was unwilling to surrender to the inevitable. Something welled up inside of him and summoned the strength and will to fight the beast off, to pummel her snout and eyes with all the fury his fists could deliver.

At the onslaught, the bear jerked her head back and blinked. Strings of saliva dripped from her jaws. Heck had once told Ned bears sometimes devour their prey alive. He hoped this one would crush his skull or tear his throat out first. Lowering her head again, her breath blew hot on his neck and cheek. It was still fresh with the leaves and berries she'd last eaten, not yet fouled by carrion. Ned closed his eyes, drew what he believed to be his own last breath, and waited.

When the bear spoke, her voice was a soothing rumble. *The Answer to what torments you can be found where all answers live. Seek truth and you'll find it within yourself.*

Ned was certain he must be delirious, that what he'd heard was his own crazed mind trying to calm him. With the clarity that can accompany madness, he remembered Red Moon's words. "Bear is the Eternal Mother, she stores nourishment for the spirits of her children while she hibernates in the womb-cave. She will always come when called by those who need her."

Had he called the bear to him? Mother Bear's liquid eyes—inches from his own—shone with compassion. Then, the beaver carcass locked in her jaws, she swung around to leave and nudged her cubs forward. A few yards away, she looked back over her russet shoulder.

Deciding not to die is not the same as choosing to live. That is the decision you have yet to make.

She and her cubs lumbered back the way they'd come.

Night fell and the world went dark. The wind picked up, agitating the trees and swirling debris up from the forest floor. Rain spattered down in fits and starts. As pain returned and blood loss weakened him, Ned's heart beat in a rapid, slipshod way. He had trouble drawing a breath that made it to his lungs. Cloud settled at his side providing what warmth he could.

Overhead, Ned heard the swoosh of wind and wings as the owl soared away and felt a pang of loss. When another squall hit with raging winds and torrential rain, he thought he'd have to respectfully disagree with Mother Bear about just how much choice he actually had in the matter of living or dying.

CHAPTER FORTY-FOUR

Rain glittered in shifting curtains.

"Ned!" Allie shouted, swinging a lantern to illuminate the dark forest. In the moving light, trees that had been shadows materialized and leaned toward each other, as if to whisper about the odd spectacle of people traipsing through their night-world.

Zeke, carrying water, blankets, and Allie's satchel, hollered, "Harper! Cowboy!"

From a short distance behind them, Luke and Joseph yelled, "Ned Harper, we're coming!"

All were drenched, their clothing—wet and heavy—clung to them and weighted them down.

"Ned!" Allie's throat had gone hoarse from hours of shouting, The wind made a wall they had to push through with every step. Often, blinding gusts of wind and rain forced them to huddle together in the scant shelter of the trees and wait for a let up to resume their search.

They called, then stopped every few yards to listen for Ned's voice or a bark from Cloud. Joseph doggedly led them on a round-about trek through the woods. Up and down the wrong knolls, along the stream—first in one direction, then the other. Finally the beaver dam—the marker the boy assured them would point the way to Ned—then back up the rise and down into the woods. When it became clear the child was spent, Luke swung him onto his back. "Straight from. . . here," Joseph murmured and rested his head on his father's sodden shoulder. He was asleep in moments.

Allie's own steps began to falter, as had her spirits. Anger festered at her helplessness in what had begun to seem like the futility of their efforts. Freezing wind and rain whipped her hair and skirt and stung her face. Her stiff hands felt frozen to the lantern handle. She'd never been in the woods at night, and the place that had always welcomed her in daylight, seemed hostile. Weariness turned her notions dark. The trees are conspiring to hide him, she thought. And the moon and stars won't even try to help.

"Harper!"

"Ned!"

"Dammit, Cowboy!"

Near dawn they heard bursts of frantic barking, muted, but not far away.

Joseph's head popped up. "Cloud!" he exclaimed. "Put me . . . down, Pa."

Lifting her soaked skirts, Allie ran in the direction of the yowling dog, followed closely by the others. As they neared the sounds, the wind struck her with an odor so foul not even the rain could cleanse it. She stopped short, her heart caving in on itself. She knew that smell all too well.

Kneeling on the soaked ground at Ned's side, Allie clasped her hands in front of her to stop their trembling from cold and terror. She was horrified by what she saw—the glint of lantern light on the ghastly steel trap, the heavy chain that shackled him to the tree, Ned's deerskin boot clamped in its jagged teeth, the ground beneath his leg blackened by a worrisome puddle of pooled blood. He lay too still, too pale, half-hidden by a soggy blanket of windblown leaves and forest debris.

The terrible odor hung above them.

"Bear bait," Zeke explained, gazing upward, a hand over his nose and mouth. His eyes went down to Ned, then back to the nails in the trunk.

"Carcass is gone," he said, bewilderment in his voice. "Damned bear must've come and took it." He looked back at Ned and shook his head. "Some damn how."

Zeke, Luke, and Joseph hovered behind Allie. Cloud hunkered on the other side of Ned watching every move she made. "Ned," she said softly, but got no response.

When she pressed two fingers to the side of his throat searching for a pulse, he stirred. When she brushed wet hair back from his forehead, he squinted up at her and managed a feeble smile. "Boston." She saw fear behind the pain in his eyes. "Joseph?"

"He's here," Allie told him. "He brought us to you."

A moment. An exhale. A softening of the lines around his mouth. Then, his gaze went past her shoulder. Closing his eyes, he groaned, "I'm a dead man."

"Ned Harper, you most certainly are not." Allie made her tone light to mask her anxiety. His breathing was labored, he was grey, cold, clammy, had been barely responsive. His pulse—when she found it—was thready. All signs of hemorrhagic shock. "That's just plain silly," she scoffed. "Yes, your leg's likely broken and yes, you may have lost a bit of blood. But you are not dying. We'll have that contraption off in a minute and get you out of here before you know it."

"It's not that, Boston." Ned drew a shallow breath. "I know you'll fix all that. It's Zeke." He closed his eyes again and gathered more air. "He's gonna kill me for missin' the game."

Zeke's hand tightened on her shoulder and Allie felt him sway behind her. A new cause for alarm seized her. When he straightened up, a wobbly knee bumped her back.

Not now, she thought. Please Zeke, please not now.

"Well, we did lose the damned game," the barber muttered, taking an unsteady step back. "But I don't hold that against you, Cowboy. Leastways not now."

Allie looked up over her shoulder. All color had drained from Zeke's face.

"But I *am* fixin' to skin the pelt off the goddamned trapper who set this . . ." Zeke's voice trailed off, " . . . goddamned thing."

With what was almost a nod, Ned said, "Me, too."

"Enough talk, both of you." As the urgency of the situation became more clear, Allie focused on what had to be done. "Zeke, you sit down right now and put your head between your knees." Staggering back, Zeke sat hard on the ground. When his father, Old Caleb Foster, passed on, Zeke had been expected to carry on the tradition of bone-setting—until it became clear he couldn't abide the sight of blood. Allie gave him a sharp look over her shoulder. "I need you fit to set his leg."

All her attention returned to Ned. He's weak, she thought, but coherent. He's lost a lot of blood from what might be a severed saphenous vein and blood is still oozing from where those teeth bit through his boot. She was certain the heavy steel trap had fractured one or both bones of his lower leg. And, he's in the later stages of wound shock. When we release that horrible thing he'll bleed more. Much more. For a moment, Allie feared she had neither the skills nor the knowledge to treat him.

Until she reminded herself she was all he had.

"Drink this," Allie insisted.

Supporting his shoulders, she held a small cup of laudanum to his lips. He gagged down bitterness worsened by honey, but in moments his pain began to ebb. Ned didn't like the idea of troubling her any more than he already had, so when she told him to drink again, he did. When he had the breath to speak, he whispered, "I s'pose you expect me to thank you for that."

"You're welcome," she said, easing him back down.

The laudanum blossomed through his body and imparted its special form of euphoria. He smiled at the memory that came to him. "Pulling out another thorn, Boston?"

Slipping her hand into his, she glared at the trap. "A bigger thorn this time, I'm sorry to say. Squeeze my hand, if you need to."

At that, he pulled his own hand free—he knew what was coming and feared hurting her. "Just something to bite on."

When he had the leather strap she'd pulled from her satchel firmly between his teeth, he nodded. Allie raised her eyes to Zeke and Findlay. "Now."

Clenching his jaw, Ned tasted cowhide. When the jagged teeth of the trap ripped free of his flesh and jarred his shattered bones, in the moment before blackness took him, he heard Allie say, "Zeke, close your eyes."

Those words. Pain. Laudanum—mercifully not laced with honey this time. Cold. Howling wind and rain like shotgun pellets. Pain. That was all Ned remembered of what transpired the rest of that night.

Morning would not be as kind.

The crack and flash of gunfire just outside awakened him. Drummers. Battle cadence. Nearer, Ned heard the moans and whimpers of wounded soldiers, the screams of amputees. He understood he was soon to be one of them—his leg blown apart in battle. Biting back a groan, he opened his eyes to a darkened tent lit by a lone lantern. In a shadowy corner, a disheveled young nurse in a blood-streaked shirtwaist dozed in a chair.

Darkness had spit him out into a world of pain and terror. Mercifully, it swallowed him up again.

Eyes grainy, mouth dry, groggy and sick, he came to again with no idea how long he'd been out. When he struggled to writhe free of the pain in his leg, a hand pressed to his chest restrained him.

"Try not to move, Ned," the nurse cautioned. When he pushed the infuriating hand away, a heavy forearm across his torso held him down. "Moving's what's hurting you," she said softly. "Be still."

It made sense, he thought, so he tried to obey her words. "Is it over?" he rasped. He'd heard medics say a missing limb could still cause pain. Phantom pain, they called it.

"Yes," she murmured and gently squeezed his hand. "I believe the worst is over."

A vague memory of flesh tearing and bones shattering haunted him, but the loss of his leg troubled him less in that moment than his thirst. As if reading his mind, the nurse offered him a cup of water. "Just a few sips." Wrapping his hands around the mug, she guided it to his lips. "Slowly." His throat still felt parched when she took the mug, but it didn't seem worth it to protest. "Now this," she said, lifting the cup to his lips again.

Ned didn't resist the bitter quaff, nor did he gag on it. He downed it like a shot of rye at the Tongue Oil Saloon and awaited the easing of pain and the sweet euphoria that should come with it. This time, bliss did not accompany relief.

Disappointed, he slipped into a strange hinterland that passed for sleep.

As much as he willed consciousness to stay away, it forced its way back. Tightening his jaw against a groan, Ned opened his eyes to a too-bright room. His thoughts were thick and slow, but he knew where he was. Will's old room at South Slope. His own clothing had been stripped off and he found himself in red long johns. Will's old long johns. And, he was surprised to find his leg still attached to his body—bruised and swollen and splinted, but definitely there.

His relief was short-lived, replaced by apprehension. He had questions, urgent questions, he just couldn't remember what they were.

Wearing a clean frock and with her hair pulled back in a neat bun, Allie sat by the side of the bed writing. After a moment of confusion, Ned realized she, of course, had been the army nurse in his dreams. He stirred and his leg delivered a stern reprimand. At his sharp intake of breath, Allie looked up. Her concerned frown softened to a smile. "You slept so long, the laudanum must have worn off."

Digging his elbows into the mattress, he tried to sit up, but pain forced him back against the pillows. "Joseph?"

"Safe," she said. "I don't know how he did it, but that remarkable boy led us to you—in the dark and rain. He and his father stayed here to wait out the storm. Without their help we'd still be looking for you."

"Cloud?"

At his name, the wolf dog gave a soft bark. Tail wagging, he rose from the rag rug beside the bed, stretched, and nudged a cold nose beneath Ned's hand.

"He's been here the whole time, too," Allie said. "Mother wanted him in the barn, of course, but he raised such a ruckus even she had to relent—despite his wet fur, muddy paws, and all."

Ned managed a sheepish grin. He remembered now that she'd answered the same questions before. The boy had found his way to town and led them back to him. The dog had remained at his side through everything. Settling back against the pillows, he realized that although his leg hurt, the pain had subsided to the persistent ache of a bad tooth.

He would have begun to relax, if Allie hadn't insisted on talking.

"Zeke and I set your leg," she told him. "Both bones were fractured—not crushed as I'd feared. But I do suspect your major saphenous vein may have been severed, because of the extent of blood loss." She chuckled and shook her head. "I had to stop you from bleeding and keep poor Zeke from passing out at the same time. You know how he is about blood, and there was quite a lot."

He listened because he had no choice.

"The teeth of that awful trap had driven dirt and cloth into the wounds. I did my best to clean them and managed to cauterize the worst . . ."

Ned raised an unsteady hand to stop her unnerving litany.

"Oh! I'm sorry." She widened her eyes and bit the corner of her lip. "I wasn't thinking. I'll save the rest of the gruesome details for Doc." Mischief played across her face. "At least he'll appreciate them."

"That would be a kindness, Boston." Ned was tiring, but her banter had eased his mind. Then, his hand went to the borrowed long-johns eliciting a new concern. "My clothes?"

Allie shuddered. "Burned. Mother insisted." After a moment's hesitation, she added, "I'm really sorry to tell you this, but I had to cut off your boot. Couldn't be helped."

His favorite and only pair, made from one of the finest deerskins he'd ever tanned. "At least you didn't take my leg with it."

When her face clouded and she didn't respond with the humor he'd expected, his own smile faded. He heard the unspoken, "*Yet.*" Aloud, Allie said, "The bones should heal with no trouble."

He understood the worry line that creased her forehead. In the army, he'd seen men with what seemed insignificant wounds die of the infections that followed. To distract them both, Ned tapped at the flannel on his chest and raised a questioning brow. Although the thought had nagged at him since he realized the long-johns weren't his, he was disconcerted by the flush creeping up from his neck to his cheeks and the backs of his ears. "You?"

"Me?" Her own heightened color matched his. "Oh, no. Of course not." She turned away to fiddle with the vial of laudanum. "I didn't. I mean . . . I wouldn't." Looking over her shoulder, she almost met his eyes. "Mr. Findlay helped you out of your clothes."

"Oh," Ned said, with more dismay than gratitude. "Findlay."

"And, he sat with you while I got some sleep."

"Findlay?" The brawny forearm that had held him down.

"Yes."

"Luke Findlay changed my clothes and nursed me through the night."

"Day."

Remembering a reassuring hand in his and the gentle palm pressed to his cheek and forehead, Ned knew they hadn't belonged to the sheep rancher. Apparently, there was much to be sorted out from the previous day and night and his mind wobbled when he tried. Still, he knew Allie had been at the center of it. "I don't know how to thank you . . ."

She lifted a hand in a dismissive wave. "Mr. Findlay also saw to it that Trickster got rescued from the mercantile and put in our barn, as soon as you were settled."

"Seems I'm beholden to all kinds of folks for gettin' me through that night."

"We all got each other through it."

"Aside from the doctoring I got from you and the bone-setting from Zeke, I owe the most to Joseph." He shot her a grudging look. "And, I suppose, his pa." Fatigue burned at the small of his back and edged up his spine. "If they're still here, I'd like to see them. Thank 'em. Get this beholden business over with."

Allie studied him for longer than he was comfortable with and frowned. "Maybe later."

"Now." The dull ache in his leg had sharpened and begun to throb, making him irritable. The heat in his spine spread to his chest and prickled the back of his neck. He tried to concentrate on to whom he was supposed to be beholden and for what. "Please."

"You really should rest."

"You and I both know I'll be resting plenty. 'Specially if you have anything to say about it." He quirked her a smile. "Which I'm sure you will."

"All right, a short visit," she relented. "The Findlays and Albert. He wouldn't take my word for it that you're most likely going to survive and insists he has to see for himself." She turned to go, then turned back. "A *very* short. Then, broth and rest. Understood?"

With his shrug of surrender, she left the room.

Balancing a napkin-draped bowl of the rich beef broth Mrs. Olney had kept simmering all day, Allie led the subdued procession up the stairs.

"Ned thinks he's fine, but he won't be if he doesn't rest." She gave them all her sternest face. "He wants to thank you for helping him, so no questions, no stories. All that can come later. Understood?"

All three nodded. She knew the boys needed to see Ned as much as he needed to see them. Joseph had witnessed so much horror in the woods and Albert had been badly shaken to see the aftermath when they brought Ned to the house.

At the door, she gave a quick knock and opened it. Ned sat tall against the pillows. His eyes were bright, Allie noted with some surprise, and his color seemed better than it had been when she'd left him. Cloud sat on his haunches on the far side of the bed and added a chorus of friendly barks to greet his pack.

Extending his hand toward Findlay, Ned said, "I understand I owe you for more than helping to find me in the woods. You rescued my horse from the storm and my. . . my modesty from . . . well, that's about all I want to say about that—except thanks."

With an easiness Allie hadn't expected, Findlay laughed and shook Ned's hand. "The less said the better."

"Joseph," Ned said, his face now somber. "When you went off to get help, I only hoped you'd make it to your pa safely. I didn't dare think you'd find your way back to me." His voice roughened. "Miss Allie says you probably saved my leg." He looked over Joseph's shoulder and met Findlay's eyes, "Maybe my life."

Joseph nodded with vigor. "I used all . . . my wolf senses just . . . like you taught me."

Allie held her breath. She imagined Luke Findlay would not take well to those words. All eyes went to the man who appeared baffled for a moment. Then, he cleared his throat. "Whatever it was you taught my boy, Harper, it saved *his* life."

Tilting his head up at his father, Joseph protested. "But Pa . . . it was Cloud." The dog's ears twitched and his tail thumped. "Cloud found me when . . . I got lost and . . . he led me all the way . . . to town."

Ned's eyes went from Joseph to the dog, then he settled back against the pillows. With a tightening in her chest, Allie realized she'd been mistaken about his appearance. His eyes were too bright and what she had taken for better color was the flush of fever.

"We all agreed we'd keep this visit short," she announced, tilting her head toward the door. Findlay took the cue, but the boys required a firm hand on each shoulder to get them moving in the right direction. "There'll be plenty of time to relive your adventures tomorrow."

When they were gone, a patina of sweat glistened on Ned's forehead and beneath his closed eyes. His leg was—as Allie feared—angry red and hot against her hand. He flinched at her touch. Blood and pus had surfaced from the puncture wounds beneath the bandages. Fighting panic, she reviewed everything she'd been taught about treating infections—carbolic, cauterization, cloves and honey, gunpowder, bromine and iodine—and found her head spinning.

Doc should be home at any time, she reassured herself. If there's anything more that can be done, he'll know. Keeping her alarm from her voice, she lifted the still warm bowl of soup. "Broth?"

"Later."

His disheartening response didn't surprise her. She busied herself mixing the laudanum.

"Doc's favorite Scotch," she told Ned, showing him the bottle. "Zeke set me straight about the honey, so you can save your scowls."

He said nothing for many moments, then, softly, "Allie?"

"Yes?"

"Joseph said Cloud showed him the way back to town." The dog gave a confirming yelp and Ned searched Allie's face. "I heard that right?"

"You did." His concern over such a small matter troubled her. She took it as more evidence of rising fever. "Joseph said Cloud came to him when he'd gotten lost in the woods and led him to town."

"That can't be." The dog rested his chin on the side of the bed and Ned scratched the sweet spot behind his ears. "Cloud stayed with me the whole time." Allie couldn't read the expression that accompanied his next words. "I tried to send him along with Joseph, but he wouldn't leave my side."

CHAPTER FORTY-FIVE

When Doc returned, and he and Allie hovered over him with faces long as fiddles, Ned understood he must be very sick and that Mother Bear was not yet done with him. The words he thought she'd said echoed in his febrile mind: *Deciding not to die is not the same as choosing to live.*

Fever had broken his world down into colors. Day was murky white, night black, pain red. People were wavering shapes of brown and blue and gray. His moods felt just as kaleidoscopic. One moment, he was so grateful for Allie's care, that he had to swallow a lump in his throat. The next, her attentions aggravated him to the point he had to grit his teeth not to growl at her to please, please, if only for a minute, leave him alone.

But when his eyes felt scorched, it was Allie's hand or the cool cloth she covered them with that soothed him.

"You've done everything that could be done, my dear," Doc assured Allie. "Everything I myself would have done. Especially under the circumstances in the woods. I've never been tested in such a way and won't even try to predict how I might have managed."

His praise, and her acceptance of it, began the rebuilding of something within her that had crumbled under the weight of her failure with Clare Winnicott. With her help, Ned had survived the trap, but now infection threatened his life and caused her to wonder if she really had done all that could have been done.

The fever that wracked his body did as fevers do. For days Ned burned, restless, hot and dry. Or, chills wracked his body and nothing could warm him. The fever would break in a cold sweat and release him for hours, then return with a vengeance. Red streaks radiated out from the wounds above his ankle. Helpless, Allie felt feverish herself. She supposed Ned had been right when he talked about the Fear Caller. Her worst fear had always been failing someone who needed her. With Ned, despite Doc's reassurances, she feared neither of them knew as much as there was to know about treating infections. Doc had been practicing in the primitive outpost of Solace Springs for more than a decade and relied on occasional journal articles to update his medical knowledge. She knew far less.

She feared their ignorance could cost Ned his leg or his life. And so, she pressed cold cloths to his forehead and warm bricks to his feet. She painted the infected puncture wounds too often, with too much iodine—despite Doc's raised brow—because she'd read of an army general's wife who'd saved her husband's life by doing so.

Whenever she asked how he was, Ned always answered, "Better."

When she offered him broth or food, he always said, "Later."

He refused laudanum, asking instead for willow bark tea. "It's more predictable."

After six hellish days and nights, he awakened from a fever-free sleep with his leg pale and cool. Allie asked how he felt.

He thought for a moment before saying, "Hungry."

CHAPTER FORTY-SIX

Mending bridles in the tack room, Heck hadn't noticed Red Moon approach the stable. There'd been a time, even though she moved stealthy as a cat, when he could hear the brush of her moccasins or the rustle of her deerskin skirt at a distance. No more. These days, he lamented, he'd gone deaf as a stump. So, when he looked up from his work to see her standing in the doorway, he was startled. And concerned. If she'd come all the way down from the house, she must have something serious on her mind.

Heck squinted, seeking a clue to the reason for the visit in her face. Backlit by the slanting late-afternoon sun, her features were obscured. "Darlin'?" Her stillness and straight back felt like a warning. "Moon?" he said, alarmed. "What's wrong?"

When she stepped out of the shadows, he saw that her expression was serene and her onyx eyes calm. "Hannah Hanover was here," she said. "She brought news of Ned."

News of Ned. Snakes coiled in Heck's belly. They had feared for him all these months. Red Moon, especially. She'd seen visions of him walking with the Warrior in White, befriending death. Heck felt sickened.

"He's been hurt," Red Moon said. "Bad." When Heck's huge shoulders caved, she added quickly, "He's all right. Now. Doc Hanover and that wise Willow Girl of his saw him through the worst of it."

Red Moon had long admired the doctor's daughter. "Like the willow," she'd told Heck, "that girl is strong, yet knows when to bend. Like the bark of the tree, she brings relief to those who suffer."

Reassured, but still shaken, Heck asked, "What happened?"

A small smile played at the corners of the Indian woman's mouth. Then, her eyes gleamed and she grinned—a wide, elated, face-splitting grin. An expression Heck had rarely seen on her. His own face tightened with the concern that his always steady wife might have gone loco. With some wariness, he asked, "What happened to him and why do you look so happy about it?"

"Because it is very good news."

"Good news?"

Her next words convinced Heck his fears for her sanity were valid.

"Because, Ox Who Hears Only With His Ears, our Ned was searching for a lost child and stepped in a bear trap. He lay alone and helpless in the woods for many hours."

He gaped at Red Moon in disbelief. "That pleases you?"

"Yes. Very much." Her smile broadened. "He called Mother Bear to him in the woods. She comes to guide those who must go inward to make difficult choices but who fear the deep cave where Answer lives." She patted Heck's arm. "He didn't die, though Hannah said Willow Girl and the doctor feared he might. Bear led him to the womb-cave and kept him safe. Our Ned faced his fear and decided to live."

Heck didn't ask how Snowy Owl had come to know all this. He just shared her relief.

CHAPTER FORTY-SEVEN

In the early days of Ned's convalescence, Allie's most daunting task was to keep him in bed. After a few nights of restorative sleep, and strengthened by a few good meals, he'd asked for crutches.

"Not yet."

As she'd expected, his mouth tightened. "When?"

Without a bit of remorse, she blamed her father. "Doc says you need to give your leg more time to heal. If you put weight on it too soon . . ."

"What I *need* is to get out of this room. " He drew a breath and exhaled slowly, what Allie had learned meant a struggle with his temper. "I'm startin' to feel like a cat trapped in a barrel." She smiled at the expletives she knew he'd held back. Giving her a surly look, he added, "I know not to put weight on a broken leg. That's what crutches are for, aren't they?"

She knew not to argue the point.

To help him pass the time and improve his mood, Albert taught him checkers and spent hours playing with him, Maude Mary tried to teach him the basics of cross-stitching—with little success, and Zeke came every few days to talk about Sarah Findlay, baseball, and Sarah Findlay. When Will or Hannah visited with the intention to cheer him up, it made him all the more restless to be reminded of the work he wasn't getting done at the ranch.

Miranda, the kitchen maid, climbed the stairs several times a day—without complaint—to bring him endless glasses of lemonade and plates of molasses cookies. Every evening, Mrs. Olney came up to get a report on what he thought of the meals she'd sent him and ask what might tempt his appetite the next day. "Thank you, ma'am," he told her each time. "Everything you fix suits me fine."

And Milady, Maude Mary's dainty grey kitten—who had never deigned to be the barn cat she was born to be—found her way to Ned's room to nap in the crook of his arm, purring in her sleep.

Cloud stretched out on the rag rug and pretended ignorance of the fluffy interloper.

One morning, Luke and Joseph Findlay stopped by.

Beaming, Joseph announced, "I'm taking my Pa out to the . . . berry bushes."

Findlay cleared his throat. "Martha packed us a picnic." He cast his eyes down briefly, then raised them to Ned's. "I'm sorry to say I've never gone walkin' in the woods with my boy before today. Thanks to you, he's got a lot to show me. Berries and beaver dams and such, I'm told. I expect we'll run into some bees while we're at it, but thanks to Miss Allie," he nodded at her, "Joseph knows just what to do if we get stung."

Ned and Allie exchanged a quick look that mirrored each other's satisfaction.

"I sure hope we can look forward to a slice of one of Mrs. Findlay's pies," Ned said, grinning.

"You'd best make room for a whole one, Harper."

Every morning, Ned asked for crutches and every morning Allie braced herself to tell him, "Not yet."

"This bed's beginnin' to feel a whole lot like that bear trap," he'd groused more than once. Though she'd had to cut off one bloody boot, she'd salvaged and cleaned the other. It sat across the room, under the window. "If you're not gonna let me use it, you might at least do me the kindness of putting that boot where it won't be staring at me."

During the endless, oppressive summer afternoons when Ned's mood grew more and more restless, Allie sat with him. They talked about anything and everything she could think of to pass the time. Her mother: "She's really not so bad." Her sister: "She really is." Her father: "He's the best man any of us will ever know."

Little's Disease and Joseph—no, sadly, there was no treatment for it. She told Ned about the difficulties facing women who seek formal medical education. Read him Lydia Brennan's letters. Expressed her admiration for the courage of Elizabeth Blackwell—the first woman to graduate from a medical college in the United States. Ned listened attentively, laughed when he should, and asked a question here and there.

She didn't tell him that when he'd been so ill, and his recovery so uncertain, her fear of failing him and the acute awareness of her lack of training had kept her awake until dawn. It had been after one of those fraught nights that she'd paid her weekly visit to the post office. From Boston, there was a letter from her father's stock broker, another addressed to her mother with Aunt Hope's exquisite penmanship, a copy of the New England Journal of Medicine, and a week-old edition of the Boston Globe.

Henry Coleman, the postmaster, telegraph operator, and chief conduit of town gossip, gave these to her without hesitation. He scrutinized a formal-looking envelope before relinquishing it to Allie. Raising pale brows to stare over his wire-rim spectacles, he watched with unabashed curiosity as she read the return address. Oblivious to the postmaster's curiosity, she tore open her acceptance to the Carver College of Medicine at the State University of Iowa, one of the few 'regular' medical colleges that accepted both men and women. Throat dry, she reread it twice, then stumbled outside and took several deep breaths to resuscitate herself before walking slowly back to South Slope.

Eager again for the advanced learning that would ease some of her feelings of helplessness, she was still torn by doubt about her own abilities. She shared the news with no one. Tucking the letter into her pocket, she carried it with her every day, telling herself she needed time and a clear head—neither of which she had had while caring for Ned those first dire days—to make a sound decision about whether or not to go.

But, whenever her hand went to the paper, her fingers tingled.

One afternoon, she talked to Ned about the Winnicotts. Ephraim and his obsession with the evil, devouring Tiger. Clare's melancholia. Allie lowered her eyes when she spoke of her own despair at feeling she'd failed the young woman. How convincing Ephraim to take his wife home had been the best Allie could do to help.

"I suppose that must count for something," she conceded. "Doc says medicine is uncertain, at best, and that physicians must 'accept their inevitable fallibility.' " She bit her lip and shook her head. "But I can't. I just keep thinking there must have been something more I could have done for Clare. Should have done."

"Her spirit got broken, Boston," Ned said. "Pure and simple. Splints and tincture of iodine can't fix that." His strong features softened. "But you figured out just the thing that has a chance of saving her and her family." His eyes stayed on her as he appeared to weigh what he said next. "You belong in medical school, Allie. You're not a debutante. You're a doctor."

Struck by the truth in his words, something in her unlocked. She had called her fear of helplessness to her and let it imperil her. *Ned's right,* she thought, *hope really is all there is when there's nothing else. And I gave that to the Winnicots when they hadn't the strength to find it on their own. I wonder if they'll teach that at the Carver College of Medicine: Anatomy, physiology, principles and practices of surgery, and hope.*

She told Ned how she'd convinced her mother to press the Ladies' Benevolent Society into service procuring donations to outfit the Winnicotts for their return to Nebraska. Despite her distaste for Ephraim, she had agreed with Allie that the children and their ill mother shouldn't suffer because of the indolence of their father. In just weeks, she had obtained all the provisions the family would need for the month—or longer—journey.

The Ladies had raised enough funds to purchase a small, worn prairie schooner and gotten donations of everything else—cooking utensils, bedding, a cast iron Dutch oven, coats, clothes, sturdy boots, and a lantern. Several people contributed assorted foodstuffs that added up to an adequate supply of flour, eggs packed in cornmeal to make corn bread, sugar, bacon, sacks of beans, rice, and dried fruit, salt, pepper, vinegar, and molasses. Water the Winnicotts would get along the way. Heck Abernathy had gifted them a yoke of elderly, but newly-shod oxen, along with a spare axle.

"They'll be on their way in a few days," Allie told Ned.

Studying her furrowed brow, he asked, "Is that good news or bad news?"

His question rattled her—she'd hoped her misgivings about the Winnicott's travels hadn't been so obvious. After a sigh that did nothing to reduce her anxiety, she said, "I just don't know if Ephraim can manage a sick wife, four children, a pair of oxen, *and* find his way across the prairie between here and Nebraska."

"Don't worry, Boston," Ned said. "Ephraim found his way out here, he'll find his way back. You can count on Etta to be looking after them all anyway."

The crease in Allie's brow deepened. "That's exactly what I'm worried about."

Whenever there was a knock on the bedroom door, Ned always said, "Come on in," and greeted his visitors with a welcoming grin. So, he was surprised to realize that as much as he appreciated any company, when the door opened and it wasn't Allie, he was disappointed.

After a few days, he began to contribute to their talks. At first, with reluctance. He started with the trivial: Baseball in the army, the Sluggers, the trick of throwing a curve ball. Watching Allie's face, he shared the intricacies of brain-tanning, expecting the unpleasant details to disgust her. Instead, she took a keen interest in the process, asked many questions, and offered some theories of her own on why it worked so well.

Then, he spoke of things closer to his heart: Raising horses, catching Trouble and Sugarplum and gentling them. Building the cabin and its furniture, Becky's delight when he surprised her with the beautiful cast iron, nickel-plated, coal and wood burning National Excelsior stove he'd ordered all the way from the factory in Quincy, Ohio. How she'd been especially taken with its embossed flowers and cherubs.

One dark afternoon, as a thunderstorm battered the windows, he talked about his brothers. Revelations often punctuated by long silences. "First," he said, "there's Nate, the oldest. Not even fifteen-years-old when our folks died within a year of each other." Left to manage a struggling ranch and three younger children. To teach them to train and tend horses so the Harper boys could make a living of sorts. Doing most of the work himself. Ned winced and shook his head at the memory. "Not even fifteen."

Ned, the youngest, hadn't realized until he was grown what it must have been like for Nate. Done to him. A boy raising three boys—six, eleven, and twelve when they were orphaned. Seeing they had food, firewood, and boots for winter. Nursing them when they got sick. Shooing them off to school when it occurred to him they hadn't gone in a while. Keeping them together when well-meaning neighbors wanted to separate them, take them in to care for them. Especially the little one. Ned. Nate had been fierce in his refusals.

"Then there's Ben." Ned went silent to fight a wave of grief that took him by surprise. He lowered his eyes, then managed a bemused smile. "That boy was afraid of nothin' and got away with everything. My closest friend."

And timid Thomas, who feared everything. "But would go along with anything."

"And me," Ned told her. "I just wanted to be with my brothers and do what they did."

After seven years and tired of the life that had been thrust upon him, Nate cajoled his brothers into coming with him on a great adventure. To war, where the battle of Spotsylvania would take two of them. After that, Nate had left Ned and gone off in search of gold in New Zealand. Asked him to come along, of course, but Ned refused. At almost sixteen, he'd had all the adventure he could stomach.

"Now I understand why he was so set on gettin' away from everything," Ned said, old pain stinging his eyes. "I didn't back then. Couldn't, I guess. I don't hold it against him anymore—taking us to war, leaving me on my own—but I did. Hated him for a long time."

When Ned spoke, his voice felt rough. "Thinking back on it all . . ." he cleared his throat. "I know I owe Nate. A lot. I want to tell him that."

On a sweltering afternoon that turned the small bedroom into a sweat lodge, Ned recounted how Heck and Red Moon had taken him in—fed him when he stumbled up to their doorstep looking for work—a half-starved, more than half-broken youth. Heck had worked him so hard his hands finally stopped shaking. Red Moon had mothered him.

"Someday ask Heck to sing you his version of the Cowboy's Prayer," Ned told Allie. "He swears to this day that dealin' with me is what drove him to religion."

The next day, when she stepped off the porch into fresh air, bright sunshine, and the caress of a late-summer breeze, Allie felt a pang of empathy for Ned—accompanied by a stab of guilt. She forgave him for the surly mood he'd been in that morning. She was accustomed to living most of her days indoors—in her house, her father's office, the homes of their patients. Ned lived outside—breathing the limitless air of the woods, the ranch, the plains and canyons. She imagined he must be suffocating confined to one room and two small windows.

"Not yet," she'd told him, when, yet again he'd asked for crutches. She was—as Ned accused—"in cahoots" with her father on the matter of not allowing a man they both agreed should not be relied on to exercise caution to be trusted with crutches too soon.

He hadn't scowled or snapped at her this time, hadn't even raises his eyes. He just kept petting the grey cat asleep beside him.

"I'm going to see the Winnicotts off," she said.

"Wish them well."

"I'll be back before noon."

He'd nodded, stroking the cat's elongated belly as the feline twisted onto her back and stretched.

"Is there anything I can bring you from town?"

He'd raised his eyes and narrowed them at her. "Crutches."

Allie returned from the Winnicotts' sendoff greatly relieved and keen to tell Ned everything. After stopping in the kitchen for a tray of lemonade and cookies, and receiving a scathing glare from Miranda, she went to Ned's room certain he'd be eager for the details. When she opened the door, his pleased expression assured her, as she'd guessed, that he'd forgiven her for refusing him crutches.

She sipped her lemonade, until he said, "Out with it, Boston."

With pleasure, she told him the tale of the Winnicott's departure.

Allie had caught up with them just as their small prairie schooner, swaying back and forth on its quirky axle, had begun to trundle away from Solace Springs. Much to Ned's surprise, her mother had sought his counsel regarding whether to find the Winnicotts two work horses or a pair of oxen to pull the rickety wagon to Nebraska. Ned had recommended oxen. "Half the price and they'll eat whatever grasses they find along the way."

Clare and Ephraim perched side by side on the bench, his arm wrapped around her thin shoulders, frowning at the slow pace of the lumbering oxen. She, staring straight ahead with a frozen expression. But, Allie told Ned, she *was* holding her squirming toddler on her lap and did appear to make occasional efforts to respond to his smiles and whimpers. She'd nodded at Allie's farewell and good wishes and echoed Ephraim's thank you.

To Allie's profound relief, she discovered that Nanny Lou would be accompanying the family on their journey. The old woman waddled alongside the wagon, spry for her age and girth. In high spirits, Etta and her younger siblings scampered around her in a game of tag.

"I'm coming along for poor Clare and these little ones' sakes," Nanny Lou told Allie. "Someone has to box that Ephraim's ears ever so often, lest he start squanderin' again," she'd whispered loudly, with an arch look back at the wagon. "I'm the one to do it. Who else? Someone has to see these babies get fed. Expect I'm the one to do that, too. With all them victuals we're totin,' I can cook' em up a mess of anything you can name in that fine Dutch oven. And, I can shoot as good as I cook—brung my own rifle—so Clare and them scrawny young'uns'll be feastin' on rabbit and squirrel and maybe even possum. If that no-account Ephraim behaves himself, he might be invited to partake, as well. And I do mean if."

Nanny had confessed to Allie that her motives weren't entirely altruistic. "I don't know if you noticed, but I *am* advancing in age and I sure don't feature dyin' alone in a slipshod shack upwind of a whore house." Etta skipped closer to listen. "I got me some family in Nebraska, just north of Saline. They'll take me in if I get myself up there. Leastways, I hope they will."

Etta threw her arms around Nanny Lou's broad hips. "Oh, Nanny, you don't need them Saline folks. You got us. We' s your family!"

And off they went, Allie told Ned. Ephraim driving the team with Clare at his side, Nanny and Etta hand in hand, and the smaller children cavorting like lambs. The wagon with its tattered canvas cover creaked along, the oxen grunting and groaning.

Just three hundred or so more miles to go.

CHAPTER FORTY-EIGHT

A few days after the Winnicotts' departure, Allie found Ned so dark and distant she felt his cool forehead to check for fever and examined his healing leg. Pulling back from her hand, he forced an apologetic smile. "It's just, thanks to you and Doc, I've got too much time to think."

Mistaking his words for an invitation to listen, she sat down and waited. He glanced at her, then looked away. At what she took for his dismissal, she stood and turned to leave. She'd taken only a step when he reached out to touch her hand and nodded toward the chair. When she seated herself again, he remained silent. When he spoke, Allie heard the effort behind each word. "I've been thinking about Becky and my son."

Everything in her went still. An elk in a clearing, she thought. Don't startle him or he'll bolt.

Eyes on his folded hands, Ned told her how Becky had stood barefoot in the middle of the cabin that winter dawn to inform him they'd be having their first child. Lifting his gaze, he smiled a thin, hard-won smile, then went silent again. More than silent. Lowering his eyes, his voice just above a whisper, he told Allie he'd felt he couldn't go on living after they died.

For the first time, she became aware of the lack of air in the small room.

"Couldn't see the point in it," Ned said. "In anything. Made up my mind to walk into the woods and never come out."

His confession closed her throat. Dizzied her. *I should have known. How did I not know?*

Holding her gaze, he hid nothing. She slipped her hand into his. "I'm so sorry."

Turning her hand over, he wrapped his fingers around it. An easier smile played at the corners of his mouth. "Just in case you're wonderin', I did change my mind about that walk. Stuck in that damn bear trap . . . " She saw him flinch at the memory. "Out in those same woods, I realized I didn't want to die." His face went somber again. "So, Dr. Boston, I'm mighty grateful you took the trouble to save my life."

"Ned Harper, it was just a couple of broken bones," she scoffed. "And a few puncture wounds—bad enough, I guess—but not even bone deep. And, well, yes, there was that hemolytic shock. Exposure, too."

He laughed and held up a hand to stop her. His other, warm and strong in hers, flooded her with yearning that was satisfying in and of itself. A carefully guarded part of her opened to him. Hesitant, at first, reluctant to relinquish her own secret, but wanting to share something of herself with him, she pulled the acceptance letter from her pocket and handed it to him. Her heart beat harder, not faster.

After reading it, he folded it carefully and handed it back. "I sure do hope this means you're heading to Iowa."

Smiling, blinking back inexplicable tears, she truly understood the meaning of the word bittersweet. "It does."

CHAPTER FORTY-NINE

In a household where unexpected events occurred on a regular basis, Doc Hanover often had the opportunity to recite one of his favorite Dickens quotations. He'd shake his head, chuckle, and announce, "Like dear old Boz, I, too 'know enough of the world now to have almost lost the capacity of being much surprised by anything.' "

But when he entered his study early that morning, he almost dropped his steaming cup of barefoot coffee. In the half-light of dawn, Ned Harper sat in one of the Chesterfield chairs, his splinted leg propped on a hassock, arms folded across his chest.

"Mornin' Doc."

It occurred to Doc that Miranda had just scurried past him in the hall, face flushed, and eyes averted. A willing accomplice, he surmised. "I would have come to you," he said, seating himself behind his desk.

"I know."

His patient looked exhausted and defiant, neither of which sat well with the doctor. Ned had asked him to make some inquiries on his behalf and Doc had prepared a report of sorts on the outcome. He'd planned to deliver it to him upstairs, where he should have been safely in bed.

"Your impatience compelled you to take unnecessary risks." Frowning, he made a sweeping gesture encompassing the stairs and the hall leading to his study. "You could have undone all Allie's hard work."

"I didn't."

"I understand your eagerness to know what I found out, but making the arduous journey down here without crutches was . . ."

"If I'd had them," Ned cut in, "I would 've used' em."

Aware he'd lost the battle at the opening volley, Doc exhaled his irritation. What was done was done. Much rested on the information he was about to impart and, he regretted, much of it wouldn't be what Ned had hoped to hear.

"First," Doc said, "I can report that dogs are permitted on most steamships. In fact, some have kennels and some even have kennel masters."

Ned made a wry face. Doc knew that anyone who'd met Cloud would have difficulty imagining the wolf dog confined to a kennel or submitting to a kennel master.

"As to the rest," Doc continued, handing Ned a sheet listing the expenses for a journey from southern Colorado to New Zealand—stage coach to Morrison, rail to Denver, then on to New York, transatlantic steamship to England, steamer from Liverpool to New Zealand.

Living costs for a year or so once there would be high. Food, shelter, transportation, prospecting equipment, and miscellany—all would be exorbitant in the mining towns. Reading the numbers, Ned's jaw tightened. He'd told Doc that in the last few years, he and Becky had saved enough to be able to buy their homesteaded land with some money to spare. He'd disclosed the amount to Doc, so both men knew Ned had nowhere near enough to cover the extensive outlay inventoried.

"I can't do that." Ned handed the paper back, his face impassive. Easing his leg off the hassock, he gripped the arm rests and raised himself to stand. steadying all his weight on his good leg. When he winced, Doc earned a hard look for noticing.

"I know your circumstances, Ned. Sit down, please. I have a proposal."

Sinking wearily into the leather chair, Ned shook his head. "I won't take a loan I'm not sure I can pay back."

"I'm not proposing a loan."

Ned's eyes flashed. "You know I won't take a handout."

"I wouldn't offer one. This is a business proposition."

In that instant, the door flew open. "Papa! It's Ned . . . he's . . ." Allie's alarmed face went slack as she stared from her father to Ned, then back to Doc. "Gone."

"No, my dear, not gone. He's clearly not where he *should* be," Doc frowned at Ned. "But he is, as you can see, quite here."

She started to speak, closed her mouth, glared at Ned, then managed, "But . . . how?"

"Best not to ask, my dear," Doc said. "When Ned and I have finished our meeting, he'll be yours to interrogate as you see fit. Heaven help him. For now, you will excuse us?"

When she had exited and shut the door, a bit too loudly for his liking, Doc said, "My proposal is this. I'd like to purchase a quarter of your interest in the H&H ranch, which should cover your travel expenses and then some. In addition," he paused before adding, "I'll stake you upfront for an interest in whatever gold you discover in New Zealand."

Clearly shocked at the generous proffer, Ned went silent for a moment. "Doc," he said slowly, "I appreciate what you're tryin' to do. More than I can say. But I can't let you do it. There's no telling what kind of profits we'll make from the ranch. Or when. Will and I just hope to make a living out of it someday. And the gold? That's a pipe dream and you know it. Most likely, I won't find a single nugget."

Doc leaned forward, eyes agleam. "That's it exactly. I can't travel to New Zealand myself. I can't sail across two oceans and adventure across an unknown land for a pipe dream. My investments are managed by unimaginative stock brokers in New York who consider the word 'speculation' the worst sort of blasphemy." Setting his coffee on the desk, he linked his gaze with Ned's. "Let me assure you the stake I'm offering you—and I hope you won't think me immodest for saying it—is a pittance of the assets I hold and will probably never use. My children have been well-provided for since birth with family money none of us have had to lift a finger to earn. Please, allow me the opportunity, the heady thrill, to—dare I say it—*gamble* on your endeavor."

Sitting back, Doc watched Ned argue with himself. Shake his head. Nod. Shake his head again. "Let me make sure I heard you right," he finally said. "You want to buy a quarter of my part of the ranch to stake my trip to New Zealand?"

"I do."

"If I find gold, you want a cut of that, too?"

"A piece of every shiny little nugget." Doc knew the offer was a fair deal that benefited everyone involved, thus must seem too good to be true.

"We'll have to run it by Will," Ned said, plainly warming to the idea. Doc saw a glimmer of hope in the young man's eyes as he seemed to realize his impossible venture might yet be possible.

"I've already discussed it with him. If you approve the terms, he's in full agreement." When Ned and Will had started the ranch, and struggled, Doc had offered help that his son adamantly refused, determined to succeed on his own. Now that the ranch was beginning to break even, Will conceded he saw the benefit of a partner's added resources to help them grow, even if they were his father's. "The only thing we need," Doc said to Ned, "is your agreement."

Ned was silent again for what Doc thought an overly lengthy time. "You're sure?"

"I am." The doctor had been accused of a tendency to meddle and hoped what he had to say next would not be seen as such. "As you know, like my youngest daughter, I am an inveterate researcher. I must confess when you lured me to the delightful Tongue Oil Saloon, got me drunk as a loon, and told me of your plans to go to New Zealand," he paused to take a long sip of now cold coffee, "inebriated as you may have believed me to be that night, I did remember everything you said. My curiosity was piqued. The very next morning I made a few inquiries. I hope you won't think me overreaching, but I have a good idea where you might find *both* your brother and our gold."

"Go on."

"It seems the west coast town of Kumara is primed to be the next significant gold field." Doc saw Ned's eyes widen a millimeter. "Something about a pair of down-and-out miners who, while trying to set up a whiskey still of all things, inadvertently discovered coarse gold nuggets in the gravel. A great deal of coarse gold nuggets. Which, as you may guess, is what set me scheming as to how I might participate in your undertaking." Doc rose and turned toward the window behind his desk. "I've taken the liberty of having the necessary papers for our agreement drawn up." Over his shoulder he said, "And, as a show of good faith, I have something else for you."

Reaching behind the curtains, he extracted a pair of wooden crutches and brought them to Ned. With a prop under each arm, Ned eased himself to a steady, upright position. Facing his benefactor, a range of emotions played in his eyes. "If I'd known all it would take to get these crutches was to give you a piece of the ranch, I'd have done it weeks ago."

When Doc grasped Ned's extended hand, the Harper and Hanover Mining and Expedition Company was established.

CHAPTER FIFTY

Ned had expected Mrs. Dr. Charles Hanover to be somewhat taken aback at having a red Indian sitting on her verandah swing. He had not expected her to come out and serve Red Moon and Heck Abernathy cups of Oolong tea herself, nor that she'd be followed by Maude Mary presenting them a plate of fresh baked gingerbread.

After making sure they were comfortable, Mrs. Hanover excused herself. Maude Mary, however, lingered. Ned knew the girl well enough to suspect she had her own reasons for joining them. As her father had said, he and she shared a passion for gathering as much information as they could, whether priceless gems or meaningless crumbs. Sitting back in anticipation of the questions he knew were coming, Ned was curious and—he had to admit—just a tad wary. The girl lacked tact as conspicuously as he lacked patience.

Seating herself in a wicker chair facing Red Moon and Heck, Maude Mary helped herself to gingerbread while Ned and the Abernathys chatted. She'd seen the couple at town events and heard tales of Ned's time working on their ranch, but—he was sure—she had never spoken more than polite greetings to either of them. They had never been guests at South Slope.

After daintily chewing her gingerbread, she napkined her fingers and mouth and folded her hands in her lap. "Mrs. Moon, I've so wanted to make your acquaintance for just the longest while."

Here it comes, Ned thought.

"The pleasure is mine, child, I'm honored to be a guest in your home." The unsuspecting guest sipped her tea, then said, "Please call me Red Moon."

"Thank you, Mrs. Red Moon. Ned says if it wasn't for your scoldings . . ." He shot her a look that warned her to choose a different course of inquiry. Not missing a beat, she said, "Why, your braids are just lovely—I do so admire them. Even when I was a little girl, Mother wouldn't allow me to plait my hair. She says it's too common . . . oh!" Ned flinched and her own cheeks reddened. "I mean, she says my hair's too fine. Oh." She bit her lip, but, as Ned had expected, her inquisitiveness got the better of her manners. "If you don't mind, may I ask please, why do you wear them?"

The old woman gave a soft laugh. "Tewa let our hair grow long because it reminds us of Mother Earth, whose hair is the rippling, sweet grass of the prairies. Ute men and women wear their hair free sometimes—flowing like the grasslands—and braided sometimes to show oneness with Spirit and each other.

"One strand of hair is weak and easily broken." Red Moon touched a loose strand at her temple. "When woven together," she patted her thick braid, "they are strong. To us, the song of the universe is 'One mind, one heart, one soul, all plaited together.' That is the sacred thought we're meant to hold. That is what our braids remind us to be."

Maude Mary peered deep into the old woman's eyes. "I didn't know anything about red Indians. Now, at least, I know about your hair. What it means. I wear my hair up now because I've become a maiden." As what she'd revealed dawned on her, color flooded her cheeks again. "Oh!"

"Yes, child." Red Moon's face stayed serious, but her eyes sparkled. "You understand how our hair can tell others important things about us."

"That's just what I meant! May I ask you something else?" At Red Moon's nod, Maude Mary continued. "On the wall at school, we keep a map of the entire world. Miss Becky had us ask folks where their families came from before they came here and we'd stick a pin in the place." She didn't say that although Miss Becky had encouraged them to do so, no one had volunteered to visit the Abernathys. She addressed herself to Heck first. "Do you mind telling me where your people are from, Sir?"

"Why, darlin'," Heck said, slapping his palms on his broad thighs. "I was born right here back when Solace Springs was no more than dust and spit."

"But what about your ancestors?"

"Ancestors?" He pondered for a moment. "Well . . . I believe my mother and father came here from somewhere over in Kansas. Before that, I can't rightly say. Hannah has the notion I've got some Scotch blood in me."

"Then your pin will go in Scotland, right next to hers." When she turned back to Red Moon, her eyes were rapt. "And where do red Indians come from, Ma'am? Where should I put your pin?'"

Red Moon's face was somber. She raised her arms to encompass the sky, hills, and land around them, then folded her hands in her lap. "We have always lived here, child, on this land. In the most ancient times, when the earth was very, very young and the day had come to increase the People, Sinawav, the Creator, gathered sticks to make the first Utes. He put us right here to live forever in these hills and valleys."

Maude Mary's eyes widened. "Oh," she breathed, "Then you must have the very first and only pin stuck right here in Solace Springs."

Red Moon studied Maude Mary with the same intensity the girl had directed at her. "I see your spirit is strong with Mouse Medicine."

"Mouse Medicine?" Maude Mary sat back. "I'm a mouse?"

"Not a mouse, but like Mouse. He is the creature who says, 'I will touch everything with my whiskers in order to know it.'"

Maude Mary sat up straighter. She lowered her eyes and, looking shy—for the first and only time Ned could remember—murmured, "Most people don't, but you understand. You understand me."

By the time Maude Mary had exhausted her list of questions and gone inside to tell everyone everything she'd discovered about the Abernathys and Utes and herself, it was late afternoon. The soft breezes of summer had turned chilly and brittle, sharpened by the breath of early autumn. After loping back from his foray into the surrounding trees, Cloud napped at Ned's feet with the grey cat curled against his belly.

"And you, my son." Red Moon turned to Ned. "Am I right in guessing you've had a lesson in Bear Medicine?"

A feather brushed the back of his neck. Red Moon was not one to guess at things. A memory, a dream lost in the mists that dissolve dreams, came back to him. Soft whooings and the swoosh of wind against wings—the owl who'd kept vigil above him in the woods that night.

For weeks, he'd been troubled by a question he knew only Red Moon could answer. Years ago, she'd hunkered down beside him in a field of snow and watched him work his arrow out of the body of a rabbit he'd just shot. She'd come to know Ned well by then—a shattered sixteen year-old, bereft and afraid in a world that had taken far more than it had given him. He'd understood her words about Fear Caller were meant to be a warning that to survive he must learn to quiet his fear. Ned had taken the lesson to heart. Or so he'd thought.

He met and held her gaze and his words came slow and measured. "Do you think I called that trap to me?"

The Indian was silent for several heartbeats. "No, Son of My Heart, you were not afraid of the trap, or of being injured, or even, I'm sorry to say, of death." The over-brightness of her eyes told him she'd guessed his dark secret. Had kept it. "Those things held no power over you. You called Mother Bear to lead you to the cave where Answer lives because you had to make a choice you didn't want to face." Red Moon adjusted her colorful shawl for warmth, turned her face to the sun, then back to him. "What you feared was that decision." After studying his features, his eyes, and the set of his shoulders, she nodded with satisfaction. "He's gone."

A weight Ned hadn't been aware of carrying lifted. Then, "Hold on," he said. "Who's

gone?"

He looked to Heck to see if he shared his confusion. The old man raised his white brows and shrugged. Tilting his head toward his wife, he said, "Best ask Snowy Owl."

"Who's gone?"

Red Moon appeared surprised by the question. "The Warrior in White Robes has left you. You've disappointed him, I'm glad to say." Red Moon patted Ned's knee. "He has wearied of your company and no longer cares to walk at your side. With Mother Bear's advice, he decided to let you go."

CHAPTER FIFTY-ONE

Of necessity, all the Harper brothers had learned to make themselves useful around the kitchen. At a precariously young age, Ned had become adept with a knife. He could skin and bone any critter or chop any vegetable set in front of him. Now, a crutch under each arm, he stood in the doorway of the kitchen with the hope of doing just that for Mrs. Olney.

Crutches had freed him from the bedroom, but done little else to lessen his captivity. Restless, he hobbled to and fro along the hallways throughout the house. Scaled the stairs. Tottered back down. Alit to have tea with Mrs. Hanover and coffee or whiskey with Doc. Spent hours on the porch alone or talking with Allie. Wandered the two well-tended, but tedious, acres of South Slope with Cloud. The grey cat, who had bullied the wolf dog into friendship, followed everywhere they went.

When no one was around, he tested his weight on his injured leg and found that every day the pain was less and freedom closer. Still, there was no escaping Maude Mary, who had embraced her Mouse Medicine. She and her questions dogged Ned relentlessly. He endured endless queries about horses and dogs and bear traps and steamships and gold mining and New Zealand and Maoris and any other thing that crossed her mind. She announced to all that the only person who had ever truly understood her—dear, wise, old Mrs. Red Moon—had said it was Maude Mary's special nature to be inquisitive. And so, she inquired. And inquired.

When she asked Ned, "Who exactly is Miss Birdie?" He had—after a spell of speechlessness—referred her to her father. One day, to escape the girl's interrogations—and desperate to be productive—he hid where he knew she would not seek him. He spent an entire day in the neglected barn fixing reins that needed fixing and bridles that didn't. Every piece of tack he could find underwent a thorough cleaning and oiling, including Doc's old riding boots. Every shelf got purged, dusted, and sorted. Every tool found a place. When he'd done everything that could possibly need doing, he'd sat on a bale of hay and searched—futilely—for more to do until suppertime.

Now, another idle afternoon loomed before him. Allie and Doc had been gone since yesterday to remove an ovarian tumor from a patient two towns over and weren't expected back until evening. Mrs. Hanover was presiding over her Ladies' Benevolent Society in the parlor, and, it seemed to Ned, Albert had been avoiding him for days. Joseph was visiting, but when Ned waved to the boys from the back porch, Joseph had grinned and started to shamble toward him, only to be tugged away by Albert.

Heck had once told him, "A man can get used to just about anything 'cept hangin' from a rope around his neck." Ned decided that was exactly what boredom felt like. A noose about to choke the life out of him

Mrs. Olney was his only hope.

Leaning against the doorjamb of the kitchen, he gave her his most engaging grin. "I'm feelin' about as useless as a button on a hat, Ma'am. Can you please give me something to do to help out? Anything."

Because she liked Ned, the cook didn't snap, "Scat!" or wave him away without looking up, as she did to anyone else who braved the portal to her domain. She allowed him into her kitchen and set him up at a table in the corner with a heap of potatoes to peel, causing Miranda to become all thumbs and spoil the gravy.

Lost in the bliss of mindless activity, he was startled when Albert burst into the kitchen, followed closely by Joseph. "Ned!" Albert shouted, "Come quick—it's Hippocrates, something's wrong with her!"

Crutching across a half acre of uneven terrain to keep up with the frantic boys left Ned winded and his leg throbbing. Exhilarated by the call to action, he barely noticed. As soon as he entered the barn, he saw what was wrong with the chestnut mare. Hippocrates stood on three legs, gingerly touching the toe of her right front hoof to the ground.

"I've got a pretty good idea what the trouble is," he told Albert and Joseph, stroking the horse's neck. "There now," he said softly to soothe her, and them, and to accustom the distressed animal to the sound of his voice. "It's serious, but we can fix her up."

Albert bit his lip. "What is it?"

"I'll show you both in just a minute. First, I want to have a little talk with our patient. Bedside manner, Doc calls it." He turned back to the horse. "You don't know me too well, yet, Miss Hippocrates," Ned told her, "but I know we're gonna be friends. Doc says you're the sweetest mare in all Colorado and I know him to be a fine judge of character, most of the time. I'll hold off telling you what he thinks of me 'til after you've had a chance to decide for yourself." Running his hand down her leg he found, as he expected, that the cannon was swollen and hot to the touch. He turned to the boys. "Feel her foreleg and tell me what you think."

"Warm," Albert grumbled, to Ned's chest.

"Warm," Joseph agreed, lifting his eyes to Ned's.

"That heat tells you there's some sort of infection going on." Still stroking the horse, Ned asked her, "Mind if I take a look at your hoof, girl? I suspect you've hurt it. When I know for sure what's bothering you, these boys and I'll set you right." Giving them a sideways glance, he added, "If they're willing."

"I am," Joseph responded eagerly.

"Me, too," mumbled Albert, still not meeting Ned's eyes.

Noting that Joseph seemed as glad to be in his company as ever, and that Albert didn't, Ned was perplexed. But, he decided, whatever's eatin' at the boy will have to wait. Hippocrates needed his full attention. Setting his crutches against the wall of the stall, he positioned himself just behind the mare's withers and leaned on her for balance, keeping his own bad leg slightly off the ground. He'd need both hands to tend to her.

"I'm a bit lame myself," he explained to the horse, "so I hope you don't mind my weight." Gently bending her leg back at the knee, he studied the hoof. "See here?" he said to the boys, pointing to a black line across the sole. "Looks like she picked up a pebble or something and it's festerin' under the hoof. That line's where the infection is. There's no place for the pus to go, so the pressure's built up. That's what's hurting her."

"What do we do?" Albert asked, half meeting Ned's eyes.

"First, we've got to open up the sore place to ease the pressure." Ned carefully lowered the mare's foot to the ground. Leaning against the horse again, he sent Albert to the house to ask Mrs. Olney for a large pot of boiling water and clean cloths that could be torn into strips. At his direction, Joseph collected the tools Ned would need from the hooks and shelves in the barn—a rasp and nippers to remove Hippocrates' horseshoe, a hoof pick and brush to clean it, a knife to open the abscess, and a tin of horse paste to pack the wound.

When Albert barreled back into the barn announcing that Miranda would bring the water as soon as it boiled, Ned sent both boys out to fill a large bucket halfway full with well water. When they returned, swinging the sloshing bucket between them, he'd already rasped down the sides of Hippocrates' hoof and removed her shoe. "Set that bucket here, close to her foot."

A few minutes later, Miranda appeared carrying a pot of boiling water and some old linens. Ned grinned and tipped an imaginary hat to her. Taking the pot, he poured its contents into the bucket of cold water. "Hippocrates and the boys and I are much obliged for your trouble."

"Oh my, you're no trouble." The maid twisted her hands in her apron. "What I mean is *it's* no trouble." Cheeks flaming, she backed toward the door. "It was Mrs. Olney. She let me. I mean, she *asked* me to bring the pot down here. I mean, I wanted to bring it down. To you. Here."

At Ned's widening grin, she turned on her heel and fled back to the house.

"What now?" Albert asked.

"Now," Ned said, "you both step over here so you can learn to treat a festerin' hoof."

"Me?" Albert asked. His father employed the farrier for such tasks.

"Me, too?" Joseph echoed.

"I said both of you. Watch me this time, 'cause you'll have to do it yourselves after supper. My leg's been givin' me fits," Ned lied. "I don't think I'll be able to make it down here again today. What we're gonna do needs doing twice a day, for about a week. Not opening the sore, I hope I only have to do that this one time, but you might as well see how it's done. Joseph, hand me the knife." The grey cat materialized on a high shelf and watched the proceedings with a critical eye. "My brother Nate taught me to do this when I was younger than you boys."

Leaning against the mare, he lifted her foot and slit the sole of her hoof. She flinched back slightly, but didn't otherwise resist. Both boys' faces scrunched at the foul odor of the released pus. Ned nodded with satisfaction. "My favorite stink. Means the poison's coming out. You're feeling a whole lot better already, aren't you, Sweetheart?

"Albert, stir a handful of those Epsom salts into the warm water." When they dissolved, Ned said, "Joseph, come over here and lift her leg like I showed you, then gentle-like ease it into the bucket to soak."

Joseph, who had never before handled a large animal, went wide-eyed, but accomplished the task. Ned said nothing. Calling attention to the success, he thought, would imply he expected something less.

"Now, we let it soak for about a half hour. Then, we'll pack it with horse paste and wrap it."

"Horse paste?" the boys echoed in unison, though Albert's pinched face didn't show the delight he would normally take in such things.

"Yep. A mash of Epsom salt and peppermint oil. Salves most anything that ails a horse. After supper the two of you'll do it again—soak, pack, and bind. Now, Joseph, you go on back up to the house and beg a few apples from Mrs. Olney. Not the good ones, just those not fit for her brown betty. Bring'em back yourself. I don't think Miss Miranda can take another visit to the barn. She prides herself on being a 'house' maid and it might be overstepping to ask her to come outside twice in one day." Joseph turned to go. As Albert swung around to follow, Ned reached out and grasped his elbow. "You stay here. I'd appreciate the company."

The boy glowered, pulling his elbow free, but stayed put.

Settling himself on a bale of hay, Ned motioned for Albert to join him. The glum child sat as far from him as he could and stared at the ground. After several uncomfortable moments of silence, Ned said, "I've been wonderin' what I might have done to make you look like a mule chewin' on bumblebees whenever you're around me."

Albert appeared to fight a smile—he had a weakness for Ned's odd sayings—but didn't give in to it. He raised bruised eyes to Ned's and his lower lip trembled. He looked away, shoulders slumped, and chin sinking toward his chest.

"What is it, Albert?" The depth of the boy's distress baffled him. "I thought we were good enough friends you'd tell me if there was somethin' wrong."

The boy lifted his chin, tears hanging on his lashes. "You say we're friends, but you don't mean it."

"Of course I mean it. What makes you think I don't?"

"You don't like any of us anymore."

The stunning blow caught Ned off guard. "You know that's not so."

"It is so." Eyes dulled with accusation, he said, "If you liked us, you wouldn't be leaving us."

Allie and Doc returned to Solace Springs earlier than they'd anticipated.

The operation, in which Doc had allowed Allie to take the lead, had gone well. To everyone's relief, it appeared the ovarian growth was a benign cyst and, just hours after the chloroform wore off, the pig farmer's hardy wife declared herself fit to get back to her chores. Doc tried to impress upon her the need for at least a week's rest after being cut open. She had agreed while exchanging a conspiratorial look with her husband. They thanked Allie and Doc and sent them on their way with five pork chops, six pounds of smoked ham, four pounds of slab bacon, and a butt roast.

Allie had always found surgery the most intriguing part of her father's practice and—second only to stopping hemorrhages—the most crucial for saving lives. The human body was a miraculous creation, Doc had taught her, but imperfect. "And mortal, my dear. Oh, so maddeningly mortal. Seeming indestructible at times, and heartbreakingly fragile at others.

"Performing an operation," he'd said, "though fraught with risks—never, ever forget the risks—allows the physician, on occasion, and only on occasion, to correct damage done to the body by illness or injury."

Allie's experience at the pig farm confirmed her belief that sound surgical skills were essential to the general practice of medicine, especially in rural areas. Doc was quick to remind her his own training had been limited and, he feared, woefully outdated. He lamented he'd taught her as much as he could and that that wasn't nearly enough. They both hoped Carver Medical College would provide her the opportunity to learn skills she could eventually pass on to him.

While Doc returned his medical supplies to his office, Allie paid her weekly visit to the post office. She had to admit to being on tenterhooks. Having confirmed her intention to attend Carver and submitting all the necessary fees and paperwork, she anxiously awaited notification regarding two significant, yet very different, aspects of her education. Weeks had gone by with no word on either. From a cubbyhole in the wall of compartments behind him, Henry Coleman handed her Doc's newspaper and a letter for her mother from Aunt Hope. Crestfallen, Allie turned to go, taking some scant comfort in the adage, "No news is good news."

Just as she reached the door, the postmaster called out, "Oh, Miss Allie, sorry. I almost missed these."

With his customary curiosity, Henry Coleman handed her the two envelopes she'd been hoping for. Although the return address on one set her heart pounding, she hid her excitement and thanked the postmaster. To avoid his prying eyes, she hurried outside and prepared herself for whatever fate awaited her. She tore the first envelope open. Closing her eyes, she calmed herself again before reading it. Twice. Dr. Archibald Clifford, the most highly-esteemed surgeon in Keokuk, had accepted her for one of the few, precious surgical preceptorships open to women.

After savoring the moment, she opened the second, thicker, envelope. It held a three page letter from Mrs. Sadie Rabinowitz informing Allie of another important, albeit more prosaic acceptance. She'd been deemed suitable to be a boarder in Mrs. Rabinowitz's rooming house. One page listed the amenities and privileges of the ten young women chosen to reside there. The other two pages outlined the house rules and the consequences for breaking them.

Smiling the whole way, Allie stopped at the clinic to show her father Dr. Clifford's letter. He rose from his chair and wrapped his arms around her without saying a word. She knew his silence meant he couldn't trust his voice. Leaving him to his tasks, she strolled the rest of the way home, composing the letter she would send to Lydia Brennan and relishing the anticipation of sharing the news with the rest of her family. And, of course, with Ned.

When she arrived at South Slope, Allie found her mother and sister in the parlor paging through a copy of *Godey's Ladies' Magazine* and admiring the latest fashions. Breathless and bursting, she stood in the doorway for a moment before they noticed her.

Maude Mary saw her expression and immediately leapt to her feet. "Tell! Tell!" she squealed. Her mother set the magazine aside and waited for Allie to deliver her news. Since Carver Medical had become a fait accompli, Mrs. Hanover—at Dr. Hanover's suggestion—had silenced her opposition and chosen to take pride in her daughter's unique accomplishments, despite what Queen Victoria might have to say to the contrary.

With Maude Mary looking over her shoulder—the better to read the missives for herself—Allie held the first letter at arms length. "Dr. Archibald Clifford is pleased to offer you a preceptorship in his surgical practice to commence at the successful completion of your year of academic studies. And," she flourished the second letter, "Mrs. Sadie Rabinowitz welcomes you as a guest boarder in her safe and well-appointed Rooming House for Respectable Young Ladies."

Allie was not surprised to see her mother's lip twitch at the decidedly not Anglo-Saxon name, but—as Doc had also suggested she learn to do in the interest of improving her relationship with her eldest daughter—she refrained from comment on what she clearly believed to be a lapse in judgment.

"But, what does that word mean?" Before Maude Mary could commence what was certain to be a litany of questions, Allie assured her all queries would be answered at supper, and swiftly exited.

Maude Mary watched her go, then turned to her mother with a quizzical brow. Allie had not read aloud the unusual salutation on Mrs. Rabinowitz's letter.

"Mama," she said, "what do you suppose 'mazel tov' means?"

Eager to find Ned, Allie hurried out toward the barn and came upon Joseph shambling away from it at an impressive pace, Cloud loping at his side.

"Hello Miss Allie," Joseph called out, without stopping. "I'm getting . . . apples for Hip . . . pocra . . . tes. Me and Albert are helping Ned Harper . . . fix her sore foot."

Although she was concerned for her father's horse, she couldn't help but smile. The boy, who had become a frequent visitor to South Slope, looked strong and brown and healthy. "I hope you can help her—she's Doc's favorite, you know."

"We will," Joseph yelled back to her. "She'll be fit as a . . . forest pig in . . . no time. Ned Harper says so."

Wondering what Ned Harper might have to say about her own news quickened her steps. For weeks, she'd shared with him her excitement and apprehension about these two last pieces of mail that would shape her stay in Iowa. About to enter the small barn, she heard Albert in solemn conversation with Ned and stopped. Not wanting to interrupt, she drew back, unseen. Though it would never be her intention to eavesdrop, she couldn't help overhearing.

Her little brother's shaky voice: "You say we're friends, but you don't mean it."

"Of course I mean it." Ned, sounding taken aback: "What makes you think I don't?"

The boy, accusing: "You don't like any of us anymore."

Ned, pained: "You know that's not so."

"It is so." Then, Albert's tearful coup de grace: "If you liked us, you wouldn't be leaving us."

Both, silent.

The boy's words shocked the breath out of Ned. He hardly had the air to say, "I'm not leavin', Albert. I'm just going away for a while. I'm comin' back, soon as I'm done in New Zealand."

Albert stared at him long and hard before asking, "You mean it?"

"I do."

"You sure?"

"Sure as a goose goes barefoot." At Albert's eye roll and grudging half smile, Ned added, "I've got to come back here. You know this town's my home. This is where everything and everyone I care about will be."

The tension in the boy's face eased. "Okay."

"Okay," Ned said, relieved that Albert was relieved. "Now help me tear up these cloths before Joseph gets back."

Reaching for a piece of linen, Albert said, "Can I ask you one more question?"

"Sure, Miss Maudie." Ned sighed in mock resignation. "Go right ahead."

"Do you love my sister?"

Before Ned's jaw could drop, Allie, cheeks ablush, quick-stepped into the barn, smiling too brightly. "Hello, you two! Papa and I just got home and I thought I might find you both in here and well, here you are! I do hope Hippocrates will be all right. I just saw Joseph and he told me she was hurt but that you . . ."

"I'm glad you're here, Allie." Ned's color had also warmed beneath the affectionate grin her presence always seemed to evoke these days. Taking her hand, he pulled her to sit beside him on the bale of hay. "You're just in time to help tear up these rags."

Albert looked from one smiling, crimson face to the other. "That's just what I thought."

CHAPTER FIFTY-TWO

I didn't tell anyone—not even Albert—everything that happened when I was out in the woods.

I told about Cloud, because I thought Ned Harper would want to know, but I didn't say anything about the white bird. When I was so scared and lost and thinking Ned Harper was going to die all alone in that trap because I got lost in the woods and then couldn't find the way home and get him help, I couldn't even move.

That's when she called to me. "You! You! You!"

People think owls say "Who! Who! Who!" But they don't. They say, "You! You! You!"

I found that out because when I heard her, I looked up and saw her glide down on her big, snowy wings and settle right on a branch close to the stump I was crying on.

"Your wings are not broken, little sparrow." That's exactly what she said to me. "Only bent. The more you fly, the stronger they'll become."

Then she flew away.

Her words made me feel strong. I got right up and found my way to the tack and feed and brought Pa and Miss Allie and Zeke, the barber, to save Ned Harper. But I knew that wasn't what the owl meant by flying.

So, today I told Pa, "It's time for me to go to school."

At first, he got all bulled up like he does and I was afraid he'd just say, "No, Joseph and that's the end of it."

But I was wrong. He got quiet for a long, long time, then he looked at me hard. "Maybe so, Joseph," he said real soft. "I suppose we can give it a try. But, mark me, if there's a speck of trouble . . ."

"Pa!" I said, "There's nothing more trouble than not knowing how to read."

And he said, "You might be right, son. We'll just have to see what happens."

Which I knew meant yes.

CHAPTER FIFTY-THREE

In the days that led up to his departure, Ned wasn't troubled by ifs or what ifs. He'd find Nate in New Zealand, or he wouldn't. Same with gold. He had his hopes, that went without saying, but no expectations. Hadn't thought much about where he was going or what he'd do once he got there, figured he'd sort it out when the time came.

And, he hadn't thought much about what he was leaving behind, either.

Didn't want to.

Allie was tormented by doubts.

Who do I think I am? she fretted. A foolish girl from a one-room school presuming she belongs in a prestigious medical college! With young men and women all who most certainly had real educations.

What if I can't keep up?

What if I can?

Leaving my dear family and comfortable home to go live in a rooming house with ten girls I've never met. What if they don't like me? What if I can't abide them? What if they're intelligent, friendly, like-minded young women who'll want to talk about all the things I've only ever been able to talk about with Doc?

What if I have nothing to say?

I almost always have something to say.

The thought soothed her enough that she could put her mind to packing.

No matter what, she told herself, folding her linsey-woolsey, I'll be home in less than two years.

No matter what, she thought dismally, sinking into the chair by her bed, I'll be gone for almost two years. She tried not to think about Ned sailing across oceans and trekking through New Zealand for at least as long.

Didn't want to.

When the day came, it turned out to be a fine morning for a send-off—sunny and crisp in the way mid-autumn can be when Colorado puts its mind to it. Even if it hadn't been, Doc guessed, most of the people gathered in front of the livery stable would have shown up anyhow. The Findlays, the Hanovers, Zeke with his new bride, Sarah, Tucker T. and his wife, Reverend Carstairs, Mrs. Olney and Miranda, Norberto and Anjelita, many of the Ladies of the Benevolent Society, and the entire baseball team came to offer their well wishes. Adding to the festive mood, Ollie Oxter and his musicians entertained folks with the lively strains of banjo, guitar, fiddle, and squeeze box.

It came as no surprise to Doc, nor anyone else in Solace Springs, that Ned Harper and his wolf dog would be escorting the lovely and accomplished Miss Allie Hanover and her mother to Iowa on his way to the gold fields of New Zealand. The way the two young people looked at each other had not gone unnoticed. Ned had offered to accompany the women to Keokuk, where he and her mother would see Allie settled at Mrs. Rabinowitz's Rooming House. From there, he would escort Mrs. Hanover to New York. Ned and Cloud would board a White Star Line steamship to cross the ocean to England, assess the merits of its kennel master, then catch another ship from

Liverpool to New Zealand, where—as all had been astounded to learn, the seasons were upside-down.

Mrs. Hanover held court in front of the mercantile surrounded by her Benevolent Ladies—including Martha Findlay—before leaving them to their own charitable devices for the next three months. When she parted company with Ned, she would take the train—Pullman class, of course—from New York to Boston. There, although it was still two years off, she and Aunt Hope would begin to plot the details of Miss Alice Maude Mary Hanover's much anticipated bud year. Sumptuous parties, pink dresses, aigrette hats, and all.

Standing apart, Doc observed the interactions of the travelers and their well-wishers. Joy and sadness can truly co-exist in one heart, he thought, watching Allie. A father's. We strive to raise our children to be good, smart, strong, and independent. Then, they break our hearts by doing so and leaving us.

Always sensitive to her father's moods, Allie came to his side. She laughed when he handed her his handkerchief and told her, "You're going to need this, my dear."

"Papa, you're such a sweet, sentimental . . ."

"Old fool? You wait and see."

Slipping her arm through his, she rested her head on his shoulder. "You did keep one for yourself, didn't you?"

Not risking a look at her, he patted his breast pocket.

Will, Hannah, and their three boys presented Ned and Allie with a tartan-ribboned basket filled with pasties, bannocks, jarred rabbit, and two vinegar pies, which they accepted with a great show of gratitude. Food available at stagecoach relay stations—for an extra charge—was notoriously unappetizing and usually consisted of bread, tea, and fried steaks of bacon, venison, or mule flesh.

Embracing Allie, Hannah sighed, "What ever will I do without ye?"

Doc's handkerchief made itself useful. "And I without you?"

Will pulled Allie close to kiss the top of his sister's head. "I won't miss you a bit."

Wiping her own tears with an impatient hand, Hannah turned to Ned, wrapped her arms around his waist, and buried her face in his chest. Composing herself, she stood back, drew up to her full height, and glared at him. "Just what d'ye suggest I tell our wee Angus when the poor bairn wails for ye?"

Ned smiled a bit sadly. "Just tell the wee spoilt bairn I'll be back by the time he's big enough to learn to ride."

Before Hannah could retort, Will took the opportunity to chide Ned. "You know I had to hire two wranglers to fill in for you when you were laid up. Don't give me that look. I'm not sayin' you did the work of two men, but now you're sayin' I have to keep them both on until Angus is old enough to ride a horse. So, partner, you'd best come back here ready to work or with enough gold jingling in your pockets to hire them on permanent."

"I'm gonna miss you, too."

With her husband proudly at her side, the new Mrs. Zeke Foster approached Allie and Ned. Sarah held out the thick, silky lambs' wool scarf she'd carded, spun, and knitted. "I wanted to give you this."

Allie pressed the impossibly soft scarf to her cheek. "I will treasure this as a precious piece of home from a precious friend every time I wear it, which I'm sure will be every single winter day."

They stood awkwardly, until Sarah threw her arms around Allie. "Miss La-di-dah, you are everything I always imagined a true friend would be, even though I didn't think I'd ever have one." Letting go, she whispered, "I will never, ever forget what you did for me."

Zeke's farewell to Ned was less sentimental. "I've been practicing' that damned—sorry Sweetheart—curve ball, just like you showed me. I s'pose it's coming along. If I can manage to get it over the damned—sorry Sweetheart—plate, I'll use it next summer."

Digging into his pocket, he pulled out a handful of coins and handed them to his wife.

Pushing and pawing at each other like rambunctious puppies, Joseph and Albert, followed by Luke Findlay, made their way to Allie and Ned. Albert gave Joseph a shove toward them. "Good-bye. . . Miss Allie," Joseph stammered. "Good-bye, Ned . . . Harper."

Bending to be at eye level, Allie grasped both his hands. "I'm going to miss you so very much, Joseph."

Ned cleared his throat. "Not a stitch more than I will."

Albert poked Joseph. "Tell'em."

With a shy, slow smile, Joseph said, "I know all the . . . letters and numbers in . . . my McGuffey's primer and I recited my first . . . lesson to the class yesterday."

Allie looked up at Mr. Findlay, who made no attempt to hide his pleasure. She held the boy at arm's length, beaming. "I do hope you're as proud of you as I am."

Albert told them, "The whole class clapped." When Joseph caught his eye and frowned, he added, "Well, almost the whole class."

"There's no one prouder than his ma and pa," Mr. Findlay put in. Clapping Ned on the shoulder, he grasped his hand. "I'm taking my son and Albert fishing out to Crain's Pond tomorrow. Sorry you won't be here to go with us." He smiled down at Joseph before looking at Ned and Allie. "I don't have to tell you what you've done for us. Both of you."

"I won't forget what the two of you did for me, either." Ned ruffled Joseph's wheat-colored hair. "That's all well and good, I s'pose, but Joseph, you'd make us all *really* proud by catching a mess of bluegill tomorrow."

Days before, Heck and Red Moon had ridden up to Ned's cabin to say their good-byes. They'd gifted him with a brand-new, coal black Stetson—unscuffed, unfaded, and lacking a bullet hole in its crown. Heck had always been aggrieved by that particular mishap. Although Ned found the hat embarrassing in its greenhorn spotlessness, it sported a three-inch bear claw fastened to its band.

"Put Badger away in your medicine bag," Red Moon had told him sternly. "And be sure you leave him there."

When the stage arrived—right on time—and the weary, hard-going mules exchanged for a fresh team, Doc embraced his wife—who he already missed. He held her face in both his hands and kissed her on the lips right there in front of everyone, before assisting her into the weathered Concord coach.

When she was settled, Allie, with Doc's now sodden handkerchief clutched in her hand, and Ned, carrying a bag of candy in one hand and Hannah's basket in the other, boarded the ten o'clock to Morrison for the first sixty miles of their journey.

With their first class tickets, Allie and her mother would ride for the entire trip. Ned, who had purchased third class for himself, would walk at bad places in the road and be required to get out and help push the stage-coach up hills. The dog would run along outside—and likely ahead of the coach—which would travel at about five miles an hour most of the way. Cloud would stop to rest when he chose or ride with the driver. All would endure whatever weather they encountered, as well as the over-stuffed mail pouches crammed under their feet.

The driver kept a rifle and sidearm at the ready and, unbeknownst to the ladies, Ned carried a loaded revolver hidden beneath his jacket. Despite his dislike for guns, he'd confessed to Doc that he couldn't ignore the faded poster he'd seen tacked to the stagecoach office door:

You will be traveling through
Indian Country and the safety
of your person cannot be vouchsafed by anyone but God

For some weeks after their departure, there would be talk in town about the protective way Ned Harper had helped Allie into that coach, one hand on her elbow, the other at the small of her back, and about their quick glances of shared amusement. It would be said, and repeated, that there certainly appeared to be something between the two. Something new and sweet and fragile that would most certainly draw them back to Solace Springs and each other.

Followed by knowing smiles and exclamations of, "Imagine that!"

Followed by deep sighs and downcast eyes. "But, goodness sakes, two years . . ."

As Ollie's lively little band stepped up the rhythm and volume of its melodies, all the folk who'd gathered to see the stagecoach off waved as it swayed and jolted down the street, with Cloud trotting alongside. Doc stood right up front with Maude Mary and Albert on either side of him, both children subdued once the red and yellow coach disappeared around the bend. Maude Mary slipped her hand into his and bent her head. Albert kicked at the dirt.

Maude Mary tried to smile. "Allie promised she'd write me every single day and tell me every single thing about Iowa."

"I'm sure she will," Doc said, squeezing her hand.

"Ned said he'd bring me and Joseph each a piece of gold," said Albert, slipping a shoulder under his father's arm and leaning into him. "When he gets back."

"Ned's word is as good as he is."

And so, Doc thought, with as much fanfare as this sleepy little town can muster, we've sent those two young people on their ways. Both adamant that all roads—rail and sea—will eventually return them to Solace Springs and all the possibilities inherent in a town so named.

But will the wider world give them back? he wondered. And if it does, who might they be when they return from such extraordinary journeys?

As the dust settled, leaving no trace of the coach and its passengers, Doc tightened his arms around his two youngest children, comforted by their closeness. As it often did, his mind turned to the words of men he deemed much wiser than himself.

Ah, old friend Montaigne, he thought, you are right, as always.

"The birth of all things is weak and tender and therefore we should have our eyes intent on beginnings."

Glossary of Scottish and Gaelic words

Aye – yes

Bhailach – (a) poor lad

Bairn - child

Bodhrans - drum

Braw – fine, excellent

Canty – cheerful, pleasant

Ceilidh - gathering

Charaid – friend (mo = my)

Chridhe – (mo) my heart

Clashmaclaivers – gossip

Crabbit - grouch

Dinna - don’t

Fash – worry, fret

Ken - know

Kent - knew

Och! – Oh!

Peeley-walley – pale or wan

Scunner – nuisance

Swither – a hodge-podge

Slinte Mhath – to your health

Verra – very

Wame – stomach, gut

Weans - children

Wee – small (or the opposite!)

Ye – you